RIVAL RADIO

KATHRYN NOLAN

That's What She Said Publishing,Inc.

Editing by Faith N. Erline
and Jessica Snyder
Cover by Kari March

ISBN: 979-8-88643-972-4 (ebook)
ISBN: 979-8-88643-973-1 (paperback)

051622

For those who barrel through life with a wild joy. Stay hungry, you weirdos.

DARIA

I could always tell it was going to be a good show by the number of questions I got about sex toys. We'd already received five of them tonight.

"My question is...can I name my sex toys?" Angel asked. "Or, really, *should* I name them?"

I leaned in, wrapping my fingers around my mic. "Does naming your sex toys make you happy?"

"It makes me *really* happy." She sighed. "I guess this question is a super-specific example of this larger issue I come up against sometimes. I'm working on prioritizing my own joy. Treating it like it matters."

"It's a challenging first step for everyone," I said. "We've been taught to treat our own personal needs and desires as the last three tasks on our daily to-do list. The tasks you *never* get to, but then you comfort yourself by promising you'll do them tomorrow."

Angel laughed. "And *you never do them.*"

"Right, yeah," I said with a smile. "Fighting the idea that this makes us selfish is a lifelong journey. I know it is for me. Can I ask what this specific issue is you're struggling with?"

She paused. "Believing that the things that make me

happy are...weird. Silly. Frivolous. It's like...have you ever gone to a wedding and no one's dancing, but then your favorite song comes on and so you just go out there, on the dance floor, and let loose? But then you open your eyes and everyone's staring at you like you're an embarrassment?"

My face warmed all over. I knew exactly what she was talking about.

"I've been there, and I *am* that girl every single time." I locked eyes with Elena through the window, who was operating the board at the mixing desk in the small room connected to the sound booth. She pointed at herself and mouthed *me too*.

I grinned. "We have a lot of fake rules in our society about joy and confidence. We don't like it when it's messy or uncoordinated. We're uncomfortable if it doesn't look a certain way. If it's too loud. Too boisterous. Not the right 'time.' Time, of course, being something other people get to decide for us. We *especially* don't like the person getting wild on the dance floor by themselves if *we* want to be doing the same thing but feel we can't."

"That's it *exactly*," Angel murmured. "I'm discovering that I like to have a lot of fun. Singing off-key and dancing in my kitchen. Buying clothes that don't match and wearing them with pride. Taking myself out to dinner just because. Naming all of my vibrators Chris Evans."

"Oh, Angel," I said. "If you're dancing and dressing up and naming your vibrators after Captain America, I don't have any advice for you. I just want to offer a sincere *congratulations*."

"And I'm not weird?"

"If *weird* means being your true, beautiful, authentic self, then we should all be that way. You're not 'taking' when you explore what you really want. You're 'giving.' That's what choosing yourself is all about." I wrapped my hands around my mug of hot water with lemon and honey. "On the topic of vibrators, I'm a huge advocate for the healing I found through solo pleasure. That's pleasure of all kinds, for all kinds of bodies—multiple orgasms, massages, hot baths, afternoon naps in the sun, a long hike. Whatever we use to achieve this pleasure isn't a toy. It's an instrument. We take care of our instruments, don't we?"

"We do. We even name them if we want."

The obvious smile in her voice sent a flicker of satisfaction through my veins. As a kid, hanging around here before school, I'd loved the blinking of the cue lights, the cozy feel of the sound booth, the ebb and flow of my mother's raspy, crackling voice as she hosted her beloved rock 'n' roll-inspired morning show.

Working at a radio station was my definition of *home*. But now that I was the one behind the mic, the "expert" answering questions live on-air, I held tight to any indication that I was the right person for this job. And not an imposter.

"Daria, can I, um…is it okay if I fan-girl for a second?"

I fiddled with the row of earrings curving up my ear. "You can. But I'll warn you that I'm not really used to this stuff yet."

"It's okay. I'm not used to calling in to radio shows and talking about my vibrators."

I laughed. "We're all in this *being vulnerable* thing together."

"I read your blog. Obsessively. The one you started after your fiancé, well—"

"Left me at the altar?" I said lightly.

"Right. Yes, that," she hedged. "I stumbled upon your first post around the time I was going through something similar with my girlfriend. We'd been shopping for rings. And houses and wedding dresses. Then I found out she'd been cheating on me and…" Angel cleared her throat. "After I ended it between us, it felt like my heart was in tatters. And I couldn't handle one more person telling me about silver

3

linings, or that I should get over it by dating someone new, or that everything happens for a reason, *blah blah* whatever. I was *furious*. Talk about messy reactions people don't want to be around. My friends and family didn't think I deserved to be so mad."

I nodded, tugging on my earrings again. "This stuff is really hard, Angel. We prefer when women only express emotions that allow everyone around them to stay comfortable. Anger most of all. What happened to you is infuriating and you deserve to feel every bit of it. The only way out is through, not stifling or suppressing it."

"And that's why I loved your blog so much," Angel continued. "It appeared in my life at the exact time that I needed to see my own rage reflected back at me. Your voice, it's like the best friend who has your back. Who takes your side and stands up for you. It's why I adore this show. Please don't ever change?"

I smirked at that. "It's highly unlikely I ever will. And I hope you do have people in your life who still support you in whatever you're going through. And that means doing whatever your weird little heart desires."

The door to the production room opened and a man stepped inside. I knew who it was even before his stupidly broad shoulders came into view. It was the change in the air, the way atmospheric pressure drops before a summer storm.

The hair on my arms stood straight up.

Dr. Theodore Chadwick pressed his tall, lean body against the wall and crossed one ankle over the other. He adjusted his square-rimmed glasses, drawing my gaze to his forest-green eyes. Anger blazed there like a wildfire.

I swallowed hard but raised my chin. I knew why he was here. And was as furious as he was.

"So, yeah, back to Chris Evans," Elena said, speaking over the dead air I'd let tick by.

Theo subtly arched an eyebrow.

"You're always welcome to call in if you need to hear that affirmation again," I added as my stare down with Theo continued.

"Thank you for making me feel less alone at a time when I was *really* lonely," she replied.

"I know the feeling," I said softly.

"Here's to being single for life," Angel sang.

Theo tilted his head, eyes narrowed.

"Here's to being single for life," I repeated. "That is, sadly, the end of our show. Don't forget to come hang with us on Twitter and Instagram, or you can reach our voice-mail to leave your questions. This is your host of *Choosing Yourself*, Daria Stone. Thank you for listening to Sunrise Beach's *only* independent radio station, K-SUN: radio for the people."

The live broadcast ended. I sat back and tugged off my headphones, stretching the tight muscles in my neck. I stood and left the sound booth, filling up on a big, deep breath. My skin prickled with the awareness of Theo's cool scrutiny. But I ignored him and beamed a smile at Elena, who was tapping away at her phone.

"Des just called," she said. "Janis needs to meet with us about some last-minute program changes." Standing, she dropped her phone into her pocket. She was dressed in black dress pants, suspenders and a sleeveless shirt printed with *queer AF*. She had light brown skin and black, curly hair shaved on both sides. Elena was Puerto Rican, had moved to L.A. from San Juan to study radio broadcasting, and had fallen in love with one of the most famous independent stations on the west coast—92.1 K-SUN FM.

She pointed a finger at me. "You were brilliant, as always. Great job tonight, Dar."

"Thanks, so were you." I lightly touched her arm. "And sorry about the dead air. I spaced, I guess."

Her gaze slid between me and Theo. "Sure, yeah. It's no

worries. We've all been there. It's a live show and shit happens."

"Having an equally brilliant board operator helps though."

She spun out the door with a grin. "You said it, girl. Theo, did you need something from me? Or did you come by to catch Daria talking about vibrators with celebrity names?"

A muscle ticked in his jaw. He smiled at Elena. Tightly. "Daria's show is always…interesting. But no, I need to speak with her about something private."

Elena's eyebrows shot up. "Well, okay then. You know where Des is?"

"Last I saw, he was working on program scheduling in the break room and nursing a beer."

She nodded, waving as she left. I crossed my arms as the door closed, shutting us into the tiny space. The sudden, unwanted intimacy only reminded me that Theo was incredibly and unfairly attractive. The man looked like a more bookish Prince Charming—thick, wavy brown hair, short on the sides and longer on top. Not a single curl ever fell onto his forehead—he was much too meticulous for that.

He was always clean-shaven and well-dressed in buttondowns that his shoulders had the audacity to fully stretch. He was white, his skin tan from the boardwalk runs I knew he and Des went on most mornings.

Theo was a few years older than me, and behind his glasses, those green eyes of his were perpetually annoyed, often studying me closely, sizing me up and finding me lacking.

Attempting to anticipate my next move.

"Did you really need to speak with me in private, Dr. Chadwick? Or did you just swing by to glower as usual?"

He reached into his pocket and unfolded a piece of paper I recognized. He tossed it onto the mixing table and smoothed down its edges. "I can glower at you any hour of the day, Ms. Stone. But instead of being irritated with you generally, I'm irritated with you *specifically* because you told *The L.A. Times* my show was, quote, 'antiquated and traditional, part of a dying breed of radio hosts obsessed with romantic love in its most narrow of forms.'"

My cheeks flushed but I forced out a dry laugh. "So? In that same article, when they interviewed you, you described my show as, and I quote, *essentially a one-hit wonder, a trendy hot take on love that won't last past the next news cycle.*"

"Was my description somehow inaccurate?" he asked.

"Was mine?"

His throat worked. "Janis won't appreciate that two of her on-air personalities are bickering with each other in the *Times*, of all places."

I frowned. "Then maybe you should have thought about that before you talked shit about me to that reporter."

He slid his hands into his pockets and leaned back against the wall. "I'd say the same thing to you. That was a fair amount of *shit* you leveled in my direction as well."

Guilt churned in my stomach. Trashing people to the press wasn't my style. But it had only been fifteen months since my radio show, *Choosing Yourself*, had gone somewhat viral, gaining me an intense cult following of local listeners practically overnight. Before I'd spoken to the *Times* reporter, I'd done just a few interviews for the press and they were all easy, softball questions about my blog and experiences.

This reporter was different. She was *supposed* to be profiling local radio hosts. Instead, she'd seemed hell-bent on pitting Theo and me against each other, hounding me about him over and over, attacking the subject from a dizzying number of angles.

Theo had been under my fucking skin for three months now. Eventually, during one of her attacks, I slipped up and spoke more forcefully than I intended to. Did Theo have the same experience? Or did he offer up an eviscerating take on my talent with ease while flashing his much-too-charming grin?

I'd seen this smile on marketing materials. Had caught rare glimpses when he was with Des or Janis or Elena, but only *just* out of the corner of my eye. Theo's good humor was an endangered species whenever I was near.

"I'm gonna go out on a limb and guess that you're not here to apologize," I said. "And I'd rather run a marathon in stiletto heels on a blazing hot day while chugging *milk* than apologize to you. That means we're back to where we were even before the interview."

"And where is that?" he mused. "I'm curious to hear your thoughts on this working relationship of ours."

"I wouldn't call it a relationship. I'd describe the two of us as currently being in a *detente*."

His eyes narrowed again. "Do you really believe the hostilities between the two of us are easing?"

"I did before you came in here to pick a fight with me," I shot back.

He dropped his finger down onto the article. "There is nothing antiquated or traditional about being a proponent of healthy and affirming romantic relationships, Daria. I'm not using my platform to force people down the aisle, dressed all in white. I've been a host a lot longer than you, have given advice to a lot more listeners, have had every complicated relationship question you can think of lobbed at me live and on the air. If you ever took the time to *listen,* you'd understand there isn't anything narrow about it. Romance is expansive."

I stepped forward and dropped my finger down, right next to his. This close, he smelled like sandalwood and sunscreen. "Celebrating singlehood isn't briefly trending, Theo. It's radical to reject the outdated notion that a person is only whole if they have a romantic partner. Promoting this idea that we all need to buckle down and find our soul mate sets people up to constantly fail. Constantly compare their lives to others and find themselves lacking. Meanwhile, we live in a society where people are *discouraged* from developing the most important relationship we'll ever have. The one we have with ourselves."

Theo made a low sound of frustration that sent a traitorous shiver down my spine. He had a voice *made* for radio, all rich, velvety notes and deep tones. That velvet had a rough edge around me, however.

"I talk to listeners every day who are lonely, who believe —and rightfully so—their soul mate is out there," he said. "Whether that's one person or three. Whether that's celebrated through marriage or not, monogamy or not. Loneliness hurts and finding love is the cure."

I took another step closer. "You have no idea how much the lie of *true love* can hurt people, Theo. I'd rather help listeners fall in love with themselves, help them celebrate the unique strengths they bring to the world instead of waiting for someone to do it for them. Some *soul mate* that may never even materialize."

The sliver of space between us was taut with restrained motion, like two predators contemplating the same prey.

Theo's nostrils flared. "Maybe if you actually *listened* to my show for once, instead of stomping around here—"

I rolled my eyes. "Oh my god, and maybe if you weren't such a smug ass—"

The door swung wide open, revealing Janis Hill, our station manager. Theo and I clammed right up, putting a more respectable distance between us.

"Hey there, Janis," I said nervously, brushing the hair from my eyes. "Did you catch the show?"

She huffed out a raspy laugh. "I sure did. I like this whole naming our vibrators thing. You did good."

I smiled in relief. Theo bristled, coughing into his fist.

Then she waved her hand between the two of us with a

knowing smirk. "I hate to interrupt this *clearly* important argument between two professionals, but once you're done bickering like a pair of toddlers over their favorite toy, can you swing by my office? I'd like to talk to you both."

"About what?" Theo asked.

Janis shrugged, smiling like she was in on the world's most lucrative secret. "Oh, it's nothin' special. Only the greatest idea in radio history. And, funny story, it involves *you two.*" She spun on her heel and left us for three unbearably awkward seconds. Until her hand hooked back around the door and she reappeared. "Whoops, I meant to clarify. It's the greatest idea in radio history and it involves you two *working together.* Now stop your fightin' and follow me. Your goddamn destinies await!"

2

THEO

I didn't generally believe that hell was other people. Quite the opposite.

Hell *was* Daria Stone, however.

I extended my hand toward the door, grinding my molars together. "After you."

Daria didn't move. "Did you know about this *idea* of hers?"

"I'm as shocked and horrified as you are," I admitted.

She whirled around, back into the sound booth, returning with a planner and her cell phone. She brushed past me, but not before tossing me a glare with her heavily lined, bright blue eyes.

When Janis had hired Daria three months ago, she'd gone from a theoretical threat to my show to a legitimate one. The year before that, I'd been all-too-aware of *Choosing Yourself*, which had garnered a passionate local following seemingly overnight at an L.A. station called K-ROX. She was Magnolia Stone's daughter, after all, and Mags was happy to share the good news of Daria's cult success over coffee in the break room or at the beginning of staff meetings.

I'd noticed the way Janis perked up at these updates, and

11

not only because Mags was more friend than colleague. Daria's show was different, edgy, exciting. The few times I'd heard it, she'd been funny and down-to-earth. Charming too, with a low, sultry voice that stayed with me long after the broadcast ended. And whenever Mags was flashing pictures of Daria around the office, I carefully avoided looking for too long.

Averting my eyes was easier than admitting how intrigued I was by her astonishing beauty.

After that, our shows spent the next year chasing each other up and down local charts and on social media. We were competitors for listeners, for fans, for future sponsorships and potential syndication.

Everything that I believed in, Daria despised. Every attitude she espoused on-air undermined my entire livelihood.

Attempting to loosen my jaw, I reluctantly followed Daria down the hallway. She had pale, smooth skin and a wide, expressive mouth often coated in red lipstick. A septum piercing glittered in her nose, matching the abundance of earrings that curved up both of her ears. Her chin-length, ink-black hair was messy and undone, as if she'd just climbed out of a lover's bed.

The woman was more *femme fatale* than radio host—the curves, the confidence, that smoky, lyrical voice of hers. Even now, buzzing with irritation, I had to resist staring at the sway of her hips in the skin-tight leather pants I assumed she wore to annoy me.

Daria pulled open the French doors to Janis's office. She had a matching set in the back of the room that led to a small deck. The rear doors were open now—they often were, given that Sunrise Beach had near-constant warm, sunny weather. The radio station was built on a narrow street that sloped down to the boardwalk. The evening held the low, ambient noise of people's voices. A mix of music. The soft roar of the ocean waves. The night sky was lit up by the Ferris wheel, slowly spinning with riders.

In the four years that I'd worked here, I'd spent more hours in this room than I could quantify. Every wall was a built-in case filled with vinyl albums, cassette tapes, a handful of 8-tracks and wobbly CD towers. Much as I tried to convince her, Janis passionately refused to throw away her collection to stream music from a laptop.

What am I, a fucking robot now? was one of the more common Janis phrases heard throughout the halls of K-SUN.

"Sit, sit." She indicated a fraying bean bag chair and a cheap plastic folding chair. I sat carefully in the folding chair to retain as much dignity as possible. Though Daria still managed to make the crumpled-up posture of a bean bag look graceful.

Janis tipped forward and clasped her hands together. "You're really becoming a huge pain in my ass, you know that?"

I opened my mouth to respond. But Janis waved her hand back and forth before either of us could speak.

"I mean it," she said. "And this is hard for me to say since I love the hell out of you both. I've been the manager here for a long time, and Daria, I'm sure Mags has told you plenty about the various dust-ups that occur when you've got a lot of big on-air personalities working in close quarters. People don't get along. People even argue, from time to time."

Janis barked out a laugh. "You two? It's only been twelve weeks since Daria formally joined the crew, and every time you're in the same room together, there's a fight. And on the flip side"—she paused, pointed between us— "it's been twelve whole weeks, and if there's some personal issue going on here, I would have expected you to work it out already. So allow me, as your boss, to more formally say: *knock it off.*"

I stared down at my hands, tugging on the fabric of my pants before hooking my right ankle over my left knee. When I looked up, Janis was watching me with the hawk-eyed gaze of hers that always made me fidget. I hadn't grown up with parents who'd cared much about me, my interests, or my whereabouts.

Janis was the first adult I'd ever met who hit me with the kind of parental stare that revealed your secrets and lies.

"Is there something you wanna say, Theo?" she asked.

"I'm sorry for my behavior," I said slowly. "Truly, I am. But I'm not sure it's as simple as that."

"Oh yeah? Stop pissing each other off and then you'll stop bickering like toddlers. How does that sound?"

I stayed quiet, afraid I was only going to come off like a petulant teenager caught breaking curfew. Out of the corner of my eye, Daria looked slightly terrified and slightly awe-struck. Not an uncommon reaction to Janis's particular style of leadership.

"I'm sorry too," Daria said. "You're right. It's unprofessional and we need to stop."

Janis frowned. "Mostly it's annoying. *Damn*, it's a radio station, kids. Have a little fun, why don't ya? And if you need some extra managerial advice, I'll mention that you're not enemies. You're not competitors. You're coworkers who do the same unique job. You've got more in common than you realize."

My lips twitched, but I held my tongue. Even the suggestion that Daria and I had things in common was absurd, as if someone had told me that reaching the summit of Mt. Everest was no more challenging than a stroll in the park.

Daria leaned forward in the bean bag chair. "Is this idea of yours—"

"The greatest idea in radio history?" Janis interjected.

"Ye-yes, that one. Does it have something to do with Theo and I being better at getting along?"

Janis traced the edge of her desk with her finger. Her expression shifted from jocular frustration to something

14

more serious. "This is going to come out at the next staff meeting, but I wanted to speak with the two of you separately. Des and Elena have already been filled in and are hammering out details as we speak."

Nerves coiled in the pit of my stomach. Nerves and a growing dread.

"Listen," Janis continued, "the station's revenue has been *lean* for the past six months. This is independent radio, so having half a year where your profit sucks is par for the course. But now it's following more of a disturbing pattern. The kind of pattern that has the larger, more corporate media companies sniffing around our bank statements. The Board told me earlier this week that they've received a few messages of interest."

"Interest in what?" I asked, brow furrowed.

She sat back in her chair. Shrugged once. "What else? Buying us out. Trying to take K-SUN, squeeze out every drop of rebellious spirit and individuality, and turn us into a profit machine."

Daria shifted in her seat. "That's what happened at K-ROX in L.A. It's why my show was canceled after only a year. They told me when they hired me that the Board was considering multiple offers. But I didn't expect the change to happen so quickly. Or for them to let go of most of their on-air personalities to replace them with people a bit more..."

"Let me guess. *Vanilla?*" Janis said with a smirk.

Daria matched her expression. "They weren't really down with the whole empowerment thing."

"It suits a lot of those companies to have shows that aren't putting forth any ideas too far out of the mainstream," Janis admitted. "I've been playing this game a long time. Long enough to spot the far-off dangers. But I'm more worried than I've been in years. The last time we had such *aggressive* interest, it was the early 2000s and stations were getting snapped up left and right. We barely made it through by the skin of our teeth."

I remembered those pledge drives. I was just a kid, but I'd idolized Janis Hill, and this station, for as long as I could remember. I grew up in a quiet house. A lonely house. One of my babysitters had taught me how to turn on the radio—like a lot of people here, she was a passionate K-SUN listener. So that was the station I turned on, the sounds of the music and the announcers filling my silent house with warmth.

In fact, I'd been a fan of *Mags in the Morning* long before I ever knew the name Daria Stone. Or that she was her daughter.

"Now I believe all we really need is a course correction," Janis said.

I arched an eyebrow. "A course what?"

"A temporary twist in our programming. Something a little spicy, a little exciting. A new idea to engage the members and get 'em to open up their wallets."

I slowly tilted forward in the chair, panic rising in me. "Janis. No. Please don't do this."

She grinned. "Janis. *Yes*. It's happening."

"Does someone want to explain what's going on?" Daria asked.

"We need to cut some costs and re-energize our listeners," Janis said. "Theo's show has been incredibly popular for years. He's our most recognizable on-air personality. But *you*, Daria, have a rapidly growing following that's taking the region by storm."

I clasped my hands together, fingers tight.

"Theo, you're going to do one more show tomorrow night. Then on Thursday, you'll combine your shows and take listener questions together and give advice together. We can easily re-air old episodes to fill in your regular spots during the rest of the week, cutting down on production and staff costs. Des will produce, Elena will operate the board, and you'll host in sound booth C since you'll need more space. We don't want you crammed in there like sardines, now do we?"

Daria let out a stunned breath. "What the literal fuck?"

"My thoughts exactly," I said through clenched teeth.

Janis reached a hand toward Daria. "I know this isn't what you envisioned when you came to work here, Dar. And I'm not angling to make this a permanent thing, I swear it. What I'm trying to do is tap into two of the greatest assets this station has. We've got folks in this town who plan their days around listening live to your shows. I'm not saying there won't be a steep learning curve to giving advice and insight as a team. I am saying..." Janis swallowed hard. "I believe the two of you have the ability to keep us afloat when we need it."

The rare dash of vulnerability in Janis's voice vanished as quickly as it appeared. That was her style, after all. It still felt like taking an elbow to the diaphragm. Janis had always been more mentor than boss to me. I understood, truly, all that was unsaid here. Understood the burden she was shouldering while Daria and I had been sniping at each other like school children.

"You're saying that we're at risk of being fucked. But we're not *totally* fucked. Yet. Because if Daria and I combine our equally obsessed fan bases into one...*super show*...it'll increase revenue and membership. A course correction, if you will."

She nodded. "This is where that whole *stop pissing each other off* stuff really comes into play."

I hid a grimace and cast a sideways look at Daria. Her gaze darted to mine then fell away. Irritation scorched through me. It was an impossible request. We couldn't even be in the same room together without fighting, let alone answer relationship questions while operating from diametrically opposing viewpoints.

"So…Thursday, then? We show up and do everything together?" Daria asked, sounding confused and miserable.

"Thursday, Friday and Saturday are the new nights you'll broadcast together. I'm thinking of calling it something like *Love and Life Advice with Theo and Daria*," Janis said. "And I want you to work with Des and Elena to come up with something entertaining to do during the week to get listeners excited and reinvested in the station. I want to energize their loyalty, want to get them donating the way they used to. Like a weekly competition. Daria Stone versus Theo Chadwick, but listeners are invited to play along. What do you think?"

"I'm sorry. A weekly *what?*" Daria asked.

Janis's smile widened. "Weekly events that listeners can pay to attend, branded to match the new show." She kicked her feet up onto the desk. "I don't care too much what you and the team come up with. Bowling, mini-golf, kickball, things like that. But it needs to at least *appear* that you're having fun or the audience isn't gonna buy it."

"What makes you think Daria and I could ever possibly have authentic-looking fun?" I asked mildly.

I didn't like—or trust—the annoying twinkle in her eye. "Let's just say, I got a feeling."

She knew how much we were going to hate this. One incredibly annoying trait about having Janis as both mentor *and* boss was realizing that she was right about things every single time. *Almost* every time.

Janis thought forcing us to work together would solve our personal problems while securing the station's financial future. Her gut instincts couldn't have been more misguided on this one.

I removed my glasses and rubbed the bridge of my nose. "Janis. With all due respect, this is going to be a disaster. You have to see that, right?"

"That vote of confidence is exactly why I *love* working

with this guy." Daria tossed me one quick, heated glare—that I returned—before Janis cleared her throat.

"I'm not asking you to partner up and diffuse a bomb or perform open-heart surgery. This is K-SUN. We do whatever the hell we want. And *usually,* that's enjoying ourselves." She hooked her thumb toward the door. "So go chill out. Lighten up. Oh, and do me a favor. Stop saying shit about each other in newspapers. It's bad for business, but you already know that."

A long, heavy silence followed. *Of course* she'd already seen it. I knew people at the station were starting to pick up on the fact that Daria and I didn't get along. But I'd thought, I'd *hoped,* we were hiding it from the outside public.

Instead, I'd made a rookie mistake and let that reporter poke and poke at me until I'd given her the hot take she wanted, throwing out a flippant opinion that was grounded more in frustration than anything else.

When it came to the subject of Daria Stone, my emotions were uncontrollable. It was a problem I couldn't allow to worsen.

I cleared my throat. "You're right. It won't happen again. It was a huge mistake."

Daria nodded, eyes down and cheeks flushed. "Yep. Yeah. I'm really sorry."

Janis nodded too, looking satisfied. She stood, rounded her desk and reached a hand to help Daria stand up from the slowly sinking chair. "Come on, up you go."

Daria rose with a relieved smile. "Thanks. And I am sorry, Janis. I'm not proud of my behavior but I appreciate you speaking to us."

Janis shrugged. "I've known you since you were a kid, Dar. I see something really special in you and in Theo. This station, this legacy, belongs to every weirdo that works here. And I want you to keep working here. Okay?"

Daria bit her lip. "Okay. I promise to keep being weird."

Janis laughed. "Now get going. Another thing I really want is to smoke a joint on the patio and then get funnel cake from the boardwalk."

Daria cracked a grin. "That's one unique way to choose yourself."

"Oh, it's the *best* way."

Janis turned around to dig through her drawer for the aforementioned joint. Daria's blue eyes landed on mine. I fought the urge to look away.

"I guess I'll...see you tomorrow...partner," she said, sounding forced.

I straightened my glasses. "So it seems. I will also...see you."

She shoved her hands in the back pockets of her pants and sauntered out the way she came in. I heard the flick of a lighter and a smoker's inhale. Janis coughed, exhaling a cloud of smoke.

"See?" she said sarcastically, "You two are so natural already. The chemistry, I mean *my god*."

I rolled my eyes and pushed up out of the chair, following Janis onto the patio, where she was already leaning her elbows on the railing with a joint dangling from her lips. She embodied this town and its reputation as the bohemian, blue-collar alternative to L.A.'s smoggy, concrete material-ism. She was anti-corporate and anti-algorithm but pro-radio for the people. In the past thirty-five years, she'd taken a tiny, independent station and turned it into a behemoth, supported by a fierce local following.

Janis was nearing seventy-one years old and had the long gray hair to prove it. She was white, her face lined with wrin-kles, and she wore round glasses that gave her an owlish appearance.

"This is some idea you've got, oh mentor of mine," I said dryly.

She exhaled, offered me the joint. I declined, like always.

"I've been your mentor for four years now. Therefore, you should know that I have the best ideas and I'm always right."

I leaned against the railing and grinned. "That would imply I've been paying attention, but you never said I was supposed to be doing that. Should I have been taking notes *this whole time?*"

She snorted. "Smile at me all you want, smart-ass. I'm not changing my mind. Deep down, I think you know I'm right about this new concept. Plus, you're getting a little too comfortable on your show. Shaking things up is good for the soul."

I bristled at the slight. "I don't think I'm getting too comfortable at all. I think I've been hitting my stride, professionally, and this will throw it into chaos. This whole thing—the show, the competitions, the events—will be an absolute nightmare."

"Then you need to get some better nightmares, kid," Janis said. "Having to work with a coworker you don't like is what this 9-to-5 gig is all about. Less nightmare, more plain old capitalism."

I glanced out toward the bustling boardwalk. "I'm not talking about my personal issues with Daria. I'm talking about the fact that I've got one single career goal right now, and that's to attract enough national attention to get syndicated. The way Magnolia's show is. It's another way to bring funds and excitement to the station. A better, more sustainable way than having Daria and I experiment on-air. How can I protect my brand, my fan loyalty, my expertise, when I'm hosting with a person who hates everything that I stand for?"

Janis nodded and stubbed out her joint, blowing one last burst of smoke from the side of her mouth. "Syndication is in your future, Theo. The tough part is that it still hasn't happened yet, as much as we've tried, and giving you increased visibility with this new show can only help. *True Romance* isn't going away, and it's not canceled. If someone wants to make an offer of syndication, I'd take it in a heartbeat. But I'm being real with you, okay? You need to learn how to compromise if you want to stay in this business. If you're open to it, you'll learn from Daria, and she'll learn from you. Your professional brand happens to be the same as your personal values. And those can change over time. *Will* change over time."

I scoffed, trying to avoid the buzzing anxiety her words were causing. "The advice I give to listeners is *not* to compromise. To stand by their own values, their own needs and only commit to someone who makes them feel like the most important person in the world. Never accepting less than what they deserve. The last thing I'd want is for something like my parents—"

I stopped, rubbing the back of my neck. Getting my show *shaken up* couldn't have come at a worse time for me, professionally. Sure, no offers had come, but that only meant I needed to reassert that I was the expert on romantic relationships in this industry—even though I'd also been single for the past six months, the longest I'd been without a girlfriend in years.

But I couldn't let Daria Stone steal these professional goals away from me.

"Theo," Janis said. "I've spent so much time with you these past four years because of what I said to Daria back there. *You* are part of my legacy. I'm not planning on going anywhere soon. But I turn seventy-one in a few weeks and won't be the Station Manager forever. You believe in independent radio. You believe in community, in *this* community. You understand what I believe our role should be."

I nodded. Slid my hand into my pocket. "We're not passive participants in this town. We don't only report on bad news, play music and move on. We are the community and we stand with them."

"We do what's right and help any way that we can," Janis added. "If some corporate asshole buys us out? We won't be for the people anymore. We'll be for profit. That can't happen to us. You and Daria, Des and Elena, everyone who works here, they've got the vision to keep it going. But it won't happen if you don't start to bend a little. Be open to changing your mind."

I gazed back out at the boardwalk, letting the weight of her words settle over me. The anxiety was there, buzzing like a swarm of flies, making me uneasy.

"Why *did* you hire Daria?" I asked, hating the jealousy that crept into my tone.

She studied me for a moment. "Because she's brave and outspoken. She helps people learn to love themselves in a world desperate for them not to. She's got her mother's bold spirit but she's even more compassionate than Mags. It's a winning combination and was an easy choice to make. I only wish our financial situation was better."

Anger flashed through me. "I help people love themselves too."

"Oh, I know you do." She patted my arm. "That's why she's not your rival in this."

"Then why are you making us literal rivals at these weekly competitions?" I asked, eyebrow raised. "You want us to get along for a show but then turn around and challenge each other to win in front of the public while...playing mini-golf?"

Janis nodded and gave me a thoughtful look. "The added fun will do you just as much good as the compromise will. One forces you to get along behind the mic. The other forces you to get along while doing something silly. Pretty soon, you'll just be getting along."

I shot her an exasperated glance. "You are awfully confident in this flawed plan."

"I know I am." She gave me a cheerful grin. "It's one of the many things you love about me. Now are we done talking so we can get some goddamn funnel cake?"

I laughed under my breath, rubbing my forehead. "Fine, but you're buying this time."

Janis grumbled as she went to go find her wallet. I pulled off my glasses and scrubbed a hand down my face.

Pretty soon, you'll just be getting along.

It was a hopeless aspiration.

Daria Stone would only ever be my adversary.

3

DARIA

*T*he next morning, I slowed to a stop at the light a block away from K-SUN. The windows of my blue Jeep beach cruiser were rolled all the way down and my music was cranked all the way up.

I drummed my fingers on the steering wheel, smiling as my mother's voice filtered through the speakers.

It's Thursday, the weather is perfect, and we live in Sunrise Beach. What's there to complain about? Nothin', I tell you. If you're tuning in and have no idea what's going on, this is Mags in the Morning. *I'm your host, Magnolia Stone, here to provide a rebellious rock 'n' roll soundtrack for the first part of your day. And this next song goes out to my only daughter, my* favorite *daughter, Daria Stone. Before you knew her as this station's newest host, she was a real wild child.*

I cocked my head, trying to guess what song she was about to play. She'd been talking about me on-air since I was a kid, gaining an added appreciation from other single parents like her. She knew I listened, knew and understood the times in my life when hearing her voice through my car speakers was like the beacon of a lighthouse, calling me home.

2

The year before Jackson and I were supposed to get married, I would sit in my parked car for an hour after work, replaying my mother's morning show and letting her voice soothe me as I tried to decipher my turbulent emotions.

Jackson and I were high school sweethearts. Had graduated from the same college together in L.A. then immediately moved into a shoebox-sized apartment near Long Beach. The next step for us was marriage because the next step was *always* marriage.

But I was only sixteen when we started dating and full of society's notions of what women in romantic relationships needed to be. So through high school and college, our young love grew more intense, and I focused on his needs, his career goals, his happiness instead of my own. I was pleasant and amenable and polite, twisting myself into a tightly wound ball of what I believed *true love* was all about.

Not even having the influence of a mother like Mags could help during those first heady years. And she viewed romance with the ire you'd reserve for a venomous snake *after* it bit you.

Once I did start rediscovering myself, my authentic self, *the wild child*, that's when my relationship with Jackson fell apart. And I learned that my future husband had wanted a polite, pliable doll to be his wife all along.

On the morning of our wedding, Jackson and his groomsmen had all bailed, escaping to a beach bar in Encinitas while I'd been left to deal with his family, my family, one hundred guests and dozens of vendors. When he finally reappeared at our apartment two days later—sheepish and apologetic—he'd confessed that what he thought had been a minor case of cold feet was him realizing he didn't love me anymore.

And hadn't, for a very long time.

The stoplight changed to green as the opening chords of

Suzi Quatro's "The Wild One" came blaring through the speakers.

"Aw, thanks, Mom," I said, singing along with the wind in my hair, the sun warming my bare shoulders. I could see K-SUN's radio tower up ahead and the large block letters that said *radio for the people*. The station was housed in a one-story white building, covered in vibrant murals painted by local artists. Just past it lay one of the entrances to the boardwalk, the narrow street covered in sand, with beach bikes chained up to stop signs and surfers strolling past carrying their boards overhead.

I drove under the curved, neon sign that read *Sunrise Beach*, past palm trees wrapped in twinkle lights, and pulled into the parking lot still singing along with Suzi. I sang under my breath as I crossed the lot. Inside, my mother's show was being piped over the speakers, but as I shoved my sunglasses on top of my head, I could see her in the first sound booth.

The cue light over the door blinked *On Air* and my mother was performing a ridiculous air guitar motion with her headphones still on. She opened her eyes and saw me. I waved, blew her a kiss, and immediately began my own air guitar, walking backward into the common room and belting out the last of the song as if I was on stage.

I swayed my hips. Tossed my hair from side to side as I sang, moving my fingers up and down imaginary frets. Then I spun around triumphantly and crashed into Theo Chadwick's stupid chest.

At first, I was only aware of hard muscle and body heat. His smell hit me—sandalwood, sunscreen. His large hands wrapped around my elbows with a firm grip, fingertips pressing into my skin. I looked up. That was a critical error. This close, Theo's face was all artistic angles: a strong nose, deviously full lips, the cut of his jaw.

Even more unsettling was the split-second of amusement

that *almost* curled the edges of those lips. I stepped back fast and pressed a palm to my racing heart.

"Are you okay?" he asked.

"Totally," I said, out of breath. "I prefer to enter most rooms that way. You're the one who ruined my air guitar."

He arched an eyebrow. "And you're the one who messed up the lyrics."

I snorted. "No fucking way, Dr. Chadwick. I was raised on Suzi."

"So was I," he replied. "I grew up listening to Mags every morning too."

I blinked, surprised. "You did?"

He nodded and turned back toward our ancient, industrial-sized coffee pot. I watched his fingers unhook the buttons at his wrists, forearm muscles flexing as he slowly rolled his sleeves to his elbows. He prepared the coffee easily and flicked the *on* button. Then he leaned against the counter, sliding both hands into his pockets.

"There was a period when I was in tenth grade when she played that song every morning, around 7:15. I woke up to it," he continued. "It would be lodged in my brain for the entirety of my school day. Would catch myself singing it all through my biology class."

"Was it lodged fortunately or unfortunately?" I asked, much too curious.

The ends of his lips twitched. "Fortunately. It's a pretty good song."

I almost said something unbelievable, like *I know, right?* But instead, I marched over and grabbed a coffee mug from the creaky cabinet. When I was a kid, I used to do my homework in this common room if Mags had to work late for meetings or pledge drives. It hadn't changed much—the couches were still oddly colored and musty. The walls were built-ins filled with vinyl records, old equipment, coils of unused black power cords and various posters from community events and in-studio concerts.

An old, cherry red jukebox that Janis had lovingly named Stevie Nicks sat in the corner, but it only played songs by The Supremes.

"Careful, Theo." I poured coffee into my mug. "You might give the impression that you actually have *fun* every once in a while."

A muscle ticked in his jaw. "I'm quite a lot of fun to be around. But then again, you don't know anything about me."

An awkward silence hung between us. I fidgeted, sipping my coffee miserably, my morning joy sapped by Theo's annoying presence—the reminder I *didn't* need that we were here early to discuss our brand-new show. The one that needed to succeed to keep the corporate robots at bay. Memories of yesterday's meeting with Janis had my stomach jumping with embarrassment all over again.

Stop pissing each other off and then you'll stop bickering like toddlers. How does that sound?

Having my professional behavior described as toddler-like was distressing enough. Having that feedback come from a woman I'd admired since I was a teenager was horrifying.

I wrapped my hands around my mug, clearing my throat. "Did, uh…did you hang back with Janis after the meeting?"

He poured his own cup, spilling not a single drop. "I did. Though I made her buy the funnel cake. Janis Hill would easily bankrupt me if I paid every time she had a late-night food craving."

"How long has she been your mentor here?"

Theo hesitated. "Does it really matter to you?"

I swallowed hard and gave him a sarcastic smile. "Of course not. I don't care."

"And neither do I."

I walked over to the meeting table and pulled out a chair.

Elena and Des would be here any minute. I didn't need to spend that time standing so close to Theo. Nor did I need to explore the boundaries of a work relationship I'd been reluctantly intrigued by for the past three months. Theo was such a smug, serious asshole around me. But those qualities softened with Janis and his friends. Overhearing him laughing at something she said or seeing them chatting over lunch caused a strange stirring in my chest.

Theo sat in the chair next to mine, putting a good three feet between us. "As much as I despise admitting when Janis is right, we should attempt a legitimate detente moving forward."

I slowly crossed one leg over the other. His knuckles whitened. "We probably should. And get on the same page about how the hell we're supposed to share a mic and collaborate on advice."

His green eyes narrowed. "You believe we'll genuinely collaborate?"

"What, you want us to duke it out on-air?"

"Of course not," he said mildly. "Though please know I'll be tempted the entire time. I assumed we'd stick to the topics we know, avoid answering the questions that we don't. It's conceivably the best way to avoid"—he waved a hand between us— "our usual patterns."

"So I'll take all of the sex questions, then." My lips curved into a sly smile. "The ones about masturbation, solo pleasure, learning how to touch your own body better than another person can. Toys, vibrators, that kind of thing."

His throat worked for a moment, but his face remained impassive. "That's a bold assumption, Daria. I counsel people through their sex questions all the time. Given my degree, it's one of my many areas of expertise."

I raised an eyebrow. "Dr. Theodore Chadwick has a degree in helping people fuck? I had no idea."

One corner of his mouth *almost* hitched up. "My expertise

contains multitudes. Sexual intimacy is a crucial cornerstone in many types of romantic relationships."

"Sexual intimacy is incredibly *empowering*," I countered. "And societal messaging tells us it can only occur between two or more people. I talk to people about shifting that priority to pleasuring yourself before you're pleasuring anyone else."

"I don't know how you could possibly think I believe otherwise. Oh wait, that's right." He snapped his fingers. "You don't listen to my show."

"Do you listen to mine?"

"I don't have to," he said. "I already know it's a snarky grab bag of whatever's trending on Twitter."

I dropped my elbows to my knees. Theo was tall and broad, his body taking up a distracting amount of space. "Just like I know yours is a boring-ass snooze-fest."

Heat flared in his eyes. They were glued to mine, stirring up those fluttery sensations in my chest. "Healthy, loving human relationships aren't boring at all. And I'll remind you that although *you* might not agree with that, my popularity, sponsorships and listener base prove it's true."

"A base I'm more than ready to win over to my side," I told him. "Describing my show as nothing but recycled internet trash is reductive and lacks imagination. What I lack in fancy degrees, I make up for with lived experiences. Lived experiences that my listeners relate to, feel seen and affirmed by. I can't say the same for you."

It was Theo's turn to duck close now. "Why is it so hard to believe that I have lived experience too, Daria?" His voice was low and dangerously rough. "Is it the fact that women have fallen in love with me and I them? That I showered them with romantic gestures and sincere affection and genuine honesty?" He leaned in one more inch. "Or is it that you can't accept that my expertise on sexual pleasure might be greater than yours?"

31

My stomach dipped. There was some disloyal, lizard part of my brain that wanted me to gawk at his large, strong hands, the smooth skin of his throat, the thick curls of his hair. I'd found it easier to focus on small aspects of Theo Chadwick because taking in his full, scholarly Prince Charming appearance was much too jarring.

"Here's a question," I said, cocking my head. "Are you a pompous dick around anyone else? Or is that a special thing you do around me?"

"I only do it because you're such a goddamn pain in my—"

Cliff Martin pushed the door open to the common room, sending Theo and me retreating to our separate corners again. He was whistling along to whatever song my mom was playing through the speakers.

"Hello there and *good* morning," he said, then rubbed his hands together. "Did you make that pot, Theo?"

"Of course," Theo replied.

"It's my lucky day. You make the best coffee, my dude."

Theo smiled at him, revealing straight white teeth and a dimple I'd never seen before. "I'm the best at a lot of things. Or so I've been told."

I sipped my coffee and muttered, "People can lie, you know."

Theo's rare smile vanished. He mouthed *you're a pain in my ass*. To Cliff, he said, "You'll be at the meeting next week to start planning Janis's party, right?"

"Hell yeah, I will," Cliff drawled, raising his mug. "We're gonna throw the greatest birthday bash yet."

Cliff was in his mid-fifties and looked like he definitely followed the Grateful Dead. He'd been a host here almost as long as my mother, with a popular Sunday night show called *The Eclectic Journey*. It was hours of randomly selected music tied to whatever bizarre weekly theme he came up with.

"You're planning something for Janis?" I asked.

Theo nodded. "Her seventy-first birthday is in a few weeks, and having planned the last four of them, I can tell you that she *hates* surprises. Her preference is to detail every single thing she wants and then we all make it happen."

"Like last year's bounce house." Cliff's tone was wistful.

I grinned, despite Theo being right there. "She's like, 'I want a horde of zebras for my birthday,' and then you—"

"Coordinate with an exotic pet store," Theo said. "And I know that because of the time she wanted llamas."

"There's usually a big dance party too," Cliff replied. "Your mom and I put together a playlist with Norris and Millie, so it's like a lot of weird shit and classic rock with some disco thrown in."

Theo sipped his coffee. "Janis loves a disco."

Norris hosted a weekly show called *Saturday Night Fever* which was described on our site as "vintage dance party" meets "Studio 54." Millie hosted a popular Friday night set called *The Mix Tape* where listeners submitted the best songs from their sweaty and hormonal teenage playlists.

"I can definitely help with that," I said. "Count me in. My overall vibes are 'weird dance party' meets 'bounce house.'"

Cliff nodded jovially and walked toward the door. "Rock on, sister. Oh, and tell Mags her show feels heaven-sent today."

"Did you catch the song she dedicated to me?"

"I not only caught it, I saw your groovy little air guitar too," he said, shuffling out the door in his head-to-toe tie-dye.

I turned back to Theo. "My skills are clearly appreciated around here."

Theo stood gracefully and set his mug on the counter. "Thank you for offering, but we don't need extra help for the party, Daria."

"But I love Janis. I've known her since I was a little girl. I wanna help, is all."

"I'm sure you do, but I'm thinking about our *detente* situation. The less time we spend together, the better. Don't you agree?"

My phone buzzed on the table with a message that read *one new email*. My pulse spiked.

"Um…yeah, fine," I said, distracted by the alert. "Have you considered taking Janis's advice and not pissing me off? That would help our situation even more."

Theo's irritated growl turned my head just as Elena and Des strolled in, mid-conversation, for our meeting. I scooped up my phone. With shaking fingers, I opened my email and felt my stomach drop when I saw the message was from one of the literary agencies I'd sent my manuscript to. I'd learned these past months I needed to click to open before my nerves kicked in.

Daria — I'm sorry to say we're passing on this manuscript. That's the bad news. The good news is that I loved this book of essays. You've got a great voice—unique, funny, bold. The subject matter is very timely and contemporary. But we're not taking on memoirs and essays right now, which is why we're declining. Resubmitting in a year isn't a bad idea, as is continuing to search for a literary house that fits what you're trying to do with this book. Best of luck to you!

I shut my eyes, very aware that I wasn't alone. *Very* aware of Theo sitting next to me again. These types of rejections were worse than the automated 'not interested' ones I also received. Telling me they liked it—*but*—hurt exponentially more. It was the dangling hope, the tease of glittering fortune. This wasn't technically a full-on rejection. I still wanted *someone* to read my essays and say, "you know what? That Daria Stone knows what she's talking about."

Especially since I was about to be spending my days being compared to Theo. As soon as Jackson and I graduated high school, we'd moved to L.A. and I began working whatever odd job or poorly paid internship I could find at radio stations. I was taking broadcasting classes at the community college and earning extra cash working at a used vinyl record shop until I landed at K-ROX.

I knew how to operate every piece of equipment in this place. What I didn't have was Theo's advanced education, experience and following. I liked to *say* I was coming for his fan base—because I was—but even bursting onto the radio stage so suddenly couldn't garner me the popularity he'd gained by consistently being the best for four years running.

I could hear Des and Elena behind me at the coffee pot. Next to me, Theo cleared his throat softly.

"Are you okay?" he murmured.

"What?" I asked, still a little dazed.

"I asked if you were okay. You seem upset."

I tore my eyes from the email and looked at Theo. The note of genuine concern in his voice was confusing. "I'm fine. It's nothing."

He nodded once, mouth tight. Until Des sat down next to him and slid a delicious-smelling bag his way with a wide grin. "I picked up an extra sandwich for you, buddy."

Theo smiled back. Beamed, really, looking comfortable and happy around his friend. His smile was compelling. His smile was *charming*.

I dropped my gaze, cutting the visual connection so that my brain couldn't latch onto the image. If I really wanted this job, really wanted this fan following, *really* wanted to publish a book, I had to stay focused on the solution to all those problems.

I had to be better than Theo.

At everything.

4

THEO

*D*es opened his laptop and the rest of us followed with whatever note-taking devices we preferred. I propped my right ankle on my left knee and pressed my notebook to my thigh, clicking my pen through a burst of unruly sensations. The ones I experienced when Daria was within my vicinity—frustration, annoyance. And something dark and primal, a scorching heat in my veins, a feeling that stretched and shook awake only when she was near.

My natural instincts tended toward curiosity. A desire to study, learn, unpack. To understand every complexity of human relationships and help others understand too.

Yet whenever I was around Daria, my emotions bucked my usual attempts at control, so those same instincts yelled *resist* when it came to the mystery of her worldview and experiences.

They yelled *resist* when it came to accepting that Daria was incredibly beautiful.

She had no idea that I'd seen her this morning before we crashed into each other. Had seen her in that blue Jeep, singing out loud, black hair flying around her face, red lips in a permanent smile. I'd even watched her dancing through the lobby and down the hallway—the sheer, unrestrained joy of it captivating me fully.

Her posture in the chair next to me vibrated with a defiance I knew was meant solely for me, from the way her plaid skirt kept sliding up her thighs, to the sly tilt of her neck and the quirk of her lips.

My pen went *click-click-click*.

Des was peering at me with a bemused look. "You two look like Janis Hill just dressed you down and forced you to start making a show together."

I grinned. "What makes you say that? Could it be the general air of misery that surrounds us?"

"Unfortunately, yes," Des said. "That's why I brought you the gift of a greasy breakfast sandwich."

I pulled back the paper bag with my finger and inhaled the addicting scent of eggs, bacon and cheese. Desmond Davis was K-SUN's director of production, and he'd become my closest friend over the past four years of working together. We spent a lot of nights in this common room, eating something fried and drinking beer as we prepped for listener questions and show themes.

He had a large extended family in Sunrise Beach, and since no members of my own were interested in spending holidays together, I now spent every single one with Des, his wife, Susannah, and their combined families. He was Black, about as tall as I was, with dark brown skin, short curls, and a beard.

Des reached under the table and extended a similarly greasy bag to Daria. She clapped her hands together when she saw it. "And I didn't forget you, Dar. Elena and I grabbed breakfast at the diner to discuss the, uh, *unexpected* program changes that Janis dropped on us."

"Did you know that Janis was that concerned with the budget and the corporate offers coming in?" Daria asked.

Elena lifted a shoulder. "It's come up in our production

meetings but this is K-SUN. We're usually in some kind of budget crisis. If she's starting to make cost-cutting measures, program changes, that kind of thing, then it's a scarier threat than the garden variety funding issues all independent stations go through."

"And we'll be making other cuts, tightening up where we can, adjusting some programs," Des added. "We're looking at a one-off pledge drive in a couple weeks too. She's dedicated to being creative about the whole thing."

I nodded. "She's extremely good at that. She's spent most of her career cutting corners to keep the station afloat."

Des hooked an elbow over the back of his chair. "I have to say, you're both taking this news pretty well given—"

"Everyone knows you can't stand each other," Elena said.

Daria and I exchanged a quick, awkward glance. "I expressed my concerns about a dozen times and all Janis did was smoke a joint and eat an entire funnel cake."

"I'm simmering with fury over here." Daria had a sardonic twist on her lips. "But we're *trying* to, like, detente or whatever."

Des chuckled. "Yeah? 'Cause your body language definitely does *not* say 'two coworkers looking forward to working with each other.'"

I rubbed the back of my neck, feeling the same anxiety and embarrassment I had last night. Janis didn't mince her words. And we'd had plenty of conversations where she'd given me advice that had forced me to learn something new or reconsider my position. They weren't easy for me, but they did happen occasionally.

Last night wasn't that. Last night was my supervisor expressing her own annoyance and disappointment in how Daria and I interacted with each other. This was a small station, a close-knit staff. Interpersonal issues had a deep ripple effect here. Giving in to the temptation to *poke* at Daria, thus far, was only ever bad for my career.

Janis was right. I did need to knock it off. I could do that —be cool and civil—without having to go along with *all* of her suggestions. Namely, the compromising and the learning from each other parts.

"I wasn't expecting Janis to force Daria and me to work together," I admitted. "My initial reaction was more shock and anger. But obviously, I would do anything to help K-SUN. I'm all in."

And the better I performed, especially in comparison to Daria, the better my chances were for syndication.

"Same here," she said. "I'm not going to tank one of our best options for keeping the doors open because—"

I arched an eyebrow her way. "Because…what?"

She pursed her lips. "Nothing. I was going to say… because Theo and I will have to adjust to a learning curve, us working together and taking calls. No bullshit, I swear. Janis was right, about everything."

Elena clicked her tongue. "She's real annoying like that."

I chuckled. "It's true. So what's the plan for tomorrow?"

Elena stretched her arms forward onto the table. "From my end, it's not gonna be much different. We'll need to figure out how we prioritize and choose the caller questions. I'd want us to divvy them up fairly evenly, though some apply to you both. With the live calls, which are sometimes total wild cards, you'll need to—" She waved her hand at Daria and me.

"Behave ourselves?" I suggested.

"That's the spirit," Des said. "On the original schedule, Daria's show aired Tuesday, Thursday and Saturday nights with Theo's on Mondays, Wednesdays, and Fridays. *Love and Life Advice* will now be Thursday through Saturday. Those are the hottest nights, from a numbers perspective. I know this isn't what you wanted, but her idea is kind of ingenious."

It absolutely wasn't. There was no way that Daria and I together could ever provide a better, more fruitful listening experience than Daria and me *apart*. We could barely make eye contact as it was, let alone sit for hours, in a small sound booth, facing each other with headphones on and mics at our mouths.

"The second piece is these competitions Janis wants you two to do with the fans," Des continued, tapping his pen against the table. "The more we can get the internet engaged with you as popular on-air personalities, and the more we can play up the fact that your shows *are* different, making it lively and competitive, the more excited folks will be to tune in."

"And become members," Elena said, rubbing her thumb and index finger together. "We need money, baby."

"We brainstormed a bit this morning over breakfast," Des continued. "Janis wants fun, nothing serious. A game of paintball, for example."

Daria cracked a smile, shoulders loosening up. "Whoa, *whoa*. I fucking love paintball."

"You do?" I asked.

She flashed me a look, like *what the hell do you know?* Which was fair. I'd said something similar when she asked me about my relationship with Janis.

"I'm down with that suggestion since it's likely I'll win." Daria's tone was laden with faux sweetness. "And how will the listeners get to be involved?"

Elena sipped from her mug. "We'd like to see members participating along with you, like a night where K-SUN staff and members take over a mini-golf course or something. We can share pictures you take that day, driving traffic to your next show, where you can tell everyone about your experiences. Play up the competitive angle as much as possible."

"We've got paintball and mini-golf, which is a Sunrise Beach boardwalk tradition," Des said. "And arcade games, you know hoops and Skee-Ball and Whac-A-Mole. I think it'll be a *great* time. Most of our fans grew up strolling that boardwalk every summer night. The paintball arena is a little outside of town, but everything else would happen in the station's backyard. Is there anything more nostalgic than playing those old boardwalk games with your friends?"

Des held my gaze for a second, face filled with a kindness that made my chest ache. Not many people knew about the hollow loneliness of my childhood, but he did. I didn't find a core group of friends until college, when I started feeling more comfortable in my own skin. That meant that although I also grew up in this town, I wasn't one of the kids eating popcorn and riding the Ferris wheel ten times in a night while on summer vacation.

The thought of doing those things with Daria had that same heat pouring through my body. Less dark though, more like the moments I had listeners describing to me all the time.

Almost like I was blushing.

"Okay, okay." Daria tapped her chin. "It feels like an old-school radio contest. It's two hosts playing fun games along with a bunch of fans of the show. And the prize is we gain even more supporters and save the station from a potential corporate takeover. Did I get that right?"

Des spread his arms wide. "Nailed it."

"It does have the hyper-local vibe that K-SUN cultivates," I said. "That's what makes us a unique voice among other indie stations. We don't report on the community, we're *of* the community. Playing games on the boardwalk doesn't have the same gravitas as when we join protests outside of City Hall. But we're still local celebrities with large followings and a passionate fan base. The listeners should see us out in the community, enjoying the things that make Sunrise Beach so special."

I felt the weight of Daria's stare but didn't return it. I'd meant what I said—about what this station was, about what it should continue to be. The reality of putting up some idealized version of my relationship with Daria still seemed like an impossible task.

Elena's lips curved up. "Are you gonna tell Janis she was right, Theo?"

"Oh, never," I said. "The more you tell her that, the more her power grows."

Des stood, closing his laptop and tucking it under his arm. "Speaking of budgets, I've got a meeting and I know Elena has to tape some promos for the weekend. Are you both good with our initial ideas?"

"I'm excited to ruthlessly beat Theo at paintball, so yes," Daria declared.

"And I'm looking forward to show Daria how short-sighted it is to underestimate me."

Elena and Des exchanged a glance. "Just, uh...keep working on that *detente* thing." Elena looked at me. "Theo, I'll see you tonight for your show."

I stood, needing space from the raven-haired menace next to me. We'd been forced into a mild civility by Des and Elena's presence and that had me feeling the need to flee. Adversarial or civil, it didn't matter.

Her presence was like a hot, flickering flame I shouldn't touch.

I refilled my coffee and tried to focus on what I needed to do for show prep tonight. But when I turned back around, Daria was standing too, palms behind her on the table. She was watching me with a feline intensity, like a cat considering a mouse. Her posture drew attention to the curve of her thighs beneath her skirt, the inch of bare stomach revealed by the cut of her top. It was a *come-hither* pose—if she'd crooked her finger at me, I would have been forced to lock my knees. But the fire in her eyes was more provocation than seduction.

"Plotting your victorious paintball strategy, I assume?" I asked.

She lifted a shoulder lazily. "Something like that."

"Will you be listening to my show tonight?"

"Probably. I always need something to doze off to."

I shook my head and gave a dark laugh. "It will be so incredibly satisfying to beat you at every single stage of this ill-advised experiment."

Daria tilted her head. "Cocky, Dr. Chadwick. If I wasn't mistaken, I'd say my presence has bothered you from the beginning because you see my rising popularity as a threat to your show and your career."

I narrowed my eyes. "Let's not pretend that hasn't been your end goal this entire time."

"You were right," she said. "I am a threat. Good luck trying to win though."

A voice in my head was screaming *control, control, control*. Janis's words from last night churned like a mantra. I ignored all of them, taking measured steps toward Daria until the tips of my shoes brushed the toes of her platform boots. Her blue eyes widened even as she lifted her chin to hold my gaze. I kept my hands by my side so I wouldn't be tempted to grip her thighs, to slide my fingers beneath her skirt and demonstrate just how expertly I understood the many definitions of *pleasure*.

"I've never needed luck," I said firmly. "And I definitely won't need it once our listeners choose love and romance in the end. When they choose *me*. I'll figure out a way to let you down easy though."

5

THEO

I could tell it was going to be a good show by the number of listeners who called in seeking advice for marriage proposals.

We'd already had seven tonight.

Though Jake's call had a unique spin—the boyfriend he wanted to propose to happened to be an actor, already followed around by the paparazzi, with his photos splashed across magazines.

"I listen to your show all the time," Jake muttered good-naturedly. "I don't know why I'm so nervous right now."

I straightened my glasses as the first flurry of ideas tumbled around in my brain. "Once you start thinking about proposals, it's going to block out the sun, metaphorically speaking. It makes it more challenging to see some of the details clearly. And I think your assumption that parts of the proposal will end up in at least one tabloid is a fair one, given that he's a celebrity." I lowered my voice. "Being nervous is normal and okay. You're sharing personal information on-air. You're in good company, I promise."

Half of the time, I spent these calls making the other person feel comfortable with whatever vulnerable question they had about their love lives. It had been an adjustment, moving from writing an advice column to answering those questions on-air—a natural separation occurred for me when I was reading emails, unable to hear the person's voice and the fear or hope or happiness in their tone.

But I'd counseled plenty of college students when I taught at my university, helped coach them through their finals stress, their personal problems, their worries about the future. Sometimes I felt like achieving a doctorate in social psychology hadn't been necessary—working alongside students never ceased to reveal the complex tapestry of human experiences.

Being the only child stuck in the middle of my parents' cold divorce had had a similar effect.

Jake laughed, loosening up. "Right, and that's why the proposal can't suck. But every idea I have sucks and isn't Instagram-worthy or fancy or glamorous."

"I highly doubt it *sucks*," I said with a smile. "Your future husband is a celebrity. That makes personal milestones more complicated, so your thoughtfulness will pay off in the end."

"You really think so? Actually, scratch that. You're basically a proposal expert, duh."

"I'm not an expert, just a guy who went to school for a while," I said easily.

Although that wasn't what I'd bragged to Daria yesterday. *My expertise contains multitudes.* But that was because we'd been talking about sex. The subject matter had activated my baser instincts with a dizzying speed, making me eager to taunt her until she broke, becoming flushed and off her game.

"I do have an idea, based on what you've told me so far," I continued. "Have you considered making the proposal an entirely private affair?"

"What, like…in our kitchen or something?"

I grinned. "I'm assuming your celebrity boyfriend has a

pretty nice kitchen, right? Or maybe a private balcony or garden? Someplace that's meaningful to you as a couple?"

I could sense him pondering this, so I took the opportunity to do some further convincing.

"I do know a *tiny* bit of what it's like to have some public scrutiny, especially here in Sunrise Beach. It can make you feel like someone, somewhere, is examining your behavior under a microscope. But this is the moment you're going to ask him to marry you. To be your committed partner for a lifetime. It's a moment of true, romantic intimacy and vulnerability. For some, sharing that in front of friends or family is important. But maybe he would want to share it only with you."

I paused, let the words sink in. Jake made a barely perceptible *huh* sound.

"No cameras, no tabloids. No magazines paying for your private moments. Just you and him." I rubbed my thumb across my lower lip. "What do you think?"

"You know, he's a homebody in real life. When we're not at award shows or Hollywood parties. And we do love cooking together. I'm going to end up planning a kitchen proposal, aren't I? How are you so good at this?"

I passed a hand across the back of my neck. I was only 32 but had had three long-term relationships. Serious relationships with women who desired marriage in the same way I did.

Yet I had never, not once, proposed to any of them.

"It's one idea," I finally said.

Jake sighed, happier this time. "I can see it, like *really* see it. He would have hated something public. Thank you for pointing me in the right direction."

"It's what I'm here for." Elena made a *wrap it up* gesture. "I do have to let you go so I can give some program updates, but please call back and let us know how it went, okay? It's going to be great."

"Absolutely. Thank you for everything," he said before the line clicked off.

I shifted in my chair, my limbs beginning to fill with a low, buzzing anxiety. "As always, thank you for choosing to spend your Thursday nights here, with me, on *True Romance*. Moving forward, we have some new and surprising program changes starting tomorrow. For the next month, I'll be joined by another K-SUN favorite—Daria Stone, our newest on-air personality who hosts *Choosing Yourself*. We'll be teaming up for a new segment we're calling *Love and Life Advice with Theo and Daria,* and it'll be broadcast, live, Thursday through Saturday evenings."

Elena clicked through onto the broadcast. "Based on the immediate reactions on our social media pages, folks out there are stoked."

My presence at this radio station has bothered you from the beginning because you see my rising popularity as a threat to your show and your career.

I exhaled through a growing tightness in my chest. "That's because we have the best fans around. Now, I know it's new. I know it's different. We've never done this before, so Daria and I are doing something new and different too."

Elena chimed back in again, clicking her tongue. "You haven't told them about the games, Theo."

I forced a smile. "Everyone at the station is looking forward to this more than I am, but then again, they're not possibly humiliating themselves in public along with their coworker."

She laughed. "It won't be that bad, we swear."

"We'll see about that," I said evenly. "Starting next week, my cohost and I will be entering into different competitions all across the city—everything from paintball to mini-golf on the boardwalk. We love the summer here and so we thought —why not get out in the community and invite the listeners to join in? Plus, members will be able to play along online or even play with us in person. Since Daria isn't here to defend herself, I'd like to have it on the record that I intend to win. Every time. At everything."

"The internet also has some thoughts on your odds of success." Elena grinned.

"I'm sure they do. This is where the whole 'trying to avoid public humiliation' part comes in."

"Eh, you'll be fine. But like Theo said, it's been a while since the station's done anything like this. Remember that year we hosted a dozen of those beach dance parties?"

"We called them *Saturday Night Beach Fever*." I laughed for real this time. "That was also the summer I remember being the most consistently hungover."

"I still think we should bring those back," she said. "But seeing a bunch of K-SUN fans lined up to play mini-golf will be pretty great."

I felt slightly better now that the announcement was out, now that I could remember, through the haze of my anger toward Daria, that there was a vital reason for doing this. She was only a true threat if I kept letting her get under my skin, jeopardizing my focus. There was a kernel of truth to Janis's strategy I hadn't wanted to admit—any amount of extra visibility this month could only increase my chances of getting syndicated.

"And with that, we're at the end of our show. We always welcome your questions on our Twitter and Instagram, and on our voicemail. Thanks for listening to Sunrise Beach's *only* independent radio station, K-SUN: radio for the people."

I sat back in my chair and pulled off my headphones before heading in to speak with Des and Elena. Crossing my arms, I propped my shoulder against the doorway.

"How'd I do?" I asked. "Are people genuinely excited or were you hyping me up?"

Elena and Des exchanged a look. "People are excited. We've got some grumble-y comments trickling in. Some people love you but don't like Daria. Some people love her but don't like you. Change is hard and folks have their sides or whatever. But we'll remind everyone in the show ads this week that 'best of' episodes will still air. They won't lose their fix entirely."

"Change is hard," I echoed. "I'm glad you're both here with me. It's an adjustment for Daria and me because we're the hosts. You've all been scrambling to make miracles work too though. I'm grateful."

"Anything for K-SUN," Elena said. "You and Dar will figure it out. I work with you three nights a week, but I also work with *her* three nights a week. You're more alike than you realize, just coming at ideas from different angles, is all. There's a lot of common ground there."

I lifted my chin toward the hallway. "Did Janis pay you to say that?"

She shook her head, laughing. "She didn't, I swear."

I tugged down my shirtsleeves and reclasped the button at my wrists. "These claims are eerily similar to the ones she made earlier."

"We'll see tomorrow night if the great Janis Hill is able to predict the future. Yet again," Des said. "Are you hanging around the office for a bit or heading home?"

"Heading home." I grabbed my messenger bag from the floor. "Want to walk me out?"

He nodded, clapping me on the shoulder while Elena finished up the broadcast.

"You did great tonight," he told me as we walked down the hallway together. "You really don't need to worry about losing your fan base. Elena and me, we see all the behind-the-scenes stuff. The numbers, the messages, the spike in listeners at the exact time your show airs every week. Trust me, your kingdom is safe."

We strolled down the hallway and out into the warm night. Above our heads, the radio tower blinked and the K-

SUN sign glowed white. I took several long inhales, clearing my lungs of the stale air of the sound room.

"Thank you for saying that," I said. "If I'm not too tired after tomorrow's show, we could get drinks at High Frequency. Bring Susannah too if she's around."

The High Frequency Bar was essentially an extension of the K-SUN offices. Just a five-minute walk down the street from here, it was part beach dive, part karaoke bar, and their kitchen served greasy food well past midnight, which was ideal for radio employees used to eating dinner at one in the morning.

"I'm down for after-show drinks," Des said. "If I bring Susannah, do you want me to ask her to invite Carly too?"

I hesitated, adjusting my glasses before giving an apologetic shrug. "The sparks weren't there between me and Carly. I do appreciate Susannah setting me up with her coworker and organizing all those double dates though. I hope she's not too disappointed."

Des rubbed a hand through his curls. "She only wants you to be happy. She won't be disappointed, but she'll be surprised. On paper, Carly's the perfect woman for you."

"I thought so too," I admitted. "There's nothing wrong with your and Susannah's instincts. Carly was sweet and lovely, and we had a lot in common. It's been six months since Stormi and I broke up and there hasn't been a single date where I've felt much of anything. Ever since—"

I stopped, horrified to realize what I was about to say.

Ever since Daria started working here.

She occupied too much space in my brain, toyed with my thoughts, had me constantly on edge and frustrated. Yet another way that Daria Stone was encroaching into my life. She had to be the reason that every date I went on felt flimsy at best. Why my motivation to get back out there and find *the one* was essentially nonexistent.

"Theo," Des said, a knowing smirk on his face. "Ever since…what?"

I cleared my throat. "Ever since Daria started working here. Her presence affects my focus when I should be directing that energy to dating. She's like some kind of true-love-hating vampire."

He was clearly trying not to smile. "Pretend you were a caller. What advice would you give them?"

I frowned. "Easy. I'd tell them they happened to have an aggravating coworker, a common complaint in every workplace. But they're giving too much energy to anger and irritation when their energy *could* be spent on cultivating meaningful, loving relationships with others." My frown slid into a wry smile. "To paraphrase Janis, I'd tell them to *knock it off.*"

Des studied me for a moment. "Just because you're the romance expert doesn't mean you have to be in a relationship all the time, Theo. No one's going to think you're less competent. You're giving advice based on your degree, on the attitudes and situations you've studied for years. But you're not a data point."

"Being single isn't that great for my brand. Especially not right now."

He cocked his head. "You're sure that's the advice you would give? I've been listening to you for four years now, and you usually tell your callers to take all the time they need. Not to rush it, but to accept that each breakup is unique so the time to heal before moving on is just as unique. Maybe you need more time after Stormi."

I paused. "It wasn't…you know it wasn't like that for us. At the end."

"Like what?"

I wrapped my hand around the strap across my chest. "It wasn't that serious. Or that passionate. Whatever connection I believed existed between us had obviously been fading for months without me realizing. If I'm taking my own advice, I'd be halfway to falling in love with someone by now."

When Stormi broke up with me, she'd admitted that our ideas of real love were not the same after all, though I could have sworn the opposite.

It seems like you only really want the symbolic gestures of love, she'd said. *And not the real intimacy and complications and tough times. I love dramatic romantic gestures and gifts and flowery language as much as anyone does. But that can't sustain a relationship for a lifetime, Theo.*

I'd spent the past six months single, brushing up against the sharp edges of loneliness that had hounded me since childhood. That made it challenging to understand how love couldn't be sustained through gifts or gestures. For so many years, I could have survived off that kind of nourishment alone.

"I see what you mean," Des said, bobbing his head. "You're saying that you *would* be out there, dating in a happy and healthy way, halfway to falling in love. Except you can't stop thinking about Daria."

I paused, mid-step, while my heart rate tripled. My mind flooded with a single image for a single second: Daria, dancing beneath the sun with a smile as wide as the horizon.

I blinked, shocked, and shoved it away so forcefully I felt dizzy.

Desmond's eyebrows shot up at my uncharacteristic silence.

"It's not…" I coughed into my fist. "It's not like that at all. That's…that's impossible."

He held up his palms. "It's a thin line between thinking about how mad your coworker makes you and thinking about her, period. Or so the old saying goes."

I started backing away toward the edge of the parking lot. "As a social psychologist, I can tell you that feelings of romantic love and legitimate hate are not closely connected in any way."

Even I could hear the shake in my voice.

"Huh." He rubbed his chin. "Then perhaps you don't hate her as much as you think. Or maybe you don't even hate her at all."

I stopped in my tracks, every counterargument in my head evaporating. Des went to turn back to the office, but not before squeezing my shoulder with a look of honest sympathy.

"Just something for you to think about," he said quietly. "Friend-to-friend."

By the time he reached the door, I attempted a casual sounding, "I'll repeat. That's impossible."

Des only cracked a smile. "G'night, Theo."

The sound of the door shutting behind him shook me from my trance. I scrubbed both hands down my face before setting off down the sidewalk that would lead me home.

"Impossible," I repeated to myself, feeling jittery.

There was nothing about the way Daria dominated my waking thoughts that suggested what Des was implying. Her siren-like beauty certainly made our adversarial situation more complicated, but the findings were no less conclusive: we were polar opposites in every way that mattered to me, which meant we had nothing between us that would ground and support the kind of relationship I desired.

The road ahead was clear: once I stopped fighting with Daria, I'd be ready to focus on dating again.

6

DARIA

*T*he article I was reading—titled *How to win a game of mini-golf and make your opponent cry*—was the reason I was walking toward the K-SUN door with my head down. I'd found it by googling the words "mini-golf success" plus "need to win" plus "can you cheat????".

I chewed on my bottom lip, scanning the screen. "I wouldn't want Theo to *actually* cry though," I muttered.

And that's when I ran into Theo's stupid chest. Again.

Or rather, his stupid chest ran into *me*.

The force of it had me stumbling back. I would have tumbled to the ground if his arm hadn't snaked around my waist, keeping me upright.

"Fuck," he said, out of breath. "Are you okay?"

I rubbed my forehead, scowling up at him. "Do you walk around our offices, waiting to chest bump my face?"

"Of course not," he said. "Do you ever walk in an ordinary fashion? With your face forward and your arms not performing some kind of air guitar?"

"Why the hell would a person choose to move through life in a way that was ordinary?" My words slowed as I realized why Theo was out of breath. And why every inch of my body tingled with delicious awareness.

He'd been coming from a run—curls *slightly* tousled, skin warm and tan, the scent of sweat and sunscreen lingering between us. His chest heaved, one hand on his hip, the other still curved around my waist. Only a single inch of space separated my lower body from pressing into his.

Like his face, Theo's broad shoulders and leanly muscled arms were a deeply unfair advantage. He passed a hand through his hair, biceps flexing with the motion.

"Your mouth is open, by the way," Theo said with a twitch of his lips.

I smacked my lips together and gave him my cheesiest *fuck you* smile. "And you're still holding me like a horny prom date."

His jaw tightened. Then his large palm slid away from my lower back. "I'm sorry. I shouldn't...I shouldn't have done that."

He took a polite step back, looking chastened.

I lifted a shoulder. "Well, I'm grateful I didn't fall, so... thank you. I'm less grateful that you hurtled into me two days in a row now."

"Getting swept up in one of the best songs to sing out loud is understandable." He reached forward and tapped my cell phone screen. "But haven't you heard these things are dangerous?"

I held it up so he could see what I was reading. "You know what's even more dangerous? The skills I'll be bringing to mini-golf for our competition."

His eyes narrowed to read, his hand wrapping around the back of mine to keep the phone steady. It was a barely-there touch, too light to even be considered a caress. It still sent a shiver of pulsing desire through my entire body.

"Your plan is to make me weep?" he asked. "How diabolical of you, Ms. Stone."

I pursed my lips. "The headline of the article is unfortunate. I'm focused more on the winning part. Not the crying part. I'm not the heartless monster you secretly want me to be, Dr. Chadwick."

An emotion I couldn't read flickered through his gaze. But I stepped back before he could speak, needing even more space. "I'm not used to seeing you look so—"

He cocked his head, clearly amused. "So what?"

"Casual," I said, choosing the word carefully. "You're usually a bit more refined around the office."

He glanced down at his running clothes. "I was hoping a long, hard run on the beach would help me keep argumentative comments to myself while we're on-air tonight."

"Is it working?"

"We've barely argued, even when I discovered you plan to make me cry in public."

My lips were curving up, and not to taunt or smirk or annoy. But to *smile*. In *response*. I looked down at the ground to conceal whatever betrayal was happening on my face. I ran a hand through my own disheveled curls, finally remeeting his eyes when I could control myself. It was probably a trick of the summer light, the split second when he seemed enthralled by my hair.

"I literally *just* said I was opposed to forcing you to weep on a mini-golf course." I put my hands on my hips. "You might not be arguing but you *are* lying. And I thought you were supposed to be a perfect gentleman? Or are your fans wrong about that?"

I realized my mistake the same moment that Theo did.

"Daria," he drawled. "How would you know that my fans tease me about being the perfect gentleman? You don't listen." He ducked his head, attempting to hold my gaze. "Or do you?"

"I don't," I said firmly. "I saw it online. On your Instagram, probably. They don't exactly hide their obsession with you."

"Listening to my show *and* looking at my pictures." His eyes crinkled at the sides. Was he about to smile at me? "This is an intriguing development in our detente."

I snorted. "So a picture came up while I was scrolling my feed. Please resist flattering yourself that much, Theo."

"Whatever you say," he said. "But if I'm the perfect gentleman, what does that make you?"

"Definitely your worst nightmare."

"So strange," he murmured. "That's exactly how I described you to Janis after our meeting the other night."

A loud, raspy voice bellowed through the parking lot. My mother's. "Is that my favorite daughter I see?"

It was a good thing too, because the only retort I could think of next was to flip Theo both middle fingers. Each interaction with him was about control and strategy. Nimbly returning every verbal volley with a precise response meant to annoy him.

But I was flustered, off my game. I didn't usually make those kinds of mistakes—like accidentally, almost, *kind of* admitting that *I'd* been the one lying this entire time.

I absolutely listened to his show. Even before I had my own, I knew who Dr. Theodore Chadwick was because he worked at K-SUN with my mom and she praised how sweet and smart and charming he was. *True Romance* was only broadcast locally, but that hadn't stopped his base of fans from growing fast in four years. I'd only ever turned it on a few times, and not recently. And only to better know my competition, to better understand the other radio host in L.A. giving out opposite advice from my own.

He was, as my mother had said, sweet and smart and charming. Warm with his callers. Vulnerable when he needed to be. And that mahogany voice of his, directly in my ears, *always* caused a liquid heat to pulse between my legs, even before we'd met in person.

My mother finally reached us. Based on the time, she must have just signed off. "Hi, baby doll," she said, wrapping me in a tight bear hug. Her hair was jet-black, like mine, cut in a Joan Jett-style shag with gray hair mixed in. She wore a jean vest that showed off the abundance of faded tattoos on her arms. "What are you doing here so early?"

"I've got a lot of work to do before my show with Theo tonight," I said. She pulled back, still holding my arms, and scowled at my reluctant cohost.

"You keep all that romance nonsense to yourself, Theodore. I see you there, trying to sneak up on me."

He tipped his head with a respectful smile. "Yes, ma'am. I'm just coming back from my run and then I'll be working all day, like Daria said. I won't kidnap you and take you to a candlelit dinner. I swear it."

My mother scowled for another second. Until she finally broke, bringing him in for a hug that looked more like a wrestling move. "Ah, I'm only fucking with you."

"I know you are. You do this to me every day," he said, still smiling.

I averted my eyes. Yet another confusing relationship of Theo's—he'd been cold and argumentative to me since my very first day. But he'd worked with my mom for four years and let her tease him without mercy. When these moments happened, I could *feel* the cognitive dissonance and it made my skin itch.

"You're gonna do great today," Mom said. "Both of you. Janis is sort of a genius about these things."

"So she has told me repeatedly," Theo replied in a dry tone.

My mom laughed. "You wanna get some coffee? I'm about to ask Daria to join me in the break room."

Theo hesitated. For one horrifying moment, I thought he

was about to say *yes*. His eyes briefly landed on mine before he shook his head. "Thanks, but I still need to shower and change. Mags, I'll catch you tomorrow. Daria, I'll...see you later?"

I swallowed through a rush of nerves. "I'll be here."

Theo turned and walked back toward the sidewalk. Mom wrapped her arm around my shoulders. "Don't worry too much about tonight, baby girl. He's nothing but a softie with some fancy letters around his name."

My mother's unrestrained, booming voice easily reached Theo, who was barely out of the parking lot.

He held out his hands, laughing. "Mags. I'm literally right here, you know."

"Saying you're a softie is a *compliment*," she yelled back.

I rolled my eyes and started to pull her back inside the station. Working here with her was, for the most part, a whole lot of fun. But every so often, she made me feel like a teenager again, the daughter who had to keep her semi-famous mother walking at a consistent pace whenever we were out—a friendly 'nice to see you, but I can't stop' speed—or I'd be stuck while she talked to fans for an hour.

She *lived* to talk to strangers, to have long, meandering conversations about music with her loud, expressive voice regardless of our plans or appointments. Or even if we had dinner reservations we were about to lose.

"He really is a sweetheart, you know," Mom said, looping her arm around my shoulders again. "And you're as much of an expert on this stuff as he is."

We pushed open the door to the staff room. Mom walked over and kicked the jukebox, the only way we'd ever figured out how to turn it on, and Diana Ross's voice filtered through the room. Mom sprawled on one of the couches, head tipped back and eyes closed. For most of her career, she'd been showing up at K-SUN by 4:30 in the morning to get ready for the top of her show at 5:00.

"How did everything go this morning?" I asked. "I caught your glam rock set on my drive in."

She yawned, lion-like. "I'd call today's set *pure* poetry."

I filled two mugs with hot coffee and joined her on the couch. "I saw Cliff yesterday and he told me to tell you that your show had been 'heaven-sent.' His words exactly."

She peeked one eye open. Sipped her coffee. "It's like I tell people, I'm the greatest radio DJ the world has ever known, but they still won't believe me. I don't understand."

I hid a smile behind my mug. "Maybe we should get one of those seaplanes to fly down Sunrise Beach with a banner that says *Magnolia Stone is the fucking best and don't you forget it.*"

"Now that's more like it." She shoved her wispy bangs away from her face and slurped her coffee noisily. If old pictures and posters were to be believed, she'd gotten this exact shag cut in 1980 and never changed it.

I nudged my boot against hers. "If you have a minute, can I get some advice?"

Her eyes widened. "What do you need me for? That's your gig, hun."

I smiled, tugging on a loose thread hanging from the holes in my jeans. "What was it like when people started to think of you as some kind of music expert? I remember when you were being interviewed in *Rolling Stone* and people were buying up albums from local bands you personally recommended. Fans seemed to take what you said on your show as like a...like a sacred truth. Just seemed like that would be a lot of pressure to maintain that level of trust."

Her head bobbed in time with the song on the jukebox. "I guess, after all this time, I could give a shit if someone thought I wasn't supposed to be there. Or if they got mad because I promoted a band that later turned out to suck. Who the hell cares?"

I arched an eyebrow. "A lot of people care, Mom. Sometimes it feels like the whole *internet* could one day have an opinion about me and the advice I gave. What if, after all of this is over, it's universally accepted that 'Daria Stone never knew what she was talking about?'"

She studied me for a moment, her dark eyebrows knit together. "A lot of people didn't like me. A lot of people still don't like me. Des said I get plenty of hate mail still even though it should be clear that I ain't going nowhere. Of course, so much of my career has involved all the usual sexist fuckery too. People have said I have the worst taste in music imaginable. That I wouldn't know real rock 'n' roll if it bit me on the ass."

She patted me on the knee. "It wasn't, and never will be, possible for me to talk about something as personal and emotional as music without pissing a lot of people off. But my job has never been to please my listeners. My job is to go into that sound booth and play the music making my heart sing. Those who don't like it, well...that's a *them* problem. Not a *me* problem." She paused. "Or a *Daria* problem."

I sipped my coffee, mulling over her words. "Back at K-ROX, my show got a lot of attention really fast, and I haven't had time to process or adjust to the reality that people look to *me* for advice on how to live their lives. When I was rage-writing my blog after all the stuff with Jackson, I wasn't as worried about getting things wrong. Now I'm speaking to thousands of people, and I'm not a therapist or a social worker. I'm just a girl who got dumped in the worst way and wanted to connect to other people going through the same kind of heartbreak. Theo's a psychologist at least. Those fancy letters around his name hold a lot of weight."

She scoffed. "After what Jackson did to you, you've had to work hard to learn how to love yourself again. To love yourself *first*. Being a sympathetic ear for listeners, sharing what you've been through...I don't think you can do that *wrong*. And you never said you were a therapist, either. These callers are still adults who have to figure things out on their own, and that's not all on you."

A large part of me knew she was right. Knew that carrying the weight of a new spotlight wasn't a life change I could rush through, much as I wanted. In therapy, I'd worked through the rawest parts of the humiliation I'd experienced on the morning I'd stood in front of a hundred wedding guests in a fluffy white gown and explained that my groom-to-be and all his best friends were missing from the ceremony on purpose.

That humiliation still lived in the back of my mind, a shallow pool of emotion that could easily surge into a tidal wave if I bumped it the wrong way. I knew what it was like to be left out in the cold, to be discarded like a bag of yesterday's trash. The glare of this shiny new spotlight had me feeling the same way, like one false move and I'd be sent hurtling to the curb where I belonged.

My mom pulled me into a side hug and kissed the top of my head. "You're nervous about tonight, huh?"

I sighed. Shrugged. "You guessed it. I also got another rejection for my book. I'm a little extra sensitive right now."

"Whoever rejected you made the biggest mistake of their goddamn lives."

I laughed, scooping up our empty coffee cups and walking them back to the counter. "It's nothing personal, Mom. It's only business on their end. And it's been almost nine months of rejection, so it might be time to take all these *no*s as a sign to stop sending my manuscript out."

"*Daria Magnolia Stone.*"

I tossed her a smile over my shoulder. "I'm right here. You don't have to yell, you know."

She fixed me with a maternal stare, pointing with her index finger. "What did you tell me right after everything happened with Jackson? The dream you had that was even bigger than being on the radio someday?"

I toed the floor with the tip of my Doc Martens. "Write a book about what happened to me and what I learned from it. A book that I wished I'd had at the time. A book that would have made me feel less alone."

"Then publishing that book is what you're going to do, baby girl," she said. "Or I'm not Magnolia Stone, world's greatest radio DJ."

I cocked my head. "You're that confident, huh?"

She stood from the couch and tugged the flaps of her jean vest across her shirt. "You're that surprised? I learned it all from you." She ambled over to the counter and wrapped me in another one of her jubilant bear hugs.

"I love you, Mom," I said, tightly hugging her back. "Thanks for the pep talk."

"I heard it's what moms are here for," she said with a wink.

Working on these essays had helped me craft and hone my voice before K-ROX ever gave me a platform, when I was a blogger sharing my most vulnerable memories because connecting with others over our shared pain made me feel seen, affirmed and understood. I wanted to express all that I'd learned from being a shocked almost-bride—that the relationship we cultivate with ourselves is vital and life-changing. That we should date ourselves *first*. Cherish our own minds, cherish our own hearts, honor our authentic desires and dreams.

We'd been sold a false bill of goods, forcing people to believe that romantic love—the kind rigidly defined by our society—should be our *only* goal in life.

I wanted to declare my single status with pride and not receive a smattering of misguided pity. In the end, the blog, the book, *Choosing Yourself*—all of it was working toward a world where romantic relationships weren't the only ones celebrated.

I touched my mom's shoulder to get her attention again.

"Hey, you wanna go to High Frequency one of these nights with me and Elena? I know how much you love to bring the house down by singing 'Jolene' during the karaoke hours."

She walked back over to the jukebox, kicking it off with her boot. "Uh, maybe? You know, this week is a little wild for me, hun."

"Wild, how?" I asked, amused.

"Just things I'm doing," she said. "Also, I've been to karaoke almost every night in the past two weeks. I need to rest up the ole vocal cords for my day job." She rubbed her hands together like she was nervous. "We should grab some dinner from the taqueria soon though. And I'll be listening tonight, of course. You're gonna do swell. Just swell. Love ya!"

I watched her leave through the door, still rubbing her hands together, an *obvious* tell when she was lying. I hadn't seen her do it in ages, either. Suddenly, I was a little less consumed by thoughts of sitting in an enclosed space with Theo for hours.

I had a sneaking suspicion my mother was keeping a secret.

7

THEO

"We are officially three minutes out," Elena said, hands on the mixing board. "Theo, Daria, you okay? Need anything?"

I pulled on my headphones and smiled her way. "I'm ready."

Across the small table, Daria wrapped her hands around a steaming mug. "Ready to rock 'n' roll, as Mags would say."

I stretched my legs out, not used to having another person with me. My shoes brushed against Daria's legs. The brief touch buzzed through my body like an electric shock. I cleared my throat and pulled back as she peeked from beneath her curls with a smirk.

"Will we need to put down a line of masking tape to mark off our respective sides?" she asked.

"I should hope not. I just momentarily forgot that I wasn't alone."

"Am I really that forgettable?"

"Of course not," I said evenly. "You're my very worst nightmare. That's not easy to forget, Daria."

"That's right." She nodded sagely. "You admitted earlier that you dream about me."

"Two minutes out," Elena called.

I tipped my head. "That was a descriptor that I used. Not an actual situation I'm experiencing. For me to dream about you, I'd have to be thinking about you outside of work hours and that's not something I've ever done."

"I'd never realized you were such an obvious liar."

I dropped my elbows onto the table, bending forward. "Aren't you the one who's been listening to my show this entire time?"

She snorted. "You wish I was."

Her bright blue eyes were glued to mine. This close, with this setup, it was going to be impossible *not* to have direct eye contact for the duration of the show. The intimacy forced me to sit with Daria's stunning beauty, from the scarlet red of her expressive mouth to the swell of her full breasts in her tank top.

As she adjusted the height of her mic, I found myself staring at her long, slender fingers and the stacks of gold rings that adorned them. She brushed a few messy strands of hair from her forehead, and all I could do was wonder what those curls would feel like against my lips.

The accompanying jolt of lust would have shocked me if I hadn't experienced the same scorching heat this morning when we'd run into each other. Again. My body's response had been pure instinct, wrapping my hand around her back and holding her against me. The timing of it all had been unfortunate. I'd convinced myself the five-mile run on the beach was to burn off the spiky anger I felt while anticipating tonight's show.

Instead, I found myself burning off a different kind of spiky energy. My feet pounded on the sand, breath thundering in my throat. I raced past tourists and surfers, dodged volleyballs and other runners. Des's words as I'd left last night were a constant reverberation through my mind—*then maybe you don't hate her as much as you think.*

But the longer I pondered that concept, the more Daria tangled with my rapid thoughts. The adrenaline of the run, the languid heat of the beach, all of it sent me spiraling until thoughts of Daria became flashes of intense imagery. Sweat on skin, nails on my back, mouths open, teeth flashing, black curls wrapped around my fingers.

Crashing into her had happened at the worst possible time. If she'd been willing, if I'd been less controlled, if we'd been *completely different people*, I would have kept Daria walking until I'd pinned her back against the nearest wall.

"*One minute till we go live,*" Elena said, breaking through my haze.

I blinked, adjusted my glasses, and caught Daria twisting her rings. "Are you okay?"

"Yep. I get pre-show… never mind. I'm great."

I nodded. "Good to hear. I'm great too."

"To be clear, we *are* arguing the entire time? Or not?"

"I've heard it's a bad look, but feel free to express yourself however you'd like."

"And when do we get to tell Janis this was a really bad idea?"

"*Ten seconds.* Don't forget to have fun," Elena called with a grin.

"Why does everyone think we need to have fun?" I muttered.

"I actually agree with that," Daria said.

We shared a bizarre look that was almost amicable. The cue lights blazed *On Air.*

"Happy Thursday, listeners. This is Dr. Theodore Chadwick, coming to you tonight with an all-new—" I said, realizing much too late that Daria was also saying, "Hey there, babes. It's your favorite host—"

We stopped, eyes locked together. Irritation blazed on Daria's face, mirroring my own.

She dipped back down to the mic. "So sorry about that,

everyone. As I'm sure you're all aware now, this is the very first episode of *Love and Life Advice*. Theo and I are in the studio together, here to answer your questions, and so that means there will be—"

"Technical difficulties," I interjected. "And a steep learning curve. Please bear with us as we learn together, on-air, with the folks brave enough to go on this journey."

Daria's lips quirked up. "It promises to be a wild ride."

"A bit bumpy, perhaps. But we're glad you're here." I extended a hand across the table. "Would you like to introduce yourself first?"

Her throat worked. "I'm Daria Stone, usually the host of *Choosing Yourself*. I've only been at K-SUN for a few months and before that, I was hosting a similar show at K-ROX out of L.A. I kept a pretty popular blog before switching to hosting. When I was twenty-three, I was left at the altar by my groom-to-be. And when I say *left*, I mean dress on, makeup done, ready for my mother—you all know her as the host of *Mags in the Morning*—to escort me down the aisle. And he didn't show up."

A burst of intense discomfort rolled through me. I knew this story in a kind of off-hand, impersonal way. Had never heard her share it directly in front of me, with no real place to look except at each other. My brow furrowed, shoulders tight. I wasn't a man prone to violence, yet every word out of her mouth had me fantasizing about dragging this guy from whatever hole he was hiding in so I could punch the shit out of his face.

"Since then, I've been all about that self-love, baby," she said, her smile curving up. "*Choosing Yourself* is about developing a deep, personal connection to your own body and mind. Extending that same connection to your friends, your family, your community. I think we should all treat ourselves as romantically as we'd treat a partner. It's helped me heal, so very much. And it's made staying single a ton of fun. I can confidently say that the date nights I take myself on are *way* better than the ones involving another person."

I sniffed, shifting in the chair. "So for those keeping score back home, Daria helps people stay single—"

"You got it."

"And I help people find, and keep, their soul-mates," I said. "I'm Dr. Theo Chadwick and I've been the host of *True Romance* at K-SUN for four years now. Before that, I wrote a relationship advice column in the *New York Times* by the same name. My actual background isn't in radio though. I'm a social psychologist by training, studying the complexities of human relationships and how we relate to one another and the world around us. And for my dissertation, I studied marriages in crisis and the factors that led to those marriages enduring or dissolving. I'd always been fascinated with love, dating and romance. I started writing an advice column for UCLA's newspaper while I was getting my undergraduate degree. I've been hooked ever since."

A few seconds of awkward dead air ticked by after. Daria pulled the mic toward her with flushed cheeks. "Right, so, uh…that's us. Theo and Daria. Clearly learning as we go here. And, you know, we're not trying to hide the fact that Theo and I often come at ideas of love and connection from different types of…" She hesitated. "Expertise. Think of it as a more *well-rounded* advice show."

Janis's feedback from the other night kept clattering around my brain, making far too much noise for the concentration I needed right now. *You need to learn how to compromise if you want to stay in this business.* It bothered me, greatly, to think that Janis heard my show every week and thought I was growing too comfortable. That she saw holes or weaknesses in what I did that were supposed to be magically fixed by Daria.

I nodded along, rolling out my shoulders. "With that, I

don't think there's a reason not to get to the first question, right?"

"Let's do it," she said brightly. But she was tugging on her earrings, a nervous tic I was beginning to recognize.

We turned to Elena, who was in the process of patching through the first call. Part of the prep work we did each week was to pull through the questions listeners submitted via email or our voicemail, and ones that were especially interesting, Elena would invite them to call during the show.

The rest she screened as they came in, using her impeccable judgment to choose equally-as-interesting spontaneous questions. This first one would be spontaneous, meaning Daria and I hadn't heard it.

"I've got Brian here on the phone. He said his question is for both of you."

My laptop pinged with an incoming message—we used a chat function to communicate things we couldn't say on-air. Her message to me said, *it's about divorce, just a head's up.*

Elena caught my eye, clearly concerned. I flashed her a warm smile and a nod. "Welcome to the show, Brian," I said easily. "What can Daria and I help you with tonight?"

A low voice patched through. "Hey, this is Brian. Thanks for taking my call. I, uh…well, I listen to both of your shows. I hope that's okay."

"The more the merrier," Daria said. "It's not like it's a competition or anything."

I subtly raised my eyebrows at her.

"So I got divorced about a year ago," Brian started. "It was pretty messy. It wasn't one of those amicable ones, you know? And things had been bad between us for a while even before we separated."

"Did you have children?" I asked.

"No, and I'm grateful that we didn't. I can't imagine going through something like that. It's been hard enough as it is without having to explain things to kids."

I adjusted my glasses but kept my eyes focused on the table. "I can't speak from the perspective of the parents, but I've shared before about my experience with divorce when I was a kid. It's unique every single time. Mine was certainly very confusing though."

"Yeah, I can imagine that." The pain in Brian's voice was obvious. "It's...man, it's been a tough time for me. In a whole lot of ways."

"I'm sorry to hear that," Daria said softly. "I know how horribly painful heartbreak can be." She paused. "And I'm sorry to hear how confusing things were for you, Theo. That sounds like it was very scary."

My gaze flew up to hers. *Scary* wasn't an emotion I used out loud when labeling those years of my life, but it was a feeling I'd tucked away in the farthest recesses of my mind. My parents were aloof and distant out in the open. That's certainly how I would describe their parenting styles. But behind closed doors, late at night when they likely believed I was sleeping...my memories were filled with their raised voices, vicious arguments, glass shattering and doors slamming.

Scary.

"Yes, well...yes." I cleared my throat. She had me slightly flustered. "Thank you. Brian, please know that we have a lot of people who call in about their divorces and they've described similar feelings. You are not alone in this."

"I figured," he grumbled. "I guess there is comfort when you know other people are miserable with you."

Daria and I shared a sympathetic wince. A hint of warmth flickered in the center of my chest at the gesture.

"My question is...it's been a year and in a lot of ways, I've moved on. I wouldn't say our relationship was *loveless* but I'm ready for love. I think? But I also feel a lot more cynical about this stuff. Like what's the point if the only outcome is

71

feeling this way. Does that make sense? Like do I get back out there or not?"

I opened my mouth, prepared to answer, but Daria jumped in first. "Not. At least that's my advice."

"And I was going to say the exact opposite," I said.

We eyed each other warily. Brian huffed out a dry laugh. "I'm not surprised. This is kinda what I needed. Daria, what do you think?"

She bit her lip. "No offense to my colleague here, but of *all* the times to embrace being single, it's now. You're on your own for the first time in...how many years?"

"Fifteen."

Daria's eyes softened. "You're grieving the loss of what you once had. You're grieving the loss of an identity, as a husband and a spouse. You're having to navigate a new daily routine and existence. Movies and television project this harmful narrative that *getting back out there* is the healthy way to move on. You can't shake off a fifteen-year relationship like a dog shaking out a wet coat. Now's the time to get to know yourself better."

"By doing what though? I don't even know what I like to do."

She tilted her head to the side. "It's hard to separate what we like and need from liking and needing what our partner wants. What about daily walks? Or sitting outside in the sun without your phone and letting your mind wander? I'm suggesting those two things specifically because I used them after my breakup. I'd really...really lost myself during my relationship, even *before* I was left at the altar. It was like drawing a map to find my way back home again. It was very uncomfortable at first. Sometimes it still is. When we're not distracted, a lot of stuff comes up that we're usually avoiding."

Brian cleared his throat. "Okay, um...yeah, I can see how that would happen. And what did it help you do again?"

Daria was staring at me while she responded. "It helped me separate what I really loved from what society tells us we should love. Helped me separate my own goals and dreams from Jackson's. To take up space again and be as loud and weird and joyful and messy and imperfect as I wanted."

My hands flexed against the table, my spine rigid. I received plenty of calls about jealousy on my show and advised my listeners that it was a sure-fire way to lose your partner's trust. I believed it to be an ugly, attention-seeking emotion that was easily managed if you knew how.

It scorched through my veins now, entwined with that same anger from earlier. Anger that her fiancé clearly hadn't appreciated all the things that made her who she was. Anger that he'd obviously diminished and dismissed her.

Not even an hour in and the forced proximity was affecting my control.

"Maybe if you spent more time on your own, you'd realize that's the way you'd like to stay," she said. "Or maybe it would make you feel excited to date again, much as I'm in the *stay single forever* category myself. Either way, I think you need to work on yourself first."

"Huh, alright," Brian said. "I see what you're saying but, you know, you are right. Dating feels weird right now but having something to do with someone makes me feel normal, so I keep doing it."

"If I can offer another set of advice," I said evenly, "if going out makes you feel comfortable, if you're continuing to turn towards it, *that* could also be a sign it's the right thing for you in the present moment. I wouldn't shy away from a new relationship because your other one remains messy and hurtful. In fact, now's the time to be brave and seek out love."

"Theo," Daria said, "bravery looks different for different people. Investing in your own wellness takes a lot of courage."

"I don't disagree. I'm merely saying that powerful inner

work doesn't happen in a vacuum. It can happen alongside another person. In fact, I believe it *should* happen. The more vulnerable you are with your partner or partners, the more you learn."

Annoyance flared in her eyes. "That vulnerability begins with the relationship you build with yourself. Romantic and sexual relationships aren't always what a person wants, whether that's based on their identity, their sexuality, their preferences. Those folks find connection within their communities, their friendships and their family. What you're suggesting is severely limiting to a lot of people."

I shook my head. "I'm not limiting, Daria. I'm offering advice based on what Brian has *told* us, which is that he was in a successful, committed marriage, until he wasn't. And that dating and being in relationships makes him comfortable and happy. If he hadn't said those things, I wouldn't be telling him to get back out there. I'm listening to him."

"Oh yeah? Because I'm listening to him too."

"Are you? Or are you only telling him what *you* would do in the situation?" I countered.

"I'm still here, you know," Brian said cheerfully. His voice cut through the tension, leaving Daria and me staring awkwardly at our mics with flushed cheeks. "I'm sorry. I kinda knew this question would get you both worked up."

I felt my molars grinding together. "Daria and I are very passionate about our areas of expertise, is all. There's no need for *you* to apologize, Brian. I'm sorry we got a little...heated."

The irritation radiating from Daria's body consumed the tight space we were in. "I'm sorry too," she said. "Does any... did any of that resonate?"

"What if I date someone and I'm not ready and I hurt them?" he asked.

My eyes met Daria's again—reluctantly. She nodded at my mic.

I dipped my head toward it. "That's one of the hardest challenges we navigate while dating. I wish I had an easy answer for that, but I never will. Hurt is possible regardless of whether or not you've been through a recent divorce."

"I feel like what Daria said is true. I mean, she's right," Brian said. "I don't know anything about who I am when I'm not with someone."

I must have looked stunned enough that Daria jumped in again. "Talk about a scary feeling. I've been there and it sucks."

"So, like, I need to take walks and stuff?"

She smiled, looking surprised. "Journaling can help too. Meditation. Anything where your brain quiets and you're not distracting it with media or the internet. Trying new things, trying out new hobbies, being spontaneous. All of it helped me find my way home."

She dreamily traced the top of her mug, rings flashing under the light. "It also helped me realize that I'm happier on my own, happier not dating. I'm not saying that's necessarily what will work for you, but I understand the cynical feelings you talked about. Sometimes when I walk past a bridal shop, I get hot all over. Kinda panicky, like I'm back in my dress again and someone's telling me that my groom isn't coming. There's nothing wrong with deciding that relationships aren't for you. Maybe just right now. Or maybe for longer than that."

Brian grumbled. "It's like a bruise and I can't stop poking it."

"It gets less tender with time. I promise," she said.

I rubbed the back of my neck, feeling itchy and unsettled. I'd witnessed divorce firsthand, so I wasn't naive enough to think that I'd never have a relationship end. I'd had three end, had divvied up shared belongings, closed shared bank accounts, had tough conversations with friend groups. But even as unbearable as those times were, that cynicism didn't exist for me.

How could Daria want to stay single *forever?*

The thought of moving through my days permanently without a partner was almost panic-inducing. The empty years yawned open ahead of me, years where I knew loneliness would stalk my heels like a pack of dogs. I didn't need to journal or take myself on long walks.

I knew myself, knew myself the way any kid who spent most of their time alone did.

"Is there anything else you wanted to add, Theo?" she asked.

"No, it sounds like what you spoke about is going to work for Brian," I said tightly. "Brian, feel free to call us back and update the listeners on how it's going. I will mention that if you're concerned about dating again, and hurting people, you're miles ahead of people who date carelessly and don't consider the feelings of others. Asking about it means that you care."

"I appreciate that," he said. "And I guess I'm flattered that I'm your first call. I think you guys did good overall."

Daria's cheeks reddened. I could feel my shoulders rising to my ears.

"Thank you, Brian," she said. "Definitely update us on how it's going. And good luck."

A voice in my head was urging me back to control and restraint, urging me to heed Janis's advice while on a public platform with thousands of people listening in. But then Daria smiled over at me, the motion *just* shy of arrogant.

My hackles rose so quickly I should have been shocked.

I leveled a searing gaze at my smug colleague. "Over the years, some of the research I've gotten to see at the university, some of the psychologists I've worked with, they've spoken with plenty of committed couples who met when one of them was going through a divorce or a tough breakup.

The vulnerability that comes from heartbreak does help you learn a lot about yourself, as you've so eloquently shared. That fresh vulnerability often makes those new relationships that much stronger. I'm happy that Brian found something meaningful with what you said. But I do think dating opens us up, makes us stronger, shows us our likes and dislikes. *That's* also meaningful when it comes to healing."

Her eyes narrowed. "I don't disagree. But sometimes people are reaching for the comfort of partnership before they've taken the time to decide what they really want. That can be unhealthy."

"Or it can lead them to their soul mate," I pointed out.

"Sure," she said flatly. "Technically, anything can happen to anyone at any time. What Brian shared was a cynicism and fear around love after *fifteen years* with another person. A year is nothing compared to that amount of time. He's got stuff to learn and throwing himself back into the dating pool could complicate that."

"What makes you so sure?" I asked.

"What makes *you*?" she said. "Or are you only mad because on our very first call, Brian took my advice and not yours?"

"And I thought you said it wasn't a competition."

"*Theo*," she said harshly. "If you're implying that my lack of advanced degrees somehow means I'm less qualified—"

I blinked, surprised. A sick feeling churned in the pit of my stomach. "Wait, I'm sorry. What did you say?"

Daria dropped her elbows flat onto the table. She was so focused on me her mouth was practically off the mic. "What makes me so *sure* is lived experience, self-discovery, interacting with the community I built online *well* before K-ROX and, yeah, that time my show was a viral hit overnight. That's how I'm sure."

My face felt as hot as asphalt under the summer sun. "I...I didn't—at no point have I ever thought not having a doctorate made you less qualified. I've never, ever felt that way."

Those words flowed from my mouth at the same time as a dozen of our recent altercations sprang to mind—the way I'd taunted her about my *expertise*. The fact that I'd called her show "recycled internet hot takes," and had flaunted my added years of experience whenever she'd pushed my buttons. Which was *always*.

Beneath the voice in my head shouting at me to *shut the fuck up* were the agitated whispers I'd been ignoring from the moment we first met in the K-SUN parking lot. It was why I struggled to maintain a measured restraint around Daria, because so much of my self-discipline was being employed to avoid what the whispers were saying.

There was a reason I was such a *smug asshole* around her. An *extremely vital reason* I pushed her away with conflict and confrontation. A multitude of startling realizations collided in my brain.

What had Des said? *Or maybe you don't even hate her at all.*

Elena's voice came on, sounding strained and uncomfortable. "You know what I think? We should probably do some program updates and reset a little."

I closed my eyes, mortified. Luckily, Daria was able to say, "That...you know, that's a great idea, Elena. You know how we get when we're...when we're getting into one of our little debates."

"Uh-huh," Elena said. "Sure. Okay, we'll be right back, listeners."

The door opened, but it wasn't Elena standing there. It was Janis and Des. I tore my headphones off and scrubbed a hand down my face. Des looked concerned, but still compassionate.

Janis's expression was inscrutable. She pulled a chair over and sat down on it, glancing back and forth between the two of us. I couldn't even look at Daria, couldn't look at my best friend, could *barely* look at Janis. I yanked my glasses off and pinched the bridge of my nose.

"You know, you were doing pretty good there for a while," Janis said. "I'm serious. Debating with each other is fine and one of the reasons why I think this new program is going to attract so much attention." She pointed at me. Pointed at Daria. "The next bit, the part where you, Theo, baited Daria on purpose? And then you, Daria, said a lot of personal shit live and on the air? It *cannot* happen again. Remember how I told you we were in a budget crisis and needed all hands on deck right now? That wasn't helping us. That was hurting us. I know you can do better than that. Am I being clear?"

"Yes, ma'am," I said.

"Yes, absolutely," Daria mumbled.

"Good. Do you need to cool off or can we trust you to handle yourselves as professionals?"

I had never, in my life, felt such a horrifying combination of regret and embarrassment. "I'm good."

"Same here," Daria said.

I cast a covert glance her way—she looked as flushed and unhappy as I felt. The regret amplified, flooding my nervous system.

Janis pushed up from the chair with an alarmingly cheerful smile. "Glad to hear it. Des has an idea for a temporary fix."

Des cleared his throat. "Elena and I can split up the calls, make sure we're giving them specifically to Daria or Theo. For now, the other person won't be giving any added advice. Only listening. So it'll be half a Daria show. Half a Theo show. Just to help with the learning curve."

I swallowed thickly and nodded again, unable to trust I wouldn't blurt out what I really wanted to say: *I'm not so sure I can do this and be successful.*

"We can work with that," Daria said softly. Her eyes shot to mine, but I looked away.

"Beautiful." Janis clapped her hands together, stopping to squeeze my arm before she left, taking Des with her. The soothing gesture made me feel even more like shit.

Elena's voice cut in. "We'll be back on in twenty seconds, first call going to Theo."

Daria blew out a breath and pulled her headphones back on. I did the same, the air thick with an awkward tension. As the music started back up, and Elena reintroduced the show, it was impossible not to face each other like two fighters in a ring, preparing to spar.

Gone was Daria's sly grin and teasing expression. Instead, the woman in front of me appeared to be cold and distant. Like I was a housefly that annoyed her, but not nearly enough to do anything about it.

I schooled my expression until it matched hers. The temperature in the room dropped another few degrees. Walls up, armor on, every wayward emotion clipped and controlled.

It was how I preferred to interact around Daria anyway.

And whatever flicker of disappointment I felt was a mistake.

8

DARIA

I sat on the low, sandy wall outside the Best Coast Cafe, holding an iced coffee in one hand and Elena's favorite breakfast smoothie in the other. The cafe faced one of the best surf spots in Sunrise Beach. This early in the morning, the waves were dotted with bobbing surfers as the sky brightened from a pale, dusky pink to the pretty cerulean blue so common here in the summer.

Behind me, surf vans sat parked next to stands selling T-shirts and frozen yogurt shops. A group of skateboarders flew by, trailing the soft beat of the reggae song they were playing on a tiny speaker hanging from one of their backpacks. The cafe wall facing me was painted with a mural of the Virgin of Guadalupe, the red of her robe as vibrant as the roses curving around her body.

Elena came walking up from the beach, wet suit bunched around her waist. She was on the phone, but grinned when she saw me.

"Uh-huh. Uh-huh," she was murmuring. "Sí, mamá. Adiós, te amo."

I held out the smoothie and she took it eagerly, plopping

down on the wall next to me. "How's your mom and how were the waves?"

She ran a hand through her wet hair. "Waves were okay today. I got a couple good ones. My mom was calling because she has the uncanny ability of knowing every single woman in the Los Angeles area. She's ready for more grandchildren."

"How many does she have already?"

"*Seven*. I have two brothers and a sister, and they all have kids. She hasn't accepted yet that relationships aren't my thing." She arched an eyebrow. "A lot of the women she sent me *are* hella cute in their pictures though. But marriage is a big deal where I'm from and people in Puerto Rico *live* for grandkids and weddings. It's why she asks me about it constantly."

I grinned, leaning back on my palms. "Do you ever date casually?"

"That's all I do," she said. "A couple fun nights, maybe a fling when I feel like it. Anything more serious than that doesn't feel right to me. I love being on my own, love being independent and doing whatever I want. Seeing my friends, working at K-SUN, traveling to surf…that's all more meaningful to me." She nudged my shoulder. "What do *you* do when you want to have sex but don't want to date?"

"I add to my ever-growing collection of sex toys," I said with a smirk. "And I basically do what you do. Casual hookups, the occasional one-night stand with a guy if the vibe is right. Sex is a form of intimacy that feels comfortable to me. It's everything else that seems wrong. Like wearing an itchy wool sweater that's a size too small."

I lifted a shoulder, pushing my sunglasses up into my hair. "It's hard to believe, since Jackson blew off our wedding to drink beer with his friends like a fucking asshole, but the whole time we were together he was really into these over-the-top, hyped-up romantic gestures. They weren't my style, even when I was younger. Flowers I didn't like, gifts I didn't need, fancy dinners we couldn't afford."

"How did he propose to you?" she asked. "I've always been curious, and you don't talk about it much on your show."

I winced, my nervous system flooding with the memory of that day. "He proposed to me in public, in front of his family. I'd told him multiple times I never wanted it to be that way. One thing about Jackson is that at first, I was too concerned with polite people-pleasing to tell him what I wanted. And when I started to tell him, he didn't listen. And then when I got louder, more vocal, he ignored me. I said yes that day because part of me still loved him in a very shallow way. And I said yes because I knew I was supposed to. And because a whole bunch of people were watching, and I felt pressure to make it special for them."

Elena clicked her tongue. "That man knew what he was doing."

Describing my heartbreak after Jackson was tough. It didn't fit neatly into any box or definition I'd seen before. Part of the pain was certainly caused by the distant love I'd once felt for him. But it was a superficial love, a love that grew out of his happiness and never my own.

So much of the pain was comprised of the humiliation and betrayal on our wedding day, the anger and regret, the dawning realization that I'd spent so many years with a man who never wanted the *real* me.

"I was stoked when Janis told me I'd be working with *the* Daria Stone on her new show," Elena said. "I don't know if I've told you that yet?"

My eyebrows shot up. "Are you being for real? Because my mom talked about *you* constantly before I joined K-SUN. Made me nervous to work with *the* Elena García."

Elena laughed. "Mags is a trip. And I'm being for real."

I nudged her shoulder back. "So am I."

She looked back out toward the ocean. We could hear the

shouts of a few happy surfers over the crash of the waves. "I listened to you when you were on K-ROX. I liked what you were about. People assume that being a queer woman is *only* about sex and who I'm attracted to. Nothing could be further from the truth. Being a lesbian informs my core self, my politics, my community, how I move through the world and how I'm treated. Your show made me feel more like myself. What you talk about is the kind of stuff my friends and I talk about, and a lot of them have different needs when it comes to sex and dating and monogamy too. There's no one-size-fits-all."

I chewed on my bottom lip. "I've learned so much about how we're all different and I've had many great teachers. A *lot* of queer folks call into the show and I'm grateful every time they share their experiences."

"You know who else has a lot of queer folks calling into their show?"

My stomach twisted. I turned to look at her, relieved that she was at least smirking. "Let me guess. Theo?"

"I've also got a lot of people in my community with soul mates and wedding dreams and babies on the way. He's not as 'traditional' as you think, Dar. Theo isn't traditional at all. In the four years that I've known him, the only person he's ever stubbornly argued with is *you*."

I stared down at my hands, stomach twisting deeper and deeper. It was Monday and our new combined show had not magically gotten better in any single way. The rest of that first night, plus Friday and Saturday's shows, had technically gone as planned based on the change Janis and Des made when Theo and I had, again, bickered like toddlers. I'd answer a caller. Then he'd answer a caller. Back and forth, with one person sitting quietly across the table while the other spoke.

We weren't fighting—an improvement over the first night. But it was awkward as hell. Because we were also barely *speaking* to each other. We kept our eye contact in the tight space minimal. Our greetings at the beginning were polite and stilted.

And at the end of every show, Theo would nod my way, say a clipped "Good night, Daria" and immediately leave. The whole thing was as frustrating as it was mortifying.

"Elena," I said, "I'm really sorry for how I acted that first night, arguing with Theo and putting you in such an uncomfortable spot. I take full responsibility and it should never have happened."

She held up her now empty cup. "Is this why you brought me my favorite drink?"

I shook my head and smiled. "I would have done that regardless. Sometimes it's nice to bring a friend something they love. The apology is sincere though."

She set her cup down carefully on the wall next to her. "I accept your apology and appreciate it. But now that you and Theo are on your best behavior, the show is boring and weird. And not in a good way."

"You're telling me," I grumbled into my coffee. "Wait, are you seeing the listeners say that too?"

She nodded slowly. "People love you. They love Theo. But together, you're either sniping at each other or behaving like two pieces of awkward cardboard. There's no spark there. No electricity. Part of me wishes you'd go back to fighting."

My laughter sounded as forced and nervous as I felt inside. I refused to acknowledge the glaring fact that I wanted the same thing. It was so unbearably contradictory it made my head want to explode.

"I, uh...that's way funny," I stammered. "That's helpful feedback though. I know that I don't feel like myself on-air right now. Probably the same goes for Theo too. We can improve."

"Or maybe you'll feel better after you paintball each

other's faces tomorrow night. That's one way to get all that aggression out of your system," she said.

I dropped my sunglasses back down onto my face, relieved that Elena was briefly distracted by a surfer riding a wave. It meant she wouldn't notice the flush in my cheeks, the one that appeared whenever my maddening cohost strode confidently into my thoughts.

My moment with Theo in the parking lot after his run was a memory my dirty little brain was *overjoyed* to play on increasingly erotic loops. Every second when I wasn't distracted was a second filled with visceral details of Theo's aggravating hotness. The sound of his heavy breathing, the rasp in his voice, the obvious strength in his muscles as he held me upright.

Being forced to stare at his face in that sound booth three nights in a row was only making it worse.

As in, making me *hornier.*

"I can confirm that I will be conquering him easily on the paintball field," I said, with as much bravado as I could muster. Even as the thought of *conquering* Theo sent a sexy shiver down my spine.

"You get it, girl," Elena replied.

My phone beeped with a reminder about a meeting I'd decided to attend at the very last minute. I slid off the wall and brushed the sand from the back of my skirt. "I wish I could hang with you here all day, but I've got an early morning meeting about planning Janis's birthday party."

She nodded, pulling up her wet suit and tugging up the zipper. "That Janis is one groovy lady."

"That she is," I said. "Hopefully she doesn't fire me after this disaster with Theo."

Elena touched my elbow. "She's also a groovy lady who's all about second chances. Not that I'm suggesting you should take advantage of her kindness. More that my impression is Janis sees something in you and your career and is willing to give it all she's got. A lot of stuff she does doesn't always make sense at the time, but she has your best interests at heart. Trust me."

I smiled weakly. Understood that if I messed up again on-air, I was probably *right* at the edge of that kindness.

I grabbed my coffee and keys, nodded toward the K-SUN building in the background. "This is random, but have you noticed anything, like, kooky with my mom?"

"More than she usually is?"

I grinned. "Yeah. A more-than-usual kookiness. I don't know. The other day she was fidgety with me, like she was lying. I'm wondering if she's keeping secrets."

Elena cocked her head. "When I happen to catch her show on playback, she does sound extra exuberant. More bellowing than usual."

I laughed, mulling that over. "Huh. That's pretty on par for her. But if you notice anything, let me know. And be careful out there today."

She raised her cup. "Thank you for this."

"Thank you for accepting my apology," I said, waving as I walked away. The knots in my stomach loosened and became flutters the closer I got to the studio. Theo had pointedly told me not to come and help with the planning of Janis's not-so-surprise surprise party. *I'm thinking about our little detente situation. The less time we spend together, the better. Don't you agree?*

I did agree, but it wasn't going to stop me from joining in. I was a new employee, but K-SUN had been a second home for my entire life. And Janis was like a salty, sarcastic, weed-smoking bonus aunt to me. If Theo Chadwick had a problem with it, he could take his aggression out on me on that paint-ball field.

At the very least, it'd be cute to watch him try.

9

DARIA

a few minutes later, I pushed through the front doors of K-SUN to the sound of my mother's voice piped in through the speakers on the wall. *You're listening to* Mags in the Morning *and I'm in the mood to play* Earth, Wind and Fire *all day. Any objections to that? Call in and let me know, but it'll have to be after this hour-long block of their songs I already loaded up.*

I waved at her through the window of sound booth C, then headed to the break room. Someone had taped up a sign that read "Janis—do not come in. We're planning your surprise birthday party and cannot realistically accommodate any more of your absurd ideas."

I laughed, tapping my knuckles against the sign. "Did you write this, Des?"

"I wrote it."

I paused, mid-tap, making accidental eye contact with a stern-looking Theo. He was seated at the table, one hand wrapped around a coffee mug.

"Oh," I finally said. "It's funny, is all."

Theo's jaw tightened but he didn't respond. Cliff and Des were there, so it was for the best. And much more professional than how we used to greet each other in the morning —with either a competitive taunt or a thinly-veiled insult. For the past four days, however, our interactions had been chilly or downright nonexistent.

Impressive, given that we hosted an entire radio show together.

The only open seat was next to my icy cohost. It was likely he'd full-on ignore me at this point, so I dropped down into it and removed my sunglasses with a smile.

"Morning, everyone," I said cheerfully. Des and Cliff responded in kind while Theo merely grunted. "I know Theo mentioned to me earlier that you had Janis's party planning covered. But she's done so much since hiring me on, I'd really like the opportunity to help out. As long as that's okay."

"I can safely say that you helping us out is the greatest idea I've ever heard in my entire life," Cliff said without a trace of irony. "It pleases Janis to know that everyone's focusing on her at all times."

"And we've got a lot to do. Something that Theo was just complaining about, so I'm not sure why he'd tell you *not* to come," Des added.

Theo shifted in his chair, fingers tightening on his mug. There was an open notebook in front of him with a page of notes filled with his orderly handwriting. He wore navy blue pants and a cream-colored, short-sleeved shirt that had me hyper-focused on the swell of his shoulders, the tiny flexing muscles of his tan forearms.

"This was before I knew Janis wanted us to pull off an extravaganza," Theo said evenly. "Now I'm seriously wondering if this is some kind of practical joke and she really wants us to throw her a party at a Burger King."

My lips twitched. "Tell me everything."

It seemed to require a lot of effort for Theo to look directly at me. But the second his forest-green eyes connected with mine, a delicious heat spread through my entire body, and I had to furiously remember every annoying thing he'd ever said to soothe my nervous system.

He tipped his head my way. "Janis has requested a 'retro roller disco' party in honor of her seventy-first birthday. She'd like us to rent out that old roller rink on the boardwalk, the one next to the Ferris wheel. Her additional requests have been"—he pulled over his notebook to read—"everyone wearing a wig, everyone dancing, disco balls akimbo—"

I snorted. "She really said *akimbo?*"

Theo *almost* smiled. "She really said akimbo. For the record, Janis has never truly known what that word means."

"She thinks it means *scattered about*," Des added. "What's she's actually asking for is glitter, sparkles, confetti everywhere and on everything."

I tapped my chin. "You know, my mom probably knows where to get us all glitter wigs in varying lengths and colors."

"I already have one," Cliff said. At Des and Theo's bemused expressions, he shrugged. "I'm guessing my vacations are more fun than yours."

"I'm guessing you would be right," Theo murmured. "But you're covering the music, yes? You and Mags?"

"Oh yeah. I'm getting Blondie's *Heart of Glass* meets *Cruel Summer* with some Tears for Fears mixed in. Mags should be good for figuring out the slow songs. For the couple's skate."

Des laughed. "That's bringing up a lot of sweaty memories. Though the couple's skate is pretty romantic. Theo, you should talk about it on a show sometime. The hand holding, the music, the lights, all the lingering glances."

I slid my gaze to the side and was stunned to find Theo watching me. I didn't back down, merely smiled as slowly as I was able. "You'll be happy to know that I'm as good at roller-skating as I am at paintball."

"And how good is that again?" he asked, voice low.

"Significantly better than you," I mock-whispered.

A spark flared between us, like an engine warming up in the cold. But then he blinked and re-focused on Des and Cliff, who were in the middle of sharing a look I couldn't decipher.

"Right, so Cliff, it sounds like you and Mags have the soundtrack under control," Theo said.

"You betcha," he replied.

"And Des, you can handle all things disco ball?"

"The theme is *akimbo* and I'm here for it," Des said with a grin.

"Daria, could you and Elena handle food? Janis specifically requested 'gourmet arcade theme.'"

I laughed, delighted. "So, like, nachos but fancy?"

"That's basically what her diet is now, and she swears it's why she's made it to her seventies," Theo's voice held real affection. Again, I felt plagued with curiosity around Theo's life—the notes of pain in his voice had been obvious when sharing about his parent's divorce during our show on Thursday night. While my mother was so clearly a huge part of my life, Theo rarely mentioned his own parents. "If you can provide all the best arcade food, expensively, she'll love you forever."

"This isn't coming from the K-SUN budget, right?" I asked, finger in the air.

"Oh no," Des said. "Janis pulls out the stops for her birthday every year and pays for it herself because even if we weren't in a terrifying budget crisis, this would send us into one. Party planning isn't even technically a staff thing. It's just…"

"A Janis thing," Theo said. "Because she's, well, who she is."

There was a comfortable silence for a few seconds, and Cliff and Des both stood to leave. Cliff gave a low bow, his long gray ponytail falling over his shoulder. "As always, it's been a pleasure. The party's in three weeks, right? A Saturday night?"

Des nodded and slid a hand into his pocket. "Maybe Theo and Daria can host a live show from the skating rink."

Theo must have made the same upset and awkward face that I did. Because Des waved his hand and said, "I'm kidding, you guys. We're not going to make you race each other in retro roller skates or anything."

I laughed weakly. "Right, no, of course not."

Cliff ambled out the door, leaving Des to scrutinize us both. "Is everything all set for paintball tomorrow? As long as you get a picture beforehand, maybe one after when you're all covered in paint, that should be the majority of content we need. And then you're both hopping onto the news broadcast for a quick interview once you're finished. Your listeners are already placing bets on who's going to win."

Theo cleared his throat. "I'm all set, thanks."

"Same here," I said. "We can try and overdo it on the paint splatter. For the sake of clickable content. We gotta keep those hungry fans satisfied."

Des shrugged. "Or you could do it because you're legitimately having fun with your coworker and enjoying your job. Just a note from your producer."

Theo grunted again. I pressed my lips together in a grim smile, my body tight, my brain full of anxious thoughts. A few weeks ago, I would have given a standing ovation to the news that Theo and I had found our way to a stifled semi-silence. But now that we had, I ached for that missing energy between us, all the taunts, the strategy, the constant quests to one-up each other.

If this had been a caller, musing about some hot, annoying dude, I would have told them to do what I'd suggested Brian do the other night—meditate or journal or go on a long hike with only your thoughts for company. I would have said something like *the less you distract yourself from what you really want, the more your mind and body will tell you what it truly desires.*

All day Sunday, I'd flat out refused to take my own advice. I'd spent the morning at an intense and sweaty spin class, where my only thoughts were *when will this end* and *everything hurts.* Followed by a long, boozy, sunshine-y brunch with some friends. Later, I filled every free moment of my remaining day with TV shows and podcasts, anything to drown out the thoughts clamoring for my attention.

My vigilance vanished around two in the morning, when I was still tossing and turning in a pitiful attempt at sleep. Those same thoughts spotted the weak link in my mental barricades and overwhelmed my senses with fantasies of Theo. In my bed, under these sheets, his big body covering mine and his hips moving sinuously between my legs.

Both of us naked. Both of us panting, arching, seeking. Those growls of frustration he made became growls of pleasure, his mouth at my ear, his teeth nipping at my skin as he fucked me senseless.

"Are we done here?"

I turned, dazed, to find Theo still in the chair next to me, rubbing his temple with two fingers and watching me closely. We were very much alone, and the break room door was very much closed.

I propped my chin in my hand. "If you say so."

"Wonderful," he muttered, closing his notebook and reaching for his phone.

"So what are you handling for Janis's party?" I asked. "Everyone seems to have a task except for you."

He paused his motions. Turned back around in his chair until he was facing me. It was like the sound booth, except it wasn't. There was no table between us.

And no one else around.

"I'm handling all the logistics. And her gift," he said.

"What are you getting her?" I asked, genuinely interested.

His throat worked, eyes darting between mine. "I want to build Janis a community pantry to place outside the radio station. She's supported the Sunrise Beach food pantry for decades. All the local news lately has centered around rising rates of food insecurity in our neighborhoods. There are other fridges and pantries across Sunrise Beach where people fill them, and can get free food, and it's truly a community endeavor."

My eyebrows shot up. "There's a community pantry outside of the Best Coast Cafe. I saw it when I was there this morning with Elena. That's..." *incredibly kind and compassionate of you* "...totally what Janis would want. A disco-themed roller-skating party followed by food-based mutual aid for the community."

His lips curved up slightly. "Radio for the people. Food for all. No one can say that Janis Hill doesn't show up as her authentic self every day of her life."

I laughed and the sound surprised me probably as much as it surprised Theo. I traced the studs in my ear, weighing the pros and cons of what I wanted to share next—a sudden memory, but a vulnerable one.

"Janis came to see me the morning after my wedding. The wedding that wasn't. I was at the apartment I shared with Jackson, though he still hadn't come home. My mom was at the grocery store. We didn't have any food because we were supposed to be heading out on our honeymoon that day. I'd been mostly in a state of shock. Exhausted and anxious. Utterly mortified."

Theo's eyes hadn't strayed from mine.

"And here comes Janis walking up the sidewalk towards my door with a totally normal look on her face. Like it was a regular Sunday morning. She'd seen me grow up, had nurtured my love of radio, had even helped me get internships in L.A. But I still opened that door and said *Janis, you cannot fucking be here right now*."

Theo's eyes crinkled at the sides. "She probably didn't like that."

I shook my head, settling back in my chair. "She barged on in which, since I had Mags as a mom growing up, I was pretty used to. But then she—" My throat tightened at the memory. "You know, she took my hand. Led me to our tiny back patio and sat me down in the sun. Brought me a glass of ice water and a box of tissues. Then she crouched in front of me and lit, oh god, the biggest joint I'd ever seen in my life. Not for me, for her."

Theo was on the cusp of a smile. Still, his low, raspy chuckle raised the hair on the back of my neck.

"Holding my hand, she said *I'm sorry, kid. Men are fucking garbage.* It made me laugh. Like that kind of out-of-control laughter that comes from your entire world splitting in two. And that became these huge, giant sobs. Janis let me cry on her shoulder for an hour. And when my mom showed up with groceries, she made us both a brunch spread I'll never forget."

He finally smiled. Just a flicker. "I'm glad she was there on your worst day. She's an excellent companion when everything's gone to hell, and it sounds like it had."

"Yep," I said, smacking my lips together. "All of that to say, I'm looking forward to this party. And if you...like, if you need...help with building this pantry, I can do it with you. It's important, not only for Janis but for everyone in this neighborhood."

He looked back down at his notebook, fingers teasing at the edges. "Thank you. I'll let you know."

I knew what was hanging between the two of us. We hadn't recognized or talked or even fought about what happened our first night of the combined show, like the look of disappointment on Janis's face when she'd stood in that doorway.

The next bit, the part where you, Theo, baited Daria on

purpose? And then you, Daria, said a lot of personal shit live and on the air? It cannot happen again.

Handing over an apology was handing Theo a vulnerability I wasn't ready to yet, even if I'd just told him a story about hysterically laugh-sobbing all over our boss. An apology was too close in a way I couldn't put my finger on.

It wasn't like he'd apologized for being an asshole to me either. I needed to stop fixating on the look of contrition on his face, how surprised he'd been as he swore he never viewed my advice as "less than" because I lacked advanced degrees.

I hadn't anticipated feeling so guilty that I'd let the substance of our daily arguments slip out on-air. And I hadn't anticipated Theo to look so stricken.

"So...you ready for paintball tomorrow?" I asked. "I'm assuming that you're spending the night mentally preparing to be destroyed by my incredible talent and skill set."

I'd purposefully kept my tone light and teasing. But I watched his expression harden and his jaw set. "I'm mostly preparing to fake my best attempt at having *authentic fun* with you so our listeners stay excited and ultimately give the station the money it needs. I'll be on my best behavior, so you don't have to worry."

I raised an eyebrow. "Is this your best behavior?"

"When it comes to you? Yes." Theo tipped forward, dropping his elbows onto his knees and clasping his hands together. "Do you have a problem with that?"

"Not at all," I said, chin lifted. "I didn't know your best behavior was ignoring me. It's boring."

I'd spoken too quickly, too honestly. Had all but handed over my queen to my much-too-clever opponent.

"You're mad that I'm not bickering with you nonstop?"

"Of course not," I said breezily. "It's just an observation."

His green eyes searched mine. I realized how close he was, how close his face was, that his body heat was warming my legs. He could have easily touched me—could have placed his palms on my knees and spread me wide open.

"Daria," he said, voice rough. "Twice I have put my career in jeopardy by giving in to whatever immature impulse you bring out in me. *Twice*. We're about to be forced into a competition tomorrow night, and I'm doing everything that I can to resist fighting with you about it. So, yes, maybe this is, indeed, boring. But what else do you want from me?"

I opened my mouth to respond. Closed it. Chewed on my bottom lip as a dozen different *wants* warred with each other inside my body. They were all pointless and stupid—Theo would always be Theo, and that meant I needed to stop wanting anything from him at all. He was not only my infuriating coworker, that was complicated enough, but he publicly stood for everything that I no longer wanted.

Where Theo wanted romantic gestures, I wanted casual sex. Theo wanted committed relationships, I wanted independence and freedom. In the Venn diagram drawing of what Theo and I had in common, the only overlap was *hosts a weekly radio show*.

"I don't want anything from you at all," I insisted. "Like you said, we both have careers and goals best served apart, not together. I'm fine keeping my head down and making it through this combined show any way that I can. At least until we can go back to the way things were."

"Sounds fine to me," he said.

"Cool."

"Great."

I gave Theo my phoniest smile. "Aces, Dr. Chadwick."

He looked like he was about to finally leave. But then he moved an inch closer and dropped his voice deeper. "Conversations would go more smoothly between the two of us if you didn't insist on baiting me into arguments."

"Are you fucking kidding me? *You're* the one who baited me on-air four nights ago. Or have you already forgotten?"

His focus fell to my mouth for a single second before rising again. "Believe me, Daria. I haven't forgotten a single goddamn second of what happened that night. But what I want to know is why you're sitting here lying to me."

I narrowed my eyes. "What could I possibly be lying to you about? If anything, I've been downplaying my paintball abilities."

There it was. That feral-sounding growl Theo made in my presence, presumably because I pissed him off. But the energy vibrating from his body was a different kind of frustrated—a coiled, controlled sexuality I wouldn't have expected from him.

"I think you're lying about what you really want. Is me, picking a fight with you over something stupid, *truly* what you want, Daria?" His gaze cut to my lips and stayed there. "Because if it isn't, you should say it."

I swallowed hard. "There isn't anything else I want from you."

We stared at each other for what felt like a thousand years but was probably only two seconds. The air crackled around us, like it usually did, but this tension had a sexier kind of edge to it. A seductive quality that had my fingers itching to fist my hands in his shirt and kiss that smug look right off his face.

"Fine. Then stop baiting me into fighting with you," he said thickly.

"Stop baiting *me*," I whispered.

Theo schooled his expression back to neutral and pushed to stand, taking his notebook and phone with him. I blinked rapidly—hot, jittery, shaken—and recrossed my legs.

"I'll be seeing you tomorrow night," he said. And if his voice held an echo of hurt and disappointment, I didn't dwell on it.

"Yeah. Be seeing you," I called back.

He didn't stop at the door. Didn't turn back around for

another verbal sparring session or one last jab. He just left, the door shutting quietly behind him.

A wave of regret washed over me just as quickly—I regretted telling him that story about Janis. Regretted revealing that I'd felt shunned by his lack of argumentative attention. And I *especially* regretted that torrid fantasy I'd given in to last night, the one that ended with me hauling out my favorite vibrator and climaxing while fantasy-Theo fucked me from behind without mercy.

At best, Theo was a workplace rival I needed to remain wary of.

At worst, he was an enraging distraction.

And either way, taunting him *or* tempting him threatened his career, my career and the future of this radio station. So he *had* been right in the end.

We were definitely done here.

THEO

J stared up at the sign outside the paintball arena located a few miles from downtown. Fields stretched in every direction from the highway, with giant pieces of metal, stacks of tires, and gym-type equipment scattered about and covered in multi-colored splatters.

A neon sign read *10 Things I Paint About You.*

"Are you sure a place called *10 Things I Paint About You* is Sunrise Beach's premier paintball establishment?" I asked into my phone.

Janis laughed. "According to the reviews. Apparently, it's all the rage among local area teens."

"Daria and I are from the local area, but we're far not teens."

"Tell that to your daily tantrums in the breakroom."

I swallowed a sigh. "Message received. And how did the call with All Star Media go? Is it bad news or worse news?"

"They're not interested in syndicating your show, Theo," she said. "They can't make the numbers work and they don't see *True Romance* fitting in with their programming right now. They are fans and this conversation wasn't a *hell no forever* type of call."

My fingers tightened on my phone. "Just a *momentary crushing of my dreams* call."

"That's how I would put it," she said. "I'm sorry, kid. Did you want me to sugarcoat it more?"

"No, it's fine," I muttered. "We've been doing this frequently enough now. I know you enjoy them about as much as a root canal."

"So much of this shit is timing. It was that way when Magnolia's show went national. It'll be that way for you. But look, it's not helping that your first week of shows with Daria didn't exactly energize our base. Elena told me that the two of you are like awkward cardboard, chemistry-wise."

I tipped my head back against the brick wall of the building. "I don't disagree with her. But I'm trying my best to stick with both my brand and my values while also adhering to the current setup. It's not exactly exciting by design. We might as well save money by cutting our individual shows in half and going back to being separate hosts."

Janis was quiet for a moment. "Then do you think you're ready to start answering questions together again? *Ready* as in won't bite each other's heads off while the cue light is on?"

I heard Daria's approach well before I saw her. She peeled into the parking lot in her Jeep, windows down, music blaring. She turned it all off, swinging open her door and hopping out of the car with wild, wind-swept curls and her piercings flashing in the sun. Her faded jean shorts revealed her strong, curved thighs, her hips swaying as she sauntered my way. Chin raised, shoulders back, a loose smile playing about her lips.

"Theo? You there?" Janis asked.

I hesitated. "What did you ask me?"

"The dynamic that's missing right now is the dynamic where you and Daria bounce off each other. Debate a little. Disagree a little. Just not to the level it was the first night. *That's* not like cardboard at all. If that worked, it would be fire. *If* you two loosened up. Right now, you're giving off seriously dreary energy."

"I see what you mean," I said, my focus locked on Daria's blue eyes. The flash of her teeth in the sun. Her smooth, bare shoulders, the glittering silver of her earrings against the contrast of her raven hair. "I'm not entirely sure if that's possible yet. Can we see if that works after this competition idea of yours?"

"It needs to be possible sooner rather than later."

I dropped my gaze to the ground as Daria arrived. "Yep. Got it. Can you let Des and Elena know we've made it and we'll do all the things they asked?"

"Only if you promise to enjoy yourself out there."

I glanced up to find Daria standing directly in front of me, as beautiful and defiant as ever. "I make no promises when it comes to my level of enjoyment."

"Don't forget to smile in those pictures," she shouted and then hung up.

Daria lifted an eyebrow. "Theo."

"Ms. Stone."

"Shall we get this madness over with?"

I extended a hand toward the front door. She spun on her platform boots and walked inside. I stayed behind for a second, taking a series of deeper and deeper inhales to regain my control. Yesterday's conversation with Daria had shaken me. Her offer to help me build a food pantry had been too sincere and too kind. The memory she'd shared of crying with Janis because of her cowardly fiancé had evoked such a spark of tenderness I'd almost reached for her.

And the worst of it, the most complicating piece of it, had been the way she'd accused me of ignoring her, while her body language had been all heat and flirtation—those parted lips, her dilated pupils, the way we kept leaning closer and closer to each other.

I'd been out of my fucking mind when I asked Daria what

she *really* wanted. Even if she had wanted to kiss me as desperately as I wanted to kiss her, she seemed to have enough sense to know how disastrous it would be.

Of course I was ignoring her. It was that or continue to argue for no reason other than my own bullshit frustrations.

It was *that* or drag her into the nearest closet and fuck us both into oblivion.

Last night, I'd gone down a rabbit hole, obsessively searching for every advice column, blog post and live radio show where I discussed the pros and cons of workplace romances. And every single time I'd counseled the person that complications would arise the longer they chose to keep the romance a secret. That they could lose their jobs, lose the trust of their coworkers, affect the professionalism of the workplace.

Every single time, I encouraged the person to let their love flourish out in the open and not in secret. And if, at the end of the day, they weren't willing to do that, it was unlikely that their relationship would last.

All of that was true when it came to this intense, out-of-control attraction I felt for Daria.

There would be no flourishing in kissing a woman who was pleased to be my direct rival.

There would be no flourishing in kissing a woman who declared that she was proudly single for life, who criticized the very essence of true love and the existence of soul mates.

There was no point in surrendering to this lust when I would always want more than she could ever give.

Inside, Daria was standing in front of a surly-looking teen with a shock of bright red hair and freckles covering his pale skin. She was holding up a mask and a paintball rifle with an easygoing confidence.

"Here's the guy I'm supposed to be competing with today," she said. "Theo, this is Aidan, our tour guide."

Aidan shrugged like we were both an annoyance and

inferior. "Welcome to *10 Things I Paint About You*, the premier paintball experience in Sunrise Beach and the entire Los Angeles metropolitan area."

I eyed the grungy gear and dimly lit surroundings. "Is that so?"

"I mean, probably," Aidan said, his voice the low, bored tone of teenagers everywhere. "This lady said she's like an expert or whatever. What about you?"

I hesitated. "Total newbie."

Aidan tossed me a zip-up jumpsuit in camouflage and a mask and then handed me the same rifle that Daria was holding. "There's a changing room right there. The jumpsuit helps keep the paint from your clothes and the mask is, like, so your face doesn't explode and stuff."

Daria was pressing her lips together, but her eyes were bright with mirth. "I appreciate the attention to safety and the protection of my face from imminent explosions and the like."

I passed a hand over my mouth, covering my own smile. Aidan frowned. Shrugged again. "Are you gonna change or what?"

I walked past him and pushed open the door, waiting until Daria swept inside. The door shut, leaving us in a similarly run-down-looking locker room with red metal doors. She set her rifle against the wall and shook out her jumpsuit.

"Should I...?" I asked, twisting to turn.

She sat down on the bench and began working her boots off. "You can, especially if you're aiming to keep that *perfect gentleman* title of yours. But nothing's coming off except my shoes. This goes on over your clothes."

I shook out my own jumpsuit and began sliding it on, eying the long zipper in the front, hoping it would conceal the fact that all the blood in my body was rushing south. The more Daria teased me about my chivalrous behavior, the more I ached to flip the lock on this door and disavow her of those courtly assumptions.

"So where did you get all of these impressive paintball skills?" I asked.

Daria slipped the bottom part of the jumpsuit on over her feet, jumping a little to settle the fabric. She looked up at me through a mess of dark curls. "About a year after Jackson left, I was still in L.A., interning at K-ROX but making money working at Atomic Records, selling vintage vinyl. There were two women there that were part of a paintball crew that competed at one of the local arenas. Their team was called *The Miss Fortunes* and they recruited me to play. It was *a lot* of fun and totally badass."

She paused, lifting a strap over each shoulder. "It was key to getting back in touch with who I really was inside, out of a relationship and back to being myself again. It's a competitive game with a lot of running and yelling and shooting at things with your friends, so it drowned out all the noise, stripped me back down to being a kid, when I wasn't so self-conscious about expressing myself."

I felt that *tug* in my chest, the same one I'd had yesterday. This had less to do with tenderness and more with the way her words showed me something I suspected I'd been missing.

"I'm sure shooting at things also helped with some of your anger," I said.

Her lips curved. "Given that you're a psychologist, my chosen coping strategies are probably glaringly obvious."

I shook my head. "Human beings, human nature, how we relate to one another, I always believed we were much too mysterious and complicated to ever be that obvious."

Daria brushed the hair out of her eyes. "How many serious breakups have you been through?"

I leaned back against the lockers. "Three."

"Theo Chadwick the heartbreaker?" she asked.

"All three of my long-term girlfriends broke up with me," I said. "Though that's nice of you to assume the opposite."

I thought I saw her cheeks turn pink, even in the dim lighting. "Well...okay, but that's only because you're the doctor of love. The perfect gentleman and all-around total catch." She shrugged. "Or whatever, I don't really care."

I cocked my head, fighting amusement. "'An all-around total catch?'"

She rolled her eyes. "The *briefest* perusal of your social media pages shows a million comments with listeners being like *Theo Chadwick is the most perfect man in existence, circle yes or hell yes.*"

I cleared my throat through a burst of jealousy. "You have your fair share of online admirers as well."

Daria relaced her boots and stood, reaching for the bottom of the zipper. "Yeah, I do okay in the comment section. My question is, how did *you* cope with three separate breakups?"

I crossed one ankle over the other, hands in the pockets of the camouflage jumpsuit. "I handle the ending of my relationships the way I handled the interviews I did with couples for my dissertation. Examining miscommunications, patterns, where our values and goals didn't ultimately line up. Differences in communication style. Whatever the reasons were for ending our relationship, I try to study with an academic eye and improve myself. My soul mate is out there, but I still believe I should be my best self when I meet her."

Daria didn't have an immediate response to that. She regarded me closely until I wanted to fidget. "What were their reasons for dumping you?"

I pushed off the wall with a mild smile. "Now why would I ever tell you something like that, Daria?"

She frowned, struggling with a stuck zipper. "It was worth a shot, wasn't it?"

Someone, presumably Aidan, pounded on the door. "Are you two all right in there? Or are you, like, dead?"

"We're getting in the right headspace for a competition," I called back.

"Anyway," Daria said, voice muffled by her hair as she looked down and wrenched at the zipper, "that's why I'm going to kick your ass today and not even break a sweat, Dr. Chadwick."

I raised an eyebrow, understanding that every minor personal detail we shared had to be immediately shrouded in insults or threats. "You'll be my *misfortune* it seems?"

"You won't be this cool and casual later when I've got you begging for mercy."

I closed the gap between us and reached for the tiny piece of metal giving her so much trouble. "Can I try?"

She looked up, lips parting, blue eyes widening. Nodded *yes*. "Are you attempting to get in my head so I go easy on you out there?"

The metal finally gave beneath my fingers. I held her gaze, slowly tugging the fabric closed as the zipper rose smoothly up the length of her body. "As usual, Daria, you've made way too many assumptions of what I can, and can't, do well. Did it ever occur to you that I've played plenty of paintball with Des and his cousins? Or that we play it so much it's now a Thanksgiving tradition in their family?"

"But you said you were a total newbie."

"People can lie, you know," I said, echoing her words from the other day. "I'm not opposed to a tactical advantage." The hand holding her zipper reached her midsection. She wrapped her fingers around mine and pulled it free, dragging it up the rest of the way.

She smirked. "If that's the case, then whatever leniency I was going to show you out there has been replaced with full-on aggression."

"It's sweet you thought you could ever handle me," I said roughly.

Another knock at the door had us stepping apart, though we didn't break eye contact. Daria hefted her mask and gun to her side, and I did the same. She brushed past me, muttering something that sounded like *fucking asshole*. Back out in the lobby, Aidan was yawning while scrolling through his phone.

"We didn't die or anything," Daria said.

"Cool." He yawned. "Oh, um, I forgot to tell you guys something. You're from that radio station, right?"

"Yeah, K-SUN," Daria replied. "A guy named Desmond Davis was in touch about doing some cross-promo since Theo and I are technically out here, shooting each other with paint for our jobs. We wanted to coordinate some deals and free passes for listener prizes. We'll even be doing a quick live broadcast from the field in about an hour." She glanced up at the clock on the wall.

"Uh-huh," Aidan said. "Yeah, whatever, my boss Kyle said it's fine. Want me to take your picture now?"

I turned around and found that we were standing in front of a mural with giant paint splatters. "No time like the present."

Aidan held out his phone, camera facing us. "Can you stand closer than ten feet apart?"

Janis yelling *don't forget to smile* rang through my ears. I glanced sideways at Daria, whose loose and confident body language had gone rigid.

The two of you are like awkward cardboard, chemistry-wise.

Swallowing as much of my pride as I was able to, I moved to Daria's side and extended the arm not holding a paint gun. Daria gawked at me like I'd sprouted three separate lizard heads.

"We need to do it for content," I whispered out of the side of my mouth.

Her wariness was obvious, as was whatever internal debate she was undertaking at the sight of me trying to pull her into a side-hug. I got it. I was just as bewildered. Eventually, she sidled over as regally as one could while wearing camouflage. We faced forward, and I placed an arm around her so gently my fingers practically floated above the ball of her shoulder. Her arm curved around my waist with the same barely-there motion. A full three-inch gap existed between us.

And still.

And *still*, my nose filled with the scent of Daria, which was floral and warm, a tropical flower on a sun-drenched beach. My body came alive at her nearness, from my fingers aching to touch her, to my cock hardening at the temptation of her curves. She shifted on her feet and the space between us vanished, her hip pressing into mine. If I turned and dipped my head, I could have brushed my lips through her hair.

"Uh...so cheese?" Aidan said.

I mustered up a smile and hoped it appeared authentic.

"Those seem fine, I guess. 'Cause you're like coworkers so everyone knows it's, like, weird," he intoned, already back to scrolling on the screen. Daria and I sprang apart to pull on our masks. Every muscle in my body was rippling with tension.

I hadn't lied—I did play paintball often with Des, and with his family, though at another arena. But I wasn't that competitive when I did.

However, standing in this dingy lobby next to my beguiling workplace rival, my only thoughts were *I need to win.*

"Oh right, so the thing I was gonna say earlier?" Aidan added. A barrage of *whoops* filtered in from outside. "This lady named Janis, she's your boss?"

"Uh-huh," Daria and I drawled in unison.

"She changed the game for today, and you're not competing against each other. You're on the same team and fighting against another group that'll start in five minutes."

"I don't get to shoot Theo with paint?" Daria asked, voice muffled by the mask.

"No, you're shooting others." Aidan picked up a piece of paper and squinted at it. "She was like...tell them if they're mad about it that I don't care, and I'm in charge so they have to do what I say. But if they seem bummed about it, remind them that I believe in them and shit." He dropped the paper. "She was kind of a weird lady."

I blew out a frustrated breath. "That sounds like our boss."

Daria flipped up her mask and flashed me a wry look. "Look on the bright side. She said she believes in us."

"And shit," I said.

A group of five rowdy people already in their gear clamored into the lobby and cheered aggressively when they saw us.

"I'm sorry, but we're playing two against five?" I asked.

"Yeah, because Janis said she was in charge," Aidan said sullenly.

Daria pinned me with a concerned look. "Well, *shit* indeed."

DARIA

I didn't know who I was more pissed at. Janis and her *I've got a secret reason for everything* eccentricities.

Or the lying, smirking son of a bitch standing next to me. The one who'd stared down at me like I was a calculus equation he *loved* solving, all while holding me still with only his hand, those fingers roaming confidently up the length of my body as if he'd zipped me up a hundred times before.

It's sweet you thought you could ever handle me.

It didn't matter how many teams we played against. I was still going to paintball Dr. Theodore Chadwick in the fucking face.

We stood outside beneath a southern California sky starting to turn twilight at the very edges of the horizon. But it was June—we had two hours of sun left at least—and that same sun warmed my hands and the asphalt we were standing on. Next to me, Theo had his mask pushed up onto the top of his head, green eyes intense behind his glasses.

"You've all done this before, but I'll repeat the rules and the safety guidelines." Aidan indicated the cluster of players behind him—all jocular, amped-up dudes who'd smirked like assholes when they saw they were competing against a woman. "Your masks stay on at all times. If the air pressure in your rifles drops down, let me know and I'll fix it. If not, you should be able to fire for the next hour. One shot, one hit, and your arms go up." Aidan shrugged. "That means you're out. Theo and Daria, I don't really know what you want to do if one of you gets hit?"

"The other one keeps playing, Aidan," I said sweetly. "And we're not going to get hit."

The opposing team of total bros rattled off a few meaningless taunts in my direction. Next to me, Theo dropped his head toward mine, mouth at my ear. His warm breath shivered across my throat.

"I'll let you take every single shot on these shitheads. How does that sound for game strategy?" he whispered.

"Are you sure? You don't even want one of them?" I whispered back.

Our eyes met. I felt a flicker of camaraderie in my chest.

One of the bros yelled, "The other team can suck my *nuts*, man."

A muscle ticked in Theo's jaw. "I'll take that one."

Aidan held up an air horn. "Theo and Daria, you start over there. This team starts behind the stack of tires. You have full use of the field. Only rules are no face shots. No shooting people more than once on purpose. Nothing too up close. Sixty seconds and then you start."

Everyone on the field burst into frenzied motion. Theo and I ran toward our starting point behind a long line of rusted-up trucks. We rounded the first car, dust flying behind us. I crouched down behind the second one, trying to get a visual.

"Do you see them?" I asked Theo, who was behind the third car.

"Not yet." His rifle was back against his shoulder, finger

curved around the trigger. "You know, I was on the phone with Janis when you got here."

"Oh, lemme guess. She didn't say jack shit about changing the rules on us last second?"

He was wearing his mask, but I heard the smile in his voice. "Of course not. And I know why she's doing this."

A flash of movement caught my eye.

I craned my neck. "Look, over there."

Theo crouched next to me. "I bet they're hiding behind those brick walls. Do you see?"

I followed his finger. Waited. A bunch of rifles waved over the top of the wall—haphazardly, like they were shuffling into position without realizing they were partially exposed.

"Amateurs," I murmured. "Follow my lead."

"Or you could follow my lead?"

"Are we really going to fight about this when I *told* you I had more—"

The player came out of nowhere, flying through the gap between cars number four and five and diving onto the ground. I half-stood, shoved Theo to the side, and shot the guy in the leg.

"Aw man, *fuck*," the guy yelled. He shoved up his mask and looked down at the yellow splatter.

"Put your hands up, dick," I sang. "You're *out*."

I was busy boasting—and rightfully so—which meant I wasn't paying attention to my periphery. One moment I was standing with my hand on my hip, and the next Theo was fisting the front of my jumper and yanking me down to the ground. A *whizz* sound flew past my ear followed by the soft *thunk* of a paintball landing barely a foot away. Stunned, I looked up to see Theo stand, aim and shoot.

There was a strangled yell and then, "*Motherfucker.*"

Panting, I tapped Theo's leg. "You got a shithead."

"Two down, three to go," he said sternly, offering me a hand. I took it, too energized and full of sparkling adrenaline to remember my pride. He lifted me easily and took off toward the brick wall. I followed, leaping over a few logs, before dropping low to slide next to him behind a semi-burned shack.

"What the hell is the theme of this place? Random garbage?" I asked.

"I think in the fall it gets turned into one of those *field of screams* corn mazes," he said.

"Given our current *field of douchebags* situation, we're not that far off."

Even muffled through the mask, Theo's raspy laughter had my stomach dipping.

I nudged his leg again. "What were you saying about Janis?"

He scanned the area before turning toward me. "She's been banging the drum of us learning the true meaning of compromise and working together since the beginning. This is like her version of a *Sesame Street* episode about the value of teamwork except with more guns and rusted metal."

I rolled my eyes so hard I probably strained a muscle. "Oh *goddammit*, you're right."

"Sometimes I am. Most times I am."

"Oh yeah?" I taunted. "Didn't our first caller Brian choose my advice over yours in the end? You've got all this academic experience of understanding human beings and you were too stubborn to recognize that our buddy Brian was heartbroken as hell and *in no shape* to start going on dates."

I felt the sear of Theo's glare through the plastic visor. Felt it and gave it right back.

"Are you still hung up on *Brian?*" he asked. "Because I'd bet every single dollar I have that six months from now he'll be in a healthy, loving relationship with someone new. Not every person turns their back on true love because it burned them. Not every person gives up like you did."

I stood up so quickly I got light-headed. "What the *fuck* did you just say to me?"

"I *said*—" Then Theo cursed, wrapped an arm around my waist and pulled us both around the corner of the shack. I shoved away, raised my rifle, and tagged the incoming shit-head in the chest seconds before he would have hit Theo.

"Son of a bitch," the guy wailed, arms raising. But I was already stalking across the field, too angry to care about exposing myself.

Theo glued himself to my side not a second later.

"You're welcome, by the way," I snapped.

"I don't recall asking you to shoot that guy."

"I don't recall asking you to pass judgment on the life I've created."

A paintball sailed past us and exploded not two feet to our right. I grabbed Theo by the arm and dragged him to the ground, where we both landed hard on our stomachs.

"Do you see them?" I asked, craning my neck.

Theo nudged my elbow with his and pointed silently with his finger. We didn't have an ounce of cover, but the guy aiming for us was a horrible shot.

"*Take him out*," Theo whispered.

I propped up my rifle, got him in my sights, and fired. A second later, his leg exploded in blue paint.

"Goddamn," Theo swore.

"Told you."

Two seconds of amicable silence followed, and then Theo pushed himself to stand and took off toward the brick wall.

"Wait, I'm not done arguing with you," I hissed, sprinting after his broad form. He'd taken up a position behind another busted-up-looking building with rows of small orange doors, like the facade of an old Motel 6. I slammed into the wall next to him.

"For the record, Daria, I don't recall asking you to accuse me of being an elitist jackass during a live broadcast," he said bitterly. "Janis is out here, forcing us to play a children's game when I know that we'll *never* work because you refuse to ever apologize when it comes to me."

I scoffed. "Do you have the ability to admit that sometimes you're wrong, Theo? Do you have the *singular ability* to apologize to me for all the stupid shit you've said these past three months too?"

A twig snapped to our right. Theo moved, hauling me against his chest and falling into a semi-dark alcove. His strong arm banded around my breasts, tight as a vice. His body vibrated ever so slightly, fingers gripping my shoulder. His lower body angled away from me even as my own hips longed to tilt back, seeking the firm length of him. That was the only reason why I was distracted when the last remaining player ambled past us, directly into view.

Theo lifted his rifle at the same time as I lifted mine, our hands knocking into each other with so much speed that the paintballs we ejected went wide. Mine smacked into a tree while Theo's hit the side of the tire next to the final player. He turned, gun swinging, searching for us.

But before he could spot us in the alcove, whatever decrepit door we'd been leaning against swung open.

With stifled shouts, we fell backward into darkness.

1 2

DARIA

*T*he door slammed shut behind us. Theo grabbed for the handle, but it wouldn't budge.

I tossed my mask to the ground. "Are we locked in here? Also, what is *here*?"

He tried to push again, hammering on the surface and calling for help. I searched for a window, a latch, a key—it appeared to be an old supply or utility closet. There was a dusty window, high in the right corner, that left us in dim lighting. I jumped up and down, trying to wave through it.

"Daria, do you have your phone?" Theo asked in a strained voice.

I patted down my pockets. "Fuck me, *no*. You?"

He tossed his mask on the floor next to mine and raked a hand through his hair. "No, I left it with our stuff back in the locker room." He turned, looking pissed, and slammed his hand against the door a few times. Yelled. And nothing.

I pointed to our sole source of dingy light. "Can you reach that window?"

His hands could easily—he waved them around and for about ten full seconds we yelled some variation of *help we're trapped*. Yelled until we were hoarse, but to no avail.

I pressed my shoulders flat to the wall and sighed. "Well, we can't get stuck out here for long. The game will end in thirty minutes and either the remaining douchebag or our bestie Aidan will rescue us. You're not claustrophobic or anything, are you?"

Theo was standing with his hands propped on his hips, glaring at the door like he thought a hole might appear from sheer fury alone. "No, I'm not. But I don't want to be trapped here with you."

It was a little hot and a lot musty. I set my rifle down, slid the straps of my jumper past my shoulders and unzipped the whole thing to my hips. "Same here, Dr. Chadwick. With our luck, the K-SUN team reverse-engineered every available space in this field to ensure that we ended up stuck until we worked out our shit."

He scrubbed a hand down his face before yanking down his own jumper. His gray T-shirt looked soft and worn and had the annoying effect of clinging to every muscle in his chest. An awkward silence hung between us in the muggy air, filled with our unfinished arguments, the lingering stubbornness, all the minor ways we'd lashed out at each other today.

Enclosed in this room, it was getting harder and harder for me not to blurt out the first of many apologies. Because my guess was that Theo would do the same. That once we began exploring a tentative truce—a real one, this time— whatever happened next between us would be the real complication.

He turned to face me, his big, lean body taking up all the space, sucking up all the air.

"What?" I asked, nervously touching my earrings.

His brows raised. "Nothing."

I swallowed. "I've got a few more points to make from our earlier disagreement. I'm happy to go down a—"

Theo closed the short distance between us in two long

strides. My shoulders hit the hard wall, my chin lifting to maintain our eye contact. His large right hand landed next to my face. Then his left hand, on the other side, effectively boxing me in on all sides.

"We are locked in a random room in a random field in the middle of nowhere and you *still* want to fight with me," he said in a gravelly whisper. "This new work setup has been a nightmare since the beginning, and it's going to be a nightmare to the bitter end, isn't it?"

My eyes searched his, shocked to find as much lust there as irritation. "You're Dr. Theodore Chadwick and you swagger around the station proclaiming yourself some kind of 'expert' on romance and thoughtful gestures and making people swoon with your advice on true love. Yet *none* of the behavior you've exhibited around me could be called gentlemanly. You've been cold and dismissive since the first day I showed up."

His eyes closed like he was in pain, an entirely unexpected gesture. My fingers twitched by my sides, dangling there though they were desperate to touch him. Theo removed his glasses and dropped them into his pocket. When his eyes opened, whatever restraint this man employed in my presence had been burned away.

My stomach pitched to the floor, my knees turning to jelly. He placed the knuckle of his index finger at the hollow of my throat. I gulped so forcefully he probably felt it. He very, very carefully traced the length of my neck, the pressure tingling against my skin.

And when he finally reached my chin, he pressed—lightly —until my face tilted up another inch. "For the life of me, I cannot figure you out, Daria. When I'm fighting with you, I'm a smug asshole, irritating you nonstop. But when I do my best to *avoid* confrontations with you—which is, I'll remind you, what we've been asked to do at our workplace—then you're telling me that I'm boring. That I'm ignoring you." He dipped his face close to mine, until his exhale mingled with my inhale. "What do you *want?*"

My chest heaved up and down while Theo was unmoving. "I don't...I don't know."

"You're lying."

"You don't know shit, Theo," I whispered harshly.

"*Daria,*" he growled. "You have spent your career advising people on listening to their bodies, to their true needs free from societal pressures. You have spent your career telling people to grab pleasure with both hands and claim it as rightfully *theirs*. I know you're lying because you *do know* what you're craving. Don't you?"

His knuckle left my chin, only to be replaced with his entire palm, cupping my cheek. The tips of his fingers dragged through my hair, sending ripples of arousal throughout my entire body.

"Fine, I do know," I admitted. "But what I want is really, really, *really fucking stupid.*"

"It can't be any more stupid than what I want," he said. "I spend every single second we're together aching to kiss that sexy smirk right off your gorgeous face."

My lips parted on a shocked gasp.

"I spend every moment we're in the same room wanting to fuck you on the nearest flat surface. A table, a desk, a chair, the *goddamn floor*, Daria. And then I go home and fall asleep and there you are, in my dreams, naked and moaning and sighing and *coming.*" His hips punched forward, pinning me back. His mouth dropped close. So close. "Trust me. I understand wanting what I shouldn't want. I understand wanting what I can never have."

In a burst of dazzling clarity, I realized how very right Theo was. Denying my body what was sexy and pleasurable had been the old, hurtful pattern of my past self. Of the person I'd been with Jackson, only ever wanting things after he gave an indication that he wanted it too. I wasn't only seeking validation *through* him when we were together, I sought approval of my own needs through him as well. *If Jackson says* x, *then that means I should want* y.

Now, right now, the delicious weight of Theo's body pressed me into the wall—shoulders expansive and rounding toward me, his long fingers tangled in my hair, his thumb caressing my jawline. This man, this clever, controlled, *disciplined* man, was glaring at my mouth with pure lust.

I stopped thinking about Theo's complicated values, my burgeoning career, all those rejected manuscripts and competitive radio contests.

In fact, I stopped thinking entirely and allowed the volume of my physical senses to crank *all* the way up. All those secret, late-night desires. The illicit, desperate attraction I'd felt toward Theo from the first moment I'd laid eyes on him. Beneath the anger beat the pure heart of *passion*.

And I'd stopped denying myself passion a long, long time ago.

I fisted the soft material of his T-shirt and pressed up on my toes. Our mouths hovered a centimeter apart, eyes locked in our most intense nonverbal argument yet.

I kissed Theo. My lips met his firmly but quickly. Still, the fire that blazed through my nerve endings was all-consuming. From a *single kiss*. Startled, I whispered, "That's what I really want, okay?"

Theo moved so quickly I barely comprehended that I'd gone from standing to hauled up around his waist. But there I was—my legs around his lean hips, his hands gripping my thighs. "Is this what you want, Daria?"

"Yes," I breathed out. "Even though you *infuriate* me every single day."

His mouth hitched up on one side. "You can stop pretending that you don't enjoy it."

I gripped his face. "Will you shut the hell up and ki—"

Theo captured my mouth in a kiss so searing my lips

parted on a whimper. But he showed me no mercy, deliberately devouring me, sweeping his tongue against mine while a sound like an approaching thunderstorm rumbled from his chest. This kiss was raw and just shy of feral, but not sloppy. His lips were as skilled as they were demanding, taking everything he wanted from me.

And I was more than happy to give in. In the office, he was a buttoned-up, highly competent pinnacle of control. Yet here he was, shoving me back against a wall with my legs around his waist, kissing me like he was an expert on sin, and I was his eager and willing student.

Theo deepened the kiss with a hungry groan. I bunched his collar between my hands, yanking him closer, letting him ravish my mouth until I was boneless with arousal. His lips roamed down my neck. As he planted kiss after deliberate kiss along my throat, I smiled through a series of breathless sighs.

"You like arguing with me too," I murmured. "You can admit it. I won't use it against you or anything."

His dangerous-sounding laughter vibrated through my skin while his hot mouth found my ear, tongue tracing the shell over and over while shivers wracked my body.

"Oh god, Theo," I whispered.

He rolled his hips between my legs, dragging his thick erection over my clit in sinuous circles. "Do you feel that?" he said against my ear, giving me another series of rough thrusts, each one setting off a wave of undulating pleasure.

"*Yes*," I hissed, head back.

"That's how hard I get *every fucking time* you fight with me, Daria." He reclaimed my mouth, our lips bruising, this kiss furious and frustrated. "And I cannot figure out *why* or *how*, only that every time you open that irritating mouth of yours, it makes me want to drag you into my bed and fuck you for three days straight."

I scraped my teeth along his jaw. "Oh, the *arrogance*."

He pulled back an inch, nostrils flaring. "Last time I checked, you don't know shit, Daria."

We glared at each other with swollen lips and disheveled hair. And then we reached for each other at the same time again, our lips crashing together, our moans loud enough for any paintball players passing by to discover our hiding spot.

I stopped us for one feverish moment, but only so I could pull off my shirt and bra. Theo's response was to grab me tight and spin us around, dropping me onto the small table shoved into the corner. My bare back hit the rough surface and Theo's lips were moving again, down my neck, tongue tracing my collarbone. While my fingers tangled in his hair, his hands rose to cup my breasts. My back bowed, my entire body tight and twisting.

"I was wrong about the three days," Theo half-whispered, half-snarled. Eyes closed, he sucked my nipple between his lips, tongue swirling, the pressure a direct line to my clit. "I'd fuck you for a *week* straight. And when it was time for you to go, I'd get down on my knees and beg you to stay."

He had me spread on a table while he devoured my breasts, and I wasn't flushing over the delicious fantasy of enjoying a growling Theo for a week-long fuckfest. *That* was currently the only kind of intimacy I allowed into my relationship-free life.

No, that wasn't what was inciting the blush.

Theo was the kind of man who would always want *more* of me, and that was setting off a riot of gigantic butterflies in my belly. Getting semi-naked with my coworker in a paintball field felt less forbidden than allowing myself to give *more* to a man, ever again.

But that train of scattered thoughts was interrupted by his teeth, scraping against my nipple. I gasped, clutching at his face. He paused, pinning his eyes to mine. "Do you like that? Or do you not?"

"L—love it," I said, shoving his face back down. He

grunted his approval and sucked my nipple again, harder this time, letting his teeth nip gently in a rhythm that had my core clenching. Theo must have sensed my need, sliding his hand down my body and cupping me between the legs.

The fabric of my jeans and underwear stood between my clit and his palm, but he didn't seem to see that as a bad thing. With a devilish twist to his lips, he put the perfect amount of pressure against my sex, using the palm of his hand. The steady, direct *push* had my eyes rolling in the back of my head.

"Daria."

Theo turned his head and kissed the inside of my knee. My inner thigh. I sank my teeth into my lower lip, rolling my hips.

"Daria, look at me."

My eyes flew open at his stern tone. Heart in my throat, I pressed up onto my elbows and watched Theo tip forward, brush his mouth over mine. When he moved the tangle of curls that had fallen across my face, that heart in my throat went utterly still. But then he pushed his palm over my clit again, and a shaky moan tumbled from my mouth.

"You know your body," he said hoarsely. "Every time I listened to your show, you...you told your listeners about learning—"

"How to make myself come," I whispered. "How to fuck myself."

He gripped my face and pressed his forehead to mine. He twisted his palm, and my legs began to shake. "Then tell me where and how you want my hand. Here, like this?"

I shook my head, mouth totally dry. "Fuck me with your fingers, Theo."

His jaw popped. His breathing came in short, harsh pants. Eyes locked, he did just that, his large, warm hand sliding past all those layers to cup my slick folds. I kissed him greedily, moaning his name through his thorough examination of my wetness, one fingertip dipping inside. Teasing.

"*Fuck*, you're so wet," he growled into my mouth. "More or less? Tell me."

"More," I panted. "You know I can take it."

Theo's hand landed in the center of my chest, shoving me back down. His other hand worked between my legs, first one and then two fingers pushing deep inside of me.

"Holy shit, Theo, *yes*," I cried. A second later and his mouth was back on my breasts again, teasing my nipples as he slowly moved his fingers inside and out. I could feel him watching me, studying my reactions, all that academic curiosity learning my every response. "I like it fast. Please."

"*Jesus*, Daria," he hissed. "Like this?"

I nodded, speechless, his thick fingers thrusting through the clenching of my internal walls. I peered up at Theo, who'd shed every vestige of his civility, so focused was he on finger-fucking me to orgasm in the middle of this room.

His hair fell messily onto his forehead. Sweat beaded on his throat. His forearm muscles bunched and rippled as he worked my pussy. I slipped my own hand between my legs and found my clit, knowing that with the slightest pressure, the orgasm coiled low in my belly would devastate me.

I didn't think it was cynical to assume we would never do this again. That Theo and I needed to furiously make each other come to find some kind of professional equilibrium. By our very natures, we had no future together—a reality I needed to cling to.

That meant if I was going to climax with Theo's fingers inside of me, then I was going to witness the fantasy I'd been playing on a loop in my head for the past two weeks.

"Theo," I sighed. "I want to watch you touch yourself while you touch me."

His body went entirely still—though not his fingers. Those kept up a steady thrusting motion that had my entire lower body trembling on the very edge. Throat working, he slowly pulled down his zipper, freeing his cock, fist wrapped around the base.

And *sweet holy hell,* of course Theo Chadwick was charmingly handsome with shoulders for days and he kissed like an expert—and had a cock I could objectively describe as *beautiful.*

"It's not fair," I moaned, eyes glued to his thick length, the smooth skin moving with his fist, the pre-cum beading at the tip. I looked up to catch his lips twitch, like he was fighting a smile, until his head tipped back on the first full stroke. I took the opportunity to run my tongue up the cords of his neck, tasting salt and skin.

And then I watched Theo work his fist up and down his cock, his fingers thrusting inside of me with the same speed. I pressed my pelvis forward until his palm was grinding against me. I wrapped my legs tight around his waist and rode his hand—our lips close, our eyes locked, the sounds of our panting breath filling the room.

"Daria," he spit out, giving me a rough kiss. "Daria, *Daria, Daria.*" His hips jerked and mine rolled, and once we were kissing again we didn't stop. Our movements were a little sloppy and uncoordinated, but that made what we were doing all the more desperate, two people so hot for each other we were nothing but roaming hands, whispered commands and soft grunts of pleasure.

I reached between us and wrapped my fingers around Theo's cock, notching mine over his, squeezing and stroking together. He was all heavy, velvet steel, and the strangled sounds he made had my internal muscles clenching, clenching, tight then *tighter.* His palm pressed to my clit. His fingers stroked and teased every nerve ending deep inside of me. A scream was building in my throat, a scream as powerful as the orgasm starting to erupt.

"*Theo,*" I cried. "I'm going to...*you're going to...*hard, harder, *yes*." I came in a blazing wave of light, dropping my face to his chest and screaming in ecstasy, my hips bucking against his through intense aftershocks. I was so turned on I kept jerking Theo in earnest—he dropped his hand and slid it around the back of my head, holding me to him as he came with a raspy shout, groaning my name into my hair.

We were still gripping each other, and I raised my head from Theo's chest just in time for him to kiss me. His lips slanted over mine with the same urgency as before, as if we hadn't come together on this table with a ferocity that had me trembling from head to toe. His tongue met mine while he slowly, gently removed his fingers from my sex. I released his cock, immediately mourning the loss, but Theo kept kissing me, sliding his hands around my waist.

"Daria," he shuddered, "what just happened between us?"

We stared at each other in the dim light, and I knew that we wore matching expressions of complete and total shock. As if a ground-splitting earthquake had rolled through, powerfully shaking every heavy object around us.

"I don't...I don't know," I admitted. Unlike before, I was telling the truth this time. What I'd experienced with Theo, what I'd felt, was an actual devastation. It had been as sexy and euphoric as it was strangely intimate—the way we'd seen each other come undone, climaxing together in a rush of adrenaline, anger and lust.

Theo had not only admitted to listening to my show but remembered how often I spoke about relearning my body's agency. He recognized that I held all the keys to my own pleasure and was eager to learn what those were.

It was night and day from the way we interacted at the station, which was essentially a stubborn, argumentative duel where any display of vulnerability was a sign of weakness.

And this moment of raw desire hadn't happened with the hottest stranger at the bar but with a coworker who pissed me off *constantly*. Whose only goals in life appeared to be bickering with me on-air and getting married to his soul mate.

The sound of heavy, clomping boots appeared, like someone was shuffling up and down the walkway directly outside the door.

"Yeah, I don't know where they are," came the voice of the fifth, and final, player.

Theo and I burst into motion—cleaning, fastening, buttoning. I yanked my shirt down and the straps of my jumper up and was almost undone again when Theo reached for my zipper and smoothly pulled it all the way closed, eyes on mine like I was some kind of beautiful, yet confusing, miracle.

He slipped his glasses from his pocket and was reaching for his mask when the heavy door swung open. Light poured in around the silhouette of Theo's body. I blinked, peeking around his shoulder to see that same final player raise his rifle and let out an obnoxious shout of presumed victory.

My hands flew forward, mouth opening to yell that we weren't wearing our masks. But he'd already shot Theo in the back of the leg, the paint flying up to coat most of the lower half of his jumpsuit.

"What the *hell*," Theo hissed, twisting at the waist and cursing again when he saw what happened. Outside, the final player was engaged in a ridiculous victory dance—one that involved more hip thrusts than was ever necessary *anywhere*.

I was already furiously yanking on my mask and reaching for my rifle. Theo called my name, but I ignored it, stalking over to the hip-thruster and grinning when he turned around and saw me.

"Oh, *sh—*"

I aimed and fired, superbly pleased I'd managed to hit him directly in the chest. Aidan was running across the field with a whistle and his trusty bullhorn.

"Arms up, dickhead," I said to the guy on the ground. He

groaned, waving a weak hand. I spun to face Aidan, pulling off my mask and giving as fancy a bow as I was able.

"Last woman standing," I sang.

"Cool," Aidan drawled. "Guess you and Theo are the winners. Now you can tell that Janis lady, the one who said she, like, believed in you or whatever."

I breathed out a wild-sounding laugh. And when I turned back to look at Theo, he was leaning his shoulder against the door frame of the closet where we'd just kissed and gasped our way through incredible pleasure.

But that forbidden memory wasn't the reason why it suddenly felt like fireflies were dancing inside of my body.

It was Theo's smile—his *real* smile, the one that lit up the darkening sky around us, dimples and all. It wasn't for anyone else either. It was aimed directly at me, calling forth my own foolish grin in response.

He raised his chin toward the guy on the ground, green eyes pinned on mine. "But what would you, Daria Stone, say to that platitude? If Janis was a listener, calling in?"

I propped a hand on my hip, my grin turning saucy. "I'd say that was a crock of bullshit. Because I believed in *myself* the whole time."

"That you did," he said softly, smile still plastered across his face.

And deep inside my chest, a *tiny* piece of my heart, a piece I'd turned my back on years ago, shivered awake.

THEO

I perched on the edge of Janis's desk, notebook resting on my thigh, and watched her pull through dusty old boxes with a mild amusement.

"And you're sure you don't want my help?" I asked.

She tossed her thick braid over her shoulder. "Last time I asked for help it was 1989, kid. Plus, I'm only looking for a bunch of old posters. I'm about to turn seventy-one, for fuck's sake, it's not like I'm some decrepit old crone."

I passed a hand over my mouth, hiding my smile. "You got all of that from, *can I help you?*"

She raised a proud middle finger my way but then exclaimed, "Holy shit, I think there's a bag of old weed in here." She raised it, sniffed it. Frowned. "Actually, it's shreds of green paper."

I stood and snatched it from her grasp, tossing it in the wastebasket. "You have a problem."

Janis snorted, indicating the open boxes around her with things like *staff meeting notes, 1996* scrawled on the side. "You say *problem*. I say *possibility*."

"What possibility is that?"

"You'll all know how to run this place when I'm gone."

She rolled her eyes at my—understandable—look of surprised horror. "Not when I'm *dead*, Theo. When I retire. If whoever comes on as station manager wants to understand why I made a decision back in the nineties, they'll have access to my brain via all of these. Though my hope is everyone will still be here. Maybe not Mags though. When I picture her retired, I imagine her joining a motorcycle club. How about you?"

Trying to envision Magnolia Stone as retired and riding a motorcycle was dangerously close to a person I was trying my best *not* to think of. Though, in all honestly, it really wasn't that much of a mental stretch to see what Janis meant.

"She strikes me as a lady of the open road," I said with a shrug. "But as long as the rest of us are here, hopefully whoever replaces you will discover that we're a much more interesting source for your legacy than 1996's meeting notes."

Janis crouched down, grumbling into an open box so musty I could smell it from here. "I *guess* that makes me comfortable. But there's also the risk that you'll leave us and go back to your cushy academic life."

I straightened my glasses. "That risk has been at the *non-threat* level for years now. Besides, if my adviser had had his way, I'd be embroiled in some post-doc program or starting a private practice somewhere, and *neither* of those things hold any interest to me. I could be at awkward wine-and-cheese functions, trying to schmooze a dean, or I could spend my nights talking to listeners about romance. And who love radio as much as I do."

I'd enjoyed the research, had always enjoyed a classroom setting and working with students. But starting that advice column had unleashed an interest that had only grown. I knew I needed to get out of stuffy, scholarly meetings and back talking to people when I'd been working on my dissertation and had looked forward to speaking with those couples every day over all the other tasks.

Janis unrolled a poster and squawked in delight. Handing it to me, she said, "Here you go. In case you need reminding of why I'm forcing the whole station to scramble around like monkeys on a sinking ship right now."

I held it up—it was from a protest in 1998. The sign read *Sunrise Beach Doesn't Stand for Big Business.*

"That was when every independent company in this town was being threatened or plain old snatched up," she said with a wince. "I'd never felt so scared. The idea of community radio becoming *commodity* is everything I've ever been against. We can't let K-SUN become another piece of property to some huge corporate monster."

I rerolled the poster, feeling the weight of Janis's fear settle in my gut. There was indeed a future where this station was stripped of its spirit, left to lurch forward without the things that made it great. I needed the daily reminder that this threat lurked in the background—that for all of Janis's jokes, she was putting her trust in all of us to do our best.

"Less suits, more tie-dye, is the legacy I swear to uphold here when you're gone," I finally said. "Not dead gone, though. Just retired and living down the street."

"Huh, did I say all of that?"

I cracked a smile. "It's one of your favorite sayings and you know it. You once told me that suits and ties should be permanently outlawed in this town."

She nodded in approval and bent back down to her task. "I'm an incredibly wise woman, Theo. Don't ever let me forget that."

"I promise," I said solemnly.

"Also, to circle back to that old *shuffling off the mortal coil* thing, I'm not ever going to die."

I hid a smile. "Another thing you've told me a million times."

She sniffed. "If I did shuffle off, I would haunt you. Not because I missed you or anything, but more for tormenting purposes."

"I'm looking forward to it."

Janis paused to give me a nod before disappearing into her boxes again. She'd never been an openly vulnerable leader, more content inspiring with her actions and her intense, immediate loyalty. In a million different ways, describing K-SUN as "her" legacy did a grave disservice to Janis and her core values, which were *community* above all else.

Over the past thirty years, what we stood for, and what we stood *up* for, came from the enduring legacies of every single person who'd graced our airwaves.

I now spent most holidays and happy occasions with Des and Susannah and their extended families. But my first year working at K-SUN, I was, as usual, all alone on Christmas Eve. I'd been skulking around the hallways, completing every minor task I could think of that would keep me there, in the warmth and chatter.

Janis, who'd been leaving unusually late, had not-so-gently told me to *stop fucking fussing around* and then taken me to get bar food at High Frequency. A tradition we still maintained, and the origin story for how she ultimately became my brash, slightly grumpy mentor.

I'd sat across from her in that booth, fiddling with the salt and pepper shakers, and admitted that neither my father—and his new family—*or* my mother—and her new family—ever invited me over during the holidays. She'd nodded and proceeded to stare off into the distance like a grizzled sea captain. Then finally said *"eh, fuck 'em,"* which startled a burst of grateful laughter from me, a moment I treasured to this day.

"How's it going with the party planning?" Janis asked in a muffled voice.

I picked up my notebook to scrutinize my list. "It's going fine. I've got an inquiry out to the owners of the skating rink. Cliff and Mags are making a party playlist—"

"What are the vibes?"

"Blondie meets Bananarama meets Tears for Fears."

She shook her head with a laugh. "How do they just *know*?"

I grinned. "They know you pretty well at this point." I glanced back down at the list. "Des and Elena are handling decor and glitter. Daria is—" I stopped. Faltered. "Daria is taking care of your gourmet food requests."

"She's aware of my devotion to nachos?"

"We are all aware and we respect it."

Janis stood and tried to lift the semi-collapsing cardboard box of vintage meeting notes she was digging through. I held still, warily watching her struggle.

"Janis."

"I don't need it."

She attacked the problem from a different angle, trying to push it, but the sides kept bulging out. I stood and moved toward her.

"I can just—"

She scowled at me, but the expression barely registered. I'd been trading all manner of glares and glowers with Daria for almost four months now and—

Fuck me with your fingers, Theo.

I tapped the box with my shoe. "You want me to stand here and watch you be in distress?"

"Yes," she said primly. "It's part of my process."

"It's amazing to me that your stubbornness has only increased the more you've aged," I pointed out. "Not that you're some decrepit crone or anything."

"Ah-*ha*. So you *do* think I'm a crone," she said triumphantly.

I laughed, passing a hand over my face. "Whoever you

settle down with in your twilight years has their work cut out for them."

She narrowed her eyes. "*Settle down with*? What the hell's gotten into you?"

I lifted a shoulder. "Nothing. I'm only remarking on your current unattached status and that in retirement, a lot of people find that they're ready to get back out there with all their newfound free time. You could be one of those people."

She brushed past me, still grumbling, but the look on her face had me spinning around, concerned. Janis had been the earliest adopter of *True Romance* and listened every week. Half of our time together was spent going over her favorite callers, dishing on the people she found the most interesting. And on the rare occasion I was struggling with my own relationship issue, she was better at dispensing relationship wisdom than most.

But in the four years I'd known her, she'd never, not once, shown romantic interest in anyone. From the little she'd shared, that had pretty much always been the case for her. It irked me more than I cared to admit, because she was a person so full of vibrancy, so willing to embrace all the best things in life, my brain couldn't handle thinking of her as being *alone*. Not when she had so much to give.

"What's wrong?" I asked her. "You're mad that I asked you about it?"

She frowned. "Course not. Being nosy about people's relationships is your whole thing."

I scoffed. "It's not *nosy*, I'm —"

"Theo," she said, tone *almost* sharp, "the way that love works for people isn't some prescription you can apply across the board. Especially for me. It wasn't my thing when I was young. It wasn't my thing when I was middle-aged. It sure as hell ain't my thing now."

I swallowed thickly. "It concerns me, thinking of you being alone. That's all."

"Well, who said I was alone?"

I extended my hand. "You did. Just now."

She dropped back into her chair, kicked her feet up onto the desk. "I think that's your definition, not mine, kid. I appreciate your concern. But I've never been alone or lonely. I've got my friends. I've got this station. I've got this *community*. I've got so much love it's filled me right on up. Even if I was, those aren't bad things. They happen to all of us, at one time or another. Just ask Daria."

I rubbed the back of my neck and stared at the ground. "I…well, she and I…"

"I think I hear her coming now," Janis said, using her feet to shove her chair farther to the left and closer to the door. "I didn't realize she was still here."

My stomach plummeted at the same instant I picked up on the sound of Daria's smoke-tinged voice, singing some jangly, sixties rock song I recognized from Mag's set this morning. Even as a sense of fight-or-flight glued my feet to the floor, I couldn't help but smile as her booted footsteps grew closer—how she seemed to sing or dance or air-guitar her way down hallways, offices and parking lots.

"*Hey, Dar,*" Janis called.

Her singing faltered. A second later, she appeared in the doorway, beaming at Janis. "How'd you like my Grace Slick impression…oh…Theo. Um. Hi."

I nodded. Cleared my throat. "You do an excellent Grace."

Both of her hands came up to grip the door frame. "Thanks. I've been perfecting it for karaoke night at High Frequency. I was supposed to go with my mom tonight and sing backup on 'We Built This City' but she bailed on me." Daria turned her gaze toward Janis. "Speaking of, has Mags seemed kookier than normal to you? This is the second time she's blown me off in as many weeks when usually it would take a visit to the ER to keep her from karaoke. And only like a serious-bodily-injury visit. Anything less and she'd show up in one of those paper gowns with all the wires hanging off."

Janis clapped her hands together and laughed. "Oh, a mother's love."

Daria raised an eyebrow. "Really, her true love has always been cheap whiskey and listening to rock 'n' roll in boisterous bar settings."

Beneath my body's Daria-inspired agitation was a sharp pang, right over my heart. It was easy to joke about Magnolia's maternal adoration because it was so damn obvious she'd move literal mountains—and happily—for her daughter. This happened to me whenever Des's parents doted on me, or Janis made me laugh, or I watched Mags hug Daria with about as much exuberant joy as a person could embody.

When I was young, before the divorce, my parents argued so loudly I used to press myself into the farthest corner of my room with my hands over my ears. It was a feeble attempt to make myself smaller, to wish the floor would open up and drop me into a place that was warm and loving.

But my parents wore their snobbish stoicism with pride around their similarly wealthy friends—even as a kid, their parties felt hollow and awkward, nothing but a way to subtly one-up each other's money and accomplishments.

Maybe if they were that cold and detached when they argued, I'd feel less like I was the problem. Yet those loud fights stood in direct contrast to how chilly they were to me. I was the child they couldn't love when they were together. And the child they didn't seem to *want* when they were finally apart. The passion in those arguments was proof they did *feel things*.

They just never felt anything for me.

"I'm glad you're here. Both of you," Janis said, dragging me from my thoughts. "Daria, do you have a sec or are you going someplace fancy? 'Cause you look it."

She shimmied her shoulders dramatically. She wore a

short red dress and large golden hoops in her ears. "Oh, you mean this old thing?"

I very reluctantly allowed myself to fully take in Daria's appearance—reluctant because I knew it would only serve to torture me later—the smooth skin of her bare thighs, her dark curls, her teeth bright against her lipstick.

It had been two days since Daria and I had unleashed three months of irritation and sexual frustration on each other in that closet. I was now a man suspended in a permanent state of desperate longing for my raven-haired rival.

"Since my karaoke plans got canceled, I called Elena and I'm meeting her and some friends for dancing at the Scarlet Lounge." Her lips curved up in a smile, even as her eyes darted nervously to mine. "But I have a second to chat."

"Come in, then. It'll be quick. I want to talk about your show tomorrow," Janis said. "And can you pick up that box on the floor and carry it over to my side table, Dar?"

I shot Janis an exasperated look. "Seriously?"

She grinned. Evilly. "Told you I have a *process*."

"Um, Theo?"

I turned around at Daria's question, moving quickly as soon as I saw her struggling to lift it. "Here, we can do it together," I said, sliding my hands under the bottom.

Daria tossed a scowl over her shoulder. "Is this *another* one of your secret teamwork exercises?"

Janis whistled, eyes to the sky.

"It's all Sesame Street episodes," I whispered to Daria. She snorted, face brightening. But then our fingers met beneath the box. Her breathing hitched. My pulse tripled.

"On three, I guess?" she suggested.

I nodded as she counted down, and we stood as one, awkwardly moving the box to Janis's table. Daria's unexpected presence had memories surging beneath the barrier I'd hastily constructed to stay focused. Over the past forty-eight hours, I'd found it alarmingly easy to get sucked back into the maelstrom of desire that had swept over me that night, knocking me from my moorings and leaving me hopelessly lost in the storm.

I understand wanting what I shouldn't want. I understand wanting what I can never have.

I'd picked up my phone to call her a dozen times—each time freezing before I pressed *send*. Hell, I'd almost stalked into her office yesterday—though I had no real plan except kissing her senseless. Years of study. Hours of training. Three serious relationships, hundreds of dates, more listener calls than I could realistically count.

None of it mattered. All of my expertise vanished. One hot, frenzied moment with Daria and I was already undone. Suddenly, I had no idea *what* to say when knowing what to say was how I earned a living.

All I could seem to come up with was something like: *I know you're my coworker. I know you're my professional rival. I know you despise everything that I love. But I've kissed you now, felt the press of your lips against mine, the vibrations of every sigh and moan. I know what you sound like when you fall completely apart. I know how beautiful you look in the midst of total ecstasy.*

How did I tell a woman I couldn't stop arguing with that she made me feel utterly alive?

"Have you two heard the playback of your interview after paintball?" Janis asked.

I blinked, slightly stunned, and managed to walk past Daria to stand in front of Janis's desk.

I cocked my head at the plastic folding chair. "You can take it this time."

Daria pursed her lips. "No bean bag chair? How gracious of you."

"So my plan worked then," Janis said with a chuckle.

"What plan?" I asked sharply.

"I think she means the time that we *didn't* get to shoot each other with paint," Daria said glumly.

Janis was pulling something up on her computer, her eyes glittering behind her glasses. "A little last-minute change of plans never hurt anybody. Maybe if the first three shows had gone well, it would have been fine to shoot paint all over each other. But the last thing you two needed was one more thing to fight about."

I cast a covert glance at Daria. She tucked a curl behind her ear. Crossed her legs. Recrossed them. Almost as if she was as nervous to be in my presence as I was hers.

"The manager from the paintball place said our joint promotion has been doing well. *Really* well," Janis continued. "And we saw the sweetest little spike in listeners when you two called in. Something our sponsors loved."

I tore my eyes away from studying Daria's profile. "I'm sorry, what did you say?"

Janis pressed a button. "People liked you and it made us money. Now shut up and listen."

We'd called in during Monday night's late re-air of that morning's news broadcast. As the evening announcer, Elena ran that show, occasionally popping in for fun live updates or to connect over to the news we also broadcast in Spanish.

"It's everyone's favorite love experts, Daria Stone and Dr. Theo Chadwick, calling in from—wait, which competition is this?"

"We're currently at the premier paintball experience in the L.A. area, 10 Things I Paint About You," Daria said, her voice crackling a bit over the line. *"Before we tell you how it goes, what's the word on all those online bets?"*

Elena laughed. "Well, it's not great for Theo. Our poll on Twitter has him losing by a lot. Facebook wasn't much better. And we received a lot of colorful descriptions of how Theo was going to lose on Instagram."

I glanced over at Daria again, chest tightening when I discovered that she was already staring back. This part of the night was a blur. I only remembered Daria shoving the phone between us and feeling a surge of gratitude that she'd remembered we needed to do our jobs. The rest of this was a memory of feeling hazy and affectionate—so much so I'd had to cross my arms across my chest to keep from wrapping them around Daria and holding her close.

"I just want to say, at this trying and emotional time, that I'm eternally grateful to the seven people who thought I might win today."

That was me—voice sounding scratchy and awestruck.

"As much as I would have loved dominating Theo on the paintball field—"

At this, Daria arched an eyebrow imperceptibly and my cock twitched.

"—Janis changed the rules on us at the last minute, so we ended up having to take on a team of five players, and though it was only the two of us...Theo, do you wanna say it?"

"You say it," I'd replied, in a tone lower and more intimate than I'm sure I intended.

"We won! We defeated the other team in the best possible way."

"And Daria did defend me in the end," I'd added.

"Anything for my cohost," she'd sung, in a bubbly, happy tone that had warmed me from the inside out. I hadn't realized how much I'd ached to be on the receiving end of something like that—the voice she used when speaking with her friends, with Janis, with her mom.

Much as I responded to the sharp, sexy edges of her challenges, every nerve in my body went haywire when she'd said that.

Janis hit a button and the playback ended. "Now *that* was damn fine radio. I want that tomorrow night. No more answering questions the way we've been doing it. As long as you can disagree with each other *respectfully*, there's no reason we wouldn't have the same audience reaction again. Only bigger." She pressed her fingers together in front of her face. "Is there any legitimate reason why you can't pull that off?"

Daria and I went silent. I was frantically trying to figure out a way to say the opposite of the words thrumming through my head. *Funny story. I can't stop thinking about what it felt like to take Daria's lush, gorgeous breasts into my mouth while finger-fucking her to orgasm. And I'm worried there's a chance both my focus and behavior will be impacted by that. Any suggestions?*

"I'm fine with that," Daria hedged. "How about you, Theo?"

I forced a smile. "Absolutely. The learning curve feels less steep."

"We should be crushing it by the time we're playing Skee-Ball on the boardwalk next week." Daria stood, tugging down the hem of her short dress. "Now, if you don't mind, I've got a date with the dance floor."

"Knock 'em dead, Dar," Janis said with a wink. "And good job with everything on Monday night. It almost sounded like you had legitimate fun together."

I kept my attention fixed on Janis. "We even remembered to smile in all of the photos."

"Turns out our improv acting isn't half bad," Daria said breezily. "Theo, I'll see you tomorrow?"

I nodded but didn't speak. I couldn't trust my voice not to be filled with obvious longing. She was dressed up—looking pretty and sparkling—and I wanted to take her hand and drag her to a candlelit dinner she'd probably hate.

Janis coughed. Slammed a drawer shut. Slowly, I turned back to her and caught the tail end of wariness in her eyes.

"What is it?"

She frowned. "Oh, nothing. Just happy to see my plan working. As usual."

I laughed—a little nervously—and hoped I wasn't blushing. "Yes, well, isn't it time for funnel cake? Or don't you have a joint as long as my arm to smoke?"

She brightened as if she'd forgotten. "It's two-dollar hot dog night on the boardwalk right now."

"Well then, Sunrise Beach's finest gourmet meal awaits us," I said, following her out the door.

But I didn't miss the way she kept watching me, like I had a new secret she was trying to sniff out.

1 4

DARIA

I lay on the couch in my office in the semi-dark, feet kicked up and my laptop balanced against my thighs. Through the back window, the pink neon lights of the Ferris wheel glittered across the carpet. I'd shut the radio feed off so I could enjoy the ambient sounds of a summer boardwalk—a mixture of arcade games, children's laughter, live music and the softest, sweetest whisper of ocean waves.

It was Thursday night, and I was due in the sound booth with Theo in fifteen minutes. So naturally, I was disregarding my own advice and clinging to distractions.

This one came in the form of a mountain of fan emails Des had forwarded my way. The note at the top said *thought you would appreciate some of these.*

As distractions went, this kind was hard to beat. I smiled, tapping my feet in time to whatever song some band was playing outside. The emails ranged in intensity—some were short and to the point (*loved last night's episode about authenticity. Thanks for keeping me company on the night shift!*) and others were heavier (*listening to the other callers makes me feel less alone*).

Still, even more felt like taking an arrow right through

the heart (*I used to make myself smaller for my boyfriend too. Took me a full year after we broke up to find my way back to my inner self. I'd ignored that voice for such a long time. Seems like you're finally listening to yours too.*).

These emails also had the bonus effect of dulling the pain of my fifth manuscript rejection—this one from the second-largest literary agency in the country. An agency that had worked with some of my favorite authors in recent years. Even worse, the message had been cold and impersonal—probably coming from an intern who'd copied and pasted my name and book title into the appropriate blank spaces in the "thanks, but no thanks" template.

It almost had me yearning for the dangling hope of the last one. At least she'd admitted to *liking* what I had to say, even if it wasn't the right fit at the time.

I recognized this pattern of thinking, this obsessive seeking of validation from external sources instead of my own internal compass. After Jackson had left, I'd spent the first year trapped in the struggle to fully reclaim my authentic self while also desperate for someone, anyone, to say *don't worry, Daria, there's nothing wrong with you even though you were publicly rejected and humiliated in front of your loved ones by a man you didn't even really love that much.*

A straight year of weekly therapy had done a terrific job at diluting the power of those intrusive thoughts. But five years later—and after even more therapy—I remained shocked at how forcefully these feelings of inadequacy could storm back in.

It didn't matter how many times I told myself I was the expert of my own experiences. I really, *really* wanted some fancy literary agency to call me on the phone while clutching my manuscript to their chest, yelling something like *eureka, she's got it!*

Eying the time, I leaned fully into this specific form of self-sabotage and pulled up the new Twitter account for my and Theo's combined show. Last week, Elena had very kindly walked me through the overall vibe from our most vocal listeners: Theo and I weren't necessarily *bad* together. But the awkwardness and stilted silence were blatantly obvious. Clicking on the post linking tonight's show, I was surprised to see a lot of kind, supportive comments mixed in with the usual *Theo Chadwick will you marry me* noise.

At the very, very bottom—a comment already garnering a large number of likes—a user had written: *How the hell does K-SUN even vet these people? You've got one guy billing himself as a psychologist, but he's never had clients. And the other lady sounds this close to selling crystals and essential oils. We're supposed to buy in that these two know what they're talking about?*

"Oh, fuck," I muttered. My face went fire-engine hot so fast it was uncomfortable. I could hear the blood rushing in my ears, my stomach flipping like a gymnast. It was at that exact moment that Des knocked on the door, startling me from my mini-meltdown.

"Hey, we're getting—are you okay?" he asked, coming to stand over where I was lying on the couch. I swung my feet to the ground, pushing up to a seat.

"Don't be mad, but I went on—"

"Don't say Twitter."

"—uh, Twitter."

He scooped up the laptop with one hand while the other rubbed his beard. "You mean, you had to read this asshole claim you're a hippie who doesn't know jack shit?"

"I should have stuck to all the nice emails." I stood and straightened all the items of clothing that had gotten wrinkled on the couch. "Which were lovely, thank you."

He set my laptop down with a wry smile. "The majority are lovely."

I pointed at the screen. "But some people think Theo and I are absolute frauds. That's not great for either of our careers if that's the consensus of the internet. It doesn't exactly scream *call in to our show and trust me with your personal problems.*

I followed Des, who was walking rapidly down the hallway toward our sound booth. "It's not the internet's consensus. That's the consensus of one single asshole. And we'll never escape that. You'll never escape that, no matter how quickly your show gets popular."

Inside the booth, I pulled my seat out and grabbed my headphones. Theo was conspicuously absent.

"You're right, you're right," I said on a sigh. "And thank you for saying it. Until I started hosting at K-ROX, I had no idea how much 'random Twitter user's' opinion of me would get stuck in my brain. And I mean *stuck*."

He nodded, face empathetic. "It's normal to react that way. Doesn't make it less shitty. And it definitely doesn't mean he's right. Have you talked to Mags about it?"

I grinned. "Yeah, but you can probably imagine her response."

"Was it, *who gives a shit about the internet?*"

"That was it *exactly*," I said with a laugh.

Des moved slightly to give Elena more room as she walked in, smiling and in rapid motion. "Have you talked to Theo about it?"

"Talked to Theo about what?"

Goosebumps broke out across my skin at the sound of Theo's gravelly voice. He strode into the room looking as immaculate as ever, except for the ends of his curls, which were still damp. His scent tonight was a woodsy soap, and his face was slightly flushed.

"Sorry I'm running late," he said. "Went for another long run on the beach and didn't want to subject you all to how I smelled after."

Des laughed while I smiled weakly. Given the wild, riotous state of my hormones the last time I'd seen—and smelled—Theo after a run, I wouldn't have minded at all.

147

"It's all good," Des said easily. "Elena and I need to check in about something really quick before you go live. You'll be okay if we leave you alone for a few minutes?"

Theo and I nervously babbled out somewhat similar responses. Des cocked his head, eyes narrowed for a second. But then he nodded and shut the door behind him, closing us in.

Theo placed my favorite mug in front of me, steam rising softly from the rim.

I glanced up at him, surprised. "What's this?"

He sat down heavily in his chair, fixing his eyes on mine. A different kind of flush was working its way up the entire length of my body.

"Hot water with honey and lemon."

I wrapped my fingers around its comforting warmth. "Thank you. I'd...I'd forgotten to make it."

His eyebrows knit together. "I saw your mug in the kitchen, next to the kettle."

I took a discerning sip, my mouth filling with the medicinal alchemy of steam, sweet honey and tart citrus. I let a smile grow slowly. "How'd you know?"

"You make that drink before every show. In that exact same mug." He pulled at the edge of his notebook, ripping at a corner. "I thought you'd appreciate it."

One time, Jackson had spent a week straight promising me a romantic night on the town. We'd both been working long hours, and hadn't seen much of each other, and he swore over and over again *get ready, I'm about to make it up to you, baby.*

It was these types of promises I was never into—his grand gestures felt insincere to me. But as the week wore on, part of me got the *tiniest* bit excited. He kept swearing he was taking me to have the best food I'd ever eaten, and I'd been oddly touched that he'd noticed some of my likes and dislikes.

And then he'd gone ahead and taken me to a restaurant I hated, a new and trendy restaurant that served food I objectively *did not like*. This was an opinion I shared often, had told him about plenty of times. Either he hadn't listened or didn't really care—that was the endless mystery of Jackson. Though not listening, to me, was the same as not caring.

The night was made worse by the fact that I decided it was best not to say a word. I'd smiled politely through a meal I hated, thanked him graciously for a week while he preened. And meanwhile I was beginning to wonder if Jackson ever really knew me at all.

I set the mug back down. "I appreciate it very much. It helps my throat, but also helps my pre-show jitters. So... thank you. I didn't think you noticed things like that about me."

Theo's smooth jaw tightened. He cast a covert glance to the mixing room, which was still empty. "Quite the opposite is true. I notice a lot of things about you."

I spend every single second we're together aching to kiss that sexy smirk right off your gorgeous face.

Except for our bizarre encounter in Janis's office last night, he'd been avoiding me for the past two days. Though I couldn't really blame him. I'd been doing the same. And I assumed it was because of the only rational, intellectual explanation that existed for what happened between us on the paintball field.

It was a mistake. A sexy, deeply satisfying and somewhat *taboo* mistake. But a mistake nonetheless, which meant it couldn't happen again.

"So what was Des talking about when I came in?" he asked.

"Oh, well, I read some troll's comment about our show on Twitter. Des happened to catch me mid-reaction and thought you'd understand."

He arched a single eyebrow. "What did they say?"

I ran my finger up and down my earrings. "Um…he was questioning whether or not we had the right to give advice because we hadn't been properly vetted by real professionals or something. You're obviously a psychologist hack with no patients. And he said I was only here to sell crystals and essential oils."

Theo pinched the bridge of his nose. At first, I thought he was pissed. But I saw his shoulders shaking. Heard the soft rumble of his laughter.

"Are you…do you think this is *funny?*" I asked.

"Yes. Yes, I do. And it's not because I think it's true. It's because this person is clearly a piece of shit."

I snorted. "Oh. Okay."

"For the record, you're clearly rubbing off on me. Before working with you, I wasn't in the business of referring to random Twitter commenters as pieces of shit. But it's exactly what you would say." Both eyebrows raised. "Isn't it?"

I cocked my head, thinking. "Wait. Of course, this guy fucking sucks. I don't even *like* crystals."

"And it doesn't matter." He leaned forward, arms on the table. "Our listeners call in on their own accord and clearly appreciate the advice we offer because they keep asking for it. It's not like we sit around, starting our shows by announcing we're perfect geniuses with perfect lives who have always gotten it right."

I raised a single finger. "While technically I agree with ninety percent of what you said, *you*, Dr. Theodore Chad-wick, do toss around your years of rigorous academic training and expertise any chance you get."

I hadn't realized I was still holding onto hurt from our first night live together, but the sulky edge to my tone was obvious in the tight space.

Theo went utterly still. "Daria…Daria, I'm sorry."

My gaze flew up to his. "What did you say?"

He tossed that same covert glance over his shoulder

before leaning closer and lowering his voice. "Our first show together, what you said, the way I made you feel. Like your right to be on this show, to speak from your experience, was inferior in comparison to my training. I…" He grimaced. "It was an awful thing to do and I'm sorry. The same goes for what I said in the *Times*. That reporter, she pissed me off and pushed me, until I said something stupid and very untrue. It shouldn't have happened, and I didn't mean it."

I let out a long, slightly shaky breath. "I'm sorry too. *I* was the asshole that first night, talking shit about you *again* in public. You don't deserve that. And I had the same experience with that reporter."

"She pushed you too?"

I nodded. "I think we got used for clickbait. But it doesn't really matter. I also didn't mean it. You're not part of a dying breed."

The ends of his lips twitched. "You're not a bunch of internet hot takes either."

This time I was the one dissolving into a slightly hysterical-sounding laughter. "Oh *god*, what a fucking mess we made."

Our eyes locked across the table. In the few seconds between the end of my sentence and Elena rushing into the mixing room, I understood that the real mistake hadn't been what happened between us in that closet.

The real mistake was letting myself be vulnerable with Theo for the very first time.

15

DARIA

"Oooh baby, okay, you two are live in twenty seconds. Everything good?" Elena asked, sliding into her chair.

We both pulled on our headphones and got into whatever position we needed. I cracked open my laptop and gripped my tea, smiling shyly at Theo while my stomach kept executing all those backflips.

He returned the gesture just as the *On Air* lights flickered on. He pulled the mic over, smile widening. "Welcome back to another week of Daria Stone and I attempting to cure your relationship woes. I'd like to say we missed all of you. But what really happened is Daria and I were too busy experiencing the euphoric thrill of victory on the paintball field."

I laughed softly. "*Euphoric* is exactly how I'd describe it."

Heat flared in his eyes. My body remembered the real euphoria of that night—the rough thrust of his fingers, his cock pulsing in my fist, his eager mouth open and roaming over my skin.

"Yes, well, I'm quite descriptive when I want to be," he said.

I stumbled a little. "It's, uh...listen, if we sound a little dazed, it's because we're still riding that high. Never thought it'd be so satisfying to shoot paint at five dudes on a field."

"And I thought you were still mad you didn't get to shoot *me*," Theo said.

"I've let go of that dream and am now focusing on polishing up my arcade skills. And that's really the perfect segue into next week's Theo-and-Daria activity." I clicked through my laptop to pull up the email Des had sent with the ticket updates. "Wednesday night, you can come play along as I kick Theo's butt at Skee-Ball, pinball—"

Theo pushed his tongue into his cheek. "So confident. It's still going to be your downfall, Daria. Mark my words. Though from what Des said, apparently a whole lot of you want to come watch me win."

My eyes widened. "Um...yeah, it's almost sold out. The boardwalk is letting us rent out the whole arcade for a private event for *free*."

"We're very grateful," Theo said, face turning more serious. "This community has seen K-SUN rise and fall with budget crises and economic recessions, and you continue to show up and commit to independent radio above all else."

"Radio for the people," I said. "Always."

We shared a friendly glance that sent a jolt of awareness through me. I brushed the curls from my forehead and tried not to read *too* much into the fun I was having.

After Elena cut to a few station ads, she pulled open the door to the sound booth. "Theo, guess who called through wanting to talk to you? Rachel and Ted."

His face brightened. "The triad relationship?"

"Yep. They've got some good news they want to share. Is it cool if we start them off at the top?"

"Please," he said. "I would love to hear from them."

"Who's that?" I asked.

He rubbed his jaw, a smile playing on his lips. "You'll

enjoy their story. It's maybe the most romantic one I've ever heard."

"Wha—" I started to ask, intrigued, but then Elena cued us back.

"Fans of *True Romance* will certainly recognize these first two," Theo said warmly. "Rachel and Ted, I'm so happy to have you back. Can you give everyone a summary on how we first met and what's been going on since then?"

I studied the loose angles of his body language, the way a smile never truly left his face, the affection in his tone. *This* was the Dr. Theo Chadwick that lit up the airwaves with his charm and charisma and honesty, the Theo that I rarely got to see.

"Hey, Theo, so good to talk to you again. This is Rachel, for all the listeners. So we first called into *True Romance* about eighteen months ago. Ted and I have always shared a best friend named Skyler. We all met in college. Ted and I ended up together but our friendship with Skyler stayed strong and only grew stronger. He was usually single, and we were basically never apart. We—"

"We loved each other," Ted said softly. "And were in love with each other before we ever had a name for the intensity of what we were feeling. When we called Theo, we'd already admitted to each other that we were in love with our shared best friend."

I grabbed the mic. "Can I ask how that went?"

"Brutally," Rachel said. "Part of me already knew Ted loved Skyler and that gave me the courage to say something. But it was also a *huge* risk, telling my soul mate I was also in love with another person."

Theo was eying me carefully. I knew he caught my flinch at the term *soul mate*.

"It was a huge risk," he said gently. "Here you are, a person devoted to honesty and trust in your relationship. And you were both honoring that trust by telling the truth.

And threatening it at the same time. Listeners often ask me how they should *know* they're in love. Of course, I can't really give them an answer since it's a feeling much too grand and mysterious to define. But, for me, what you're describing, Rachel, is how I would describe love. Honesty, vulnerability, trust." His throat worked. "Authenticity, most of all."

I opened my mouth to respond but stopped. Rachel and Ted weren't some theoretical story, they were real people, sharing something deeply intimate with us. I could use this question as a springboard to pick a fight with Theo—on-air, *again*—or I could sit with my discomfort and hear the rest of what they had to say.

But I couldn't help my first, rash reaction—I'd had very little exposure to couples like Ted and Rachel in my life. What I *did* have exposure to was my relationship with Jackson, where the more I demonstrated the qualities of authenticity and honesty, the less he loved me. So much so that he opted to publicly humiliate me as his way out.

The thought of risking that much hurt ever again was about as appealing to me as diving into a pool filled with starving alligators.

From the line came some muffled whispers. Theo looked sweetly bashful, eyes full of hope, and all I could think about was the raw emotion on his face the other night when I'd said that his childhood with divorced parents sounded *scary*.

"Uh, hello, am I on the line?" came another voice.

The smile that blazed across Theo's face put the California sun to shame. "Is this *Skyler?*"

"Yeah. Hey. I'm a little nervous."

"Being on the radio is nerve-wracking," Theo said.

"Our *really, really awesome news* is that we came clean to Skyler about being utterly in love and devoted to him," Rachel added. "And then the best thing happened, which is that he said he loved us too. And we all went on a first date one year ago this week and have been living together, as a triad, ever since."

"Like, a three-person couple?" I clarified.

"Yes," Skyler said. "It took a second for my parents to get the lingo but now they go around on their retirement cruises, bragging about how lucky they are to have a son-in-law *and* a daughter-in-law."

Theo rumbled with laughter, the sound sending shivers up my spine. "I cannot tell you how happy I am right now. You were brave and open and love made it all happen. Congratulations, I'm—well, I'm just overjoyed."

I chewed on my lower lip as a wave of embarrassment washed over me. In an interview with a major newspaper, I'd called Theo *antiquated* when here he was, supporting a queer triad that bucked all the same societal norms that *I* often raged about on my show.

Theo must have caught me wincing, arching his brow with the subtlest shade of *told you so*. But it lacked the snark of our past interactions. It was more sincere and curious than anything else.

Flip, flip, flip went my stomach.

"Theo and I have a tendency to disagree on a lot of things," I said, eyes searching his, "but one thing we do have in common is celebrating bravery in all its forms. There is no act of bravery too small or insignificant."

"I wholeheartedly agree," he said roughly.

"We're happier than we ever thought possible. And obviously, our relationship looks different from some others," Rachel said. "Though we've met more folks with situations similar to ours than we initially expected."

"It's nice to remember acts of bravery are happening all around us," Theo said.

"And that we don't truly know anyone's situation until they explain it," she continued. "But *of course* we have plenty of family members and friends and, I don't know, people at the grocery store who don't understand us. Don't want to be around us. Or straight-up hate us. Now that we've spent our first year together, how do we handle these expectations? I care less about overall society. It's more like…man, I want my brother to support me again."

I shut my eyes, heartbroken at their loss of support from the people they loved so much. "Of course you want that. You're happy and in love. You deserve for this relationship to be cherished and adored the way you cherish and adore it."

Theo tilted his head. "Daria, why don't you answer this one?"

"Me? Aren't romantic expectations kinda your thing?"

"Yes, they are," he said simply. "But isn't living life boldly kinda *your* thing?"

Nervous laughter spilled from my lips. "Sure. I just…"

Theo waited expectantly. I thought about the influence of my mother, and even Janis, those first few weeks after the wedding. The two women in my life who barreled through each day with a wild, joyful hunger—and who never, not once, stifled their appetite for *more*.

For the entirety of my relationship with Jackson, I tiptoed around taking mouse-sized bites of life, careful to make sure I wasn't bothering anyone around me while doing it.

"At the end of the day," I said, tipping forward in my chair, "your job is to love each other as boldly and beautifully as you're able to. The world is a better place because the three of you opened up to doing what is *right* despite all the ways our culture loves to create arbitrary limits based on a whole lot of hot nonsense. Your authenticity will attract others like you, will draw other brave souls your way. These are the folks who will love you all the way back. Not despite your relationship but *because* of it. Because every brave choice makes space for others to do the same."

I swallowed around a lump in my throat. "I really, really

hope people like your brother and other important folks in your life begin to see that."

There was a short pause. I almost said more, if only to fill the dead air. But then Skyler said, "Thank you, Daria. This is the kind of advice we can work with: things we *can* do. And that's loving each other and attracting other people doing the same. I obviously wasn't on the first call that Ted and Rachel made, but I've been a big fan of the station since I was in college. Of all the places to call in and talk about stuff like this, K-SUN has been the most welcoming. Oh, and Theo, my mom wants me to let you know that my sister is single."

Theo chuckled, his cheeks turning pink. "Good to know, thanks."

"Be honest with me here, guys," I said. "Does Theo get a lot of callers asking him on dates?"

"We even got a proposal once," Elena chimed in.

"*Theo*," I exclaimed, jaw dropped.

He was rubbing the back of his neck shyly. "That was a few years ago. Elena does a much better job now at screening out marriage offers."

"And we are so grateful to you both," Rachel said. "Thanks for letting us share our happy news. We couldn't have done it without you."

Elena disconnected the call and cheerfully sent the show to a few commercials.

I shifted in my chair, stilling when I saw Theo's face. "What is it?"

"What you said, about bravery and loving each other and authenticity," he said, voice low. "That was excellent advice. I thought you'd feel a connection to them. Even though they're, you know, in a relationship."

"Why did you think that?"

"Because they're proud of who they are," he said. "Just like you."

"Oh, well." I cleared my throat through a burst of nerves.

"I know now how wrong I was to call you traditional or whatever."

I didn't hear his answer. The door to the sound booth opened and Des stood there, wearing a big smile.

"Shit, are we in trouble again?" Theo asked.

Des shook his head. "This isn't my *shit, you're in trouble* smile. It's my *where has this been hiding all along* smile. I don't exactly know what happened, but whatever you're having to do to fake getting along and sounding like you're having fun is working. Keep it up."

He hit his palm against the doorjamb and left us, stopping to chat with Elena on his way out.

I turned back to Theo and tightened my headphones. "Do you think this is some kind of sign of the apocalypse? And, if so, should we be warning people?"

"You know, at one point I did think I heard a lot of screaming in the streets," Theo said. "But I wouldn't be too worried. There's plenty of time left for us to fall into our usual conflict patterns."

"Right," I said. "Looking forward to baiting you into an argument in the near future."

His smile looked forced. "Same here, Ms. Stone."

And I clearly imagined the flash of hurt in his eyes before we took our next caller.

16

THEO

One day later and I was back in the sound booth for my next show with Daria, staring at a list of radio hosts who'd been newly nationally syndicated. Talk shows, news programs, music—it ran the gamut, and there were plenty of people hosting call-in programs like I did. There were even some with programs running for less time than *True Romance* already syndicated and being heard on stations and streaming internet radio across the country.

I sighed irritably, trying to remember what Janis had said. That these things were about timing. That these kinds of numbers didn't happen overnight, that four years was short compared to other hosts considered titans of the industry.

But her steady, rational reasoning paled in comparison to the thoughts churning like a spin cycle in my brain. I'd laughed when Daria had told me about that Twitter user's shitty comment questioning whether we deserved to be giving advice or not—but that was mostly because the thought of rebellious and edgy Daria Stone selling crystals was too amusing to ignore.

The other part though, the part where the commenter had said I was *clearly a psychologist hack with no patients* had planted vicious, ugly roots in my head that had grown forest-sized by morning.

I didn't read reviews for a reason, because I didn't need a million different opinions on why I didn't belong—why I didn't belong here, at K-SUN. Here, on the airwaves. Here, offering advice on love when every romantic relationship of mine had ended in failure.

For all my own posturing, I longed to admit to Daria I felt like a fraud sometimes. And the more I overanalyzed every breakup I'd ever been through, the more my last girlfriend's words felt increasingly prophetic rather than descriptive: *It seems like you only really want the symbolic gestures of love and not the raw intimacy or complications or tough times.*

After Janis had announced she'd be making Daria and me work together, my most secret fear, the one I never dared to share, was less about Daria's impact on my brand and show. Though that was always a concern, floating around in the background.

No. My most secret fear was that Daria Stone would expose all that I *didn't* know about love.

As if reading my mind, my phone buzzed with an automated alert from one of the many online dating sites I'd used in the past. *It's been 117 days since you last logged in and we've missed you!*

I didn't have time to react. Daria pushed open the door to the sound booth and paused, looking surprised to see me. She brushed a mess of curls from her forehead, sending her long, silver earrings swaying.

"You're here early," she said.

I looked up from my phone, arching an eyebrow. "Or you're here late."

Her lips pursed in a smirk. "You wish, Dr. Chadwick. We're finally out of the fucking doghouse, so to speak. I'm doing my best to keep it that way."

"You mean because we managed to remain pleasant throughout an entire radio broadcast?"

"Yep." She smacked her lips together. "Though to be honest, I expected more of a hailstorm of frogs or a swarm of locusts on my drive home."

"I *thought* I noticed a few locusts hanging around my front door last night."

Her eyes brightened with amusement. Then she spotted the mug of hot water, lemon and honey that I'd made for her. I knew she'd spotted it because of the ripple of motion across her shoulders. The almost imperceptible movement of muscles in her throat.

I wasn't sure why it mattered so much to me, that she seemed both pleased that I'd brought it but also that she trusted I would do it again.

She sat down gracefully and pulled the mug toward her with a smile more shy than her usual sultry. Contrary to what Des had said last night, I wasn't faking getting along with Daria *or* enjoying myself. Hearing Ted, Rachel and Skyler's joyful love story had boosted my spirits sky-high. And then Daria had sat there, eyes pinned to mine, and said *every brave choice makes space for others to do the same.*

If you had asked me ten days ago if Daria was capable of hearing a call like that—one filled to the brim with real romance and three soul mates—without rolling her eyes, I would have said *no fucking way*. I would have assumed she'd think it cheesy or too precious.

But in a space this small, it was impossible to disguise our reactions. I'd seen Daria pissed, bored, annoyed and frustrated, all in the course of one show. I knew she'd seen the same in me.

Yesterday, her entire body lit up as she heard their story and stayed blazing and brilliant as she'd offered them advice so perfect for their situation I was stunned.

That had to explain why I'd felt so disappointed immediately after, as she'd teased about baiting me into future arguments. It didn't matter what transpired between the two of us in the closet—an experience we *still* hadn't spoken about. Our entire relationship was grounded in pointless bickering.

Therefore, it was equally as pointless for me to feel like it was a step backward for us, instead of a step forward. Because when it came to Daria, what the hell would we be stepping forward *into*?

"Thank you for making this for me," she said, pointing at her drink. "I wasn't aware I could have been asking you to make me the perfect combination of steam, honey and lemon this entire time."

I lifted a shoulder. "Yes, well, the doctorate thing is all a ruse. I've been waiting for someone to recognize I'm as talented at boiling water as I am at paintball."

Her lips twitched. "But I still had to defend your honor in the end."

I pressed a palm to my chest. "And I'm still grateful."

My phone chimed again, and Daria's brow furrowed when she saw the message on the screen. "Apparently Match.com misses you. Or is that all the women you're chatting with on there?"

I turned my phone over, hiding the screen. "It's the website. Not the women."

"I'm sure a dating and romance expert is a hot commodity on a site like that."

"Especially for a total catch like me," I said with a wry grin.

She cocked her head. "At least now I can say with certainty that you're no gentleman."

"And what makes you say that?" I asked, my mind filling with far too many filthy memories for the workplace.

"Unsportsmanlike conduct on the field."

I breathed out a laugh. "Name one thing I did that broke the rules."

Her lips parted, chest rising and falling. I let my gaze travel down her elegant throat to the swell of her breasts in her baggy sweater, the ball of her shoulder exposed against the corded fabric. I remembered, distinctly, what it was like to take her nipples between my lips, to feel her body's electrified response when I grazed them with my teeth.

"Never mind," I said thickly. "I can think of a few broken rules."

Cheeks pink, she twisted back and forth in her chair. "That's funny. So can I."

We were still alone, ten minutes left to air. The temperature in the room was slowly rising, keeping pace with the tension. I unhooked the button keeping my cuffs closed and began rolling the material up to my elbows.

I nodded down at my phone again. "I know you don't date."

"No, I do not."

"But do you ever use these sites for something temporary?"

I forced the words out through the grinding of my back molars. Picturing Daria swiping right on a bunch of other men was spiking an unsettling jealousy in me.

She shook her head and wrinkled her nose. "Not my style. I'm too busy personally testing all the vibrators and sex toys sent to my show from companies looking for ad opportunities."

My fingers twitched. "Do you really rate all of them?"

Her smile was a slow, sexy reveal. "My personal motto is that life's too short not to test every elite sex toy that lands on my desk."

Trying not to smile, I said, "As a researcher, may I ask what your rating system looks like?"

She curved her hand through the air like she was describing a theater marquee. "Made me come like a freight train in thirty seconds."

I coughed out a laugh. "And what else?"

"Floating through a stratosphere of multiple orgasms," she said dreamily. "That one was like *all* knobs."

"This is very illuminating, thank you."

"You're so welcome." She reached into her hair and stroked her earrings. "So, uh, cohost to cohost, are you actively on Match.com…dating?"

"No, I'm not," I said firmly. "And I haven't been for 117 days, according to the alert."

She nodded, licking her lower lip. "Why not?"

Elena and Des burst into the production room, meaning our brief moment of privacy had ended. But I still leaned across the table and kept my eyes pinned to hers. "I haven't been on that dating site, or any dating sites, because I've been very distracted."

"By what?"

"By you."

Her teeth sank into her bottom lip. "Theo."

Nothing else. Just my name, murmured in a tone full of so much affection it was difficult to recall our months of animosity. The sound of it, the pure *ache* of it, had me yearning to reach for her hand and say, "I know you don't date but I'd *really* love to take you on one. Immediately."

The more I cracked open these complicated feelings, the more I was forced to admit that they'd existed from the first moment we met. I'd been eager to classify my preoccupation with Daria as mere professional curiosity, turned strategic opponent, turned irritating coworker. Those first few weeks she was here at K-SUN, our slight aloofness slowly became passive-aggressive debates, which morphed into sarcastic taunts and then full-blown arguments.

So it was tough for me to accept that the first morning we met, in the K-SUN parking lot beneath a dazzling sun, her pretty pictures had been no match for her breathtaking beauty.

And when she'd shaken my hand with her usual sultry smile, the flare of sensation that shot through my body had left me momentarily speechless.

Elena patched her voice through to get our attention. "Five-minute countdown to broadcast. Are you both feeling okay? You need anything?"

"I'm perfect, thank you," Daria said. "A little birdie told me the surf today was incredible."

Elena grinned. "Waves were killer. Did you happen to catch your mom's show this morning?"

"No, I missed it. Wait, did she share another one of my embarrassing childhood moments?"

Elena pulled her headphones on, her fingers moving over the mixing board as she prepared us to go live. "Mags asked listeners about what there was to do on Valentine's Day in Sunrise Beach."

I frowned. "She didn't realize she could come ask the romance *expert*?"

"She didn't realize it's only *June*?" Daria said in an equally shocked voice. "And why the hell..."

"Could Magnolia be dating someone?" I asked. "She's pretty stridently opposed, but maybe that explains why she's canceled plans on you twice while seeking out advice about chocolate-covered hearts and cupid cards."

Daria visibly shuddered. "I don't know...I guess? The last person I knew she was officially 'with' was my dad, but he didn't even stick around for the eight-week ultrasound before bailing for good."

My brow furrowed. "I didn't realize he wasn't in your life at all. I'm sorry to hear that."

She waved her hand like it was no big deal. "Thank you, but it's fine. Really. Technically he's one-half of the reason why I exist. But he's not the reason why I'm *here*. I'm here because my mom raised me with help from our family, and folks at this radio station, and even Janis. Does that make sense?"

I thought about being a lonely kid, hearing Magnolia's voice on the radio in my kitchen while I picked at my breakfast and unsuccessfully tried to attract my father's icy attention.

Or the fact that once I made friends in college and then grad school, I spent a series of birthdays and holidays with families that were never my biological one. I thought about Janis buying me dinner on Christmas Eve. Playing football in a backyard with Des and Susannah on Thanksgiving, surrounded by heaps of food and cousins.

"It makes perfect sense," I said.

We shared a tentative smile and a liquid warmth spread across my collarbone, down my shoulders and all the way to the tips of my fingers.

"I thought her talking about it was hella weird too," Elena said. "But I know you've been asking about her, so I figured I'd pass it along. You two were fire on the show last night, by the way."

"*Fire?* That feels slightly exaggerated," Daria said with a smile.

Elena rolled her eyes. "Mostly I mean, you didn't awkwardly argue. It's a step though, and it worked for our listeners. Lots and lots of love for you across the internet today. There was even a mention about the show on K-ROX's Twitter."

Daria and I exchanged a glance.

"But they only air syndicated programming now," I said.

"All I can say is that whatever you were doing last night, keep it up," she said. "You're on in five seconds."

Daria's eyebrows flew up and she mouthed *for real?*

I straightened my glasses and mouthed *the apocalypse?*

The cue lights blinked on as Daria laughed. "Hey listen-

167

ers, happy Friday," she sang into the mic. "Sorry about those first few seconds there. Theo's got jokes now."

"I've always had jokes. You chose to ignore them."

"That's exactly what someone who never had jokes would say."

I laughed while giving her the middle finger, which only amused her more.

"Dr. Theodore Chadwick, romance expert, is giving me the middle finger here in the sound room."

I arched an eyebrow. "And I thought this space was sacred."

"You thought wrong, I guess."

I waved a hand across the table. "For the public record, and folks tuning in at home, I've never been the kind of person to flagrantly flip someone off, but that's what I get for spending so much time with both Daria *and* Magnolia."

She scoffed. "Excuse me, but my mom and I are more than just women who express ourselves through flipping the double bird. We also curse like sailors."

"My apologies for the inaccurate description," I said with a rueful smile. "Now to get to our show, the real reason we're here with you all, late on a Friday night. Who do we have first, Elena?"

"Our first caller is Sami," she said.

Daria pulled the mic closer to her mouth. "Sami, you're on with me and Theo. What can we help you with?"

Sami blew out a nervous-sounding breath. "Hey, Daria, hey, Theo. I know this is corny, but I'm a long-time K-SUN listener, first-time caller."

"We live for corny. Keep it coming," Daria said. "So what's up?"

"Um, well, I just dumped my boyfriend about a week ago and I feel like total garbage. We were *not* meant to be, and he was kind of the worst. It's just that, this is my fifth failed relationship. Each time I'm less and less happy. But each time,

I'm also growing and learning and setting more boundaries. It's not like how I was in my twenties, being some fake version of myself so that my boyfriend would keep liking me."

Daria hummed a sound of understanding. "I spent a lot of time securing my boyfriend's approval and admiration. Over time, his opinion and his permission became more important to me than whether or not I was honoring my true self and my own needs. It's so *sneaky*. I don't think our partners are always doing this maliciously either—though some of them do. But it's easy to fall into learned patterns of behavior, especially if you're a woman and you feel that pressure to be polite, pliant, agreeable."

"Happy, helpful and eager to please," Sami added.

"And perfect," I said.

Sami and Daria went silent. I paused, not wanting to intrude too much on their experiences. But I'd spoken out loud without realizing it.

Daria propped her chin in her hand. "Yeah. *Perfect*. Wait, do you have more to say about that, Theo?"

I straightened my glasses. "Perfectionism doesn't discriminate when it comes to gender, and people of all genders often feel trapped by perfectionist tendencies. But there's a specific way that perfectionism affects women in relationships—physical appearance, perfect. Living situation, perfect. Behavior on the date, perfect. And what that 'perfection' looks like in each of those scenarios is problematic enough. I just wanted to add that it also gets in the way of true intimacy. There's no authenticity when perfection's in the way."

A weighted silence followed. Then Daria said, "Oh my god, *yes*. Thank you, Theo."

"See, that's my problem," Sami said. "Every guy I've been with, once I stopped being perfect, I got dumped."

"Hard same over here," Daria said—but through her bemused smile, I could see the tense lines bracketing her mouth. With every allusion to Jackson, my blood pressure spiked, and I hadn't figured out a way to manage that reaction. I needed to, since Janis hadn't given us an expiration date for this experiment, and I wasn't itching to end up in the emergency room.

"I wish there was a Magic 8-Ball I could shake up that could tell me whether or not I even really *want* to be in a relationship with someone," Sami said. "So many of my friends are happily paired off and my parents are so obviously in love. But most days I really want to chill out, do my own thing, and not get hurt over and over." She sighed. "Sorry, that's my long, rambling lead-up to my question."

"And what's that?" Daria asked gently.

"How did you figure out what you really wanted after you were left at the altar?"

Daria lowered her mouth back toward the mic, and I was compelled to keep watching her—the gold glint of her septum piercing, the long sweep of her dark lashes, the curve of her berry-colored lips. "I should start by specifying that the things that helped me are unique to my own life. Based on your experiences, your sexuality and identity, your brain chemistry, it could be different. Or it could be similar. But I never want to appear like I have all of the answers when I don't. And I'm speaking for Theo here a bit, but I'm sure he feels the same way."

"Absolutely," I said. "There's never a one-size-fits-all when it comes to giving advice."

Janis's sharp words from the other night rattled through my brain—*the way that love works for people isn't some prescription you can apply across the board.*

I knew that, *of course* I knew that. But it was worrying that she felt like she had to say that to me. Worrying in the same way that Daria had called my show *antiquated.*

Did I really come off as that strict and unyielding?

"I was lucky," Daria continued, "to find a therapist who

helped me process what happened the day of the wedding, my feelings of shock and betrayal and mortification. And *relief* too. That was a tricky one to navigate. Over time, she began asking me a lot of questions I didn't have answers to. Questions about my goals and dreams, my comfort levels and needs. There wasn't any pressure to have answers either, but whenever she asked me something, I took the time to really think on it and process it. That's when I started writing my blog. That's when I started romancing myself with as much passion as I'd put into my previous relationship. I took myself on a lot of dates. Bought flowers. Tucked little notes of affirmation into my mirror so I'd see them when I woke up."

Daria chewed on her lower lip, eyebrows knit together. "None of these caused any immediate changes or dramatic realizations. It was just me meditating, or going on long hikes by myself, or writing in my journal. With time, I remembered who I'd been all along and could live again without hearing that critical voice in my head, or feeling guilty, or worrying obsessively about what people thought of me. There are still good days and bad days."

The lines on her face smoothed away, lips curving into a sweet smile. "But five years later, the relationship I've developed with myself is the most fulfilling one I've ever had."

I swallowed a few times, throat tight. Separate from my ambitious career goals, my dream had been *marriage*. When I had a girlfriend, my comfort level was usually tied to hers. And when I was single, that comfort level plummeted. My needs were love, companionship, affection. My needs were a lifelong commitment with another woman filled with trust and honesty.

I'd only ever yearned for romance that was real. So why the hell did I want Daria with a desperation that made rational thinking impossible? If I admitted all these needs to her, would she only ever tell me I had no legitimate relationship with myself?

"That's…wow, that sounds like a lot of hard work," Sami said dazedly. "But I like those ideas. I feel like some of this stuff I've been avoiding, to be honest."

"I've been there, trust me. Every day it's hard," Daria said. "It's worth it though. Theo, did you have anything you wanted to add?"

"I don't, no," I replied, as dazed as Sami. "I think that's excellent advice."

"But what if I do all this stuff and then I realize, hey, you know, I actually *do* want to be with someone? Is there any hope for me?"

Daria arched an eyebrow my way. "Now that does sound like a Theo question."

I rubbed my thumb across my temple, turning over a response in my mind. "My hope that people will fall in love has been my own version of a North Star. I chart every decision in my life around that hope. So yes. If after you've spent more time understanding what you're looking for, you decide you want to start dating again, then I have complete faith that you'll find the one for you. That you'll find the person who loves your authentic self just as you'll love theirs."

Daria's physical reaction to what I'd said was difficult to unravel—she was nervously stroking her earrings, but I could also feel her foot and leg shaking next to mine under the table. She didn't appear angry or annoyed. She did, however, seem *unsettled* in a way that I'd never seen before.

Sami laughed a little. "You really do stay optimistic, don't you?"

I smiled in response. "I was young when my parents divorced but that didn't stop it from having a profound effect on my outlook on love. Seeing a marriage fall to pieces like that would turn a lot of people cynical and that's understandable. Instead, it turned me into a social psychologist, studying relationships as my job before this one. I learned that love really does prevail."

I breathed out a laugh. "I know how cheesy that sounds. And"—I pinned my gaze to Daria's— "and I mean love in the way that Daria mentioned as well. I've spoken with people who survived life-changing traumas, who suffered incredible losses, went through divorces, lost jobs and struggled with money and felt very, very alone. With time, love reentered their life. For many of them it was romantic love, even if they often stated it wouldn't ever happen to them. But I think…"

Daria's eyes were searching mine and I was finding it hard to focus.

"I think one aspect that Daria has spoken so well of is all the kinds of love in this world, from friendship to family to community. And love of self."

Her lips quirked. "The hardest one of all."

I nodded. "Very true. Maybe that's where my optimism springs from. I've been single for the past six months, and I still feel hopeful."

Daria dropped my gaze. My fingers tightened on the mic. "Does any of that resonate with you, Sami?"

"What you and Daria said really does. At the very least, it's helping me to understand that I've got work to do on myself and it's not selfish to do so. And to recognize that, either way, I'm very lucky to have all kinds of love in my life already. I…I feel very grateful."

"Plus, you don't have a garbage boyfriend anymore," Daria mused.

Sami laughed. "It does make life more enjoyable."

"I'm so glad we could help," Daria continued. "Please call us back with updates. And have fun romancing yourself."

Elena disconnected the call and played an ad to give us a minute to breathe.

I cleared my throat, snagging Daria's attention. "You were

really good with Sami. That…well, it was really enjoyable. The two of us just now."

She tucked a strand of hair behind her ear. "What you said about perfectionism…" She nodded. "It really got me. It was, you were…great. No wonder all these people love your show."

"No wonder all these people love yours," I murmured.

Talk about a *distraction*.

I'd given Daria a lot of shit about keeping us arguing instead of getting along. I shouldn't have been so eager to press the issue. The barest hint of her sweet, tentative respect had me seeing stars like a cartoon character after taking a hit to the head.

Like I'd told Sami, I didn't think true intimacy was possible without true honesty. But it didn't matter how this relationship with Daria progressed, whether we were friendly cohosts or two people who had desperate, angry sex in closets. Our authentic selves were at permanent odds.

And for the first time in my life, I couldn't find it in myself to care.

17

DARIA

*I*t was just after 2:30 in the morning when I slid my key into the front door at K-SUN and let myself in. The station was almost entirely dark, though the building still hummed with a glowing, ambient energy.

Theo and I had finished up our show at 11:00 and then *The Mix Tape* had aired until 1:00. But the producers and engineers had either all gone home or hit up High Frequency for a round of drinks.

I walked quietly down the empty hallways, my ears picking up the low sound of the broadcast we aired every night from this time until my mom and the rest of the morning show crew arrived before dawn. It was a playlist curated by Cliff for people who worked the graveyard shift or who were up at odd hours. He called it *Echoes,* and it was mostly eerie and dreamy techno beats that never failed to help me sleep when I needed it.

And tonight, I needed it.

I'd been miserable for two hours now, nothing but a restless bundle of nerves until I'd finally gotten up, pulled on some random clothes, and walked here in a meager attempt at clearing my head.

After Sami's call, the rest of the show had passed without incident. Except that was a good thing. A *great* thing. As Theo and I were leaving the sound booth, Des mentioned that our numbers were way up and we'd officially sold out tickets for next week's arcade night. Janis had marched by, given us both a brisk hug, and yelled, "Knew you could do it!" over her shoulder.

It had left me with a floaty feeling of dazed amusement. And that, combined with my body's rosy response to Theo's earlier compliment, was the source of my tossing and turning.

Because I wasn't supposed to be enjoying myself while cohosting with Theo. I wasn't supposed to be listening, or learning, or developing a back-and-forth rhythm of sharing the airwaves with him that was becoming relaxed and comfortable.

I was *supposed* to be gritting my teeth and getting through the new programming until K-SUN's budget was safely back where it needed to be, all while focusing on proving my own expertise to Theo every chance that I got. That was how I was going to grow my listener base for *Choosing Yourself* while enticing a fancy literary agent at the same exact time. All of this had been crystal clear to me two weeks ago.

Now I was a super horny hot mess who was barely sleeping.

It wasn't a good look.

Humming softly beneath my breath, I turned the corner and paused, mid-step. Golden light spilled from Theo's open office door. I set my raised foot down as quietly as I could while blood rushed in my ears. There was the sound of ice against glass. And then Theo's velvet voice said, "Daria? Is that you?"

Limbs heavy, heart racing, I closed the remaining distance between the dark hallway and the warm light. I peered around the doorway and had to remind myself to breathe.

Theo was stretched out on his couch in navy blue joggers and a worn-looking gray T-shirt emblazoned with the logo of one of K-SUN's old pledge drives. He was barefoot, glasses off, with a shadow of scruff on his jaw.

Even his curls looked more disheveled than normal, like he'd woken up and decided to make bedhead sexy.

I spend every moment we're in the same room wanting to fuck you on the nearest flat surface. A table, a desk, a chair, the goddamn floor, Daria.

"Couldn't sleep?" he asked.

My mouth had gone dry. "Just a little…worked up is all. How'd you know it was me?"

One side of his mouth hitched up. "I'm familiar with the sound of your Doc Martens now. Plus, you have a distinctive style of walking."

I leaned against the doorway. "Oh yeah? What's kind of style?"

"Bold," he said after a second. "Like you're on your way to someplace exciting but you won't rush to get there."

The eye contact we shared sent an electric shock through my system. His gaze traveled slowly down the length of my body in a manner just shy of haughty. Then his face broke out in a full grin. "Daria. What the hell are you wearing?"

I glanced down at my outfit and laughed. I did a mini-twirl in the doorway so Theo could get the full visual. "Where's the disconnect for you? Is it the boots paired with these neon-pink shorts printed with dancing mustaches? *Or* is it the David Bowie shirt I bought out the back of some dude's van on the boardwalk that's five sizes too big for me?"

Theo pressed his lips together in an ineffective attempt at hiding a smile. "Each of the items, separately, are one of a kind. So to see them all together like this is startling."

I shrugged. "I wasn't expecting company. What are you

doing here so late anyway?"

He sighed and pinched the bridge of his nose. "Also couldn't sleep. I went home and everything…" He trailed off. "I had the ludicrous idea that I'd get caught up on work but I'm too tired to even open my laptop."

"But not tired enough to sleep?"

"You got it," he said softly. "Something about this station feels like a comfort to me."

I stepped fully into the warmth of his office before I could stop myself. Theo started to sit up, making room for me on the couch, but I waved him off. Instead, I perched on the coffee table, my knees pressed to the cushions, my upper body turned toward him. Next to me was a half-empty glass of whiskey with a melting ice cube. I picked it up with a questioning look and he nodded.

"There's more if you want it," he said.

I swirled the ice and took a sip. My eyes stayed glued to Theo's face while his eyes lingered on my lips.

"Thanks," I said, balancing the glass on my thigh. "When I was a kid, this place felt like a second home. When I moved away with Jackson to L.A. so we could go to school, I missed this physical building almost as much as I missed Sunrise Beach as a whole."

"I'm sure everyone here missed you too."

I glanced back at the glass on my leg. I hadn't realized how tempting it would be to have Theo's big, lean body stretched out on display a few inches from my fingertips. I'd never seen him look so relaxed and indulgent. It was a tanta-lizing reminder of what transpired between us in that closet, the many ways Theo's infamous control had snapped as he'd shoved me back against that wall and claimed my mouth like he owned it.

"Do you ever feel hungover after a show?" Theo asked, shaking me from my thoughts. I immediately looked down at the whiskey, but he laughed quietly. "No, not from drinking.

178

More from sharing so many pieces of ourselves with perfect strangers and large swaths of the internet."

"Ah." I grinned. "I know exactly what you're talking about. And yes, I do. I'll feel kind of like I do tonight. Buzzy, but not in a pleasant way. A little itchy and on edge. Worried that I'd shared too much or said the wrong thing."

Theo was nodding along as I spoke. A mop of curls fell across his forehead. "I never mind being so open with our listeners because they're being open with us. Feels like an even exchange of vulnerabilities so I'm willing to share. But it's a risk."

"It can be used against us," I said. "Or we could hurt someone with our words. It's…" I cocked my head, thinking. "There's a price that we pay for being so vulnerable."

"Sometimes it's a higher price than usual."

I traced the rim of the glass with my finger. "What does your vulnerability hangover feel like?"

He blew out a long breath. I handed him the glass. "Wiped out, like I could sleep for a day. I'll get a tension headache if it's bad. Buzzy, like you said."

I cracked a smile. "It is like walking around naked and not in the totally hot way."

He watched me for a second. "When you told me about crying with Janis after your wedding, I didn't share anything back. In fact, I think we got into an argument immediately after."

I brushed the hair from my eyes. "Oh. I wasn't worried about it. I wanted to tell you, so I did."

His brow creased. He pushed himself up gracefully to sit on the couch, wrapping his arm across the back and pointing to the newly opened space next to him. A low, delicious heat had been pooling in my belly from the second I'd seen his light on. The air in here was thick with the same tension that hovered between us before our kiss.

Mesmerized, I moved myself to the couch, turned my

upper body to face Theo and discovered he was barely a foot away from me.

"I know you asked before about why I'd been dumped by my previous girlfriends," he said.

"Theo," I said quickly, "you *do not* need to—"

"It's okay. I think it's important as…as cohosts. An even exchange," he said carefully. "I threw myself passionately into my three serious relationships but, with hindsight, they were more comfortable than fiery. That's not bad. It's certainly what a lot of people are looking for. I was overly focused on putting what I'd learned, and what I advised people on, into immediate practice, including probably going overboard with the romantic gestures. I wanted everything to *mean* something to them. Wanted every day and moment between us to be positive. Happy. When my partners were unhappy or stressed or worried, I'd fill the house with flowers and gifts but—"

"But what?" I tipped my head to catch his eye.

His throat worked on a swallow. "What I learned is that they were looking for me to listen. To not be there with a bouquet and a solution, but rather to sit with their discomfort and love them regardless. I even avoided arguments."

My eyebrows shot up.

He rubbed his forehead. "I know. Shocking. But I did. When Stormi broke up with me, she said she felt that I was too easily swept into the romance and much too eager to disregard the hard stuff. The complicated conversations and the compromises that take work. All the emotional ups and downs that come with loving someone authentically. It appears that I can give that advice on my show but not…do it in real life. With real women who deserved someone to be there for them."

He stared down at the table, tracing his lower lip with his thumb. "I've studied emotional intimacy and healthy communication all my life. And at the end of every relationship, I was told that I'm apparently shit at it." He looked up at me through his mussed curls and I felt the rhythm of my heart change patterns. "My biggest concern is that everything I tell people on that damn show is flimsy. Nothing but a lie wrapped in pretty radio packaging."

"Oh, Theo," I said, "I'm sorry. I know what it's like to have other people's parting words stuck in your head. It fucking sucks."

His nostrils flared. "For the record, I think Jackson's an asshole."

My face warmed at the rough edge in his voice. "I know he is. But you're not. You're a person doing their best and learning along the way. That's the horrible and beautiful part of being human. Besides, look at Rachel, Ted and Skyler. Your advice helped them find their way to a loving relationship even though it was scary and hard to do. Your advice isn't flimsy. You just haven't—"

I stopped, realizing too late what I'd been about to say.

"Haven't what?" he asked, sounding vaguely amused.

I raked a hand through my hair and mumbled, "Found the right woman yet."

"You're not sitting on this couch and telling me you believe in soul mates now, are you?"

I shot him a pleading look. "I'm *saying* that the way your girlfriends felt was important and valid. You also might feel differently when you're with, you know…the one. Not that it means you can smother her with flowers whenever you feel like it."

His lips twitched. "An overexaggeration at best."

"But, you know…you learn. You grow. You change. When it's right, maybe those complicated conversations won't feel so hard. Maybe the compromises will come a little easier. I imagine the emotional ups and downs would feel more natural too."

I finished talking, my hands falling to my lap, and realized

Theo was studying me with open, affectionate appreciation. I squirmed back a few inches on the couch, tugging on my boot laces to give my fingers something to do.

"What?" I asked breathlessly. "Is the chemical color of these shorts giving you hallucinations or something?"

"You, Daria Stone, gave me advice on love."

I scoffed. "That's not even remotely what happened here. I was only offering words…"

"Of wisdom?"

"Nope. Just plain old boring words."

"Like…a suggestion?"

"The only thing I would suggest is that you should ask Janis to invest in a more comfortable couch for you."

"It's almost like you were giving me guidance based on the question that I asked you. Some call that *helping*." He tapped his chin.

"Oh my god, shut up." I scooped up the whiskey and finished it off. With a bemused smirk, Theo stood, took the glass and walked over to his desk. He refilled it, and as he handed the glass back he gripped it tight, keeping it still while I tried to free it.

"Thank you, Daria," he said, catching my eye. "Seriously. I forget this is why people call in to our show. Unburdening helps me feel a bit lighter. And your plain old boring words are appreciated."

He released the glass, and I pressed it to the center of my chest, watching him sit back down with looser shoulders.

"You're welcome," I managed through a tight throat. "If it helps, I spend a lot of time afraid that all the advice I give is flimsy too. I haven't told you this yet but if we're unburdening tonight…I wrote a book. A book of essays, like a memoir. About what happened to me on the wedding day and everything I learned from it. It's *Choosing Yourself*, in chapter form."

Theo's delighted smile caught me entirely off guard. I

almost kissed him. "Wait, you're serious?"

"Yeah, I am. I've been sending it out to agents for, shit, nine months?"

"Daria, that's an incredible accomplishment," he said. "Have you told anyone else here?"

I shook my head. "My mom knows, of course. But it's... it's not exactly something to shout about. Especially since I'm currently living in Rejection City. I'm getting a lot of *we love your voice but* emails."

"Again. Assholes," Theo said.

"That's what my mom said." I took a sip of whiskey and then handed Theo the glass. "But uh...I guess I wanted you to know that my secret fear is that I'm a fraud, sitting behind a microphone. Because right now no one who reads what I have to say in the written form thinks it's deserving of publication."

He winced in sympathy.

"Being left like that, the way Jackson did it, made me feel worthless," I said. "I don't feel like that often anymore, but the weekly rejections have hit that trigger point a lot recently."

He nodded, understanding dawning on his face. "And then I told you your show was a one-hit wonder."

Now it was my turn to wince. "Yeah, well, I said a lot of shitty things too that I'm sure hit some of your trigger points."

He looked down at the now half-empty glass, swirling the amber liquid. "Your words are deserving of publication, but your advice and experiences carry weight all on their own. When the right agent for you finds your manuscript, it'll feel easier."

I took a big breath in, slow and steady. Theo's affirmation didn't, and couldn't, solve the mess of emotions I felt surrounding my book. But the muscles in my chest relaxed a few helpful degrees, and I was grateful for the respite.

"Unburdening," I said with a grateful smile. "Thank you for your—"

He arched an eyebrow. "Plain old boring words?"

My smile widened. "Yeah, yeah, okay, I see your point."

He returned the gesture before glancing back down at his hands. "For the past couple years, Janis and I have been trying to get *True Romance* syndicated, like your mom's show. Professionally, it's all I've ever wanted—to be trusted on a national scale, to expand the reach of K-SUN's influence, to remind people that independent radio isn't inconsequential or some ancient relic. It's the backbone of any vibrant, cultural community and the more we fight for our space on the airwaves, the more we keep what is rightfully ours."

The passion in his voice had me leaning in, compelled, same as when we'd sat in the break room and he'd talked about what made this station so unique: *we don't just report on the community, we're* of *the community.* That, combined with his idea to build a food pantry for our neighbors painted this side of Theo I was now starting to see—a person as fiercely devoted to the cause as I was.

His green eyes slid to mine. "I've been so focused on maintaining my brand and my expertise because I've been assuming that, any day now, we'll get the call. And it keeps not happening."

I grimaced. "You're hanging out in Rejection City too, huh?"

"It appears so," he sighed. "Even Janis told me, that night she gave us the news about our new show, that she thought I was getting too comfortable. That I needed a cohost like you. It…" He swallowed. "I understand feeling like a fraud. What's the point of all those years of intense studying, all these hours of answering questions, all my romantic relationships, if the general public thinks I don't know what I'm talking about?"

"The general public is also an asshole," I said, nudging his knee.

A smile flickered across his face.

"It's awful though," I continued, "putting yourself out there, over and over, only to be turned down. Feeling like you don't belong makes total sense. There's a lot of competition in our industry, and not just the way it's been between you and me. It's a surefire way to feel like shit."

He rubbed the back of his neck, his smile growing shy. "Maybe we should start selling crystals after all."

I experienced a full-on blush attack—it was the sweet quiet of the station, Theo's tentative reveals, the way his secret fears so closely mirrored my own. My fingers itched with the need to find this *general public* and demand they treat him better—couldn't they see he would be wonderful?

I twisted my fingers together in my lap. "Have you ever thought about…choosing yourself a little?"

He stilled. "Like…taking myself out to a candlelit dinner?"

"That's a super-specific example. I mean, like, spending some planned time alone. Maybe it would help you figure out some of your relationship questions or process some of the rejections. This stuff is really hard, Theo."

The openness on his face rippled shut, like a lamp flicking off. "I've spent a lot of time alone, Daria. I'd prefer not to make it a priority when love and companionship are all I've ever wanted."

My eyes narrowed. "Okay. I think it could help, is all. If we're going to keep being cohosts for God knows how long Janis makes us, is there any harm in trying out some of my advice for our listeners? They're already jazzed about these weekly competitions. And there's this hiking trail called the Rose Point Lookout that I used to do when I first moved back home. It's ideal for getting in a certain kind of headspace. I could give you directions or—"

"And what headspace is that?" he asked.

"Learning about yourself. Understanding what you want despite what other people say."

"I've already done that work," he said crisply. "But thank you for the suggestion."

Theo was closing himself off again and it was sending my hackles up. He'd welcomed me in here and given me whiskey and then bared a tiny piece of his soul.

The quick pivot was giving me emotional whiplash.

"Cool," I said blandly. "Well, it's getting late, so I should probably—"

His jaw clenched. "If I did what you said, would you agree to do something romantic?"

"What, like go out on a date to a candlelit dinner? Who's gonna take me, some random guy I pick up at the bar?"

"I'd be the one taking you," he growled softly.

Goosebumps shivered down my arms. His expression shifted again, an intense, hungry yearning carved into his features. I had an inkling where the whiplash was stemming from now.

"Theo," I started, "if this is about the other day, what happened between us, I'm sorry if you felt like I was avoiding talking about it. But I think it's obvious we needed to burn off whatever prickly, argumentative energy that existed between the two of us. It was only a one-time thing. Right?"

My body was rioting even before I finished talking—stomach churning, mouth dry, a cold sweat on my skin. Any one of these symptoms by themselves was a physical reaction to stress or nerves. But together? It was a surefire way to let me know that I was lying.

Theo looked positively mutinous. "No. I wasn't aware that anything like that was obvious," he said in a clipped tone. "When we were stuck in that room, we were forced to tell each other the truth, Daria. The only thing obvious to *me* is that every time we argue, it's because we're not being honest with each other."

186

"Really? Because we argue *constantly*. That can't be a healthy sign, Theo. It can't be *good* that every time we talk, we end up lying to each other."

He leaned in close, refusing to drop eye contact. "You pick a fight with me whenever you don't want to get too close. I know you're doing it because I've been doing it too. So I'm going to *unburden myself* of what I should have said days ago. What happened between us in that room changed everything for me. I've never wanted someone more than I want you. You were so astonishingly beautiful, you were *breathtaking.*"

He reached out and tucked a few curls behind my ear. "I can't stop thinking about you, Daria. Why do you think I'm not sleeping at night?"

As though all the air had been sucked out into the starry night sky, I couldn't seem to catch my breath. Theo was, again, awakening emotions I'd stopped feeling *years* ago. Awakening emotions I now made a career out of saying didn't matter to me. Because they didn't.

Except why was my stupid heart trying to climb right out of my chest?

I licked my dry lips. "What...what you said to Sami tonight about authenticity and finding partners who love your true selves. If what we did on that field wasn't a one-time thing, then what was it?"

His brow creased. "I don't know. And I don't care anymore about trying to define it."

"Theo," I said, exasperated. "We want completely opposite things in our lives. How could we ever explore whatever this is while knowing we'll always disagree? Besides, we're coworkers. More than that, we're *cohosts* at a radio station with a budget crisis looming on the horizon. We *have* to care. If not, this doesn't end well for anyone."

Irritation sparked in his forest-green eyes. "Do you really expect to be single forever? I understand why you've avoided relationships since Jackson. I get it. But you're going to turn your back on anything romantic that comes your way for the rest of your life?"

"Yes," I said, even as a roar of nerves rose in my chest. "I mean…Theo, it's who I am. I have an entire radio show *based* on that. A show, an online following, a fucking book that I wrote to help me process the worst years of my life. I can't toss that out because it doesn't make sense to you."

"I'm not asking you to toss out anything. And I don't need the reminder about how complicated my feelings for you make our current work situation. I know…" He raked a hand through his hair. "Telling you this is a risk for me, professionally. I know that."

My feelings for you. The part of my heart that Theo had sparked to life was doing more than blinking awake. It was like an entire cheerleading routine was being performed inside my ribcage. And I was one back handspring away from climbing into Theo's lap and begging him to kiss me.

I softened my tone, feeling like my entire body was melting into a puddle of want and confusion. "I promise I'm not bringing up these complications to be an asshole. Theo, I *know* what you want in life. I know it because you tell our listeners every week. You've built the same brand and image around these romantic dreams of commitment that I have around being single. Are you really going to date a woman like me who's never going to get married? Who doesn't even want to be in a *relationship*? How is that fair to you?"

His eyes searched mine, chest rising and falling with each frustrated breath. His fingers flexed against his thighs, his body rippling with a restrained motion. My words hung in the tense space between us, but every single part of me ached with desire for this man.

"God*dammit*, Daria," he finally whispered. And then he cupped my face in his hands and kissed me.

I knew why he did it, could *feel* him pouring his passion

and confusion and lust into the firm press of his lips against mine.

He tilted his head, deepening a kiss that already had my head spinning. The tips of his fingers dragged through my hair and his thumb stroked across my cheek. His mouth moved ravenously over mine until I wasn't sure where I ended and he began.

The kiss broke me wide open, overwhelming me with the signs my body had been giving me all along about my radio rival. My feelings for him were a contradiction. They were terrifying. They were absolutely outside of whatever bullshit Venn diagram I imagined we existed in.

But the only way to deny what these feelings were was to lie. To wrap myself back in the same restrictions that kept me polite and perfect when I was with Jackson.

If I was committed to honoring my authentic self, I had to admit to Theo he wasn't alone in this risk.

He broke the kiss, pulling back enough that I could see the hint of panic in his eyes. His lips parted on a shaky exhale. "Daria. Daria, I'm so—"

I covered his mouth with my hand. "Don't," I whispered. "If I don't say it now, I'll lose my nerve. I have feelings for you too, Theo. And I'm as confused as you are but I'm also just as willing to take the risk. Whatever *this* is. No more lies."

I slowly removed my hand, and he stared into my eyes for a long, intimate second. The slightly crooked smile that lit up his face would have sent my heart tumbling around in my chest if that hadn't already been the case this entire time.

That's when I realized it wasn't Theo's academic career or years of experience or obsessed fan base that had me feeling like a fraud these past few weeks.

It was that I was spending my shows telling listeners I was *so over* this "romance" business when I had so foolishly, so *obviously*, wanted Dr. Theodore Chadwick all along.

18

THEO

No more lies.

The relief, the want, the *desire* that soared through my body at Daria's admission was overwhelming. I was a psychologist and no stranger to research, yet for almost four months now I'd been ignoring whole swaths of evidence indicating a glaring fact.

I didn't want her because of our complications. I wanted her *despite* these complications, was willing to risk more than I ever thought possible to kiss her one more time.

I ran my hand through her hair and brushed my lips over her temple. "Are you sure?" I whispered.

"Yes." Her fingers twisted in my collar. "Yes." Her mouth found mine again, kissing me urgently. "I'm very, very sure."

I had Daria flat on her back on that couch not a second later. I reached behind my head and pulled off my shirt, tossing it over my shoulder. Heat flared in her eyes, gaze traveling down my chest and widening the lower she got. I took advantage of her distraction to hook her left foot up and yank open the laces, tugging off her heavy boot.

She pressed herself up on her elbows with a sexy grin. "I can do that, you know."

I kept my eyes on her as I gently worked her other shoe from her foot. "How about you take that shirt off for me instead?"

She pursed her lips, looking adorably defiant. "Just how bossy are you, by the way?"

I matched her insolent expression, lowering my hips between her spread legs and pressing my chest to hers. She arched beneath me, our lips dancing close but not touching. I slipped my hand beneath her shirt and skated my palm up to cup her bare breast. Her nipple hardened beneath my fingers. I hissed out a breath and dropped my mouth to her ear.

"That depends, Daria. You're going to tell me how to make you come with my tongue. And then I'm going to do that over"—I kissed her neck— "and over"—I kissed her jaw — "and over again. If that makes me bossy, so be it." I pinched her chin and brought our faces close. "Now take off your goddamn shirt."

She captured my mouth with a hushed moan. Her fingers threaded through my hair while her tongue stroked mine. She rolled her hips beneath me, urging me to move, to grind against her in a rhythm that matched the motion of her lips. One hand left my hair and roamed down my neck, the curve of my spine, sliding beneath my sweatpants. Her fingernails bit against my skin, tearing a ragged curse from my throat. I reared back just in time to see her smile indulgently.

"Sorry." She pouted. "What did you say again?"

I let out a strained laugh that ended in a growl, nipping her throat harder than I intended. But she sighed out a *yes* that had me yanking off her shirt without any finesse. I pressed my forehead to hers and didn't look down—knew that once I saw her semi-naked body under my own there'd be no turning back. Instead, I went back to circling her nipple with my thumb, slow circles that had her eyelashes fluttering and her fingernails digging into my shoulders.

"I get it," I said softly. "You're going to make me work for it the way you make me work for it in every fight and argument we've ever had. Is that right?"

I paired the motion of my thumb with the motion of my tongue, darting out to lick up and down the shell of Daria's ear. She was shaking beneath me, moaning my name in between panting breaths. "That feels...*god, so good.*"

I dipped my mouth down to her nipple, using both my tongue and thumb to tease her sensitive peak. Around and around, each desperate, keening cry she made sending flames of arousal through my entire body. My cock was hard to the point of pain, every sense and every ounce of focus poured into this one motion, this one point.

When I dropped my thumb and sucked her nipple into my mouth, Daria gripped my hair like a vice. Smiling around her skin, I curved my hand down her smooth belly and under those ridiculous shorts. Her cunt was slick with arousal and when my index finger nudged her clit, I groaned louder than she did.

Keeping a close eye on her reactions, I lightly circled the bundle of nerves and was rewarded with her brilliant, breathless smile.

"Daria," I said, helpless not to smile in response, "I'll play any bedroom games you want. In every way that you need. Just say the word." I lifted my head from her gorgeous breasts and pinned her gaze with mine. "But I'm not going to play around to avoid the truth of what's happening between us."

One more piece of her external wall came tumbling down. I saw it in the way her blue eyes softened. Felt it in the caress of her fingers across my forehead. I didn't resent her for it—we needed high walls so we could plausibly deny the dizzying attraction between us. But I was looking for an equal exchange, same as when we hosted our show, one small hint of vulnerability at a time.

We didn't need to bare our entire souls, but I wanted some shared recognition of the risk she promised to take.

"Okay," she whispered, kissing me softly. "No more teasing. It's just me."

I started those circles on her clit again. She shuddered, curling her hands around my biceps. "I like just you," I said.

"I like you too." She sank her teeth into her bottom lip. "And you can boss me around all you want. Please."

I brushed my mouth over her ear. "Then be a good girl and show me how you come."

She hissed, nipples hard, chest flushed. "Theo."

"Take your shorts off," I commanded. "I want you to see what I'm doing."

She did this time, eagerly, revealing the sweet curve of her hips, her long legs, the fine dark curls covering her mound. And my finger, tucked between her folds. She was squirming beneath my touch, arms tossed over her head. I wrapped my other hand around the back of her neck, squeezing firmly, and my name fell from her lips in a nonsensical rush.

"Is this what you like?" I asked, watching her beautiful, naked body in full-on amazement. "You want to be told what to do while I say the dirtiest things imaginable?"

She nodded and whispered, "*Yes*. But I need more."

"Do you want me to fuck you with my mouth?"

A cheeky grin appeared on her face. Then she grabbed my head and tried to shove it down her body. I chuckled against her skin and nipped her ear lobe. I caught both of her wrists and pinned them over her head, our fingers entwining on the pillow. Still wearing my joggers, I rocked my erection against Daria's bare, slick sex, both of us groaning at the impact.

"*Fuck*, you feel amazing underneath me," I said with a kiss. "Now were you trying to tell me something earlier?"

She hummed through a breathless laugh. Her wrists twisted beneath my hands, her legs wrapping around my waist as her lower body moved with mine. I could have stayed here, like this, forever—not even fully naked, just the two of us on this couch, suspended within a sweet, mounting pleasure that made my very skin feel electric. Daria parted my lips with her tongue, drinking me in, filling me with the taste of her, the smell of her, her yearning inscribed in every breath we shared. I pulled back to catch my breath and knew I looked dazed. She did too, with swollen lips and heavily lidded eyes.

"Lick my clit," she murmured. Then she closed her teeth around my lip and pulled. The growl that surged from deep in my chest was more animal than human. "Now."

I released her wrists to clutch her face and kiss her hard. "This smart mouth of yours is filthy too, huh?"

She raised a single eyebrow. "I'm guessing no more than yours, Dr. Chadwick."

Pure instinct took over, sending me moving down her body, cupping her breasts, kissing every single inch of her. She was poetry beneath my hands, all flushed, pale skin, her fingers tugging my hair, her head thrown back and neck exposed.

This was the vulnerability I wanted to see from her—the release, the trust, the openness. It was strange to think that we'd earned this through months of arguments. But the intimacy had grown alongside the attraction in every heated look and glimmer of understanding.

When I finally, *finally*, reached her pussy, I held her legs open and pressed my face into her folds, inhaling her warm, musky scent.

"*Daria*," I whispered, darting my tongue out to taste her. "Sweet *Christ*, why did we fight this for so long?"

"Because we can't take our own advice?" she said, tossing me a grin that sent my already racing heart into overdrive.

I closed my eyes and rubbed my mouth through her folds, along her inner thighs, loving the way I could feel the muscles of her thighs tensing and flexing. I circled her opening with my index finger, dipping in an inch and then retreating.

"Oh, yes, *that*," she moaned.

I did as I was told, eagerly. Then I circled her clit with my tongue the same way I'd been touching her earlier—and her back arched off the couch.

"Is that something you like?"

She didn't respond verbally. But she did twist her fingers into my hair and direct me back to her clit. I was more than happy to oblige, would have stayed there for hours if she needed me to. I lapped my tongue against her while working my fingers deep inside of her, twisting. Curling. Thrusting my hips against the couch because tonguing Daria to orgasm was hotter than anything I'd ever experienced before.

She was all need, all want, rocking up and into my tongue when she wanted me to go harder. Begging me when she needed faster. Squealing my name when I found a certain spot deep inside of her.

"Oh god, oh god, *oh god*," she chanted, so out of breath it was barely more than a whisper. "I'm close, Theo. You're so goddamn good at this, *fuck*."

"Show me," I demanded, licking her with the fast, firm pressure she liked. "I've got you, Daria."

She pressed up onto an elbow and shoved her fingers into my hair, watching me with luminous eyes and wild curls. I wrapped my lips around her clit and sucked, fluttering my tongue and stroking that spot she loved with two of my fingers. She came like a firework in the sky, bucking against me so hard I had to press my hand to her stomach so I could lick her through every second of her orgasm and the aftershocks that kept her trembling and gasping.

Not once did I look away from Daria. Not once *could* I look away. I kept my face buried between her thighs, tasting her pleasure, while grinding my cock into the cushions. Every nerve ending vibrated with the need to come, every muscle was clenched and aching—and I was so tuned to Daria's reactions it took every bit of willpower I had not to climax along with her.

When her body finally settled, I very gently slid my fingers free, crawling up her naked body to find a very pretty, very relaxed Daria staring up at me with smug satisfaction.

I nudged my nose against hers. Kissed her—groaning as she licked deep inside my mouth.

"Theo," she murmured, "if I told you that all your fancy academic degrees were bullshit because you're *really* an expert in cunnilingus, would you be able to take the compliment without becoming utterly supercilious?"

I hummed against her skin, pressing kiss after deliberate kiss up the length of her neck. "Keep using five-syllable words in bed with me, Daria, and I'll prove I'm an expert as many times as you'd like."

She sighed. "I knew it would go right to your head."

"There are a lot of things going to my head right now," I said, kissing her temple. "The feel of you on my tongue, your taste, every sweet sound that you made." Her eyes were closed, a dreamy smile playing on her lips. She liked this. "I love that you showed me what you needed and when. Expert or not, I'm here to learn. And I mean that."

I was too enthralled with the elegance of her profile to notice what she was planning. Only that in the blink of an eye, I was the one flat on my back, gazing up in amazement as Daria straddled me and pinned my hands down. My hips lifted involuntarily, seeking more of her. All of her. She dipped her head close to tease with an almost-kiss, eliciting a growl of frustration from me when she danced away.

"I'm here to learn too," she whispered, kissing across my chest. Nuzzling her cheek against my chest hair. She moved lower. And lower, finally releasing my hands so she could trail her fingernails down my rib cage. I shivered, hissing out a breath as her nails dragged along my skin. I watched with my heart lodged in my throat—her curious blue eyes, her pink tongue, her ass raised behind her in the air.

"Daria," I gasped.

She slowly removed my sweatpants with a grin so sly and seductive I had to grit my teeth to keep from begging. Daria wrapped her fingers around the base of my cock and squeezed, traveling upward.

"Oh, *fuck*," I grunted.

"That's what I wanted to ask you about," she said. "Can I use my mouth on you, Theo?"

"*Please*," I spit out.

She didn't tease or linger. She took the length of me between her warm, wet lips with a greediness that roared through me. She'd wanted me with the same ferocity, the same hunger, that I'd wanted her, and the knowledge of that was dizzying. I slipped my hands into her snarled curls and lowered her mouth back down my cock, my thighs already trembling.

"Close your eyes," she said, "and think about how you want to fuck me, Theo. I need to come again but I want you inside me when it happens."

My head fell back in pleasure on that vague image alone —but when her mouth descended again, tongue flat against the side of my cock, I let every filthy fantasy run through my mind. Daria sucked my cock and hummed, and I twisted her hair, remembering how often, in the middle of an argument, I only wanted to drag her onto my desk and fuck her senseless.

"Up," I managed to say. "Stand up. And get on my desk."

Daria sat back on her knees, wiping her mouth with a smile. I raised an eyebrow and she stood, walking naked and confident to the edge of my desk. She leaned back on it, displaying every curve and dimple for my eyes to feast on. And feast on it I did, grabbing a condom and stalking toward her as her eyes widened and her lips parted on a tremble. I reached for her face, kissing her hard. Then I took her hips and spun her fast, her palms landing on the desk.

"Oh, *yes*," she sighed. Her head fell back against my shoulder. I kicked her feet wide and took her earlobe between my teeth, working the condom on at the same time.

"I spent way too much time wanting to fuck our way to agreement after every fight," I whispered. My hands slid from her hips, up her stomach, to palm and squeeze her breasts. "Way too much time wanting you like this, bent over for me, needing it as desperately as I did."

"I'm here now," she said, arching into me. "So take it."

I buried my head into the crook of her neck, scraping her with my teeth. Daria shuddered and shoved her ass back so hard I let out a pained laugh. But I looked down and saw the head of my cock at her entrance and every bit of humor drained from my body. I squeezed her hips hard and kissed the back of her neck.

"Yes?" I asked.

"*Now*," she demanded.

I grinned. "You're going to kill me, Daria Stone." Then I slid inside of her, the tight muscles of her pussy squeezing my cock. A full-body euphoria washed over me, and I punched my hips forward, fully seating inside of her as she cried out my name.

"Oh, Theo, *thank god*," she sighed, pushing up on her toes as I rocked into her. "This is what I love. This…this…*this*."

I drove my fingers into her hair, tipping her head back, my thighs slapping against her legs as I started to move. "What about this do you love? Tell me."

"Hard. I like it —"

I pushed her face down onto the desk and she cried out again.

"Harder. *More*. You know I can take it," she begged. Her hands shot forward, fingers scrambling through the files and books on my desk. A jar of pens and a stack of papers fell to the ground. The desk shook with each of my thrusts. I grabbed her right leg and lifted her knee, gripping the side of the desk while I rode Daria as rough as she liked. Hell, as rough as *I* liked.

I'd admitted to her in a burst of terrifying vulnerability that my relationships, while serious and committed, were more tepid than fiery. I hadn't realized that I needed *fiery*—craved this intense lust that demanded I pin her to this desk and fuck her with a passion bordering on obsession.

I bent over her, grabbing her hair and tipping her head back so I could press the side of my face to hers. She turned, meeting me for a wet kiss full of our own moans. I wrapped my hand lightly around her neck and moved even faster.

"Jesus, Theo," she panted. "You're so good, *it's so good.*"

I could feel the orgasm building in my body like a storm. With every thrust, I sank deeper inside her pussy, her muscles tight and fluttering the closer she got to her second climax. I let the hand not holding her neck slip between her legs and find her clit again. She wailed.

"I made a mistake before," I breathed in her ear. "I promised I would drag you into my bed and fuck you for a week straight. But how could I ever get enough of what we have right here?"

Her head fell back against my shoulder. A deep red flush covered her chest and throat. I felt a bead of sweat slide down my spine, everything inside of me coiling *tight.*

"It's perfect, you're...perfect, oh god, *oh—*"

I covered her mouth with my hand, and she screamed against it, coming so hard I couldn't hold back one more second. An orgasm tore through my body, had my hips bucking against her, my face pressed to her neck. My vision dimmed, the sharpness of the climax removing my ability to do anything except groan Daria's name like a goddamn prayer.

She started to fall forward. I wrapped an arm across her chest, catching her and holding her against me. We stayed like that for a minute, until our breathing slowed together. She wrapped her hand around my own, squeezing tight, sparking a languid happiness in my chest.

"Some perfect gentleman you turned out to be," she murmured, her laughter warm and a little raspy.

I chuckled, pressing my lips to her cheek for a long second. "You can't stay away from my Instagram comments, can you?"

"Like you never looked at my selfies."

"Maybe." I kissed her cheek again. "Okay, all the time."

She started to poke me in the chest, but I bent and scooped her up instead, moving us both so we could collapse onto the couch. I disposed of the condom and fell back against the cushions, happily surprised to have a naked Daria crawling into my lap. I brushed the hair from her eyes while she traced my lips with her fingers. I caught the tip of one between my teeth and tugged.

She wrinkled her nose. "Theo Chadwick the dirty talker. Who knew?"

I took her wrist, turning it over. Dropped my lips to her pulse point, smiling as I roamed up her arm. Goosebumps shivered across her skin. "Only with you."

I heard her breathing hitch. "Really?"

My eyes flew up to hers. I nodded. "No more lies, remember?"

Another shift occurred in her eyes. Another softening. I traced the array of sparkling, studded earrings that curved up the shell of her ear. "I like these. Is there a reason why you got so many of them?"

"Well, I've always been a nineties riot grrrl at heart."

I grinned, stroking my thumb up and down her ear. "I wouldn't expect anything less from someone essentially raised by Magnolia *and* Janis."

Daria leaned into my touch like a cat seeking a scratch. "After everything that happened with the wedding, I worked so hard on learning about and loving myself again that I realized that I'm deserving of decoration."

"Decoration," I whispered, rubbing one of the earrings between my thumb and index finger. "It suits you, Daria."

Her eyes studied mine and I discovered it was far too easy to get lost in every shade of sapphire. "No more lies, right?"

I swallowed. Nodded.

She chewed on her bottom lip. "Having sex is easy for me. It's everything else that I tend to avoid. *Have* avoided, for five years now. But what just happened, what we just did…I haven't felt this close to someone or had sex like *that* in…" She hesitated. "I'm not sure."

I stilled, not wanting to jeopardize this rare moment. But when her gaze returned to mine, the worry there was extremely real. I kissed her palm again, held my lips there as I spoke. "I'm not sure if I've felt this way before either."

The dazzling truth of that slammed into me, knocking the air from my lungs. All the diligent post-relationship analysis I'd done over the past ten years and Daria had shown me in an instant what I had missed, every time. Whatever powerful connection existed between the two of us—and even I was afraid to label it—must have been absent in my relationships before.

It had to be—one glorious night with Daria and I was hooked on it.

The worry in her eyes changed to wariness and everything we'd said, everything we'd argued about before we'd had sex crowded back into my memory.

Are you really going to date a woman like me who's never going to get married?

"What does…" I cleared my throat. "What does that mean to you?"

"I don't know yet," she said simply. "But it doesn't change

what I said, about taking the risk with you."

She wrapped her arms around my neck, cheek resting on my chest, and I was bowled over by the affection. I curled my arms around her back, stroked my palm up and down her spine. I had to be okay with *I'm not sure*. Because the risk was real for us both, and we hadn't even broached the subject of K-SUN, and *that* was going to be—

"Shit, do you hear that?" she hissed.

Our late shows basically guaranteed we were never here when the dawn crew arrived to start prepping for Magnolia's broadcast. But I knew the sounds of the station waking up— the flipping of light switches, the tread of shoes in the hallway, the buzz of equipment and electronics being turned on for the day. Daria fumbled for her phone and cursed again when she saw the time.

"I don't think K-SUN's new cohosts should be discovered having spent part of the night together," I said gently, worried that would somehow hurt her feelings. I didn't need to—she was pulling on those ridiculous shorts and yanking her David Bowie T-shirt over her head.

I followed suit with my sweatpants, raking a hand through my hair and finding my glasses. Daria scooped up her boots and tiptoed to the office door. But just as she quietly turned the knob, a burst of voices filled the hallway outside. I reached over and pressed the door closed, holding a finger to my lips.

Her shoulders were shaking with laughter she could barely suppress. I covered her mouth with my palm and whispered, "Can you slip out the back window? Might be the easiest way to avoid our coworkers seeing us with incredibly obvious sex hair."

She pulled my hand down and whispered back: "Thanks for the great advice, Dr. Chadwick. I'm so glad I called in this evening."

"Such a smart mouth," I growled against her ear, turning

her toward the back window behind my desk that faced the boardwalk and the beach. She cast me a smirk from over her shoulder, pushing the window up and peering out. A warm ocean breeze floated in, catching the ends of her hair.

Another realization slotted into place, made more obvious by the thrill of our spontaneous sex, Daria's sly humor, even the adrenaline coursing through my veins at the risk of getting in trouble for doing something forbidden. It was almost five in the morning, and my beautiful rival was climbing out my office window after we'd shared a secret tryst.

I was having *fun*. Unanticipated and unexpected fun.

Daria slid one leg out the window, still holding her boots. "I think I can make it without being seen. Promise not to rat me out to the boss?"

I stroked the curve of her cheekbone with my thumb. "That's a promise I can easily keep."

She flashed me a toothy grin, turning to go. I halted her mid-motion, pulling her against me for one last, searing kiss. Her arms came around my neck, holding me close, her fingers trembling slightly against my skin.

"Thank you," she said, "for being honest with me tonight. That…that's the kind of thing that means a lot."

I nodded and squeezed her fingers. "Thank you for being yourself, Daria."

The smile on her face widened. She winked, sliding through the window and dropping softly onto the ground. She only paused for a second to lace up her boots, and then she was walking through the grass and toward the cool sand with the ease of a Sunrise Beach local.

I could see the Ferris wheel, dark now, and the very edge of the boardwalk. Beyond that, the white foam of the waves and a pale smattering of pre-dawn stars.

And to the right, past the bay filled with gently rocking sailboats, I could just make out the first pink rays of sunrise.

19

DARIA

*T*heo was calling me.

I bit my bottom lip, but there was no stopping the enormous smile that flew across my face when I saw his name on the screen. My heart began beating in the pattern I could only blame on Theo, because it went something like *oh girl, you're in so much fucking trouble.*

I peeked around the door of the store I was about to step into. Elena was already inside but far from the front. Still, I stepped off the boardwalk to stand in the small alley, leaning against a wall with a colorful mural of psychedelic-looking palm trees.

"This your host, Daria Stone, speaking. What burning questions about love can I help you with this evening?"

He laughed, the velvet, rumbling sound vibrating against my ear. "Thanks for taking my call, Daria. Any advice for someone forced to work in close quarters, three nights a week, with a woman he can't stop thinking about?"

I hummed under my breath. "Has anything happened between the two of you?"

"We had the best sex of my life on the desk in my office."

Every single muscle in my body still ached from that sex in the most delicious way.

"You see, I was having trouble sleeping before, what with the thinking about her all the time. And since our hot office sex, anything that involves sleeping or focusing or breathing is a lost cause."

I bit the tip of my thumb. "I'm no expert, but it sounds like your only option is to see her again."

Trouble, trouble, trouble.

"Funny, I was thinking the same thing."

"So we agree?" I teased.

"It's been occasionally known to happen."

A group of skateboarders flew by on the boardwalk with loud music trailing behind them from a speaker hanging from one of their backpacks.

"Are you on the boardwalk? Let me guess," he said, "you're practicing for our public competition on Wednesday?"

"Hardly. I'm outside The Wig Shack—"

"The one next to The Fry Shack?"

"The one and only. Elena and I will absolutely be having a dinner of only French fries after we pick up some costume items for Des for Janis's party. He got pulled into a planning meeting for next week's pledge drive so he begged us to go buy a bunch of wigs, costume jewelry and decorations that we could find with the *disco balls akimbo* theme."

Mentioning the pledge drive had a dampening effect on Theo I could feel through the phone. Janis had sent out a budget update this morning and her tone had been neutral, which was Janis-speak for *grim*. The numbers for our second quarter fundraising just weren't cutting it, even with her creatively rearranging as many buckets of money as possible.

For the first time in five years, the K-SUN board had authorized the use of our meager reserves. And to offset the rest, we were launching the emergency pledge drive.

Buried within an email full of bad news and worse news

was a glimmer of hope I hadn't thought possible. The numbers for the second week of *Love and Life Advice* had been higher than expected, higher even than Theo's show. Des and Elena were fielding twice as many calls and emails with listener questions, and tickets for our arcade night event were sold out.

Against all odds, it was maybe, sort of, kinda...*working?*

And that meant no one could find out that we'd slept together two days ago.

"I'm sure you'll find all the best and most outrageous wigs and Janis will adore you for it. Glitter is her love language," Theo said. "Though I am calling for a legitimate reason and not only to flirt with you."

"Ah, your inner scoundrel comes out."

"I prefer perfect gentleman, as you know," he said smoothly. "The hiking trail you were telling me about. What was it called again? I was going to check it out tomorrow." He paused. "Per your advice."

"Oh," I said, tucking my hair behind my ear. "Rose Point Lookout. "It's about twenty-five minutes from the station. Want me to text you the directions to the trailhead?"

"I'd like that," he said. "And this doesn't get you out of doing something romantic with me, so you know."

"If it involves anything resembling red petals, sprinkled into the shape of a heart, I'm fucking out."

The smile in his voice was obvious. "Got it. No petals on the premises. Could you sneak back into my office? I'll leave the window open for you."

I laughed, if only to hide how desperately I wanted to. I popped my head back around the side of the wall and into the store. Elena was staring outside with a quizzical expression. "I've gotta go. Text me when you get to the viewpoint tomorrow?"

"How will I know I'm there?"

"You'll know it when you see it. And, Theo…thanks for calling."

"Thank you for answering."

I slid my phone into the back pocket of my jeans. Relief washed over me—I hadn't realized I'd been waiting for us to talk, a sensation I hadn't experienced since the early days of dating Jackson. But after Theo had fucked me into a blissed-out stupor in the early dawn hours of yesterday, we hadn't been able to speak properly. We *did*, however, cohost our show that night with a relaxed energy, though I knew neither one of us had really slept.

Other than the stray intense look or the rare blush, we stayed professional. Except when Des threw his arm around Theo's shoulders after we wrapped, dragging him to late drinks at High Frequency, Theo had given me a parting glance full of so much pining I'd felt it all the way down to my toes.

I shoved the door open to The Wig Shack and pushed my sunglasses into my hair. This place was a boardwalk institution—it was primarily a store for Halloween costumes but stayed open all year round with an assortment of party wear, plastic jewelry and whatever leftover Halloween wigs they didn't sell in October.

Elena brightened when she saw me and immediately launched a purple object at my chest.

"What is this?" I asked warily.

"Your new look," she said, clicking her tongue. "It's fashion show o'clock and you're the model for this evening."

I fanned my face with the purple monstrosity. "I've been waiting my entire life to do a wacky wig-wearing montage." When I reached Elena, I grabbed her by the shoulders. "Dreams really do come true."

"You're doing a lot of talking and not a lot of montage-ing," she said, raising her brow. "I've already pulled together some of the best ones with the most glitter."

"Fantastic." We wandered to the back wall, covered in large panel mirrors and so many wigs hanging on hooks I felt dizzy just looking at them. "Do we know if Janis intends on changing into all of these possibilities during the night? Or are they for her friends and family to wear?"

"My impression is Janis wants us whirling around the rink while wearing them," Elena said. She rubbed her fingers over the shaved sides of her head. "I already snagged an orange one for me."

"A great color on you." I picked up a long one made of crinkly, silver tinsel and tugged it over my curls. "Where's the runway again?"

Elena clapped her hands together. "Hold up, we need music for this." She queued up a funky dance number on her phone and propped it on top of a low white table. "Let me see what you got."

The store was completely empty, and we hadn't seen any employees. Though even if it was milling about with people, I wouldn't have hesitated to model a half-dozen glitter wigs for my friend. Hands on my hips, I did my best strut toward the mirrors, tinsel flying around my shoulders, and spun around to find Elena struggling not to laugh.

"Am I not *elegant*?" I said, waving my hand down the length of my body. "Am I not the definition of *poise*?"

"The tinsel makes you look like a fancy alien."

I tipped my head and let her yank it off. "So that's a *yes* on the poise?"

"Oh yeah, this is so Janis's style."

I modeled a highlighter yellow one, a sleek, lime green one and the purple monstrosity, which was cuter than it looked. In between struts, we scooped up glittery disco ball lights, rainbow-colored glow sticks and pink feather boas that we carried around our necks while shopping.

"Uh, hi, sorry I was in the back for so long."

I spun around and the wig toppled from my head.

Standing in front of us, with a name tag that read *The Wig Shack*, was Aidan, the red-haired teenager from the paintball field.

"Oh, *hey*," I said. "Aidan, right?"

He snapped his fingers at me. "I met you last week with your coworker."

"I was the victorious last woman standing," I said, struggling to free myself from all the feathers, glitter and sequins covering my entire body. "Do you work here on the side?"

"Yeah, I'm trying to save up for a car," he drawled. He began loading up our party supplies with the enthusiasm of a sleepwalker. "I told everyone at work about how you and that guy got stuck in the closet."

"You told them what?" I sputtered.

"Who the hell did you get stuck in a closet with?" Elena asked. "Theo? Because that sounds like a hilarious disaster waiting to happen."

Every time you open that irritating mouth of yours it makes me want to drag you into my bed.

I busied myself with opening my purse and grabbing my wallet to pay. "Disaster is how I'd describe it. We fell into one of the old buildings on the field and the door locked behind us. It wasn't like we were in there for that long—"

"It was like half an hour," Aidan said. Traitorously.

Elena nudged my arm with hers. "Dar. You left out the best part of the story when you called into the station that night. How long did it take for you to start arguing?"

A polite smile froze on my face. "Not long." *That wasn't a lie.* "But long enough that we did, I don't know...work through some of our..." I waved my hand in the air. "Core issues."

Also not a lie.

She shrugged amiably. "It worked. The shows after have been gorgeous. I wouldn't put it past Janis to figure out how to plan something like that. Really force you to get along."

209

I laughed nervously. Aidan handed me our giant bags full of party wear and gave me a small nod. "See you around, I guess."

"Thanks for the help," I said over my shoulder as we stepped back outside onto a boardwalk crowded with tourists and locals. I cast a sideways glance at Elena and my stomach tied itself into knots. What happened between Theo and me in that closet, and in his office, was new for me. It was a lot confusing and more than a little bit terrifying. Even if Elena and I didn't work together, I wouldn't be ready yet to expose something so delicate and fragile.

But still. We *did* work together and were friends beyond that. And what happened between Theo and me could make things even *worse* for K-SUN if things went badly. If I was a listener calling into my show with this question, I'd urge them to honor themselves and tell the truth. Instead, I'd lied right to Elena's face.

"Hey, are you okay?" she asked, hefting one of the bags higher. "You need me to carry something?"

"Oh no, I'm good," I said as four people on rollerblades cut around us, leaving the smell of sunscreen in their wake. "I'm happy to hear that you think the show's getting better. It does seem to be bringing in some much-needed revenue right now."

"I know I told you it was more interesting when you and Theo were arguing on-air, but that was mostly a joke," she admitted. "You two getting along is *way* more fun. The questions have been interesting, you're both charming, all the easy chemistry you had on your own shows is doubling. The show is getting mentioned by other stations in L.A., not just K-ROX. Up north, past San Francisco, and even a station in Portland. It's all local stuff but people are wanting to tune in to"—Elena dropped into her announcer voice— *"Love and Life Advice with Theo and Daria."*

"It's still only temporary, right? A way to boost some ratings and raise money?"

She nudged her sunglasses back in place. "Would it be that bad to keep doing something that's working? Seems like you're both enjoying it."

"We are," I said, dazed. "I was thinking about our brands. That kind of stuff. Is it that smart, long-term, when we're more famous for our separate shows and diametrically opposing opinions?"

"Yeah, maybe." She gave an easygoing shrug. "Except you're not really that opposed. Wait, hold up. Can I run in here and grab tablecloths? Des texted about needing some."

Elena left me with the bags and I leaned against a tall palm tree, enjoying the warm summer sun on my face through the shivering green leaves. I took a few long, even breaths until my nerves calmed. In the space of one outing to buy disco balls, the heavy weight of what Theo and I had done, what we were *doing*, had settled firmly over my shoulders.

I wanted to sell my book and wanted my radio show to be famous on its own. But I also wanted K-SUN to thrive and would do literally anything to make that happen.

And as strange as it was to fully admit this now—I wanted Theo too. Desperately.

"'K, I'm back." Elena reappeared with a plastic bag, scooped up half of our other stuff, and we set back off down the boardwalk again. "I never thought I'd have the kind of boss where I willingly, in my own spare time, went out to buy glow sticks and tablecloths for her overly dramatic birthday parties."

I shook my head with a smile. "She's always been something else. Theo's building a community pantry outside the station as her birthday present."

"Oh, she'll love that. She's been wanting to increase the station's coverage of food insecurity in Sunrise Beach, really start putting pressure on elected officials." We walked past stalls selling funnel cake, crispy French fries and soft pretzels, the air smelling like fried bread, butter and salt. "So this was about two years before you came to work for us, but you know that community organization, The Rivera Center?"

"Of course," I said. "They're an advocacy group for queer and transgender teenagers, right?"

Elena nodded. "I got involved right after I moved here because they run a mentorship program for kids who speak Spanish and when I was new at K-SUN, the center went through this awful budget crisis. Lost all this funding. Lost their building, including where they would hold their programs. We were reporting on it at the station, and Janis knew I had a personal connection there. She let them use our break room for three months, free of charge, while they figured out how to get their funding back. And we threw a fundraiser for them too."

"I remember that," I said quietly. "My mom said it was one of her favorite times working there, having the staff triple in size overnight."

She laughed. "I think we all legitimately missed having the staff and kids of The Rivera Center there every day. That's when I learned that Janis Hill was the real deal. No bullshit or fake words or performance. She says it, she does it."

I smiled at Elena, my heart squeezing with that feeling of *home*. "Radio for the people."

"Radio para todas las personas," she repeated, but her brow furrowed. "Hey, isn't that Mags over there?"

I spun on one foot, arms full of bags, and through a burst of pink feathers I could see my mother's trademark black hair. She was stepping out of High Frequency.

"Hell yeah, it is." I beamed, then raised my voice to yell. *"Mom! Hey, Mom!"*

She was distracted by something, giving no indication she'd heard a word that we said.

"For a woman who spends the majority of her life bellowing, you'd think she'd be better at hearing it herself," I said. We walked toward her, through groups of people that kept getting in the way. When they finally parted, I called, "*Magnolia Stone!*"

She did turn then. And she did see us. And I'd never seen such a complicated mess of feelings cross her usually cheerful face.

"Is she okay?" Elena said under her breath.

"I don't—"

But I realized my mother wasn't alone. She was standing next to a woman about her same age. Standing and holding her hand.

"Well...shit," I said. "Theo was right. My mother *is* dating someone."

DARIA

*T*he four of us stood facing each other, frozen in place. People spilled out of the bar and brushed past us, jostling our feather-boa-filled packages, but my mother was still speechless. She hadn't let go of the other woman's hand—she was about my mother's age and height. Pretty, with light tan skin and dark blond hair in a long, thick braid.

She was smiling at me nervously, but her dark eyes widened when she saw Elena.

"I thought that was you," she exclaimed. "Elena, right? From the radio station? Cómo estás?"

Elena shoved her sunglasses up, cocked her head. "Oh, *Martha*." She moved forward to give her a long hug. "Tanto tiempo. Que bueno verte de nuevo."

When I shot my mother an amused and curious look, she seemed as nervous as Martha had been.

My mother had been proudly single for my entire life—according to her, Magnolia Stone didn't give a *good goddamn* about any man. But to see her exchange a shy smile with Martha, while holding her hand like her life depended on it, explained the past few weeks of her strange behavior—her suddenly busy schedule, her magnified elation, asking her listeners about *Valentine's Day*, of all things. But she hadn't told me, and we told each other everything.

Though it wasn't like I'd been planning on telling her about Theo just yet either.

Elena tapped my elbow. "I was *just* telling Daria about when the folks from The Rivera Center worked at our offices for those three months. Daria, I met Martha Rosales through the mentorship program. She's one of the counselors there."

"Oh, amazing," I said brightly, shaking her hand. "My mom still speaks fondly of that time. Is that how you two met?"

My mother couldn't contain the smile on her face. "Technically, yes. Though we bumped into each other doing karaoke here a few months ago."

Martha lowered her voice. "Your mother asked me to duet with her on 'Ain't No Mountain High Enough.'"

My jaw dropped. "Mom. You sang *Motown together*?"

She rubbed the back of her hair. "Martha's got a stunner of a voice. We sound good up there on the stage."

They exchanged a look that spoke volumes, a look that sent a shiver up my spine and had my throat closing.

"Well…I was just leaving," Martha said carefully. "Elena, it was lovely to see you again. And Daria, so nice to finally meet you. I listen to your show, by the way. I love it."

I bit my lip through a smile, suddenly feeling as bashful as my mom looked. "That means a lot to me. You listen to *Mags in the Morning* too though, right?"

She pressed a palm to her chest. "Every single day."

"Ah, I try my best," my mom said. "It's not a big deal."

"Says the woman who routinely describes herself as the best radio DJ of all time," I teased.

"Like fourteen times a day," Elena added.

Martha laughed sweetly. She kissed my mom on the cheek and said, "That I believe. Call me later?"

"Wouldn't miss it," my mom said. And while my mother gazed after Martha, looking awfully lovesick, Elena and I exchanged twin expressions of *what the fuck just happened?*

When she turned back around, I hefted the bags onto my hip and said, "Uh, Mom?"

"I can go," Elena said slowly.

Mom waved her hand through the air. "Please, Elena. You're family to me. Stay. Do you want to sit over there on that picnic table? Sorry I'm so—" She blushed, a physical reaction I'd never seen on her before. "I'm a little shocked and embarrassed."

We followed her to the picnic bench on a plush patch of grass facing the ocean. She shooed away a pair of seagulls squawking over a half-eaten hot dog and sat down. I dropped my bags on the table and came to sit on the same side, right next to her.

"Mom," I said, taking her hand, "what do you have to be embarrassed about? Martha seems wonderful."

She fiddled with her leather bracelets and gave me another bashful smile. "I didn't mean for you to find out like that, like I was keeping some big, shameful secret when really I was only waiting for the right time to tell you. But Elena's right, we met when she was working at the station for those three months. Became pretty fast friends, especially 'cause I would see her at karaoke every so often. Martha had a partner and it was serious, so even though I felt…"

She took a deep breath. "Damn, I felt so *fluttery* around her, I thought it was like, I don't know. Heartburn, maybe? It was the first time I'd been attracted to anyone besides Daria's father, almost thirty years ago. And even that was, you know, kinda iffy for me since he ended up being such a fucking asshole."

I wrapped both hands around her forearm. "That's pretty

understandable, Mom. You loved him, and he left you to raise a kid all on your own."

She snorted. "His goddamn loss. I told him that I just *knew* you were going to be a girl and a real ass-kicker. Told him he should hang around and be your dad because it was going to be a lot of fun." She looked at Elena and cocked her thumb at me. "She *was* a lot of fun. And as far as I can tell, got 100% of my genes."

"I would never doubt that," Elena said.

My mom's eyes fell back to her hands. She plucked at the leather, hesitant again. "I didn't want you to be disappointed in me, Dar. For dating again. For...for falling in love."

Emotion swelled in my chest. "You're in *love*?" I blinked. "Wait, *disappointed*? Why? Mom, I—"

"Because this dating stuff's not really your thing," she explained. "We used to bond all the time about being single, and I loved that. I'm so proud of you for what you learned after Jackson, and for your show and how you talk to people about loving themselves first. That's important work. It's who you *are*. I didn't want you to think I was a sellout."

I sat back, a cold clamminess breaking out over my skin. I hated that my own mother thought I wouldn't support her falling in love because I'd spent so many years dismissing it.

But it was true—very awkwardly true—that ever since Jackson left, I'd been surrounded by people also relearning how to love themselves. Like everyone I met through my blog and then *Choosing Yourself*. Or I was surrounded by women like Elena, Janis and my mom—they'd worked hard to cultivate their independence above all else.

It was only when I first met Theo—and then, later, when I was listening with him as he took calls—that it became harder to dismiss these stories. Because it meant I was dismissing *people* and I'd never, ever set out to do that.

Was I really that *unyielding*?

I wrapped my arms around her neck and pressed my face

to her shoulder the way I used to do when I was a kid. After a second, she hugged me back and patted my hair.

"It's not possible for *the* Magnolia Stone to sell out," I said firmly. "I don't care what you do. I *do* want to hear more about how you feel for Martha and when we're going to get to spend more time with her, as long as that's okay with you."

The smile that blazed across my mother's face was her real smile. That shit-eating, life's-too-short, I-don't-give-a-fuck smile that had carried me through some of the worst moments of my life. "Hell, I already started a calendar of fun stuff we could all do together."

Elena propped her chin in her hand. "Martha's basically an honorary member of K-SUN already. You should take her to Janis's roller rink birthday party."

The blush on my mother's face deepened. "I did ask her, and she already said yes."

I nudged my mom's knee with mine. "So, the flutters. It wasn't heartburn, huh?"

"Sure wasn't," she said. "All I knew was that I thought about her nonstop. And wanted to be with her all the time. And I love all the interesting, funny things she says. She's... she's very beautiful."

Theo's hushed, intense words from the other night rippled through my thoughts and sent a fizzing heat coursing through my limbs: *how could I ever get enough of what we have here?*

"You know, Dar, what's funny is that I've basically dated myself for thirty years now," she said. "I loved it. Wouldn't trade that time for anything. I know myself, I respect myself and I trust my instincts. That's why when I started having feelings for Martha, I knew to pay attention. Because I'd never experienced anything like it before. If I hadn't spent all that time listening in here"—she paused, tapped her temple—"I would have missed it."

I reached forward and squeezed her hand. "Oh, Mom. I'm so happy for you."

She cast a curious look over at Elena. "I'm not super sure what this means for my sexuality."

Elena squeezed my mom's other hand. "We get to spend our entire lives learning new things about our identity and sexuality. It means you can take it at your own speed, Mags. You know what I mean?"

My mom cleared her throat. "Yeah. Think I do."

I threw my arms around her again. "Can we *please* finally get dinner? You've bailed on me three times in the last three weeks, and now I want to hear about all the dates you and Martha went on."

She *whooped* and clapped her hands together. "Alright, then. It's two-dollar hot dog night at Shady Sandy's so…"

I shoved one of the bags into her hands. "If you carry all these wigs, I can buy us the hot dogs."

Elena very gently placed the hot pink wig on my head, sending another shower of glitter all over my body. "New plan. You wear this the entire night, and I'll buy you both dinner."

My mom clicked her tongue. "You can't get a better deal than that." We stood up, gathering our things, and she bumped my hip with hers. "I listened to your and Theo's broadcast this morning after I finished my set. You're starting to sound good together. Told ya he's just a big softie."

In the moment, I could only remember the unexpected affection he'd shown that night in his office—his lips on my temple, fingers in my hair, the way he'd carried me to the couch with ease. He'd kissed the inside of my wrist as if the act was *sacred* to him, then gazed into my eyes like he was literally starstruck.

Bouquets and Hallmark cards didn't do it for me and probably never would. But Theo tenderly brushing the hair

219

from my forehead with a shy, crooked grin made my entire body feel like liquid gold.

If I hadn't spent all that time listening in here, I would have missed it.

"Yeah, he really is," I said, stumbling a little. "I guess you could say we're finding our groove."

My mom tossed her arm around my shoulders. "Whatever you're doing, it's working."

And as the three of us strolled down the bustling boardwalk toward the scent of hot dogs sizzling on a grill, all I could think about was the last chapter I'd written in my manuscript, the chapter I envisioned would tie up the themes of my essays in one tidy little bow. Declaring that I planned on being permanently single hadn't made me feel nervous or worried at the time. The opposite, in fact—it made me feel safe.

I still believed it was absurd to think I had a soul mate out there, wandering around and waiting for me to find them. Over the past fifteen months of hosting *Choosing Yourself*, I'd only met people who believed the same.

But I couldn't get Rachel, Ted and Skyler's brave love story out of my head. Couldn't stop thinking about Sami, who'd been burned before but remained curious about love. And now my mother, who embodied both independence and a fierce pride—and had stared at Martha like she hung the moon.

I was so used to thinking of romantic love as a direct *contradiction* to my values. But maybe 'contradiction' was too rigid a description for something so wonderfully vast and mysterious.

21

THEO

*D*aria had been right about the scenic overlook on this hike—I'd known it as soon as I crested the final hill and was able to take in the magnificent view in front of me.

After four miles straight up, following a well-worn trail that rose above the city, I finally stood at the top, beneath a fierce sun, and was instantly mesmerized.

The whole of the horizon opened in front of me—the rocky coastline trailed off to the right and there was a cluster of seals sunning themselves on a tiny outcropping. The sky was the same aquamarine color as the ocean. They melted into each other until it was impossible to tell where water ended and sky began.

It made me feel like a speck of dust in the face of grand, awe-inspiring nature. I had a sneaking suspicion that had been Daria's point, to lead me somewhere that could bowl me over with sheer beauty.

I'd sent her a picture from the top with a message that read *You were right about the view.*

But by the time I finally made it back to my car—another two hours later—the poetry of natural beauty had vanished, only to be replaced by a tired and sweaty hunger. I'd been alone with my thoughts for four and a half hours and everything inside my head felt tender and exposed. One block from my bungalow, I scrubbed a hand down my face and turned my car down the street, fantasizing about food and beer and a shower.

And Daria. And then Daria *in* the shower.

So by the time I was pulling into my driveway, dreaming of warm water cascading down Daria's naked body, I fully believed the sight of her blue Jeep parked in front of my house was a full-on mirage.

Except there she was, looking like a literal sight for sore eyes in a loose tank top, yoga pants and sandals, attempting to sneak down my front yard like a pretty bandit.

I climbed out of my car with a whistle and a smile, spinning my car keys around my finger.

Daria winced, shoving her sunglasses up into her dark hair. "I was trying to be mysterious."

"We're in broad daylight. The sun hasn't even set yet."

"Not all of my ideas are incredibly well-thought-out."

Behind her, nestled in front of my front door, was a white plastic bag. "Daria. Did you bring me a gift?"

"No."

I arched an eyebrow.

"Okay…yes. I did. But it's not a big deal."

I took a few steps closer, and her eyes fell to my lips. "What did you get me?"

"That hike is incredible but killer. Especially the first time. I thought you'd appreciate a chicken burrito from La Isla Bonita. Also some Gatorade and there's a packet of Tylenol." Her lips curved up. "And a cold beer."

A strand of hair blew across her face. I caught it, tucking it behind her ear. "This is the perfect gift. Some would even call it *romantic*."

Her throat worked. "I don't really think giving someone Tylenol is that romantic, but you're the expert."

I dipped down, nudged my nose against hers. She pressed onto her toes and kissed me—sweet at first, until she grabbed my shirt by the fistfuls and licked her tongue into my mouth. I let out a low groan of pure happiness, sliding my palms up and down her back as the kiss went deeper. And deeper.

Somewhere in the back of my head, I knew this public display was a legitimate risk—Theo Chadwick and Daria Stone couldn't be openly making out on a quiet side street in Sunrise Beach. But as with everything when it came to Daria, my own limits kept eroding by the second.

When we finally parted, I whispered, "Are you getting romantic ideas from cohosting our show?"

She laughed, dancing away when I tried to tug her back. "Keep it up, Chadwick, and that'll be the last gift you get from me."

I studied her loose, comfortable body language and the slight flush in her cheeks. We weren't at the studio. Or in a sound booth. Or even running through a paintball field. We were at my house, and I was suddenly desperate for her to stay.

I cocked my head toward the front door. "Can I convince you to sit out back with me for a few minutes? I should warn you I'll be inhaling a burrito while that's happening."

She held out her hands. "You're not even going to offer me half?"

I held up the bag as I pushed open my front door. "This was a gift, Daria."

I was grateful that I'd turned around at the last second. I had no control over how the sound of her delighted laughter made me feel and knew it was written all over my face. I once measured every interaction with Daria like the skirmishes they were, full of strategic victories and the occasional retreat.

Now a moment like this was the victory—her easy flirting and capricious smiles better than any other triumph.

Daria followed me inside as I flicked on lights in my small bungalow. I dropped the food onto the kitchen counter and planted a quick kiss on her cheek.

"Patio's out back, make yourself at home," I said. "I'll be right back."

Her eyes widened as she peeked around my house, fingers trailing down the wall. I heard her say, "Holy fucking *bookshelves*, Theo."

I smiled to myself. "I was in school for a very long time," I called over my shoulder. Once in my bedroom, I ditched my sweaty hiking clothes and pulled on clean ones, then strolled back into the kitchen to find her in my living room, staring up at my books and looking adorably astonished.

Every muscle in my body ached to go to her, to pull her into the shower and pick up where we'd left off in my office. But she'd openly admitted that sex was easier than whatever tenuous connection was hanging between us today.

I wanted to explore that connection—very, very badly.

I busied myself in the kitchen while she continued to pull out some of my old textbooks, flipping through them with a goofy grin, exclaiming when notes and stickies fell to the floor. "Sometimes I forget you were a social psychologist before you were a radio host."

I opened the beer and split it into two glasses. "I'm a better radio host than a psychologist, trust me."

"Is this vinyl collection all yours?" she asked.

"Janis's influence," I called back.

Her voice was muffled. "You've got a lot of non-psychology books too."

I stilled but then ducked my head around the door. "I was a big reader as a kid. Books and K-SUN helped me not to feel so lonely." At her questioning glance, I said, "It was just me when my parents divorced. They never thought to set up playdates or whatever when I was younger, and I didn't have siblings or close cousins. Things changed in high school and college, but until then..." I lifted a shoulder.

She stroked her finger down the spine of a well-worn novel and gazed back up at me. Whatever she was going to say was interrupted by me handing her a plate and a glass. She brightened, pushing to stand. "You *did* give me half of your burrito."

I stroked my knuckle up the front of her throat. Lifted her chin. "Of course. I could tell you wanted it."

"Am I that obvious when I want something?"

Our lips brushed together. "Not always. It would have been more obvious if you'd picked a pointless argument with the food first."

A mischievous smile spread across her face. She raised her middle finger between us, looking cute as hell. "I liked you better before you had all these jokes, Theo."

I grabbed her finger and kissed her hard on the mouth. "You like me better now."

She sauntered out toward the patio with swaying hips and a haughty smirk. I followed her eagerly, stepping into the sunny space with a relaxed contentment filling my limbs. We stretched out together on a long bench I'd built beneath a spray of pink, flowering branches and two palm trees. I spread my legs so that my feet bracketed her hips, while her legs fit easily between mine. We propped our plates of food and glasses of beer on the small glass table next to us.

Daria and I faced each other the way we had so many times for the past three, now almost four, months—first in various stand-offs and disagreements, and now through the intimacy of cohosting. It was different though. *We* were different.

I dropped my hand to her ankle and squeezed, stroking my thumb along her skin, and I felt a corresponding hum of electric pleasure spread through me. She tipped her head back to drag her fingers along the pink petals and I was happy to watch the play of light and shadow across her face through the palm leaves. Meanwhile, the sounds of birds, and my neighbors grilling, and people playing loud music in their cars filtered in and out.

"Did you know that gifts are considered one of the five love languages?" I asked.

She eyed me over her beer, but with less wariness, more sincere curiosity. "What are those again?"

"It's an interesting concept," I said, "and relates to both of our worldviews, believe it or not. It's about how people connect differently with one another, and not only through romantic love. One of the more popular languages is receiving a gift, as long as it's sincere. I tell listeners that giving sincere gifts carries the same weight."

She tilted her head. "The first night you brought me tea. Was that a...a love language thing?"

I hesitated. That impulse hadn't come from any analytical part of my brain. I'd only registered *need*—as in, Daria needed something and I wanted to be the one to fulfill that need, no matter how small.

"Yes, but I didn't think of it that way at the time. I wanted to get your attention, wanted to do something that you'd appreciate. Because I'd let three days go by after kissing you in that damn closet and I felt, quite literally, tongue-tied."

Her lips parted. "Oh," she said, breathless. "Even if that's not a love language, bringing someone tea after you've sexed each other up in paintball gear should be added to the list."

I squeezed her ankle. "I agree."

"What else is there?" she asked, pulling a piece of marinated chicken from her burrito and popping it into her mouth.

I indicated the patio. "Quality time. But not hanging out just to say you did. It's about giving someone your undivided attention. Listening, being sincere. Being open, that kind of thing."

She nodded, chewing slowly. "I like that one."

I made a mental note of her liking it, but it wasn't surprising—Daria had been betrayed on her wedding day, left by a person she was supposed to be able to trust. Her life was all about *showing up* now. Showing up for herself and for others with her undivided attention.

"And then there's words of affirmation," I said. I brought her hand to my mouth and kissed her palm. "That's something like...I'm grateful that you recommended I go on this hike today, to be alone with my thoughts and achieve something that was physically challenging. It was good advice. The right advice. When you first suggested it, I shut down and said no like an asshole and I'm sorry I did that when you were trying to connect with me."

A quiet understanding dawned on her face. "So what if I said something like...the night you told me you had feelings for me, regardless of all the risks, meant more than I can say. Because you were honest. Honest and brave. And I can't stop thinking about it. Do you feel affirmed?"

She'd ended with a sweet grin, but I still held her gaze and said, "Yes, I really do."

Daria bit the tip of her thumb, still smiling. "I like this."

She was so beautiful, awash in sunlight, framed in flowers. As vulnerable as I'd ever seen her.

"I like you," I said quietly.

She set her plate down and shifted, crawling the length of the bench until she could touch my face and kiss me. I kept my hands at my sides, content to let her slide her palms up and down my chest, her lips warm and inviting. My willpower snapped a mere three seconds in. I curled my arms around her waist and pulled her close, letting my mouth roam slowly, sweetly down her neck.

"I like you too," she whispered back.

My body glowed with sensation like the summer sun above. At the same time, I was startled to discover that the euphoria filling my chest at Daria's whispered words was an entirely new feeling for me. I sat behind a mic every week and declared myself an expert, yet here I was realizing I'd been *lying* about everything that had ever come before this moment.

Daria's gentle *I like you too* was enough for me to understand that I, Dr. Theodore Chadwick, didn't know the first goddamn thing about falling in love.

22

THEO

*D*aria hummed under her breath as my lips reached her collarbone. "Is this one of the gifts?"

"It is." I nipped her neck. She gasped, swaying. "Physical touch is one of the more powerful love languages, in my humble opinion."

"Yeah, you would say that."

I pulled back, pinching her chin. "If my memory serves, you kissed me first, Daria."

"If *my* memory serves, you fucked me on your office desk."

I laughed, dragging her against me and kissing her hair. "You were right. I'm a scoundrel. But only when it comes to you."

She turned and settled comfortably on my lap. "What's number five, then?"

"Acts of service." I brushed the curls from her forehead. She turned her head and kissed my palm. "Actions over empty promises."

She bit her lower lip. "My husband-to-be not showing up on our wedding day is one of the more dramatic examples of empty promises. But he was always like that, and not to give him *too* much credit, but in a lot of ways, he was a victim of societal pressure to behave a certain way in relationships just like I was. We were young, he loved these flashy romantic gestures, and he loved how much his friends and family would say he was *such* a romantic guy. An old soul. But they were gestures absent any real sincerity, more performance than anything else. It's why it bothered me so much. I only wanted him to see me and love me for who I was, and not who he wanted me to be."

I hesitated over my response. We were two chess pieces on opposite sides of a board, inching closer and closer to the middle with every personal revelation.

"Sitting with you these past weeks, and hearing callers who have been betrayed, hurt, shamed." I swallowed hard. "Lied to and pressured. I never wanted to come off as naive on my show. Only hopeful. With some of the people we've talked to recently, I can see why it's been so important for you to point out how we prioritize romantic love over all other kinds. It's not only a fair criticism, it's warranted. A Hollywood-style happily-ever-after will garner more attention than anything else. That automatically leaves behind a lot of lives and stories that should be celebrated just as much."

Daria's eyes searched mine. Her fingers roamed across my forehead, shifting a strand of hair back into place. "Theo. You were right, the other day. I found out that my mom *is* seeing someone. She's dating again after all these years of being against it like I was."

My eyebrows shot up. "You're serious? But I thought Magnolia Stone didn't give a good goddamn about any man?"

"It's not a man," Daria said with a smile. "Do you remember Martha Rosales, from The Rivera Center?"

"I do. Come to think of it, they did seem to become friends during that time. That's who she's dating?"

"Yes, and it's *serious*. They've been singing karaoke duets together."

I sat up a little straighter and wrapped an arm across Daria's thighs to keep her close on my lap. "Then they're obviously getting married. Your mom doesn't just sing duets with anyone."

She grinned. "That's what I said. You know, I was shocked when I saw them together only because she'd been more adamant about her single status than I was. And she hadn't told me yet and we don't..." She paused. "We don't keep secrets from each other. Usually."

I heard the unspoken words hanging around that *usually*. Whatever was blossoming between the two of us was doing so in secret. We both had enough self-awareness to understand how that couldn't continue for much longer.

What came after that, however, was completely unpredictable. So I didn't poke at that *usually*, choosing instead to enjoy the simple comfort of Daria Stone curled up in my lap and her fingers idly playing with my hair.

She bit her lip, frowning. "My mom thought I'd be disappointed because she was 'selling out.' Her words. She thought I'd see her happy and clearly falling in love and be *mad*. What you said reminded me of how I felt in that moment, almost like the opposite of you. I never wanted to come off as *anti*-love on my show. Just critical of how shitty it can make us feel when we don't love ourselves too." She sniffed, her arm sliding around my neck. "A hell of a lot of people seem to think you and I know what we're talking about three nights a week. It still worries me."

I laughed, relieved. "I've been thinking about that a lot too."

"Any advice, Dr. Chadwick?"

"None whatsoever."

She stole my glass of beer and took a sip. "Well, you're no help."

"Now we sound like the trolls who comment on our Twitter posts."

Daria set the glass down and turned until she was fully facing me. "Say a girl wanted to know which of the, whatever, love languages you were into…how would she go about learning that?"

I bit back a smile. "She could ask. Many listeners would consider me to be an open book."

She rolled her lips together. A tiny bit of nervousness shone in her eyes, and that had my heart ricocheting against my rib cage. Daria carried herself with a bold confidence that had enthralled me from the beginning. Yet I couldn't deny that seeing this other side of her, this stumbling-through-something-new side, was just as captivating. Romance expert or not, I felt like I was stumbling around too.

"Okay," she finally said. "What are yours?"

I reached into her hair, rubbing a dark curl between my fingers. Tugged on it until some of the tension around her mouth disappeared, curving into a smile instead. "They all work for me in different ways. But if I had to choose the most meaningful…acts of service, same as you. Quality time. Spending time together, being there for another person, really listening to them and being accountable—that, to me, is love. And not only romantic but every single kind, in every single way. To me, a lot of what you talk about on your show is how to spend quality time with ourselves, to give our own inner worlds the undivided attention we deserve. I appreciate that about the advice you give."

"That's important for me to know," she said. "For the normal, cohosting type reasons. Not for anything else."

"Sure," I teased. "I also like knowing yours for typical cohosting type reasons."

We shared a grin that quickly turned goofy, but my heart still beat like a boomerang.

"So speaking of quality time with yourself…how was the

trail today? And congrats on making it to the top. It's not easy."

"It was brutal," I said.

She hummed in agreement.

"And...beautiful. I can see why it helped you."

"I started doing that trail when I moved home a few months ago. But I did something similar the first years after Jackson, when I needed to force myself to sit with my thoughts and rediscover my innermost wants and desires. I used to cry when I made it to the top. Out of, I don't know, sheer relief? Sitting with all these confusing thoughts and memories was truly terrible and then, later, enlightening." She tilted her head. "How about you?"

I pressed my head back against the wall. "I was young when my parents divorced, only five, and I spent most of my time at my dad's new house. His office was behind these heavy mahogany doors that were always locked. I would play in front of those doors or read. On the rare occasion that he'd come out, he'd stare at me like he forgot I existed and then bark at a nanny or babysitter to come scoop me up."

I pinched the bridge of my nose as a wave of old, familiar embarrassment washed over me. "I used to *beg* for these table scraps of his attention. Whatever he tossed me was never enough. But that was because I was a child my parents did not want. They were, they are, very wealthy and I was cared for in a material sense. I do find myself resisting—"

I paused, collecting my scattered thoughts. "Yes, *resisting* doing some of the internal work you talk about, like being alone with my own thoughts on a hiking trail. And that's because I was such a lonely kid, I mentally dig my heels in and try not to ever go back there. Does any of that make sense?"

Daria was utterly quiet. She nodded, blue eyes wide, hand wrapped tightly around mine.

"I was drawn to social psychology because I wanted to

233

understand why my parents' marriage fell apart. Why they weren't overflowing with unconditional love like the parents and guardians of my friends. They were chilly people. Before the divorce, there was so much fury and anger between them, but only at night when they thought I was sleeping. I could...I could *hear* it. Their shouting. Their hoarse screaming. Glasses breaking and doors slamming, it was..."

"Scary?" she offered.

I squeezed her hand. "Yes. I never saw that side of them during the day, except that only made me feel like I needed to tiptoe around and not wake up their anger. It was somehow worse being so hidden, like a figure in the shadows I was constantly waiting to jump out and startle me. Later, as I grew older, it only made me more interested in love. Studying it. Finding it, having it, marrying someone who felt it for me the way I felt it for them. It seemed like the antidote to how I was raised."

She stroked the hair at my temple. "I'm so sorry that happened to you. I'm so sorry that all came up for you today on the trail."

I took a deep breath and was surprised to find it easier than before. "You know, it's the unburdening, like we talked about. It feels good to say it out in the open. I never—"

I stopped, a glaring truth making itself obvious. Between the long hike and Daria's calming presence, it must have been waiting for the right time to pounce.

"In all my past relationships, I never went into that much detail about my life growing up. My girlfriends knew I had parents I wasn't close with but that was..." I rubbed the crease in my brow. "That was all."

"Were you worried if you were too vulnerable, they would leave you like your parents?"

I shook my head. "My parents didn't do that."

"I guess I meant, like, emotionally. Sounds like they abandoned you. Left you to your own devices, which isn't very fun for a kid."

This revelation settled over me like a wool coat—warm and heavy but itchy at the edges. "Yeah," I said, rubbing that same crease in my brow. "I guess...yes, they did leave me. And I shouldn't have been so worried. All those girlfriends left me in the end anyway."

"It fucking sucks."

I breathed out a laugh, surprised. "It did suck."

"That's basically the theme of my show. Love sucks."

I was still laughing, pulling her tight to my chest and wrapping my arm around her legs. "I *know*. That's why your show is bad for my business."

"Says an absolute *scoundrel*."

I tugged the edge of her ear between my teeth and growled. "Scoundrels can believe in love."

"They can't. They can only tempt highbrow, well-bred ladies into drawing rooms so they can ravish them during parties."

"Daria," I drawled, kissing her neck again, "you ravished me on my *office couch*. The tempting seductress in this story is you."

She straddled me with a look of pure mischief. Brushing her lips over mine, she said, "I brought you a *gift* and it was kind of a big deal, if you'll recall. This unfair treatment is uncalled for."

My hands skated up her sides. "Ah, so you admit it after all."

She was mid-eye roll when her phone rang. Daria sighed and checked the screen, wrinkling her nose at whatever she saw there. "I have to go. I'm meeting Elena to try some gourmet party food recipes for Janis's party."

"Fancy nachos?"

"The fanciest," she said. She touched my hair again and kissed me sweetly—so sweetly it made me ache in entirely different ways than before. "What we talked about, everything you said, that's a lot to share and then be alone. Do you want to come with me? Or do you want me to come back later and keep you company?"

I was already shaking my head. "No, I'm good. Strange as this sounds, I think I'd like to keep being on my own for the rest of the night, maybe think about some of the stuff we talked about. Although I want to see you again soon. Very soon. Immediately, if possible."

She blushed. "Um…yes, yeah. I'd like that. There's this radio station thing on Wednesday night. Just a bunch of cool people hanging out and playing pinball or whatever. You can tag along if you want?"

I pushed forward a little, catching Daria before she fell back and wrapping her legs around my waist. I stood up, taking her with me and walked us backward into the house, wearing an arrogant smile. "So the trash talk before we compete in front of all of our listeners is already starting, huh?"

"I can't trash talk you if I know I'm gonna win," she said, tightening her knees around my hips. "These are facts, baby."

I pressed her gently against the first wall we came to. I nuzzled up and down her neck, enjoying the delicious weight of her ass in my palms and the glorious way I fit between her legs. "Cocky girl and a smart fucking mouth," I whispered at her ear. "What am I going to do with you?"

She scratched her nails along the base of my scalp, making my skin shiver. "I don't know, Theo. Maybe you could humbly concede defeat on Wednesday night?"

"Not a chance in hell," I said with a smirk. "But don't worry. When you lose, I'll make it up to you."

"Would you call that an act of service?"

I chuckled, brushed my lips through her hair. We were no longer sitting beneath the sun, yet everything around me felt golden. I carefully set Daria down at the front door, but not before kissing her so hard, and for so long, she was out of breath when I finally let her go.

Her eyes fluttered open, and I made sure to hold her gaze as I said, "Thank you for today. For the gift. For your time. For listening."

"Thank you for trusting me," she said back.

I leaned in the doorway and watched her climb into her Jeep, crank her music up high and roar off down the road. While I was learning I didn't know a goddamn thing about love, I did know a thing or two about hope. Could recognize its buoyancy in the center of my chest, could recognize I was starting to feel it every time Daria was near, and even when she wasn't.

The odds were stacked against us in every conceivable way. It made this hope all the more appealing.

It made this hope all the more dangerous too.

23

DARIA

*J*anis and I stood outside of Sunrise Beach's most famous arcade, *Retro City*. And though we were both animated in the moment, it was for entirely different reasons.

Janis was sitting on top of a picnic table, eating a paper basket of standard boardwalk nachos with an enthusiasm I'd only ever seen from people being informed they'd won a huge monetary prize.

Meanwhile, I was leaning back against the wall in an attempt at effortless cool. This was a ridiculous endeavor— Theo was due in a minute and the cheerleading squad that had taken up residence around my heart was undertaking a floor routine.

Above my head hung a pink-and-yellow arrow, lit with bulbs, that connected to a neon sign blazing *Retro City*. Music pulsed through the glass doors, and inside, people's voices rose and fell, mingling with the jangling melodies of the games.

The owners were long-time fans and devoted to the station, and had offered us the entire space for free tonight. K-SUN hadn't had a true community event in over a year.

I peeked over my shoulder and caught a quick glimpse of the crowd inside. In the middle was a hastily put-together dance floor where my mother was tonight's DJ. I recognized her exuberant dance moves as *her* version of air guitar, smiling when she called one of the dancers over to air guitar with her.

The other dancer was, of course, Martha, looking as flushed and happy as my mom. I caught Elena's eye by the air hockey table and cocked my head toward the lovebirds. Elena's hand flew to her mouth at the sight of them, the other pressing to her chest. To me, she mouthed something like *too fucking cute*.

She was right—they were too fucking cute.

What appeared to be a small group of listeners noticed me peeking and burst into motion—waving, pulling out cell phones, nudging each other with looks of excitement. I hadn't thought it possible, but it was undeniably true. The tickets sold out. The place was *packed*. And to hear Janis tell it, it was because they wanted to see me and Theo.

I turned my head toward Janis, who was licking bright yellow cheese sauce from her fingers. She winked at me. "You look nervous, kid."

I hooked a thumb over my shoulder. "That's a lot of people in there. When you started talking about wanting to get me and Theo out in the community, hosting these competition nights, I had no idea it would end up as popular as *this*."

Her eyes twinkled with mischief. "Have you talked to Des yet? The team is working on the details for next week's pledge drive, and he said you and Theo have been requested to use your star power for good. Tickets for the mini-golf night Des is planning are selling like hotcakes, and he thought you could give a few tickets away on-air during the drive. Turns out you and Theo are pretty popular together. Who the hell knew?" She gave a little wave like she was the goddamn Queen. "Wait. I did. I knew."

I sized her up and down. "Theo told me that any time someone admits that you were right about one of your completely fucking bonkers ideas, your power grows exponentially or something."

Janis paused to consider this. "Theo is right." She set her basket down and dropped her elbows to her knees. "I didn't place you for a person with stage fright."

I peered up at the surrounding palm trees, the leaves a dark green against the pale blue sky. "I still feel the pressure sometimes. Or all the time. I knew my blog was popular, but it was hard for me to really *feel* the volume of readers the way I felt the surge of listeners immediately after I launched my talk show at K-ROX. A following this size feels… unwieldy. And unearned, in some ways."

She shrugged. "You started talking about something a lot of people don't and that's why they responded to you so quickly. There was an open space that you walked right into. Made people feel seen, and that shit's contagious."

I glanced back over my shoulder at the people inside. "Every day I'm like…is today the day they all realize I've been faking it this whole time?"

She laughed. "You and everyone else on this planet. Dar, your *only job* when you're behind that mic is to be true to yourself. No one else's opinion matters because no one else has the unique worldview, personality and life experience that, combined, makes you such a great radio host. No one else can say they're Daria Magnolia Stone, and that's why, when I found out that K-ROX had let you go, I moved to hire you so quickly." Janis set her hand in the middle of her chest. "I knew it in here."

I softened. "In your heart?"

Janis frowned. "No, I meant in this great set of tits I have."

"*Aw*." I sighed.

She tossed the empty nacho basket into the trash can and stood, brushing the crumbs from her hands. "You were always a rock star, Daria. And Theo is too. When I realized that shit was going to hit the fan, budget-wise, I thought of you two immediately. Knew that combined, your rock star powers had the potential to get people excited about K-SUN again. As long as you stopped fighting over every little thing." She cocked her head at the very full arcade behind us. "You stopped fighting and look what happened."

I want to see you again soon. Very soon. Immediately, if possible.

"Yep," I said weakly. "Just had to figure our shit out."

Her phone rang and she scowled down at the disruption. "I'll be right back. It's the board."

"'K," I called after her, feeling a flutter of unease, but I turned back just in time to see Theo approach. My stomach dipped and spun like the old wooden rollercoaster he was walking past on the boardwalk to get to me. But then my eyes met his forest-green ones, and those full lips curved into a charming grin, and I had to brace myself against the wall.

Two days ago, I'd showed up at Theo's house with food and beer because I remembered the mental and physical toll that hike used to take on me, and I couldn't resist the urge to *do something* for him. But then Theo had arrived, managing to look devastatingly handsome even after hiking eight miles on a summer day. And he'd been so adorably pleased by me, so goddamn *cute* about everything, I followed him inside his house with barely a second thought.

Once again, I found myself navigating the same conflicting crossroads—how was it possible that I felt like my authentic self around Theo when the feelings he awoke in me were so wildly different from what I swore I wanted?

The only solution I had was temporary—follow the instincts I'd worked so hard to trust again. Those instincts went up into a full cheer whenever I even *thought* about the man striding toward me right now.

Behind the glass doors, I could hear the laughter and music of the community who'd come out today to support us, who were devoted listeners of our show, who called in to share vulnerable truths so that others might feel seen and heard.

I wanted to do right by them, *needed* to do right by them. My one, desperate hope was that the huge risk Theo and I were taking by dating in secret wouldn't ruin the tenuous success K-SUN needed right now.

Theo closed the remaining distance, and my body hummed with a bright happiness. I saw him take note of Janis nearby, but clearly distracted on her phone. Still, I watched his jaw tighten and his hands slip into his pockets, his posture turning more rigid.

"You're here early, Ms. Stone."

"I am," I murmured. "Smart fucking mouth and all."

He rubbed a hand across his jaw, drawing my attention to his tan forearms, the dusting of golden hair there. "I'll be spending this entire evening wanting to kiss that mouth but being unable to. Maybe I could make that up to you later?"

I clicked my tongue. "I see more acts of service in your future, Dr. Chadwick."

His laughter was deep and gravelly at the edges. My core tightened at my last memory of Theo servicing me, how possessive he looked as his mouth roamed down my body. His firm, heavy hands pressing my knees open, his skillful tongue swiping through my sex, tasting all of me. *Sweet Christ, why did we fight this for so long?*

Janis ended her phone call and marched over to us. Theo straightened up further, pulling his shoulders back and giving his mentor a tight smile. "That didn't look like good news," he said grimly.

"When does a member of our board ever call me with

good news?" she said. "But there are more important things going on than revenue reports. And that's asking if you're prepared to lose mightily to Daria today?"

His lips twitched at the ends. "What's the basis for these assumptions?"

"All the polls Elena ran this morning online," Janis said. "The listeners do not think you have what it takes to win, I'm afraid."

I tossed Theo my haughtiest smile. His answering grin was just as smug. "As both my mentor *and* boss, your confidence in my abilities has been an inspiration. I'd say *thank you* for believing in me, but the words *thank you* seem almost trite."

She clapped him on the arm. "You chose the wrong mentor, kid. And don't be such a smart-ass."

Theo squeezed Janis around the shoulders in a rare display of affection between the two of them. But it made sense once he said, "What's going on with the buyout threat?"

She frowned out over the boardwalk, toward the ocean. "The money stuff is really not great. Next week's pledge drive, however, should help. As will all of these great ticket sales. And I don't know how much Des and Elena have gone into the numbers with you, but the show is really taking off. I've been getting *nice* emails from our ad sponsors, and that's saying something."

He rocked back on his heels to peek through the doors —I saw his look of genuine amusement at the crowd in there, though there were lines of tension bracketing his mouth.

"That is excellent news," Theo managed. "And unexpected, to say the least."

Janis reached forward to grab the door handle. "I'm more worried than I've been in years, though I'm real proud of how every person at the station has offered up all kinds of creative solutions. That's what keeps me going every day and helps me sleep at night. *That's* what these big, money-hungry corporations lack. Creativity. Imagination."

She pulled open the door. "They only have power because they've bought it, but in my experience it's *never* as powerful as what we have. And that's a whole bunch of weirdos willing to play Skee-Ball together because they love this town and this radio station. People are more powerful than profit in the end. Now let's go have some fucking *fun*."

Theo took the door from her and nodded for me to follow. But not before we shared a look that was more emotional than our easy flirting a few minutes ago.

His vulnerability on Monday had left me shaken with a fierce urge to protect him at all costs. And given me a much more intimate understanding of the way he'd been abandoned by the two people meant to love him the most.

I used to beg for these table scraps of his attention. Whatever he tossed me was never enough. But that was because I was a child my parents did not want.

We weren't only risking our blossoming careers and professional reputations. We were risking what Janis had correctly identified as the most important thing in this world —our people. Our community. For Theo, K-SUN was his family as much as it was mine.

I released a shaky breath, and the moment passed. Theo's smile turned completely wicked. He tossed me a wink that could have been seen by *anyone*.

My body didn't care. I felt my heart skip, dance and *twirl*.

And as I stepped into an arcade room filled to the brim with excited fans, I suddenly had more in common with Theo's infatuated listeners than my own.

24

THEO

I followed Daria inside the *Retro City* arcade room and was happily stunned—though not surprised—at the number of people there for a night of food, music and vintage games. Janis wasn't lying. Our listeners showed up when we asked for help.

The fact that they were all here because they loved my show with Daria, however, was humbling on another level.

In the far corner, I spotted Mags, a stereo setup and a small dance floor with people already dancing. There was a makeshift bar and boardwalk snacks. And the room itself was full of games, from Skee-Ball to Pac-Man. There was an intensity to the energy, but a good kind—brought on by the easygoing crowd, the jangly game sounds, the machines spilling long reams of tickets onto the floor.

It should have been impossible to feel a crush of nostalgia at the scene in front of me. That would imply that my child-hood was full of memories like this when the exact opposite was true. But the nostalgia *was* there, a bittersweet ache curled up in my chest that made me think of those first sweet days of summer vacation as a kid.

I suspected these heady sensations were a side effect of

being with Daria, who was currently flashing a pretty smile and shaking an excited fan's hand. I'd continued taking her advice since the hike on Monday. Like she'd suggested to countless listeners these past weeks, I didn't have to do anything dramatic. I'd gone on a few meandering walks. Went down to the beach to see the sunset two nights in a row, watching every wave and appreciating the inevitability of each white-foamed crest.

I let my thoughts spread out without distraction. Chased down a few memories I typically avoided. That's where I discovered my anger. It wasn't particularly dramatic. It was just *there*, a part of who I was, an ambient noise like the sound of a ceiling fan on a hot day.

Daria's astute observation had shaken loose this emotion. My parents *had* left me. Not physically, but emotionally, stripping my formative years of affection and love. Abandoning me so they could have horrible arguments at night and ignore me during the day.

I'd buried this anger in academic study and a cool acceptance. Until midway through last night's sunset, when one of those wayward memories bumped hard against this core of quiet animosity, and I'd walked home *seething*.

For the second time in as many weeks, I had to admit that Stormi was right to accuse me of being more concerned with romantic symbolism than substance. No wonder my partners had all felt like I was constantly swooping in with boxes of chocolates to *fix it*. I didn't even let myself acknowledge my own tough and complicated memories, let alone the tough and complicated parts of being in a relationship.

To use Daria's vernacular, I'd chosen myself for a few days, allowed moments of quiet instead of noise and distraction, and had happened upon something important.

Daria turned in the crowd, searching for me as if she could sense I'd been thinking about her. Her smile was a cautious flicker, and I understood the attempt at restraint.

We *barely* kept our interactions professional at the height of our hostility. Now the energy between us burned white-hot with a different kind of passion, and it was straining the absolute limits of proper behavior.

I started to move toward her in the crowd and saw groups of fans peek over at me. I angled my body toward them, raising my hand in a wave. But instead, Des swooped in, wrapping me in a hug and clapping me on the back.

"You finally made it out to the arcade," he said. "Be honest. Did I talk it up too much? Get your expectations too high? When my dad and I used to come here to play the air hockey table every Saturday, I *was* in sixth grade and things can seem cooler then."

I shook my head. "Not at all. In fact, I don't think you talked it up *enough*."

He laughed with a hand on his chest. "I'll ask my cousins if we should switch from paintball to Pac-Man every Thanksgiving."

I nudged his elbow with mine. "Des, what you did here, all these people, selling out the tickets…it's incredible."

"I'll take the compliment because I'm one hell of an event organizer, but the star power is all you and Daria. Elena and I had to start asking some of the assistants from other departments to help us field the inbox we set up because you're getting so much fan email. And that's not counting the questions filling up the voicemail and every one of our social media sites. If it keeps going like this, we'll have to create a new system because we're almost at the limit of our people power to handle it."

Goosebumps rose on the back of my neck. "It's really that intense? I know we've been overwhelmed this past week but I guess I thought it was a bit of a fluke."

He took a swig from his beer. Shrugged. "At this point, I'd call that fluke a pattern." He squeezed my shoulder with a sympathetic gleam in his eye and lowered his voice slightly.

247

"Your separate shows were already incredibly popular. So please don't take this the wrong way, but there's something about the two of you together that's resonating with this audience. I mean, now that you're not biting each other's head off every other sentence."

A floaty, out-of-body sensation spiraled through my veins. Janis was right. I had been safe and too comfortable in my show for too long, because even though I had a large and devoted fan following, it was nothing like the keyed-up, crowd-before-a-concert vibe in this room.

And we'd certainly never had to bring in people from other departments just to sort listener emails.

This was the popularity I'd been seeking, the kind that all-but-guaranteed national syndication if the timing was right. And this surge in popularity was coinciding with my attraction to Daria which, like our show, was also increasing at a surprising rate every single day.

"Why..." I cleared my throat. "Why do you think that is? I'm not complaining, merely curious."

He rubbed his hand through his hair, gazing around all the people in the room with satisfaction. "What makes you and Daria so popular is that you're firm in your convictions. I think Daria makes *you* better at giving advice because you have to be more thoughtful and hear her perspective. But I think the same is true for her. I don't mean to sound too much like Janis, but that kind of on-air charisma is what we call *damn fine radio.*"

There wasn't a single word to describe the riot of emotion fizzing through my nervous system. I agreed about our chemistry on-air—now that we weren't constantly on edge around each other, our shows were fun and laid back while also engaging. I'd find myself chewing over something Daria had said for days, studying how her opinion slotted neatly into mine. Studying how it didn't but not in a way that was bad.

That was the good part of this emotional riot. The complicated part, the part where my nerve endings were in severe turmoil, was the whole *every time my cohost smiles at me, my heart tries to punch through my chest and I forget my own name* issue.

"This is hard to admit, given how often I described working with Daria as being a 'nightmare' and 'a disaster waiting to happen—'"

"I do *not* miss those days."

I grinned. "I was *wrong*. I'm having fun. A lot of fun. And not only because we're about to spend a night playing arcade games for our job."

Des shrugged good-naturedly. "I don't want to jump the gun, but at this rate Janis might try and convince you both to keep working together past the budget crisis."

I knew this was where the conversation was going. Knew it because it was physically impossible for Janis Hill to be subtle, and she'd been raving about us ever since that paintball interview.

Even still, I stumbled out, "Uh…why? Really?"

"You're getting along and all of *this*"—he indicated the crowd around us—"is happening because of it. I can't think of a reason why not."

My gaze landed on Daria's face in the crowd. Mags had joined her—they were both chatting animatedly with a few fans. Daria's black hair shone beneath the reflection of multi-colored lights, her teeth flashing as she smiled.

"Theo, are you okay?" Des asked. And when I turned at his voice, it was obvious that while I'd been watching Daria, he'd been watching me. It wasn't a critical look. Yet. But it was the kind of curious look only a best friend can give you, like they're this-close to sniffing out all that you've been keeping from them.

For the first time ever, I'd been keeping a lot from everyone.

I plastered a smile on my face. "I'm spacing out due to competition nerves. Janis told me the internet is predicting I'll lose across the board, and it's getting in my head. If it comes true, Daria will never let me live it down in the most annoying way possible."

He relaxed and pointed up to a large scoreboard I hadn't noticed when I came in. The staff must have let the station commandeer it for tonight's shenanigans. In white block letters, it said, *THEO VS. DARIA* with two big zeroes beneath our names.

"Don't tell Daria, but I know you're gonna win," he said. He bent back and cupped his hands around his mouth to yell, *"Welcome to K-SUN game night!"*

The crowd clapped and cheered. I rubbed the back of my neck, my eyes connecting with Daria's. She assessed me with an imperious look and mouthed *get ready to lose, Chadwick*.

Cocky girl. Smart mouth.

We hadn't even begun, and I was already a goner for her.

THEO

*D*es was quick to get us moving to our first game—the aptly titled Super Shot.

About half the crowd was off playing arcade games or hanging at the makeshift bar. But there was a core group of fans who eagerly followed as Des pushed Daria and me by the shoulders to stand in front of the two basketball nets, handing us each a ball.

"I'm sure you're familiar with the Super Shot," he said, "or as every kid knows it…arcade hoops."

The crowd's raucous cheer at this game had me smiling in response—something about the shared experience of arcade nights on this very boardwalk, the iconic symbol of Sunrise Beach that could never really be taken from us, no matter how many tourists came through. It hadn't been part of my childhood, but I felt grounded in this moment just the same.

Daria lightly tapped my ball with hers and winked. And I felt grounded again.

"When the buzzer goes off, you'll both have two minutes to make as many baskets as you can," Des continued. "The host with the most, wins. Then we'll move on to the next one. Our first set of games tonight is more of a rapid-fire round to test Theo and Daria's reflexes. And on that note, I'll be right back. Oh, and this whole next part is a surprise."

My head turned at the phrase *this whole next part is a surprise*, but Daria hooked her arm around the side of the game and smirked, pursing her dark red lips. "It's not too late to humbly concede defeat. You can tell the listeners now if you want. Might be a better look than, you know, begging me for mercy later."

I raised an eyebrow and lowered my voice so only she could hear me. "You still think you can handle me, Daria Stone?"

She gave my body another one of those lazy perusals. My fingers tightened on the ball. "You should know by now that I absolutely can."

The arcade game in front of us wasn't the only one we were playing tonight, and she knew it too. I was surrounded by loud, cheering people and flashing lights, and Daria was *still* the only thing I could think about. The way her nails felt, dragging down my side. Her fingers hooking and tugging down my clothing. Her hot breath feathering along my skin, her tongue, sliding—

"And I am *back*," Des said. He had his arm extended to introduce a listener. She was tall, about our age, and had long blond hair tied back from her face. She wore the board-shorts-and-sandals combo that was essentially the Sunrise Beach uniform. A bright smile slashed across her face when she saw us.

"So *this* is Misty and she's a K-SUN member," Des said.

I reached forward to shake her hand. "Theo Chadwick. It's nice to meet you."

Daria did the same. "Hey, I'm Daria. Thanks for coming out tonight for our K-SUN game night."

Misty bobbed her head. "I'm a huge fan of you both. *Huge.* I started off listening to Theo's show religiously, then when Daria joined the station and I started tuning in, I got totally,

totally freaking obsessed." She clapped her hands together. "So you can imagine how excited I was when Des informed me that I'd won the contest to ask for your advice, in person."

Des leaned forward. "That was the surprise. Are you up for it?"

I glanced over at Daria, who gave an affable shrug.

"Hell yeah," she said. "I'm only, like, four thousand percent more nervous because we're not in the anonymous safety of our sound booth. What could possibly go wrong?"

Des and Misty shared a conspiratorial look. "The hook is...you'll be answering Misty's question *while* playing."

I laughed behind my hand. "Whose idea was this? Janis?"

"All mine, actually," Des said. "You two are experts on giving advice, on-air, in public, with very little prep ahead of time. So I thought...wouldn't it be even more fun to have them do it spontaneously and while playing games?"

"Oh shit," I said, still laughing. "Also, we can curse since we're not on the air. Which means I can tell our illustrious program director, Desmond Davis, that he's a pain in the ass."

He squeezed my shoulders and turned me back toward the game. "You'll love it, I promise. And Daria, the internet odds are in your favor tonight, so I'm letting you go first. You and Theo are free to answer back and forth regardless of who's playing."

Daria waved Misty over with a warm smile. "We're doing this for K-SUN, right?"

The small crowd behind us applauded as people jostled into closer positions surrounding us. Des raised his hand in the air, and Mags cut the music. Though the room was still full of noise, it was considerably easier now to hear Daria and me lightning-round Misty's question about love while aiming for a basket.

"Misty, babe, what's the topic of your question?" Daria asked, twisting the ball between her hands.

"I want to ask about soul mates," she said cheerfully.

Daria stilled, eyes darting to mine. Three weeks ago, this topic would have been fertile ground for an argument. There was a weighty pause between Misty's response and Daria's answer, but a glimmer of a smile appeared on her face.

"Misty, you are bringing the heat tonight."

Misty pressed her lips together and nodded. "I could use some advice from my favorite radio hosts."

Daria touched her arm gently. "If our answers come out sounding totally fucking bananas because we're trying to beat each other at basketball, I promise we'll give you a better one before the end of the night."

"That sounds good," Misty said. She turned to Des. "I think they're ready."

"Ask your question and then the buzzer will sound for Daria," Des said.

She took a steadying breath. "For most of my life, I've believed there is one person out there, waiting to find me or for me to find them. I've dated lots of people, but it never seems to work out and I'm starting to worry that I keep getting older and it keeps getting harder to find the one. But this past year, I let go of that idea. I started dating more casually. If it wasn't a good match, I didn't get so worked up about it."

She shrugged. "And there's this guy, we've always been friends, and now we're dating. We have a good time, and he makes me laugh. But sometimes I get so *terrified*. What if I'm so busy messing around that I miss my chance? Should I stick with the guy I'm seeing? Or should we break up so I can be more serious about finding my soul mate?"

Daria and I locked eyes again, but her gaze lacked the wariness that was usually there before an argument. She looked a little intrigued, a little flirtatious, a *lot* amused.

I rolled my shoulders back and straightened my glasses,

realizing that we just weren't the same people we were three weeks ago, bickering on-air over every question.

It was almost as if we were made to host a show on love together.

I tipped my head toward Misty. "I'll let my cohost speak first since she's up at the basket."

"I'll gladly take the lead," she boasted. "Des, you can start the countdown clock. I'm rea—"

The buzzer went off and Daria cursed. Her first throw missed the basket entirely but her next two went in solidly with a *swish*. She aimed a smug grin my way before tossing the basketball again.

She missed.

"Fuck," she said, laughing. "Anyway, so Misty," she began, keeping up a steady stream of movement, "if you're enjoying this friend of yours and he makes you laugh, I don't see any problem here whatsoever. I want to say *who cares* but I don't mean that in a snarky kind of way. I mean literally: who cares?"

Her next three throws sailed right in: *swish, swish, swish*. There was a smattering of applause, and Daria's eyes were a bright, dazzling blue. "Life's too short to put a bunch of labels and restrictions on what's bringing you joy. Sounds like you found this person who makes you laugh after you stopped worrying so much about this soul mate stuff, and that, to me, says you don't need it."

"Wait, don't need a soul mate?" Misty asked.

Daria missed two baskets but made the next two, with thirty seconds still on her buzzer.

"I'm not saying"—*swish, swish*— "it's this binary, yes or no. But our culture tells us to ignore developing a healthy relationship with ourselves in order to focus on this"—*swish, swish*— "concept of a soul mate that I think is really harmful." Daria was just slightly out of breath now. "We're told that we need to fall in love someday to discover true happiness."

The buzzer beeped a ten-second warning. Flustered, she shot baskets as fast as she could, most of them going wild, while her laughter spilled over. I hid a smile behind my hand, captivated by her breathless charm. She threw her hands up in victory as the buzzer rang out and gave a cheesy bow to the crowd. Panting, she faced Misty.

"It's this false narrative that happiness is a highly guarded secret that only married people get to know. And the key to that happiness is finding a mysterious soul mate, who's out there wandering the planet." Daria shrugged. "Whether you decide to keep dating this guy or not, it's worth thinking about if you believe finding this person will magically make your life better. Or if you've been the magic all along."

Misty cocked her head with a thoughtful expression, and Daria tossed me the basketball. She blew the hair from her eyes and said, "Score is twenty-four, Chadwick. Think you can beat it?"

Chuckling under my breath, I brushed past her and murmured, "Watch me."

There was another round of cheers and clapping as I took my position. It had been years, of course, but some things really were like riding a bicycle. Des started the buzzer, putting two minutes back on the clock.

"And...*go*," he shouted.

My first shot sailed into the basket with a whisper and the audience cheered. I couldn't help but smile, rolling out my neck and tossing in three more, back-to-back, while getting my thoughts about Misty's question in order.

From a macro perspective, I agreed with Daria's answer. It was the personal perspective that had me hyper-focusing on the feel of the ball beneath my fingers to keep them from shaking.

I knew what was right for me, and that *was* the labels, the commitment, the soul mate. I could be patient, especially since the more Daria and I stumbled through our disagreements, the more trust we built. Despite our conversation around love languages and what she appreciated, it was glaringly obvious to me that she valued *trust* above all else.

I wanted her to trust me. I also wanted to believe that, with time, she'd want the same kind of long-term commitment that I did. It was too easy to forget her strong, anti-marriage stance when it was just the two of us, kissing on a bench under the sun, without a single sliver of reality getting in our way.

"Okay, Misty," I said, holding the ball in front of my face, "this isn't going to surprise you, but I'm a huge believer in soul mates. While I agree with a lot of what Daria said, if *you're* serious about it, I think it's time to move on from your friend."

One eye on the clock, one eye on the basket, I made the next two shots with more applause. I could feel the weight of Daria's attention on my skin, but knew if I chanced a glance, I'd lose my advantage.

"He *really* makes me laugh though," Misty said.

Swish. Swish. Swish. I had thirty seconds left. "Then how do you know he's *not* the one you're supposed to be with?"

She wrinkled her nose. "I guess I thought it would feel more dramatic. More like fireworks, or this desperate need to see him all the time. Sometimes we go a week or two without hooking up. Wouldn't I need to be with him constantly if he *was* my soul mate?"

I made basket after basket as the clock ticked down, relying on muscle memory so I could stay focused on Misty. "That's pretty much up to you. Every person's identity and orientation is different, so if you like this person and you like the way it feels, stay. Relationships are unique ecosystems. What sustains yours will never be the same as what sustains another. *But—*"

There were two seconds left. I flung the ball up with one hand and it sank in as the buzzer sounded. "Only you and your friend have the authority to say that. If you don't like the way it feels, leave."

I looked up at the scoreboard and noted the points. Rubbing one hand across my jaw, I gave Daria the slowest, most self-satisfied grin I could manage. "What was that thing you were saying about humbly conceding defeat? Might want to try it since I just beat you by a whopping ten points."

Des was laughing. The crowd was clapping and bustling around us. Daria looked flirtatiously mutinous, eyes narrowed while she tried not to smile.

I cocked a thumb at the scoreboard again. "Well?"

"You did this before paintball too," she said. "What, do you and Des sneak in here on the weekends and play basketball nonstop?"

I lifted a shoulder. "More that I played actual basketball all through high school. I was on a team and everything."

She rolled her eyes. But I didn't miss the flare of appreciation across her face, the almost sultry toss of her hair. She gave a curtsy that was so sarcastic I burst out laughing. "Well done, sir. You managed to beat me *one time*."

Des came round and looped his arm around my shoulders. "I forgot to tell Daria that Theo was a minor basketball star back in high school."

Her jaw dropped. "You were *in on it*."

He shook his head with a grin. "Come on, everyone. We've got Theo with one victory so far, but we've still got two more games on this rapid-fire round."

"And Misty to help," Daria said, scooping up one of the smooth, wooden Skee-Balls and hefting it in her hand. "I feel like you've still got some questions about what you should do."

Misty closed one eye and pinched her fingers together. "A *little* bit."

"We got you," I promised, then turned to eye up the game in front of me. I wasn't totally in the dark—I'd played it a handful of times throughout my life, but the way Daria was swinging her arm back and forth, like she was loosening up on the pitcher's mound, had me slightly nervous.

Des tossed me my own ball and faced the crowd. I gave Misty a friendly smile and waved her closer. "Tell us the truth," I asked. "Was it too bananas, as Daria said? You're asking a thoughtful question with a lot of layers. We wouldn't want you not to get the thorough answer you're looking for."

She returned my smile. "The only reason I've got more I want to ask is because you both brought up so many valid points."

I arched an eyebrow at my cohost. "We've heard we have a tendency to do that sometimes."

"Or a lot of times," Misty said excitedly.

Des interrupted us. "Skee-Ball is fast so we can do a couple rounds. Best two out of three, okay?"

The balls came rumbling down the incline and a series of white lights lit up the ramp. Next to me, Daria wore a sexy half-grin that sent a similar zap of electricity racing up my spine. We were on the furthest thing possible from a date, but that didn't stop me from feeling a lighthearted pleasure that fixed a permanent smile on my face.

"How's your ego?" I whispered to Daria out the side of my mouth. "Bruised? Dented? Shattered?"

"*Kiss my ass,*" she whispered back.

I didn't respond verbally. I did, however, give her the same lazy perusal she'd given me earlier, lingering on the curve of her ass in tight, high-waisted jeans I fully intended to peel off later tonight.

And I considered Daria's bright red cheeks to be an additional victory.

"And...*go,*" Des said.

Our Skee-Balls hit the incline at the same time—Daria's

flying up and sinking into the ten circle while mine hit the fifty.

"I know a lucky break when I see one," Daria said.

"Really?" My next one hit the forty circle. "Because I can only see a sore loser."

We rolled twice more, getting into a groove, and paper tickets began snaking down onto the floor. "Okay, Misty," Daria said, "you wanted to dig deeper and we're here for it."

Misty was watching us play with a wide, sparkling smile. "Are soul mates real or fake?"

"Real," I said firmly, just as Daria said, "*Fake.*"

We made hasty, startled eye contact, and both of our balls missed.

Misty waved her hand and laughed. "Sorry, sorry. I should have known that was a nonstarter. What I mean is, how do *I* figure out what they mean to me? I think what you're both trying to say is that it's based on the individual, which I get and that is helpful. But then, how do I know what to believe?"

"You date yourself," Daria said, just as I added, "By dating other people."

We paused. Shared a *slightly* irritated look. As one, we rolled the ninth and final ball, but we were both distracted.

Daria won by ten points but didn't twirl around and boast about it. The game reset, the nine balls reloaded, and Des called out, "Game number two!"

I waved a hand between the two of us, swallowing a sigh. "Daria. You go."

She reached beneath her hair and tugged on her earrings —the only real display of her nerves I'd seen all night. But she shook it off, beamed a smile at Misty, and rolled her first ball right into the fifty circle.

While the crowd cheered, she and I began the same rhythm again—roll the ball, sink the ball, grab the ball.

"*So,*" Daria said, "the ultimate question around soul mates is really a question about if you want to end up in any kind of romantic relationship. You can't know *that* until you take the time to really know yourself so you can honor what you truly want. Not what society *tells you* you should want. Real, fake, it doesn't really matter. What matters is if you know what's in your own heart, and you're not going to get that by going on a bunch of dates."

I shook my head. "I disagree. To hear you tell it, you've wanted this your entire life, Misty. And I understand how culture and society play into that. But what if you feel that way because it's an authentic goal? I don't think you need any more time to figure it out on your own. *I* think getting out there and dating will demonstrate that it's a priority. Plus, you'll learn what you're looking for in a partner, which is invaluable."

Daria raised her chin. Tossed her hair. And scored fifty points, back-to-back, handily beating me for the second time and negating our need for a third. This time she did twirl, but only to face me and Misty with her hands propped on her hips.

"Theo," she started, "I really don't think Misty can commit to being with someone if she hasn't committed to *herself*. It's the foundation every healthy relationship grows from, and not just romantic. Developing that personal relationship is another variation on commitment, and commitment is basically your jam."

"My jam?" I asked, bemused.

Her shoulders softened down. "That's the academic term, I'm assuming?"

"It's not only considered academic, but I also personally used it when defending my thesis," I replied. "Countless times. Perhaps even…dozens."

"*That's* how you became a doctor."

I shrugged. "I don't make the rules. *But*, even though commitment is my jam, if Misty has already done that work and wants this for her life, then believing in the existence of her soul mate is just another variation on empowerment. She's choosing what *she* wants, above all else. And that is basically…your jam."

Des was standing next to us, looking like an excitable ref at an amateur fight night. "Not to break this up but, uh… Daria won."

She gave another bow to the crowd, who was loving this. Through a gap in people, I saw Janis with Elena, laughing as they shared a drink with Cliff Martin. She saw me, raising her glass. I returned a mock salute.

"That means you're tied," Des said, "and going into the most important round yet. *Air hockey.*"

I touched Des's shoulder, stilling him for a moment. "Misty. Before we head to do our next children's game—"

"Doesn't mean I'm any less of a winner," Daria interjected.

"—were any of the things we said *your* jam?" I finished.

Misty gazed up at the ceiling, like the answer lived there. "I don't know. It could be that this guy I'm seeing is a tough example. On the one hand, it's easy when we hang out but there aren't any fireworks or a ton of passion. It's like…is he the problem? Am I the problem? Or am I happier being alone? If I'm not so focused on the pressure of 'am I doing this right,' I feel a lot less stressed out."

"That's really good," Daria and I said. In unison.

"*Whoa,*" Misty said. "Do you finish each other's sentences now?"

"Not a chance in hell," Daria said, shaking her head. "Just a fluke. Though I do know Theo well enough now that I can say we do love it when our listeners are stress-free."

"It's the goal," I said. "Bottling questions like this up, or worrying nonstop without some kind of release valve, can make it harder to see what you really want."

"Yeah, that's true," Misty said, following as Des shuffled us to the bright white air hockey table. "Listening to you guys on the radio does feel like a mini-therapy session sometimes."

Des handed us both small, flat mallets to defend our goal. There was now a number one beneath both of our names on the big sign, and a kind of careless laughter threatened to escape every time Daria and I made eye contact.

Janis's bizarre advice from the night she changed our programs raced back into my memory, and the smug expression she wore tonight suddenly made a lot more sense: *One forces you to get along behind a mic. The other forces you to get along while doing somethin' silly. Pretty soon, you'll just be getting along.*

Goddammit, she was always right.

"This one's pretty straightforward," Des said. "First one to ten, wins. But keep talking because I really want to hear what else you have to say about Misty."

He dropped the puck onto the tiny table, and Daria lunged forward and hit it hard.

Right into my goal.

I picked up the puck and cocked my head. "Was that cheating?"

She mimicked the motion. "Are you just a sore loser?"

But mid-sentence, I dropped the puck and slammed it into her goal, bringing us tied within the first minute. Her eyes widened, head tipping back on a laugh.

"Fine," she said with an eye roll. "Let's fucking go, Chadwick. And Misty, keep those questions coming."

"Actually," I said as Daria and I exchanged hits of the puck back and forth, "can I ask you a question, Misty?"

"Please, of course," she said.

"As soon as I told you to move on from your friend, you pushed back on that. Which tells me you probably like him more than you think. Are you genuinely having fun with him?"

I scored a goal, and then Daria scored a goal while Misty ruminated on my question.

"When you told me to break up with him, my whole body was like *oh, hell no,*" she admitted.

"See, I don't think either of you is a problem," Daria said. "Every time we rely on a rigid limitation to give us joy or love—of any kind—I believe it's setting us up for failure. Like the whole, *you must find your soul mate to achieve lifelong happiness* thing. It's the same as *you must get married and have children* or *you must find your dream career immediately.*"

The puck ricocheted around the table with a smack. For a few, furious minutes, Daria and I were locked into a back-and-forth that wouldn't end, until I finally hit it neatly into her goal.

"Fuck my *face,*" she hissed. "Wait, what's the score?"

"Nine to six. Me," I said.

She pinned me with a look across the table that was so adorably defiant I was tempted to flip the table over, haul her against my body and kiss her in front of everyone.

Daria deviously took advantage of my bewilderment and sank her puck into my goal.

"I think that's nine to seven now," she said primly.

I cracked a smile. "Are you done making your point to Misty or can I say something too?"

"Oh, you don't agree with what I said?"

"The opposite. I'm opposed to those limitations too, of course, *but* in the case of Misty's question, I wanted to add that pursuing real romantic love *in spite of* all those rigid definitions is, to paraphrase Daria, brave as hell. It takes courage to keep searching for what's genuine, buried beneath all that's fake."

The puck was floating between us easily, almost mindlessly. Neither had made a goal, because Daria was staring at me, transfixed, and I was just as captivated by her interest.

"What is it?" I prompted.

"Do you think that telling our listeners that marriage is the *only* kind of commitment you want is embracing your own version of a rigid limitation?" she asked.

My throat tightened, mind whirring in response to what would have felt like a direct hit two weeks ago. But the sincere curiosity laced through her tone made the difference. Made this question, this moment, much too intimate for this extremely public setting.

I wanted to sit with her someplace private. Pull apart every single thing we'd said tonight like loose threads from a sweater, let it unravel until we found middle ground.

"I don't…" I started.

"She's got a point," Misty said. "Though Daria's all about staying single forever so—"

The puck rattled into my goal. I looked down, shocked, and learned Daria was just as surprised. "Nine to eight," I muttered.

"—that's a rigid limitation too," Misty finished.

I raised a questioning eyebrow at Daria, who seemed to be genuinely turning that statement over in her mind. It was probably my imagination but the whole room felt hushed, even the games. There was only the *clack-clack-clack* of the puck and the puff of generated air on the table.

Before Daria could respond—and I was desperate to hear her answer—Misty rubbed her hands together expectedly. "I'm going to try and summarize everything because you've both given me a *lot* to consider. What you're telling me is… there's nothing wrong with being with this guy—"

"Correct," I said.

"—because life's too short not to have fun—"

"*Absolutely*," Daria said.

"—and since I don't truly know what kind of relationship I want yet anyway, this *could* be the kind that works for me—"

"Yes," I said emphatically. "Only you know what works."

Misty cocked her head. "—because at the end of the day, predicating my happiness on bullshit limitations that don't work for me is the *real* problem, not whether or not I believe in soul mates. If I'm brave enough, I'll find my magic either way."

"*Exactly*," Daria and I said at the same time. And with the same amount of force. So much so, that no sooner had I finished speaking than I was smacking the puck directly into Daria's open goal.

"Did you just straight up *agree?*" Misty asked.

"Did Theo straight up just *win?*" Daria asked, turning to Des.

"He sure did," Des said to the rowdy cheers of the small group of fans that had followed us from game to game. "Official tally so far is Theo two, Daria one. *But* the night is young, and later there have been requests that you partake in Pac-Man, maybe some table tennis. And we can't let you leave without learning which of you dominates on the pinball machine."

I dropped the mallet onto the table, shaking out my fingers. My smile could not be contained, but neither could Daria's, and even now I watched her face flush and knew mine was doing the same.

A person barreled into me—Misty. Her arms wrapped around me in a quick hug and then she turned and did the same to Daria. "Thank you, thank you, *thank you*."

"Are you sure we deserve it?" Daria asked. "Maybe you should call in next week so Theo and I can do a redo, free of any and all pucks and balls."

"No, are you kidding? That was way more fun seeing you in action, in person. You're really great together." She glanced over at Des. "Is K-SUN going to keep doing these community events with Daria and Theo, you think?"

Des passed a hand over his hair and shrugged. "I know I'd love it, and the members seem excited. It just depends on our cohosts. They're already working together nonstop, so as long as they don't mind seeing each other even *more*."

Misty laughed and I did too, though it sounded nervous even to my ears. Daria's shoulders tensed even as she was all smiles for the fans. I could guess why—easily—and it had everything to do with how often she and I were already seeing each other in secret.

The abundance of new empathy I felt for all those listeners with calls about workplace romances was staggering. I'd been cavalier with my advice, urging them to declare their new relationship to the world because the consequences of keeping it private would only continue to pile up. This was *definitely* true for me and Daria.

But the thought of jeopardizing this sweet, tentative happiness between us made me want to keep it a secret forever. And I *knew better*.

I'd still do it anyway.

"Can we take a picture?" Misty asked.

Daria nodded, moving close to me and Des. "Come on over, all these people who willingly watched me lose to Theo."

Des got us semiorganized beneath a banner that read: *K-SUN. Radio for the people.* Talking with fans and meeting listeners in person was one of my favorite parts of this job, but the faces and names blurred as Daria pressed next to me for the photo.

"Dr. Chadwick," she mused, eyes sparkling.

I tipped my head. "Ms. Stone."

"Everyone get close now," Des said, waving his hand. Janis, Mags and Elena stood next to him, watching with pleased expressions. Mags cupped her hands around her mouth and yelled, "Great job, honey! Way to stick it to Theo even though you lost!"

Daria snorted. "Thank you, Mom. Love you."

Her arm slid very gently around my waist. My arm slid

very gently around her shoulders. Almost every single coworker we had was in this room, most of them watching this display of professional camaraderie.

We stayed perfectly still, smiling on command for Des.

It was my heart that wouldn't obey, pounding in my chest, probably changing my amiable expression into something utterly foolish. I was awash in the most powerful feeling, surrounded by my fans, surrounded by my coworkers, perfectly at home with this found family I'd cobbled together because my own had never wanted me.

And in my arms—Daria, my gorgeous rival and charming cohost. The woman I was absolutely falling for, so quickly it should have been terrifying.

This feeling coursing through my veins was what Daria had been talking about all night.

Magic. All of it. *Magic.*

26

DARIA

*T*heo and I barely made it through the front door of my house.

It slammed shut, leaving us in the semidarkness of my front hallway. He had me pinned to the wall a second later, his lips crashing down on mine. He growled and tipped my head back, giving him better access to ravish my mouth. His tongue swept inside, rhythmically caressing along mine, until I was boneless with want.

"I wanted this, wanted *you,* all fucking *night,* Daria," he whispered fervently.

He tilted his head, kissing me with a roughness that revealed the depth of that desire. A depth that easily matched my own. While his lips trailed down my neck, I cupped his thick erection and bore down, so out of my mind with lust I would have eagerly fallen to my knees if Theo hadn't snatched my wrist away with a hiss.

"Is this you making it up to me like you promised?" I panted.

He kicked my feet apart so he could push the hard muscle of his thigh between my legs. His big hands landed on my ass, squeezing possessively as I gasped out his name. His hands encouraged me to rock and I did, because the second we'd stumbled inside, the connection between my brain and body had completely vanished.

His mouth hovered at my ear. "A promise is a promise. Though I'm more in the mood to make you beg for mercy."

I started to smile, but it quickly became a moan when Theo pressed his thigh harder against my sex, kneading my ass, kissing me dizzy and senseless. We were stuck at the arcade for another two hours after our air hockey game finished—two hours of competing and flirting, unable to touch each other. As the night wore on, he only got cockier, which only made me more insolent, until every interaction between us became one long, sexy challenge.

I'd watched Theo all night. His amusement had been obvious, his smiles charming and his body relaxed. He'd moved with an effortless confidence among the fans and listeners, who gawked at him with starstruck expressions.

I understood completely. My body had been in a state of permanent blushing since he'd strolled up to me on the boardwalk.

But while both fans and games jostled for his attention, he only had eyes for me. I'd felt it like a flame against my skin, tracking my movements, studying my reactions.

I'd already spent the night feeling worshiped by Theo, and he didn't even have to use his hands. Which had led right to this frantic moment in the hallway, with me grinding on his leg and our mouths locked together in a bruising, groan-filled kiss.

I dug my fingers into his shirt and pulled hard.

He got the message.

Theo ripped his shirt off with the same cocky smile he'd worn at the arcade. Goosebumps scattered across my skin, and I rocked, helplessly, up and down his thigh, each press providing a delicious friction of fabric brushing my clit, though nothing dulled the relentless throb pounding between my legs.

I raked my nails down Theo's lean chest, gazing in wonder as the muscles in his stomach flexed and jumped beneath my touch. He bent at the knees and lifted me high with barely any effort. Then he walked us down the hallway, peering up at me through slightly disheveled curls.

"Where's your nearest flat surface?" he asked.

"Ki-kitchen," I whispered.

"Perfect." The hallway ended and he turned toward my small kitchen table, dropping me gently onto the edge. He gripped the back of my neck, keeping our faces close. "I need to make you come right the *fuck* now or I'm going to lose my goddamn mind."

I darted my tongue out and licked Theo's bottom lip. His mouth curled wickedly. A feral-sounding rumble came from the back of his throat.

"Then get on those knees and prove that you can handle me after all," I murmured, knowing the taunt would snap the last of his control.

And snap it did. He yanked my hips to the edge of the table. My back hit the surface. Theo discarded my shoes and peeled my tight jeans from my body with trembling fingers. Those same fingers curled into my underwear and dragged it down my legs. I watched all of this in a sexed-up daze, my core already tightening in anticipation of his skilled mouth on my slick skin. He fell to his knees and curled his upper body toward mine. He propped my legs up on his broad, golden-hued shoulders, flexing with sinewy muscle.

Theo stared down at my pussy, and a muscle ticked in his jaw. His fingers tightened around my thighs, holding me open for his decadent scrutiny. When his eyes flicked up to meet mine, heat scorched over my skin. Then he descended, and the moment his face pressed to my cunt, he groaned so forcefully I felt the vibrations through my core. His tongue swiped up firmly, just once, and my back bowed off the table.

"*Oh god,*" I moaned. I drove my fingers into his hair, the other hand scrambling behind for purchase on the edge. Theo was true to his word—within a minute I was begging for mercy, but only because I was about to set my own personal record for fastest climax. I'd been turned on to the point of pain for hours, so his tongue, lapping at my clit, sent spirals of intense, mind-bending pleasure through me.

He licked me eagerly, flattening his tongue to make firm, fast circles. My hips rose over and over, and each time they did, Theo growled his approval, finally using the strength of his arms to lift my lower body right off the table.

I came so hard and so fast my vision went dim, and I cried Theo's name until my voice grew hoarse.

"Jesus…*Christ,*" I said, completely out of breath and shaking. "I think…I think you proved yourself."

He nuzzled his face along my inner thigh and bit down, making me jump. "I'm not done with you yet."

"Is that so?" I asked lazily.

"Can we play with some of your toys?" he asked.

My eyebrows shot up in surprise. "Uh, yeah. *Yes.* We sure can."

He nodded, looking determined. Scooped me up off the table and started toward the narrow hallway that led to my bedroom. "I'm assuming your den of pleasure is this way?"

I scoffed. "Every room in my house is a den of pleasure. I take that shit seriously."

"I know you do, Daria," he murmured at my ear. A shiver raced up my spine. "I've spent too much time fantasizing about what you look like when you use these toys you rave about. And not enough time seeing you do it in real life."

He shouldered open my bedroom door. I reached out and flicked on the light. Theo hummed with approval before tossing me backward onto the bed. With that same haughty smile, he worked off the rest of his clothes like he knew I was watching. And I was. He snapped his fingers at me and said, "Take off your shirt, Daria."

I did as I was told, but when I stood, I bent and clamped my teeth around the meat of his pec. In the large dresser mirror, I was able to enjoy the sight of a very naked Theo groaning, head back, as I kissed across his chest, stroking and teasing his cock. He was thick and heavy in my hands, skin warm, and when I licked his throat, he tasted like salt.

He wrapped his hand around mine, moving us together up and down his length. I felt every stroke like he was moving inside me, every rough breath feathered across my skin.

"Show them to me," he demanded, removing my hand from his cock. He didn't have to clarify *what*. I tugged him over to a large drawer and pulled it open, revealing my sex toys. But it was also filled with all manner of self-care objects, things that made my body feel loved, held, pleasured —body oil, candles, lotions.

Over the years, I'd learned that masturbation, massage and long baths all served a similar purpose for me. They taught me about my body—its likes, its dislikes, its beautiful quirks. It taught me to love my body, to worship it, to give what it asked for without judgment. Sometimes my body asked for soft, chenille blankets and a good book. Sometimes it asked for hot porn and fast vibrators. There was a lesson each time, even if that lesson was merely to *listen.*

I followed Theo's hungry gaze as he stared down at all the colorful toys, laid out in a pretty pattern. He touched some of them—reverently—and my toes curled into my plush carpet.

I had a feeling today's lesson was something like *get ready for the ride of your life.*

I grabbed Theo's hand and rested it on a favorite dildo of mine. It was purple and curved and vibrated in an extraordinary range of patterns and speeds. An idea blazed into my brain.

"Theo, I've had this fantasy."

His eyes rose up sharply. "Tell me."

I licked my lips, a heady arousal coiling in my belly. "Fuck me with this," I said, touching the dildo, "and lick my clit. Again."

His fingers closed tight around the vibrator. "*Daria*," he growled. "Get on the bed."

I bit my lip. "So that's a yes?"

He dropped his head and kissed me. "Go."

I went. Crawled across my soft, scarlet sheets and knew Theo was staring.

"On your back," he said. "And spread your legs."

He was there a second later, stretching his big, naked body next to mine, dildo in one hand and a small bottle of lube I had in the drawer in the other. I applied a few drops to my fingers and covered the toy with it. Tipped my face up so I could kiss Theo. Kiss Theo and feel his firm lips slanting over mine, his fingers holding my face still. I needed a second to collect my thoughts, and Theo seemed to sense that. He was, after all, in my house, in my bedroom, in my *bed*.

Listening to what I wanted. Remembering what I needed. Giving me an intimacy I hadn't experienced before—not with Jackson, not with any of the men I occasionally brought home for sex that was enjoyable but ultimately meaningless.

To me, this kind of sex with a partner was the epitome of meaningful. Like I'd declared tonight, in between basketball and air hockey, it defied limitations and rigid definitions.

It was *magic*.

We parted on a shared, shaky breath. Eyes locked together, I wrapped my hand around his, and together we dragged the tip of the dildo down the center of my body until it rested between my legs.

"What feels good?" he asked softly. He notched the toy at

my entrance. With a furrowed brow, he slowly, slowly began sliding it inside. The blunt intrusion, guided by his hand, felt *amazing*. My mouth opened on a soundless cry and my eyes fluttered shut. I felt Theo's palm pass over my forehead, pushing the curls from my face. The tender gesture only increased the desire spiking through me.

He pushed the toy in a few more inches. I bit my lip and whimpered. "A lower…a lower speed at first."

Theo clicked it on. The soft vibrations echoed through my sex. I tilted my hips up, already seeking more. My eyes flew open in time to see his lips curving wickedly. "Like this?"

I nodded. Gasped. "Deeper, *please*." I stared down my body as Theo's hand worked the rest of the dildo all the way in, to the very hilt. We'd barely done anything and my cells felt on the urge of detonation. My fingers clutched at Theo's strong shoulders and a keening cry was building in my throat. He began moving the toy in and out, fucking me with my dildo in a frustratingly consistent rhythm that had my head thrashing back and forth.

His warm breath caressed the shell of my ear, the only thing grounding me through the rapidly building ecstasy. "You are so beautiful, just like this," he murmured. "I've never seen anything so damn sexy."

Before, I might have joked or teased or let loose a string of pretty, affirming words for the unbelievably handsome man working me over with a dildo like he'd spent years practicing for this very moment. But we'd traded words for sport all night long, and I was finally, blissfully out of things to say. I was pure sensation, a body floating in a sea of euphoria, so when Theo clicked the vibrator up a single speed, setting off a flurry of mini-orgasms, I simply shoved his shoulders as hard as I could and said, "For the love of god, *now, Theo*."

He didn't hesitate for a second to give me what I asked

for. He fell back in position between my legs and curled his soft, wet tongue around my clit.

I screamed.

I couldn't help it. The deep penetration plus the vibrations plus the sweet caress of his tongue was the most exquisite combination of sensations I'd ever experienced in my life. He grinned but didn't stop, lapping at my clit and fucking me with the toy. All of a minute went by before a sharp, piercing second orgasm had me screaming again into my pillow. I writhed, bucked. Theo pressed his hand to my stomach and held me still until the very last wave ebbed away.

I flopped back onto the bed like a ragdoll. I covered my face with my hands and tried to slow my breathing. A bead of sweat rolled between my breasts. After he very gently removed the dildo, he moved slowly up my body, inch by inch, kiss by kiss, until he could lick up that bead of sweat with a deep, gravelly sigh of satisfaction.

"*Daria*," he breathed, in a tone filled with awe. "You are a marvel. You are a *miracle*." His mouth kept traveling, until the length of his body was pressed to mine. His weight, his warm skin, was a delicious relief. His hips pressed me down into the mattress and his hands curved up my waist, cupping my breasts, stroking up my throat. He dragged his nose down my jaw, kissed my cheek. I opened my eyes and grabbed his face. His lopsided grin was much too adorable following an orgasm that literally shattered me.

"You made one of my fantasies come true," I said, softly tracing his lips with my finger.

His smile grew. "Watching you with one of your vibrators was my own fantasy. Thank you for trusting me with it."

I hummed under my breath. "Thank you for being trustworthy. I don't…" I cleared my throat. "Theo, this entire night is a first for me. You make it easy to open up. You make it easy to be myself."

His lips brushed my temple. "I'll never get enough of being around you, Daria. Just the way you are."

My heart felt like it was on fire. Emotion crowded my throat. I trailed my hands down his back, rippled with muscle, until I could grip his ass. He hissed out a breath and rocked against my still-sensitive clit, which sent a barrage of aftershocks rippling through me.

"I want you, Theo, just like this. I want more...*more* of you."

His eyes searched mine. He shifted his hips again, grinding down, and it was *so damn good.* Because I was still sensitive, still aching, still *needing* to feel every inch of him inside me. It was sweet and sultry, this slow and steady movement, our bodies clinging together. I nipped at his bottom lip and said, "*Please,* fuck me."

He captured my mouth in a kiss that quickly turned rough. He palmed my breasts, rolling my nipples against his palms. I cried out against his mouth and thrust my fingers into his hair. He replaced his palms with his hot mouth, sucking and licking and scraping his teeth.

"How?" he asked in a strangled voice. "Your fantasies are my fantasies, Daria Stone."

"Just like this." I sighed. "And I'm safe. Protected too, with my IUD. I'm fine with no condom if you are."

A shock wave went through his body. He grabbed my hands and pinned them above my head, our fingers entwining in the sheets. Whispering my name like a prayer, he leisurely thrust his cock inside me, slow inch by slow inch. He was thick, stretching me, filling me. Going deep and then deeper still, until my toes curled. My hips rose to meet him, urging him on. Our bodies moved together with an indulgence that built to a wicked frenzy. I moaned with each deliberate stroke of his cock, each grind of his pelvis against my clit.

It didn't take long until Theo was fucking me harder.

Faster. His mouth stayed at my ear and every husky growl and heavy breath only got me hotter. My third orgasm hovered close, spurred on by his deep strokes and steady rhythm. But I was also captivated by watching Theo unravel in front of my eyes—his body shuddering, his teeth grazing my skin.

"I can feel you on the edge, Daria," he said. Our bodies slapped together. My hips moved with every drive of his cock. "I can feel you. *So fucking close. So beautiful.*"

"*Theo*," I whimpered. I was on the brink of climax for a third time and I wasn't sure I would survive it. "Please, *oh god*. You're so good, you're so good, *you're so—*"

He released my hands and pushed up, hitting a new and perfect angle. I arched my back right off the bed, and Theo's tongue was there, running between my breasts, his mouth dragging up my throat.

"A marvel," he panted, "you are a marvel and a miracle." Then he swore under his breath and kissed me. His cock plunged between my legs, and I came in a series of long ripples that had me gasping. I wrapped my arms around his back and held him close as his breathing turned rough.

"Daria, *fuck*," he swore. He shuddered and groaned through his climax, and I continued to hold him tight with a giant, satisfied smile on my face. His lips moved over my face. He kissed the space between my eyebrows. The tip of my nose. My hair. A warm, languid feeling suffused every limb, from the top of my head to the very tips of my toes. He lifted his head enough that our eyes could meet. He chuckled softly, brushing my hair back and smoothing his hand over my forehead.

"Are you okay?" he asked, lips quirking.

"I'm in another stratosphere, thank you very much," I said. "And I mean that literally. Thank *you* very much."

Theo cracked a boyish grin. "Do you think it was naive of me to declare the sex we'd had in my office to be the best of my life when I hadn't yet experienced the singular ecstasy of whatever the hell happened here?"

I pushed up onto my elbows and stole a kiss. "Arcade-games-as-foreplay is what happened."

Laughter rumbled from his chest. He reached for the sheets at the end of the bed and softly dragged them up and over our naked bodies, smoothing his hand down my back and curling his arm loosely around my waist. We lay on our sides facing each other, dreamy and satisfied, and the sweet affection in his eyes had my toes curling again for an entirely different reason.

For a moment, we didn't speak—rare for the two of us. I surrendered to the temptation to continue touching him, tracing the shape of his face with my fingers—his strong jaw, the curve of his cheekbones, his clever mouth. Theo seemed content with my exploration, gazing at me with gratitude in his eyes, and my heart ached with the memory of his childhood loneliness, his parent's cold dismissal, his years of study about love because he'd been denied it at such a pivotal age.

His palm moved in big, soothing strokes up and down my back. I cuddled in closer, and he kissed the tip of my nose. "What did you think about Misty's question tonight?"

"I think Misty was a *really* good sport," I said with a grin. "But in the end...I really liked the advice that we landed on. Together."

"No limitations or rigid definitions," he echoed softly. "Which I can work on, for you. Would like to work on *with* you."

My breathing hitched. For two people who often swore publicly that they were opposed to narrow labels, we had certainly chosen hard lines to stand upon: *only marriage* versus *single forever*. What Theo had said right before that had shaken the very foundation I'd clung to from the moment my mother had to unzip me from my wedding dress.

Pursuing real romantic love in spite of all those rigid defini-tions is, to paraphrase Daria, brave as hell. It takes courage to keep searching for what's genuine, buried beneath all that's fake.

"I would like to work on being more open too," I whispered. And meant it.

A smile lit up his face, smoothing away the lines on his brow. "I'm discovering that our listeners love us more because we clearly *don't know* what we're doing. That's more relatable than an expert. Or so I'm learning."

"Ah," I said, sighing as he stroked my hair. "So you're telling me that the love and romance expert isn't an expert after all?"

"I'm really not," he said mildly. "I promised you a grand romantic gesture the other day and that promise hasn't been fulfilled."

"Theo," I said, kissing his cheek, "we played games tonight with our fans and coworkers. And at one point I laughed so hard I cried. *Then* you made me come three times. This *is* my idea of a romantic gesture. You nailed it on the first try."

His smile widened. "Please allow me to shower you with these specific gestures every day of the week. Twice a day, even, if you're feeling extra romantic."

I brushed the curls from his forehead while my heart cartwheeled around in my chest, letting me know with every physical response possible that what I felt for Theo Chadwick was as genuine as it gets.

And when sleep claimed me a few minutes later, it was with my head pressed to his chest, his strong arms holding me tight, and the rhythm of his heartbeat like a lullaby in my ear.

27

THEO

I finally understood the true definition of the word *gift*.

It had nothing to do with the way I'd once showered my girlfriends with gifts that were given sincerely but ultimately lacked meaning. And it had everything to do with waking up to the soft, comforting weight of Daria's head on my chest, her dark hair splayed everywhere, her quiet breathing synced to my own. I turned to press my lips to those raven curls, inhaling her floral scent. She shifted but didn't wake, and gratitude washed over me so strongly my throat tightened.

Last night, we'd had sex so hot and intimate, I knew it would be seared into my memories forever. Even still, I'd fully expected not to sleep here, much as I longed to. She was honest about her boundaries more than anything else—it wasn't hard to imagine that she probably had one about staying the night.

But we'd reached for each other instead, Daria curling up beside me as if we'd done this a hundred times before.

It certainly felt like that to me.

I stroked my fingers lazily down her spine, content to stay beneath the covers in her cheery, sun-drenched bedroom. She grumbled adorably, stirring, then she lifted her head with a bleary expression.

"Good morning," I drawled, brushing the hair from her eyes.

She scowled sleepily.

"Now there's a look I know well."

Her lips pursed. "I'm angry because you also look super-hot when you first wake up in the morning and I find it deeply unfair."

Her voice was raspy with sleep, hair a snarled mess, her naked body warm against mine. I caressed the side of her neck, lifting an eyebrow at a bite mark.

"Consider it payback for all those months you wore those leather pants to distract me," I said with a grin.

She scoffed. "I've *never* done *anything* like that in my *life*, Theodore Chadwick."

I rolled us easily, loving the sound of her surprised laughter and the feel of her now beneath me. I cupped her face and kissed her, our lips moving as sweetly and languidly as the sun's rays sliding across the floor. I took my time with her mouth, moving unhurriedly. Letting the moment unfurl between us without limits or hesitations. I could feel her lips curving into a smile. Could feel the loose happiness in her body. And when I finally pulled back, the look of warm affection on her face cracked my heart wide open.

"Okay," she admitted, "maybe I wore those pants to distract you *just* a little."

"Just a little, huh?" I teased.

She kissed me again, bringing my head down while she vibrated with laughter. "You were right. Maybe *I'm* the scoundrel."

"A very, very, *very* beautiful one," I whispered at her ear.

Daria bit the tip of her thumb, her sapphire eyes searching mine. "About last night," she started, and my heart stopped. But she reached up and stroked my cheek. "I haven't stayed the night in over five years. And I haven't let anyone sleepover here, either."

"Not in five years?" I murmured, my heart restarting chaotically. "Did you want me to—"

She shook her head firmly. "If I wanted you to leave, I would have felt comfortable asking, and I know you would have understood. But I wanted you to stay with me, Theo. Want you to keep staying."

"I'd like that," I said hoarsely. "Staying over with you"—I paused, realized I was blushing— "it felt different with you. Waking up with you this morning was extraordinary. You are extraordinary."

"So are you," she whispered, "and that's why I think this feels different. You make me feel safe and comfortable, Theo."

The depth of emotion in her hushed voice was like nothing I'd ever heard from her before. As were her trembling fingers on my skin, her throat working on a delicate swallow. Her promise from last night rose in my thoughts: *I would like to work on being more open too.*

Bathed in morning light with Daria in my arms, it suddenly didn't seem so foolish to hope we'd stumble our way toward something *more.*

I nudged my nose against hers. "Can I cook you breakfast?"

She arched an eyebrow. "Theo. You made me come three times last night, including once with my vibrator. If anyone's cooking breakfast, it's me."

I brushed my lips along her jaw. "And I'd do it again, breakfast or not."

Daria pushed playfully at my shoulders, swinging her legs over the bed and standing fully naked and utterly gorgeous in front of me. I rolled onto my side, astonished and aroused and already reaching to pull her back. She swatted my hand away and tossed on her oversized David Bowie shirt from the other night.

"Come on," she called over her shoulder, "allow me to 'gifts of service' you."

I scrubbed a hand down my face with a laugh, reluctant to leave the paradise of her bed but physically unable to resist her commands. I tugged on my briefs, found my glasses, and raked a hand through my hair.

"What was that again?" I asked, following her into her kitchen.

She banged a skillet and spatula on top of the stove. "I gotta quality time your affirmations and stuff."

I banded an arm around her waist and tugged her back against my chest. "You know I get hard when you talk about love languages," I growled, nipping at her ear.

She laughed. "A girl brings a cute guy some Tylenol *one time*."

I gave her a loud kiss on the cheek and then sat on top of her counter, watching her turn on her coffee pot and pull out eggs, bacon, cheese and set them next to a plate of biscuits beneath a glass cover. She had black-and-white tiles on her floor and light blue appliances, her counters and fridge covered in pictures and art.

"What are you making me?" I asked, lifting my chin toward the spread.

She coated the skillet in butter, cracked two eggs and dropped in a few strips of bacon. "On show nights, especially if I'm wired up, my late dinner is usually a cheesy fried egg sandwich with bacon on a biscuit. I would have made it for you last night, but I was too busy falling asleep on your impressively broad chest."

My lips twitched. "I promise to be less impressive next time."

"You better, because you're about to discover how delicious my egg sandwiches are." She spun in her bare feet and danced over to me with a steaming mug of coffee. Before she could spin away, I caught the front of her shirt and tugged until she was standing between my legs, wearing a pretty smile.

I tucked a strand of her hair behind her ear. "Would you believe me if I told you I make the exact same dinner after late shows?"

Daria brightened. "Janis was right all along. We do have things in common."

I chuckled softly. "Do you think we've finally learned a vital lesson about teamwork and compromise?"

She cocked her head. "That depends. Do you take hot sauce on your fried egg sandwiches?"

"You're goddamn right I do," I whispered fiercely.

She walked backward to her fridge with a salacious look, then pulled open the door and grabbed a red bottle with one hand, tossing it to me.

I caught it, amused, and held it up. "This is the exact kind that I use too."

"Well, whaddya know," she crooned, sprinkling cheese on top of the bubbling eggs, "four months of animosity ended over a sandwich."

"Maybe some other stuff helped too," I said with a wink.

She bit her lip, cheeks pink, and placed the biscuits into a toaster oven. "I can think of a few notable examples of…compromise."

I eyed her over my coffee, watching her move around her kitchen with ease, plating sandwiches and licking bacon grease from her fingers. The ordinary, peaceful domesticity of this morning couldn't be ignored, especially in comparison to the night before—which had been full of flashing arcade lights and eager fans, then urgent lust and sex toys.

That we could slip into the bliss of bedhead and bare feet together, only hours later, made me ache with happiness I struggled to fully define.

Daria tipped her head toward the other room and said, "Go sit on the couch, and I'll bring it to you."

I obeyed, but not before stealing a kiss. Her living room had a large sliding glass door that, like mine, led out to a sunny patio. Her walls were painted a light yellow and on them she'd hung vintage surf pictures and K-SUN posters. White lights were wrapped around her flourishing potted plants and a short palm tree. I settled down on her couch, next to a bowl filled with ticket stubs. With one finger, I tugged out one of the orange milk crates beneath the table to reveal a lot of slightly dusty records.

"You've got one hell of a vinyl collection too," I called over my shoulder.

"Magnolia Stone's influence," she said, the smile in her voice obvious. She appeared a second later, balancing our food and her own mug of coffee. I took a plate of delicious-smelling breakfast while she curled up next to me on the couch, entwining her legs with mine. Daria glanced over with uncharacteristic shyness as I took my first bite of crumbly biscuit, melted cheese and crisp bacon.

I groaned so loudly she burst out laughing.

"So I did okay?" she teased.

I nudged her foot with mine. "Daria Stone, you are absolutely astonishing in every way."

She rolled her lips together, looking pleased with herself, then broke off an extra piece of bacon and held it toward me. I pulled her wrist to my lips and pressed a kiss over her pulse point, then snatched the bite from her fingers with my teeth.

She clicked her tongue. "Such a flirt."

She tracked my gaze to the picture, framed on her coffee table—it was a younger-looking Mags sitting in the sound booth at K-SUN, wearing headphones and a gigantic smile aimed at a little girl with long dark hair holding the microphone up.

I reached for it, stroking my thumb across the image. "Is this you?"

"Sure is." Daria twisted at the waist and grabbed another picture from behind the couch. "Check out this one."

I cupped the frame in my hands and grinned. "Holy shit. That's Janis and your mom at the protests in 1998 about the corporations snatching up all the independent businesses."

Magnolia carried a bullhorn. Janis held the sign she'd given me the other day—*Sunrise Beach Doesn't Stand for Big Business.* She was, of course, holding this with one hand while her other raised a defiant middle finger.

It had been simpler to avoid the deep roots of my connection with Daria—my years of friendship with Mags. The fact that Janis, my mentor, was essentially Daria's grumpy, foul-mouthed aunt. Our shared devotion to this town, this radio station, and all the things that made it such a special place. There were too many threads, binding us together, and until recently, discarding them had made it easier to ignore my growing feelings for her.

"You're only a few years older than me," she said, "and I spent a lot of mornings with my mom, in-studio, while she was recording her show. As I got older, she even let me choose some of the songs. There are probably days that you were listening to her show at home, while I was there listening too."

My gaze rose to meet hers. "Were you responsible for her playing 'The Wild One' every morning for a week straight?"

She shrugged cheerfully, eyes on the ceiling. "*Maybe.*"

I swallowed around a lump in my throat. "Wouldn't that be something."

Daria placed her now-empty plate on the table and turned to face me. We rearranged slightly until her feet were in my lap and my hand was squeezing hers.

"Can I ask you a personal question?" she said.

"Always."

"Why did you really leave academia to become a radio host? I can't stop thinking about how much you'd invested, all that dedicated time you had to give up to come to K-SUN."

"In some ways, it was a lot to give up," I admitted. "But I was only twenty-eight when I started hosting, so I mostly just feel grateful that I chose the career I wanted and not the one I was feeling pressured to go into by my advisors, my professors, even friends in the field."

I paused, lightly squeezing her ankle. "Studying human relationships was fascinating to me because of what happened with my parents, but once I started writing that advice column, I found that I most enjoyed connecting with regular people about their questions around love. People who were just as confused and hopeful and curious as I was. That, combined with the fact that I'd been obsessed with radio since I was a kid, made taking Janis's offer the easiest decision I've ever made. Talking with our listeners every week makes me feel less alone."

She nodded and stroked her thumb across my knuckles. "That makes perfect sense to me. And I get the not wanting to feel alone. Hosting our show does that for me too."

"Did you always want to be like your mom?"

"Oh yeah." She laughed. "There was never any doubt in my mind about where I was meant to be. Back in L.A., I worked every station job I could for the experience, until the producer at K-ROX was willing to take a chance on a recently dumped, pissed-off girl wanting to scream about self-love."

"I'm grateful they did," I said.

She propped her other elbow up on the back of the couch and leaned her head against it. "Radio is everything to me too," she said softly. "Indie stations are like this voice in the wilderness. It's your favorite song being played at the exact moment you turn on the radio. It's friendly company on long road trips and comfort in the middle of the night."

I hummed my approval under my breath. Let my eyes wander to her framed posters, the steady presence of the beach in the background of all of them. "Radio is like the constant of an ocean wave. You hear a song you used to love or listen to a story on-air that makes you feel seen, and it's like you're returned to a specific moment in time, no matter what you're doing in the present."

She smiled at me, all warmth and tender affection, and I realized that this was the only place I ever wanted to be. That recognition softened the edges of the goals I'd clung to for years—national syndication, larger fame, a happy marriage. It wasn't that I didn't want them. I did. But it felt okay to release some of my own urgency because simply being here, with Daria, was starting to feel like enough.

I tilted my head when my eyes landed on the little blue desk in the corner, next to her palm tree. On top of it was a laptop, a large stack of papers and a series of worn-looking notebooks. She saw me looking and covered her eyes with a bashful smile.

"Daria," I said, "is that where you wrote your book?"

She blew out a heavy breath. "Uh-huh, yep. Though I wrote a good portion of it here on the couch. And on the floor. Some of it I wrote in bed, and in coffee shops, and on the beach. It took me two years of transforming my messy, emotional, stream-of-consciousness blog posts into essays and it was…" She hesitated, chewing on her lip. "It was the best thing and the hardest thing I've ever done. I know you and I have talked about vulnerability hangovers before, but seeing my innermost thoughts and fears and opinions sprawled out over a stack of pages was the most exposed I've ever felt. Sometimes I can't *believe* that I sent that hot mess of feelings out to agents. For them *to read*."

I shifted back against the couch pillow and crooked my

finger. With a flicker of a smile, she crawled up my body until she was straddling my lap. Her hands landed on my bare chest while I slid my palms up her bare thighs, stopping just below the curve of her ass.

She arched a flirtatious eyebrow, but I only lazily lifted a shoulder. "I missed you and you were too far away."

She flashed me a cheeky smile. "It's *so* obvious that you like me."

I pulled her flush against me until our faces were mere inches apart. "Says the woman who can't stop bringing me food."

She tried to look sly for all of a second, but grabbed my face and gave me a long, hard kiss. "I like you a lot, Theo Chadwick."

"You're *so* obvious," I whispered against her cheek.

She laughed but I held tight, needing to look her in the eye. "And to get back to what you were saying about your writing, I just want to reiterate the advice I've heard you give countless times now to our listeners. People love mess and they love a hot mess even more. There's no room for perfectionism in authenticity, and you're the most authentic person I know. Exposing all of your feelings like that is incredibly brave."

Daria traced the outline of my mouth with her fingertips, looking pensive. "I worry that I might have written something in that book that I'll change my mind about, three years from now. What if I discover I'm wrong about everything? The more you and I cohost, the more I feel like we're making all of it up as we go."

I brushed the hair from her face and stroked the jewelry curving up her ear. "I think it's likely that three years from now you'll have changed your mind. Not because you're not an expert in your own experiences. But because ever since we started cohosting, I feel more and more like a total amateur."

Her hands flew to cover her eyes. "Oh my god, so it's not just me?"

"Not at all," I said on a laugh. "Every time I'm with you, I learn something new, or contradict something I'd said earlier, or scrutinize a former value. As much as I resisted accepting this, I'm starting to understand that maybe we're amateurs forever."

She grinned. "None of us know what the hell we're doing."

"But we try anyway," I said, bringing her in for a kiss. She surprised me, wrapping her arms around my neck and pouring a passion into this kiss that was more emotional than sexual. She smiled against my lips, deepening the moment and sliding her fingers into my hair. I gave her everything she wanted—no walls, no barriers, no hesitations. She sat back to pull her shirt off and then she was naked and beautiful on my lap, joyful and open.

I could only peer up at Daria in total astonishment, unsure how I'd been so wrong about this woman who was so incredibly right for me. And as my lips roamed leisurely down her throat, and she sighed my name sweetly, the only thing I really knew was how desperately I wanted us to stay like this forever.

DARIA

Two weeks later

$\mathcal{I}$ smoothed my hands down the cherry-red jukebox in the break room while making soothing noises, like it was a dog refusing to swallow a pill.

"Come on, Stevie Nicks," I crooned. "I know you can do it."

I gave a kick in the same spot as always.

Nothing.

"Here, let me try," Theo said, coming up from behind me. His velvet radio voice held just a *hint* of hoarseness. With a sly grin and a well-timed kick, the jukebox clicked on and began playing The Supremes, as usual.

I pointed my finger at his chest. "Looks like you've got the magic touch today."

He tossed me a wink that tripled my heart rate. When he turned back toward the table, he raised his hand and snatched the tennis ball Des had lobbed at him out of the air.

"What if I hadn't turned back around?" he asked, lobbing it back.

"I had faith in you." Des was sitting on a chair at the table with his legs propped up on the edge. Elena sat by the window in a similar pose, gazing longingly at the sparkling blue sky outside. It was a Saturday, and even though we had a show tonight, the warm July weather and overall *weekend vibes* were fracturing our focus.

Theo settled in the chair beside me and caught the next throw. Tossed it back. Des nodded at the steaming mugs in front of us and said, "Drink. Both of you. You must be giving each other head colds in the sound booth, and I don't want you sounding nasally during the broadcast."

I fiddled with my earrings and avoided looking directly at Theo. "But I'm not sick. I don't think Theo is either."

"Well, you sound froggy as hell," Elena said. "You're all raspy on playback and we've got listeners asking about your health. Some sweet lady even offered to drop off chicken noodle soup for you."

Theo dutifully took a sip. "Could be all these community events. I am doing a lot of victorious screaming."

I raised an eyebrow. "Victorious? I won the mini-golf competition last week."

He held up a finger. "By one point, Daria."

"That's still called *winning*."

Des laughed, rubbing his palms together. "I had no idea it was going to be this fun watching you duke it out all across Sunrise Beach. I even took Susannah mini-golfing last night for a date because I'd forgotten what a blast it was. Janis hasn't given the green light for any additional events, but I have a feeling that's gonna change."

"The fans want more Theo and Daria," Elena said, raising her own mug at us. "Big time."

Theo caught the tennis ball and squeezed. "Then it's lucky that Daria and I are so evenly matched."

I twisted my mug in a circle, spilling hot water down the handle. "Sure is."

The mini-golf competition that Des had planned had been just as successful as our arcade night and raised even more money. K-SUN fans had milled around the courses for hours, enjoying drinks and food and music provided by my mother, of course. *Greg's Golf House* was dinosaur-themed, the greens filled with giant prehistoric creatures we'd all known and loved as kids. The peeling paint hadn't been updated since the eighties—the same was true for the entire establishment—so my mother curated the evening's playlist around a collection of new-wave-era classics.

After that night was over, Theo and I didn't leave his bed for hours. I'd pushed him onto his back and ridden him in a slow, sexy grind that had both of us gasping as we came. And in the morning, when I woke up a little sore and a lot satisfied, his clever mouth had roamed leisurely down my naked body until his head was between my legs, his tongue licking me to a breathtaking orgasm.

Two weeks had passed since the first morning we'd spent together, when I'd cooked us breakfast and blushed myself silly over the presence of a bare-chested Theo in my kitchen, with sleep-tousled hair and an easy half-grin.

We hadn't spent a night apart since.

It was true we'd been hosting our show with hoarse and raspy voices, but it wasn't due to head colds or victory cheers. It was the combination of our hot sex that was only getting hotter.

And the very adorable fact that we'd been staying up way too late, talking for hours.

"Janis had so much fun at golf she told me she's considering asking for her seventy-second birthday to take place there," Theo said with an affable smile. "Speaking of, sounds like everything's set for this coming Friday?"

"Wigs, glitter, signage, check," Elena confirmed.

"Gourmet junk food, check," I said.

"Music is almost set. Venue is secure," Des replied. "When are you setting up the community pantry?"

"In a couple days, on her actual birthday," Theo said. "I just need to find one of those comically large bows to place on top."

My phone rang with a number I didn't recognize so I silenced it, flipping it over on the table. "I have one of those. I can bring it by if you still want my help setting up?"

Theo shifted uncomfortably in his chair. "Sure. Yes. That's, uh…that would be great."

"Cool," I said casually. *Hopefully* casually. "We can find a time when I see you after work. Or *during* work, I mean. During all those work hours we spend together."

"Yes." His tone was careful. "The many work hours."

My phone buzzed with a text. I scooped it into my lap to see who was calling and texting me.

"I never thought I'd see the day when Daria Stone and Theo Chadwick were getting along *famously* and even building food pantries together," Des said. Theo chucked the tennis ball a little harder at him. Des laughed but still caught it. "These are strange times, indeed."

My stomach flipped nervously. This was a common occurrence now. There was a relaxed happiness in the air at the station—the budget was slowly improving, the weather was beautiful, Theo and I had settled into an engaging on-air chemistry. Our popularity was on a steady, upward trajectory that was re-energizing the entire base of K-SUN fans, which only lent itself to the dreamy atmosphere.

And at the same time, Theo and I were keeping a secret from our closest friends, family and coworkers, and I felt a mounting pressure weighing me down. Part guilt, part confusion, part worry I was going to slip up and kiss Theo square on the mouth every time he made me laugh at work.

It was as unsustainable as it was foolish, yet we continued to tiptoe around it.

My deepest fear was that we were starting to use the fact that we were cohosts to protect us from the actual issues between us, the ones that had bred so much professional animosity in the beginning. But it felt impossible to sift through our opposing wants and needs when, in the moment, everything between us was so *delightful*.

My phone buzzed a second time. I clicked open the text messages while Elena and Theo were going back and forth on the logistics of roller skate rentals for the party.

Hi Daria, this is Joanne Campbell from Keller Literary Group. I'm sorry for the texts but I figured you might not pick up for a number you didn't recognize. I've had your manuscript on the top of my pile for a few weeks now but finally got to it and loved it. I would love to chat if you have a minute?

Blood rushed in my ears. Nine, almost ten months now of obsessively checking my inbox only to be disappointed and *now*, here it was. A literary agent had loved my book of essays where I declared proudly that I intended to be single forever. And I was sitting next to the man I'd woken up with for the past fourteen mornings, often on my side with Theo's arm wrapped around me and his face buried in my hair.

His voice interrupted my scattered thoughts. "Daria? Are you okay?"

I gulped. "I need to make a quick call. I'll be right back and don't let Elena give the pink glitter wig away because I already called it."

I grabbed my things and left the room, speed-walking to my office. I shut the door and pressed my phone to my chest, filling my lungs with slow inhales until my nerves settled. I rounded my desk and pulled up my email, squealing against my hand when I saw Joanne's message at the top of my personal inbox. The subject line: *Inquiry regarding your manuscript.*

An email, a phone call, a voice mail and text messages. I was a total literary newbie but I knew enough to know these were good signs.

I held tight to the memory from a few weeks ago, of my mother in the break room reminding me in her usual boisterous fashion that writing this book had been my dream for five long years. My relationship with Jackson, from beginning to dramatic end, felt like one long betrayal of the messages about true love I'd been bombarded with since puberty.

Writing about that betrayal saved me.

I hit "call back" on my phone and placed it at my ear. It rang twice and then a friendly voice said, "Hi, this is Joanne Campbell. Is this *the* Daria Stone from K-SUN?"

That startled a laugh from me. "It is, but I didn't know you were a fan?"

"Recent," she admitted. "Once I came across your manuscript, I started tuning in to that show that you do. The advice show with that other guy, Theo?"

"That's the one," I said, chewing on my thumbnail. "Being a radio host is as glamorous as you've always imagined. We spend a lot of our time eating burritos at our desk and recording shows in our pajama pants."

"I love that," she said, sounding amused. "And I *love* your voice. Your writing style is fresh and young. And *funny*. You sound like everyone's best friend who takes them to a bar after some awful guy breaks up with them and tells them true love is a scam, while plying them with shots of tequila."

I looked up at the ceiling, overwhelmed. "Wow, um... that's so great to hear. I'm a little starry-eyed, to be honest. I swear I'm not this awkward."

"Well, I'm just sorry it's taken me so long to get back to you. We've been behind on our memoir acquisitions, but things are finally moving ahead, and I'd love to set up an actual call to talk to you about representation and hear what your interests are. I swear every other self-help manuscript that lands on my desk is all the same. I want something edgier. I want a self-help book with *teeth*. Someone firm in their convictions, like you are."

There was a knock at my door, and Theo's head peeked in. I held up a finger. "I would love to talk with you about representation."

"*Great*," she said. "My assistant will work with you on scheduling, and we'll hash out those details. But Daria—I loved this book and everything you had to say. I want to live in a world where people are encouraged to love themselves *first*. Seeing it on the page, the way you laid it out, was extremely persuasive. Your defense of being single as a choice and a preference was so powerful when we're told marriage is our only option for inner happiness."

"Thank you. That means so much," I said in a shaky voice, as memories of what I'd written at the end made my hands clammy. The fears I'd shared with Theo from that morning in my kitchen raced back through my thoughts: *What if I put something in that book and I've changed my mind? What if I read it three years from now and discover I was wrong?*

"So my assistant will get with you and then we'll talk, okay?"

"Sounds amazing, yes, *thank you*," I sputtered. Joanne hung up and I set my phone down on the desk through waves of full-body jitters.

"Holy fucking shit," I whispered. Theo knocked again, drawing my attention back to the door. I waved him in as some of those worries were drowned out by an electrifying excitement that had me grinning like a fool.

"Hey, are you okay?" Theo asked. "Based on that smile, I'm going to say it's good news?"

I peeked around him—the door was open and any of my coworkers could hear.

But maybe this book didn't have to be a secret anymore.

"That was an agent named Joanne, who happens to work for one of the best literary agencies in the country," I said slowly, "and she read my manuscript. And loved it. She wants..." I swallowed past a lump in my throat. "Theo, she wants to set up a call to talk about representation."

Too late I realized that my eyes were flooding with tears. Regardless of the ending and what it might mean—for me, for the book, for the handsome man standing in front of me —there was something so very gratifying about what Joanne had said. I'd written that book because I needed to feel seen and she'd seen *me*. My authentic self, my rage and relief, my humiliation and healing—it was *all in there* and she'd described it as powerful.

"Daria," Theo said, voice rough with emotion. "This is incredible. You're—" He glanced over his shoulder as coworkers passed by. "This is brilliant news and I'm so happy for you. And proud. Proud to...to know you. Your story, your voice, what you give to people, it's much too important to stay on a stack of pages in a drawer somewhere. It deserves to be read."

I breathed out a fluttery-sounding laugh. "It's been a long journey, finding my way home again."

He stood frozen in the doorway. And I stood frozen at my desk. His fingers curled around the door, jaw tight. I wanted to leap into his arms and knew he wanted to be the one to catch me.

"I know it has," he said. "You've worked so hard. It's...it's made me think about a lot of things recently." He took a step farther in, a mess of complicated emotion scrawled across his face. "Daria, do you think we should—"

"*Knock, knock*," Janis said, appearing behind Theo with a slightly muted expression. "Sorry, Dar, are you okay? *Who do I have to kill?*"

I laughed again, pressing the heel of my hand to my eyes.

"No, no, I'm fine. Better than fine. No need to kill. I just got some incredible news like three seconds ago."

Janis hooked her thumb over her shoulder. "Wanna swing by my office and tell me about it? I was actually looking for you and Theo to talk about some stuff. If you've got a minute."

"When don't I have a minute for my favorite mentor?" he said. "Although, so help me god, if this meeting is you giving me a list of exotic animals you want at your birthday party, I will find your stash of weed and throw it in the ocean."

She barked out a laugh. "*Ha.* And what, get all the fish high? I'm calling your bluff, Theo. You love animals too much."

His lips twitched. "I will not organize a group of flamingos to put on roller skates."

"A group of flamingos is called a *flamboyance* and I'm *not asking you* to do that," she huffed out. "But come on, we all need to talk for real. It's about your destinies again."

29

THEO

*F*ive weeks had gone by since the night Janis had dragged us to her office to announce her idea for our new combined show. Last time she'd found us mid-argument, furious with each other about quotes in the *Times*. I'd stalked in here and couldn't even make eye contact with my raven-haired rival.

Today we were walking into her office moments after she'd interrupted Daria's glorious news about her book. News that had made her shine like a constellation in the sky. News that had made her so heart-achingly beautiful, I was seconds away from suggesting we say *fuck it* and tell all of K-SUN we were dating, consequences be damned.

"What's your good news, Daria?" Janis asked. "And Theo, make sure that door is shut tight, will you?"

Instead of sitting behind her desk like usual, she was leaning against the front. And instead of weird furniture masquerading as chairs, she'd pulled two real ones for us to sit in. The unusual formality had a nervous anticipation rising in me.

Daria sniffed and brushed the hair from her face. Her

cheeks were still pink, sapphire eyes even brighter than normal. "I wrote a book of essays, like a memoir, using my blog posts and all that I learned from Jackson leaving me at the altar. I sent it out to agents like ten months ago and assumed I wasn't going to hear back. But I just got off the phone with an agent who loved my manuscript."

Janis clapped her hands together. "*Hot damn.* Good for you, kid. When life hands you a piece-of-shit fiancé, you take those lemons and turn them into a lucrative book deal."

"As the classic saying goes," I said, hiding a smile.

Daria's hands flew to her face. "I'm completely and totally overwhelmed. *Anyway*, what did you need to see me and Theo about? Something with the show?"

Yet another thing that had changed so dramatically as to be laughable. We weren't just getting along on the air, we were very obviously enjoying ourselves. My mind was filled with a steady stream of memories from the past two weeks: Daria, naked and under my sheets, rehashing listener questions with a sleepy smile. Daria, lying on my porch swing with her head in my lap and my fingers in her hair while I pointed out the stars. Daria, barefoot and wearing only my shirt, sitting on the floor with my old psychology textbooks spread around her, brainstorming future themed episodes based on things she'd read.

Janis noticed her cheerful tone too, cocking her head with narrowed eyes. Beneath that grizzled-sea-captain exterior was a leader who didn't miss a goddamn thing, and I was extremely aware that our secret relationship was living on borrowed time.

"Your show is gold," Janis said. "Better than gold. The board is happy, our listeners are thrilled, and the two of you are becoming legitimate local celebrities here in town. I couldn't be more impressed with how you've pulled it off."

I hooked my ankle over my knee. "And our finances?"

Her lips thinned. "Better. We're not out of the woods yet, but at our last meeting, the Board was confident that we won't have to capitulate to a corporate buyout. For now." She waved her hands in front of her. "This shit is cyclical. We'll stay vigilant and keep up the fight, but I don't want to diminish how much of that is because of your hard work."

Janis cleared her throat, clasping her hands in front of her. "I received a call from All Star Media yesterday. They're the company that syndicated Magnolia's show back in the day. They were asking about your new show. Given the very sudden spike in popularity and that you're gaining traction fast regionally, they wanted to inquire about purchasing the show for syndication on their internet streaming platform. That means any person with an internet connection here in the States would be able to listen to your weekly shows. They see the potential for *Love and Life Advice* to become a major hit and they want to jump on the opportunity before someone else does."

"What?" I asked, stunned. "They want...someone wants to syndicate...us? Not our separate—"

"Nope," Janis interrupted. "This was an offer for both of you, long as the intention is for the show to continue in its current format. People call in. You answer their questions about love and keep up the super active social media presence. It doesn't affect you being local celebrities or us staying out in the community. What it *does* affect is your growth and your reach on top of that."

She shot me a discerning look—she knew I'd been waiting for this conversation for years and now that Daria and I were working together it had come in a matter of *weeks*.

"This would be good for the station, right?" Daria asked, sounding dazed.

Janis hesitated. "It means a lot more stable money. More

press, more attention. Easier to get and keep members when their favorite DJs and hosts are popular. I'm not gonna lie, when your mom got syndicated it changed things big time around here. But the spotlight on you is only going to grow locally. This would mean it would also grow nationally. There will be a lot more eyes on you and a lot more opinions *about* you. And a bigger platform to manage plus a larger fan base."

A slow, creeping dread was spreading through my limbs. "Janis, whatever you think might be—"

She held up her hand but there was such an intense kindness behind those glasses that my breathing hitched.

"I'm bringing this decision to you and placing it in your hands entirely. I have every confidence that you could handle this. Listening to your show these past few weeks has been an absolute joy. You're funny, you're interesting, you play off the questions and each other and"— she rubbed her palms together again, and I realized I was seeing her nervous tic for the first time— "you've made me very proud."

"I don't understand," Daria said.

"I know that you're dating each other," Janis said. "And I'm no expert in this stuff, but I'm sure growing your show exponentially could be a lot of pressure. And we haven't even talked about what that means here, at K-SUN. What it would mean for the cohosts to be, you know, romantically involved. I wish I could say there won't be scrutiny, but of course there will be."

All the air left my body. I dropped my elbows to my knees and scrubbed my hands down my face, the stress warring with the relief.

"You are dating, right?" Janis said.

My eyes slid to Daria's, and I saw the same collision of conflicting emotions. Our secret had weighed on her as heavily as it weighed on me. She bit her lip but gave me a short nod.

"Yes, we're dating," I said hoarsely.

Janis finally cracked a smile. "Don't worry, I'm not mad, so you can stop looking like you're about to throw up on the carpet. It's a delicate situation though, and I understand the complicated place this puts you in."

I looked back and forth between Daria and Janis. "Wait, you're not pissed at us?"

She shrugged, looking a bit more like the sea captain. "Maybe if you'd been doing this for six months. I'd be hurt, mostly, that you didn't tell me. And yeah, of course I'd be pissed. This is a goddamn workplace, not a dive bar, much as I've been trying to manifest that energy here for years. But I've known you both long enough to know that you wouldn't do that on purpose."

"How do you know that?" Daria asked.

"You have a lot of integrity. Both of you do. And I trust you. That's what this *building-a-community* thing is all about. But I can't protect you from the staff, who might be angry or concerned and would have every right to be. I can't protect you from the public either, and they'll have as many opinions about your relationship as there are blades of grass."

"What about the Board?" I asked.

She frowned. "Fuck the Board. I do feel a *little* bit responsible. I did force you to work together, spend all that extra time together, so I can't really be too mad."

"But how did you know?" I asked carefully. "We haven't told anyone."

Janis glanced between us with an exaggerated look of shock. "I'm not sure how to put this nicely, but you are extremely, extremely obvious." She reached her hand out. "Not obvious the way you were when you were fighting. But if you thought this was a secret, it is *not*."

Daria and I hadn't exchanged a word. I wasn't even sure I'd taken a full breath. My emotions warred between surprise, relief and a low-key embarrassment.

"If we did anything unprofessional or made people feel uncomfortable, please let us know. We...this wasn't..." I waved my hand between us, feeling much too tongue-tied for a person who gave advice for a living. "We would want to apologize."

"Yes, please," Daria said firmly.

Janis shook her head. "No, it's nothing like that. It's just, like, your faces."

"Our faces?" I asked.

"The way that you look at each other."

Yet again, for the millionth time, Daria had reduced me to nothing more than a novice. An amateur. If a caller had admitted they were falling in love with their coworker and couldn't say anything about it, I would have absolutely advised them to *not make it obvious on their face*.

"This is excellent feedback, thank you," I said.

Janis snorted. "I told you to loosen up and have fun and it seems you took that managerial suggestion swimmingly. *But* none of this solves the question of what we're going to do about this. The way I see it, you've got two options. We go for syndication, your show gets a ton of attention, the station makes more money. Or you don't go for syndication...*yet*... stay local, build a base here, and we make less money at first, more money in the future."

My brow furrowed. "Syndication is huge, it's all we—it's all *I've* wanted to have happen since I first came here. It seems like an obvious *yes*. We need the money, don't we?"

I'd spoken without looking at Daria. Janis did though, and whatever she saw had lines tightening around her mouth. "Yes and no. The complication is your personal lives. I think you can inform the listeners that you are together, knowing that you'll lose some people. Knowing that you could lose the syndication offer. Or you can keep hiding it. But I guarantee it'll come out somehow, and then you'll have lied when you're both pretty into the whole honesty thing. You'll absolutely lose people because you've built their trust and broken it."

"We wouldn't be the first couple to host a talk show," I said. "Why would that risk the offer?"

The word *couple* tasted strange on my tongue because Daria and I had had zero conversations about any of this— what we wanted, where we were going, who we were to each other. A quick glance at her wide-eyed profile confirmed my worst fears. A voice inside my head urged me to stop this meeting, urged me to drag Daria someplace safe and hash out what we wanted before everything went haywire.

"It risks the offer because things, you know—" Janis shrugged. "Things could get messy. Or something. It's not that you're together, it's more what happens if…"

Ice water flooded my veins.

"What happens if we break up." I could barely force the words through gritted teeth. The agonizing loss I felt at the mere suggestion of not being with Daria was chilling. If at any point I needed an indicator of how far gone I was for Daria Stone, the fact that the words "break up" had black dots dancing across my vision would have been it.

"Yeah, that you could break up," Janis replied simply. "Dar, are you okay? You haven't said anything in a minute."

"I'm okay. My head's spinning is all. Between the agent call and this…this *news*, I'm not sure what to think." Daria's hands fluttered nervously in her lap. "Even with everything you said, national syndication is still what's best for K-SUN, right?"

I turned sharply at the anguish in her voice.

"Let me be clear here," Janis said. "What's best for my *employees* is what's best for K-SUN. I could give a flying fuck if people don't like your show because you're dating. I could give a flying fuck if they think that makes us look bad. I haven't cared about the opinions of a bunch of strangers for a long time. Now, from a bottom-line perspective? Yeah, having another show go big makes everything easier. From a *personal* perspective? Forcing two people I happen to love very much into a position they don't want to be in just to make a little extra cash will never be an option for me."

She held up her finger when she saw my face. "Don't get smart, Theo. We both know I would have split *Love and Life Advice* apart if either of you was hurting that bad. That first week was so awful I almost did, but I'm glad I didn't." She softened her voice. "There will be an added level of scrutiny and pressure on your relationship. That's all I want you to think about before giving me your decision."

I rubbed a hand across my mouth and stared at the floor. Daria must have seemed equally upset because the next thing I knew Janis was touching my arm.

"You've got a show tonight, right?"

Fuck. "Yes. Why?"

Her eyes moved between us. "You've both been working really hard, and I just dropped a couple bombshells. Why don't you take the night off, and I'll have Elena play a compilation of your old shows or something?"

"Sure, whatever." I was still dazed. Until I saw Daria's deep frown, her knee shaking nervously, and my heart sank. "That's probably a smart idea."

"Thank you," Daria said quickly. She pushed to stand. "We'll talk. I appreciate your understanding." She turned on her heel to go but Janis stopped her, shifting back and forth on her feet.

"I'm not super great at all the feelings stuff, as I'm sure Theo has told you," Janis said.

I nodded. "The two times you expressed any kind of tenderness around me, you swore me to secrecy."

Her face lightened. "Exactly. And I'll preface this by swearing you both to secrecy again. The work stuff, the syndication offer, I know it's complicated. I don't want to make it more so by forgetting to mention that I'll support whatever you choose to do. I love you both." She coughed into her hand. "Very much. If you're making each other happy, then the person who gives you any shit about it is gonna get punched in the throat. By me."

Daria's entire body softened, and the ghost of her real smile appeared on her face. She gave Janis a very fast hug, though Janis just patted her on the back. All I could think about was the story Daria had told me, of Janis sitting with her in the sunshine while she cried for hours after the wedding.

"I love you too, Janis," she said. "I'm sorry to make you share your feelings but I'm glad you got to mention throat punching."

"You can make it up to me by bringing those flamingos Theo mentioned to my party."

Daria grinned, looking much more like herself. Though as she turned to leave, I saw that smile vanish, saw her fingers tighten into fists at her side.

I moved to follow her but stopped in the doorway, turning back to Janis who was studying me with a wry smile. "I love you too, you know."

Her eyebrows raised. "Then bring me more exotic animals."

"I will not."

"Then I guess you don't love me."

I breathed out a laugh, twisting at the waist to spot Daria turning right down the hallway.

"Theo."

"Yes?" I muttered, distracted.

"You and Daria bring out the best in each other on your show and that's why All Star Media called me so quickly. *Even still* I would never want you to think of it as 'proof' of your talent and skill one way or another. You've been the face of this station for four years because you love people and you love this town, and that's not something that can be measured in dollar signs."

I rubbed the back of my neck. "Thank you," I said gruffly.

She nodded, cocked her head in the direction where Daria had gone and said, "Now go get her."

I slapped my hand against the doorway and did just that.

30

THEO

The door to Daria's office was cracked open. The second I reached it, I heard her say, "Theo?"

I slipped inside. She was curled up on her couch and tugging on her silver earrings.

"Can I join you?"

She nodded, distracted, but patted the spot next to her.

"Daria," I said quietly. "Your book. You did it. I know that was a lot back there with Janis, but *you did it.*"

"I finally did it." Her throat worked on a swallow. "And that book, my show, my whole brand, is based on the fact that I fully intended on never being in a relationship again. It's why this agent liked my manuscript. She said I was *firm in my convictions.* And now we get this amazing career opportunity, but it definitely means everyone finds out about us. How does that look, when I'm the so-called expert on being single but I've been dating my cohost in secret?"

I clasped my hands together tightly. "Whenever you sell yourself that way, I feel like you're selling yourself short, Daria. I haven't read your book, but I've sat with you for weeks now, hearing you with listeners, and you're *more* than that. Your story is more than that. Who says the ending of that book can't change?"

A line formed between her brows. "That's easier for you to say. You've had four years to establish yourself in this industry while I'm only starting. You dating your cohost is literally on-brand for you. For me? It makes me seem like a fraud."

Unease slithered down my spine. "When did our *brands* become the focus of this conversation? I came in here to ask you what you wanted to do about us, not compare market research on how our relationship plays out in listener satisfaction."

Irritation flashed across her eyes. "Don't pretend that this national offer means nothing to you and your career. This is what you've been working so hard for. One of the reasons we fought so much when I first came here is because you saw me as a professional *threat.*"

I pinched the bridge of my nose and sighed. It'd been a while since we'd fallen back into our old patterns, but the source of these conflicts was the same: we weren't telling each other the whole truth. We were hiding from what was hard. And if my past partners felt like I ran from compromises and tough conversations, this was my chance to show Daria otherwise.

I pushed the coffee table back and got down on my knees in front of her, putting us on eye level. I wrapped my hands around hers and squeezed. She let out a long breath and relaxed forward, pressed her forehead to mine. My heart rate slowed immediately.

"It's just me," I said softly. "It's just me and I'm here with you, same as I've been every night for the past two weeks. Whatever professional risks we take, I'm willing to take them together."

She turned her head and kissed my cheek for a few sweet

seconds. "I'm sorry. I'm here with you too, I promise. Risks and all."

I bent my head until I caught her eye. "Forget the show, forget having to make a decision about anything right now. What's making you afraid?"

"That call from that agent and what Janis said is kind of setting me off," she admitted. "I want my book to be published. I even want to keep making our show together."

"I want to keep making our show together too," I said, as a tenuous hope blossomed in my chest.

"But suddenly, I realized how much I'd be opening my life up again. That there would be a lot of critical eyes on what we're doing. Last time that happened to me, I was standing in a wedding dress, having to inform one hundred guests that apparently the groom wasn't coming. I had to stand there, mortified, while people asked me questions I did not have the answers to. And later some of those same people blamed *me* for him not showing up. Then I had to call Jackson and beg him to tell me where he was and have him say that I wasn't lovable. Not anymore."

The amount of unchecked violence I felt toward this man could have powered a jet engine.

"I'd finally stopped being so amenable to his needs while ignoring my own. I stopped play-acting and let my true self shine through, and he told me I was *too much* to love. Too loud, too weird, too joyful, too greedy." Daria wiped her cheeks, but her chin was raised, expression proud. "He did me a big favor. I didn't love him. Not really. Our marriage would have been a disaster. It's still hard for me though, to remember that the second I started to take up my own space, I was left in the most embarrassing way possible."

I smoothed her hair back and stroked my thumb over her temple, every muscle aching with the gravity of her story.

"It makes me scared to put our new show and our new"— she waved her hand— "new *us* on a national stage because I

313

think Janis is right. We'd have to disclose that we were dating because having it come from some other source will only make us look like shady liars. But you and I want different things. How can we declare this to our fans when we haven't even defined it ourselves? When I'm not even sure…."

"Sure what?"

"What if I never want to be married? What if long-term commitment doesn't work for me, so we break up and it ruins our show, and everything here at K-SUN is horrible? And then we've shattered this perfect *place*, this little family that means so much to us both? There's risk and then there's *ruin*."

It felt like a fist was closing around my throat. I thought about the bravest choices, the ones that Daria and I had been privileged to listen to in the sound booth we shared now. There was no room for *perfect* in this moment, only honesty. In the past, I would have filled this room with roses or taken Daria to a candlelit dinner after planning out what I wanted to say for days.

Instead, I was kneeling on carpet that hadn't been updated in twenty years, next to a table covered in takeout containers and show notes, while in the hallway my coworkers were loudly discussing the best place to pick up lunch before the pledge drive.

But this was Daria. I knew what mattered to her.

It had never been *ambiance*.

"I understand all of those fears, Daria. I really do. They're serious and losing this place we love worries me too. I don't want to lose it. But I can't lose you either."

She bit her lip, cheeks pink. "What's making you afraid?"

My stomach hollowed. "I'm afraid that I'll only ever want more of you. And you'll only ever want less. Every time I've reached for love, I've been left too. By my parents, most of all. I thought unconditional love was something you had to earn. And I tried to earn it by being perfect and quiet and never asking for much. I understand taking up space and being told you don't deserve to."

"Oh, Theo," she said, reaching to cup my face.

I grabbed her hand and kissed her wrist instead, keeping my eyes on hers. "You taught me that I don't know the first thing about falling in love. With you, I finally understand what true love *is*. And it is far more terrifying and exhilarating and *beautiful* than I could ever have imagined. Anything romantic that I felt before is a pale comparison to how I feel whenever I'm around you."

I kissed her wrist again. "Daria, you cannot be quantified. You cannot be studied or measured. I couldn't distill the magnificence of who you are into a pithy piece of advice if I tried for a hundred years. You are a marvel, and I love you. I'm *in* love with you."

Her smile was a revelation. Her breathing hitched, eyes shining. "What did you say?"

I slid my hands around her hips and tugged her close. "I'm in love with you—"

Daria kissed me, flinging her arms around my neck and sinking against my body. As her lips slanted over mine, I could feel her smiling, could feel the joy in her limbs, our breath tangled together. I slid my hands up her back and relaxed into a moment that was perfect without the pressure of perfection. Let my heart sing as Daria kissed me with a sweet and breathless passion that was addicting.

"You are so worth every risk," she whispered, both hands pressed to my face. Knowing her history, I didn't expect her to say those same words back to me—in fact, like everything else I'd shared with her recently, keeping them to myself *was* the burden.

My love for Daria deserved to flourish in the light of day.

"Theo, I want to be with you, and I want to keep our show. We just have to figure out in what way. No matter what decisions we make, as long as we make them together and stay honest, I *know* it can work."

"I agree. And for what it's worth, I have too much trust in this community we've created here to think we'd be truly ruined. I don't think it's possible." I brushed my mouth against hers. She parted her lips, stole a kiss. "What do you need in order to make our decision?"

"I need time," she said firmly. "A few days by myself with my own thoughts, listening to my own heart."

I nodded. "That I can definitely do."

"What do you need?" she asked.

I held her gaze, filling it with as much obvious trust as I could muster. "All I need is for you to come back to me when you're done."

She wrapped her arms around me. "I will come back to you, Theo. And that's a promise."

But an hour later, after Daria had left and I'd stumbled out an excuse to Des and Elena about Janis giving us the night off, I found myself right back where I started all those weeks ago. Standing on the deck behind Janis's office and staring out at the boardwalk, my thoughts consumed by only one woman.

I clung to trust. I clung to hope. I clung to the emotion in her voice when she whispered *you are so worth the risk*.

The anxiety was there too, spiky and sharp beneath the surface. I'd been so swept up in the moment, baring my heart and my love with full honesty, I hadn't stopped to think *what if I'm doing this all wrong?* If I wasn't an expert on love, then I wasn't an expert on *this* part either—placing my heart in a position to be broken.

"You're still here?" Janis appeared at my elbow, taking up a similar position, staring out at the sparkling lights of the Ferris wheel.

"I just needed…"

"I hear ya."

We were quiet for a minute until I said, "Daria and I are going to talk in a couple days about the offer."

"We've got a few days," she said. "I'm not worried. Might be a little worried about you though."

I didn't answer.

"I've known you through a couple relationships, Theo. This is the first time I'm seeing you in love."

I exhaled a ragged breath. "I told Daria the same thing." I nudged her arm. "Was this your plan all along?"

"What, have you fall in love with your cohost?"

I shot her a wry look.

She huffed in indignation. "I lied before when I said you were super obviously in love the past few weeks. I knew it four months ago. When she first got here."

I turned to face her, stunned.

"I was at Daria's wedding. The wedding that wasn't," she said. "I didn't really know the guy she'd been with since high school, but I knew that before they got together, she was this total *firecracker*. She was young, only a kid, but with this confidence that came straight from Mags. Even then I could tell she was gonna be one hell of a radio personality."

Janis cleared her throat. "When she had to give everyone the bad news about her groom, I watched her stand up there like a queen, even though I knew it cost her everything." She rested her hand on my arm. "I knew that if Daria ever fell in love, it would have to be with someone as extraordinary as she is. And last time I checked that person was you. Since I've been your mentor for a while now, I'm an expert on your best qualities."

My chest felt much too tight, but I still managed to loop an arm around her shoulders. "That's now the fourth time you've shown emotion around me, you know."

"And it'll be the last if you tell anyone."

"I'll take it to my grave. The one I'll be going to well before you, apparently."

"Because I'm never going to die." She reached down and lifted a white plate in the air, bringing with it the smell of powdered sugar and fried dough. "Also, do you want this funnel cake I got for you in case you were sad?"

I laughed and snatched the plate from her. "I'm not too sad but I will eat this cake. Thank you."

Janis did her usual shrugging off my gratitude while I pulled apart pieces of cake and enjoyed the simple pleasure of sugary boardwalk food on a warm Saturday night. It was funny the way love continued to show up, again and again. You could live in a cold house with stoic parents receiving the bare minimum of affection, and then, years later, it could appear in all the places you never even thought to look.

Love was persistent like that.

DARIA

Three days later

$\mathcal{I}$ sat cross-legged in the back of my Jeep, surrounded by flowers, about to possibly lose the interest of the only agent who'd seemed to like my book.

"So why the early call?" Joanne asked. "Is everything okay?"

I rubbed a pink petal between my thumb and forefinger. "Everything is great, but that's the reason that I'm calling." I stared up at the roof. "When I wrote the essays that you read, I *was* intending on being single for the rest of my life. I wasn't lying in that last chapter. But I hadn't met Theo yet."

My face went hot. Just saying his name out loud made me blush.

"Theo Chadwick, your...cohost on the radio?" she asked quizzically.

"Yep, that's the one. That's not public knowledge yet, so I'm trusting you'll keep it to yourself," I said lightly.

"Of course, that's not a problem. I'm just pretty shocked."

"Well, so was I," I muttered. "I want to be honest with you. If my book sells, I can't publish it with the last chapter as is. It's not the reality and it's not true. I know that *Choosing Yourself* is about more than being single, but I do go hard on the whole *permanently single* angle, and it wouldn't be right when I'm clearly in a relationship with someone."

I chewed on my bottom lip, thought about authenticity and bravery and change. "I've been sitting with this problem for a few days now and I...I believe the book would be stronger with this new ending. I believe it's stronger because I still loved myself first, before I met Theo, and it made all the difference for me. I want the last essay to be this experience right here, of falling for my cohost and discovering I was right about so many things. And, because I'm only human, wrong about some stuff too."

There was a long, weighted pause, then Joanne said, "I'd have to see these new pages, of course, and make sure the voice still matches the overall theme, but I agree with you. Perfection is outdated. Readers want to feel like the person who wrote their book is a human being full of flaws."

"I got a few of those." I winced when I pricked my finger on a thorn. "If I send you a new chapter, you'll read it over?"

"I'd love to. We can tweak some of the beginning, make it clear that you choosing yourself doesn't negate choosing to love another person either. Which, to be fair, was the theme of your book all along."

My mother strode through the parking lot to pick up the final round of bouquets for my grand, romantic gesture, her black hair flying behind her shoulders, her walking speed forever set at *bat-out-of-hell*.

I tipped my head back on a long sigh. "If you haven't already figured it out, I give advice for a living, but I don't know what I'm doing myself."

Joanne laughed. "Thank you for telling me the truth,

Daria. And if you're rewriting the ending of your book for this guy, that tells me he must be some kind of wonderful."

You cannot be quantified. You cannot be studied or measured. I couldn't distill the magnificence of who you are into a pithy piece of advice if I tried for a hundred years.

"You have no idea how wonderful," I said softly. "Thanks for taking a chance on me. I'll write like the wind, I promise."

Joanne and I hung up as my mom popped open the rear of my Jeep with a triumphant grin. She scooped up a bunch of roses by my feet but was attacked by the same thorns.

"Shit, *fuck*." She sucked the tip of her index finger into her mouth and glared at the red petals. "Why are people always going on and on about these things when they can hurt you?"

I brushed a few curls from my face and a shower of leaves fell out. "I have no clue. You know what can't hurt you? A good old-fashioned mixtape."

A grin slashed across her face. She reached into her pocket and pulled out the tape she'd made last night—with my very minimal help—using a dual cassette player she'd bought at a garage sale and a stack of cassettes that Janis had lent her from her mighty collection. "Do you really think Martha's going to like it? It's not too cheesy?"

"Mom," I said, "if the lady wasn't obsessed with you before, she'll be obsessed with you now."

She nodded to herself, confidence restored, and dropped the tape back in her pocket. She knew I was going to be here early this morning and had promised to stop by and help on the thirty-minute news break during her show. One of the best parts about having a mom who was regularly up at dawn was the bizarre number of places she knew in Sunrise Beach that sold fresh flowers and vases at the oddest hours.

I reached my hands forward and she helped me climb out, sending even more cuttings and leaves to the ground. With our arms overflowing with bouquets, we left the Jeep and made our way to Theo's office.

It was a skeleton crew this early but every bleary-eyed production assistant we bumped into took one look at the flowers and said, "Are these for your boyfriend, Theo?"

"I really thought we were doing a good job of keeping it a secret," I muttered out the side of my mouth.

Mom frowned. "What's your definition of 'good job,' baby girl?"

Inside, it looked like a floral bomb had gone off in Theo's office—empty vases, piles of leaves, clusters of flowers on every flat surface. I fingered the small white card in my pocket, still blank.

"How long do you have until Theo gets here?" she asked, dropping the last few stems onto his desk. "Also, I crushed some of the flowers here." She pointed. "And here. Also, some of these don't look right and that's probably because of my boots."

I hid a smile. "I only have an hour but all I have to do is take *this*"—I indicated the minor catastrophe of flower petals — "and arrange them in such a way that conveys *I'm stupid in love with you.*"

Mom pulled me into a side hug. "I haven't had a lot of opportunities in this life to convey *I'm stupid in love with you* but if anyone can pull it off, it's you."

I arched an eyebrow. "What kind of energy do you think that mixtape is giving off?"

She blushed. "Ah, hell, you're probably right. I'm lucky that Martha's so patient with the fact that I don't know anything about this *having a girlfriend* business. There's something freeing about being almost sixty years old and realizing you don't know shit, you never knew shit, and you never will."

I sank to the floor and pulled handfuls of daisies into my lap, haphazardly arranging them into a vase. "I'm going to seriously start considering using *I'm Daria Stone and none of us know shit* as my show sign-off." I held up the vase for her perusal. "Do you think these daisies say *I'm looking forward to cohosting a radio show with you?*"

Mom shrugged. "Sure, why not?"

I'd told Theo I needed a couple days to think, and I'd embraced that time eagerly. Had even hiked the long, eight-mile trail that he'd finished the other day, spending time at the lookout point as revelations crashed over me like the waves breaking against the coast.

That call from Joanne had shaken up a burst of excited nerves. And Janis telling us we'd gotten an offer for national syndication had shaken up a burst of insecurities. But on a day full of surprises and shake-ups, Theo saying *I love you* made the most sense of all.

It was more than *I love you*. I knew that because my mind had recorded what he'd said as if it was making its own mixtape.

You are a marvel and I love you. I'm in love with you.

There were love languages. And then there was Theo, putting his heart and his fears and his deepest vulnerabilities on the line because he knew I'd appreciate that kind of open-ness most of all. His honesty didn't eliminate our differences or our challenges ahead. I trusted that we would figure things out together.

Deciding to fill his office with flowers was a paltry gift in comparison to all that he'd given me. But it was the best option I had to show him the way he made my heart feel: bursting over with love.

The idea had come to me last night in the middle of mixtape-making with my mom. After two days of being alone, I'd driven to my childhood home, crawled onto the couch, and lay with my head in her lap the way I used to as a kid. She didn't bat an eye, merely patted my hair with one hand while recording cassettes with the other. At first, she assumed I was there to drink the bottle of champagne she'd bought for the news about my agent.

Instead, I spilled the entire story of me and Theo, stream-of-consciousness style. Because I had learned from my listeners that it was easier to figure out what to do next when our messy thoughts were brought into the light of day.

Halfway through the telling, I knew exactly what I needed to do. It helped that my mother had suspected we were dating all along, confirming Janis's description of our overly obvious pining.

Mom's hand landed softly on the top of my head while I was wrestling another bouquet into submission. I looked up, and she brushed the hair from my forehead. "There's no doubt in my mind that he's going to love all of it," she said firmly.

I sighed, closing my eyes. "I really hope so. I really, *really* hope we can figure things out together."

She crouched down next to me. "I didn't say this to you last night and I should have. Do you remember when you and Jackson got those engagement pictures done?"

I grimaced. "Vaguely. I was deeply unhappy that day."

"Maybe if I wasn't your mom, I would have been able to look at those photos and not feel like my heart was being torn in two," she said. "But I am your mom. When I saw them, you looked like his accessory. You looked like his *side-kick*. All of twenty-two years old and feeling like you had to live your life for another person instead of yourself."

My stomach twisted at the memory of that feeling—a distant memory, but a powerful one.

"I knew what you and Theo had was serious that night at the arcade," she continued. "It's hard to describe, but it was like your body language together radiated this *joy*. You were so in sync with each other, so in tune." She snapped her fingers together. "You know what? You and Theo *looked* the way a great song *sounds*. That make sense?"

"Perfect sense," I whispered, much too overcome with emotion.

"Most importantly, baby girl, you looked like *yourself*." She kissed the top of my head and clomped through another clump of roses. "That's how I know he's the one for you." She glanced at her watch. "Oh *shit*, I have to get back. I'd say good luck, but you won't need it, I swear."

She barreled out through Theo's office door at the same speed she'd barreled in, leaving me vibrating with love and my cheeks wet with tears. Then I released a slow exhale, grabbed my scissors, and got to work.

The next hour passed in a blur. I hung a garland of flowers around his door and stacked a dozen bouquets on his desk. Wildflowers dotted his windowsills, and his coffee table was all thick stalks of sunflowers, heads bobbing in their vases. I scattered rose petals in a path from the door to his desk, from his desk to his couch, leaving a spray on the cushions. But I was still only halfway done—my body a mess of cuts and dirt, his office a floral maelstrom—when his velvety voice echoed a greeting down the hallway.

"Oh my god, he's *early*," I hissed. I stood up too quickly, scattering supplies and flowers, and tried to clean up as best as I could. I shoved the card into the spray of daisies, realizing a second too late I hadn't gotten a chance to write anything on it.

I was in the middle of picking up all the leaves on the ground when Theo appeared in the doorway. I stopped, mid-motion, and was suddenly grateful that this position allowed me to see the full panorama of emotion that appeared on his face when he saw the flowers—surprise, relief, gratitude, *love*.

It hadn't even been a full three days since we last saw each other, and my knees were weak from missing him.

He took a step inside and shut the door. "Daria," he said gruffly. "What...what is this?"

"I think they call it a romantic gesture?"

His green eyes flew to mine. "No one's ever gotten me flowers before. It's usually the other way around."

I dropped the leaves and scratched the back of my head, feeling proud and bashful in equal measure. He reached for the bouquet of daisies and the blank card.

"That was supposed to have a message for you but…"

His brow arched. "But what?"

I twisted my fingers together nervously. "You got here early before I could write it."

His jaw tightened. "What was it going to say?"

"This morning I spoke with that agent, Joanne, and told her I didn't want her trying to sell the book yet because I needed to dramatically rewrite the ending."

One end of his mouth hitched up. "Is that so?"

"This wild thing happened where I'd written an ending declaring I was going to be single for life. Until I fell in love with my radio show cohost. A cohost who was also my former enemy." I tilted my head to the side. "Really, it's a way better ending for the drama alone."

A ripple of motion went through his body. He set the card down and said, "Come here."

I closed the distance between us easily, stopping when the tip of my boots touched the tip of his shoes. There were shadows under his eyes and scruff on his jaw. A single curl fell across his forehead. He was so handsome it hurt. Especially when that half-smile grew into a full grin that took my breath away.

"Can you please say all of that again?" he asked.

"I'm in love with you—"

His lips were on mine before I finished, but I didn't care one bit. It was a full-body kiss, a complete assault on my senses. I wrapped my arms around his neck while his hands pulled me tight against his chest, our lips moving hungrily.

"I love you, Theo," I said when we finally broke apart. "I love you with my whole heart. I know, growing up, you felt like you had to beg for scraps of love from your family, and I don't want you to ever feel that way with me."

His eyes crinkled at the sides. "Is that why you filled my office to the brim with flowers?"

"Yes, *and* even though you've been shifting your opinion on some things, I know you're still a hopeless romantic. I'm not a bouquet type of girl but I can be the type of girl who buys them for you."

His hand curved around the back of my head and held me still as he kissed my forehead, inhaling for a long, sweet second. "I love you, Daria. So very much." He slid away, but only to step farther into his office and slowly turn around. The morning sun filtered in through the windows, making his office look like a woodland field.

"There are gifts," Theo said softly, "and then there are *gifts*."

I was all big, cheesy smiles as I watched him study each bouquet with an academic curiosity I now knew well.

"Before I met you," he said, head ducked to examine a spray of lavender, "I would have never wanted to admit that I didn't have much of a relationship with myself. Would never have admitted that my *own* rules around love had become so restrictive. I don't want us to ever stop learning from each other, Daria."

My heart was nothing but backsprings now. "I secretly believed I was done learning. Then I met you, Theo, and I discovered that there's nothing fraudulent about being a work in progress like every other confused human being who calls in to our show. Our names mean something to people, but that doesn't mean we don't deserve to change. There's no end to who we're becoming. There's no arrival. Fighting for people to love themselves *is* my goal in life, but that doesn't mean I can't also love you completely."

He stepped forward, careful not to crush any petals, and dipped his head for another kiss. This one softer, sweeter. We took our time, surrounded by sunflowers, drinking each other in with a kiss that felt like the beginning of everything.

When we parted, he pulled a leaf from my hair with a bemused grin. "Thank you for coming back to me."

I traced his jawline with my fingers. "Thank you for knowing that I would."

I felt his gaze land on the bag of supplies by the door, basically the only thing not covered in flowers. He toed the edge with his shoe. "What's this?"

"We're still building the community pantry today, right?"

Theo's smile blazed across his face, heating up every single inch of me.

"No empty promises," I whispered. "And this is important. For Janis. For the station. For our neighbors."

He caught my chin and pressed a firm kiss to my mouth. "I love you so much."

My toes curled in my Doc Martens. He grabbed the bag then my hand. "Come on, I was just getting set up outside. And we've got decisions to make about our jobs."

It was early enough to still be breezy and cool, the sun low in the sky. Seagulls flew overhead, and the ocean sparkled in the morning light. The boardwalk was empty of tourists but full of locals. We walked around to the side of the building, to the wall that one of Elena's friends had painted in a mural of rainbow-colored vinyl records. Leaning against it was a box with an unassembled narrow outdoor shed inside.

I reached into my bag and tossed Theo a box-cutter. He sliced down the sides, peeling open the box and laying the pieces onto the parking lot.

I pulled out the instructions and laughed when I saw how unbelievably simple they were. "It says here we'll be able to build this in ten minutes or less."

He rubbed the top of his hair. "I *might* have purchased the easiest one to assemble, but in my defense, this was back when we couldn't even turn on the coffee pot without fighting about it."

I tapped my chin. "Huh, was that *us?*"

He winked in response and handed me one of the long side pieces.

"So," I said, snapping one half of the roof together, "we've both had a few days to consider our options and the one thing I definitely want is to keep doing our combined show. How about you?"

His eyes shot to mine, full of that same relief and gratitude. "Me too. I want to keep working with you, Daria. But I've been doing a lot of thinking about the national syndication offer and I—" He took a breath. "I don't want to do it yet."

I stepped back to make eye contact. "Wait, you're being serious? I thought that's what you wanted for your career."

He rubbed the back of his neck. Smiled a little shyly. "One thing I've learned through all of this is how easy it's been for me to seek external validation that I belonged. I was this kid who grew up with parents who didn't love me. And then this love expert with girlfriends who only ever dumped me. I just wanted someone to say, *everything you went through, all those years of study, all that loneliness and hurt, was for a reason.*"

Theo held the side of the pantry tight as I slid the first panel of the door into the hinges. I grabbed a screwdriver while he held the door steady for me to tighten in the bolts. "Saying that out loud is hard to believe. I've told callers hundreds of times that it's impossible to find happiness when your validation only comes from outside forces."

I swung the door out, testing the hinges. Handed him the screwdriver for the other side. "It's hard but normal," I said gently. "You're only fighting decades of messaging telling you otherwise."

He finished the other side, and we closed the door together. I smiled when it clicked in tight, my gaze rising to meet Theo's. I used the tip of my boot to flip up the wire shelving for the inside.

"The thing is, Janis is right. Getting our show syndicated is a lot of money, but also a lot of pressure and a lot of scrutiny on our relationship. A month ago, I wouldn't have hesitated but now…" He reached into my hair, amused, and pulled out yet another leaf from one of the bouquets. "Right now, I'd rather focus on the two of us and keep Sunrise Beach at the center."

I released a giant sigh I didn't realize I'd been holding.

He cocked an eyebrow. "Do you feel the same way?"

"My fan base growing so exponentially this past year has already been stressful," I admitted. "I *like* being in Sunrise Beach and cultivating these fans first. I never want to grow for growth's sake. That doesn't mean I'm not interested in the future, just not right this very instant."

Theo settled the first shelf in the pantry, and I slid in the second and third.

"Let's not grow then," he said softly. "Until we're ready."

"Until we're ready," I repeated.

I went to reach for the fourth and final shelf, but Theo pulled me against his chest for a hug, pressing his face to my curls as my arms locked around his neck. He squeezed me tight, leaning back so my feet dangled off the ground and I burst into laughter. I peppered his face with kisses until he dropped me back down, wearing an effortless smile that matched my own.

"You're sure about this?" I asked.

"I've spent a lot of the past month feeling like a fraud and an amateur." He brushed his lips across my temple. "But not right now. Not making this choice, with you. Daria, I've never been so sure of anything in my life."

"On that, we most definitely agree," I whispered.

We snapped in the fourth shelf and stood back to admire our handiwork.

"She's a beauty," I declared.

"She sure is," he said, watching me.

The sound of shoes crunching across the asphalt had us spinning around to find Janis heading our way. I squealed and threw Theo the big bow I'd found. He stuck it to the top, proceeding to lean casually against the wall with his arms crossed.

"Mornin'," Janis called out as she reached us. "Today is the joyous day of my birth, in case you weren't aware."

"I was very aware," I said with a laugh. "My mom wanted me to tell you she dropped off a gift basket and it's on your desk. It's marijuana and junk food-themed."

"Seventy-one," she cheered. "The more you eat corn chips, the longer you live. It's a well-known saying."

Theo grinned. "No one has ever said that before."

"And yet here I am, smartass," she said fondly. She walked around the pantry, studying it with a delighted smile. "Well, well, well…what'd ya get me?"

Theo placed his palm on top, looking handsome and proud. "Happy birthday, oh mentor of mine. Daria and I built a food pantry for the radio station. A community endeavor, perfect for a place that embodies community. We'll keep it filled with food and our neighbors can take whatever they need."

She looked at him like he'd invented a new type of board-walk snack. "How did you know this would be a perfect gift?"

He shrugged good-naturedly. "You've been my mentor for a long time. That means I'm basically an expert in your best qualities."

An emotion passed between the two of them that was part mutual respect, part teasing affection, and part the crunchy love that Janis showered around this world like confetti.

"I love it very much," she said, voice cracking. Theo squeezed an arm around her shoulders and winked at me when she wasn't looking.

"So what's the word, kids? Have you figured out a game

plan?" she asked while opening and closing the pantry doors with a toothy grin. "Holy shit, we can really fit a lot of food in here."

"That's the idea," he said warmly. "Radio for the people. Food for all. Call it a theme."

Her head popped out from behind the door. "I call it being part of the resistance."

Theo's eyes slid to mine. His smile felt like a secret only for me. "That too. All tie-dye, no suits. And to your earlier questions, yes. We have a plan."

Janis nodded toward the front door. "Then let's get going. Those destinies are waiting for you again."

"How many destinies do we have?" I asked.

She shrugged. "Twelve? I don't know. I don't make the rules."

And as we turned to follow our boss inside, Theo wrapped an arm around my shoulders and pulled me close. He buried his mouth in my hair and whispered, "And you are my destiny, Daria Stone."

3 2

THEO

I knew it was going to be a good show. Not because of the number of marriage proposals, but because of my beautiful cohost.

It was our first since Janis had informed us of the syndication offer. And our first since we'd politely declined the offer, choosing to nurture our local base first. It meant less money, and we'd be disclosing our relationship to our listeners tonight.

But Janis was unperturbed in the end. We had a growing membership base thanks to *Love and Life Advice* and a newly energized radio community thanks to our events—it wasn't perfect, but it never would be.

We'd keep fighting because we understood we had a right to be on these airwaves.

Daria and I sat across from each other at the table, headphones and microphones in front of us, same as always. The difference now was that I'd wedged my foot between hers under the table, safe from view. Every so often she'd squeeze her feet against mine with a comforting smile.

The pop of a champagne cork startled us both. It was Elena, laughing as bubbles spilled down her hand. Des held

333

cups beneath it, catching as much liquid as possible before it dripped to the floor.

"Champagne already?" Daria asked. "Damn, Janis really celebrates her birthday all week long, doesn't she?"

"I'm right here, you know. And yeah, I do," she said. She was also in the mixing room with Des and Elena, feet kicked up on the sofa and a peaceful smile on her lined face. "I also thought it could help with any pre-show jitters."

My eyes slid to Daria's bright blue ones, smudged with dark eyeliner. Her black hair was wild and curly, her earrings glittered, her red lips curving into a knowing grin.

"What jitters?" I mused. "I've never been so calm and prepared."

Janis barked out a *ha*. Des and Elena stepped into the sound booth with their cups, cheering us with goofy grins.

"Is telling everyone we fell in love like the worst idea? Or a brilliant idea?" Daria asked.

Elena peeked around at the board. "We'll find out soon, since you're on in five minutes."

"And after, there's always the collection of extremely strange and very erotic fan fiction you two have been receiving," Des said soberly. "I've been saving the best ones for a drunk reading at the next K-SUN holiday party."

"Jesus." I laughed, rubbing my jaw. "Perhaps the listeners won't be that surprised, like Janis said."

"Yeah, 'cause the whole staff here was *shocked*," Elena said in the driest tone imaginable.

After speaking with Janis, we'd gone to talk with whoever was in the building that morning, continuing to do so every time we caught someone new. Cliff had stared, open-mouthed, and said, "I thought you were dating this whole time?"

Des and Elena had already guessed, though Daria and I still apologized. They'd taken it in stride, but we were still cooking dinner for them next week, with Susannah and

Des's parents coming too. Because as Des had said later, giving me a long hug and a meaningful look, *my parents are dying to meet the woman you fell in love with, on-air, with thousands of people listening in real time.*

"Who the hell is hogging the champagne?" Janis yelled. She popped into the sound booth and stole the bottle right from Elena's hands.

"Everyone, please do come into the world's smallest sound booth while we record," I said, spreading my hands over the table.

From the hallway came a bellow I knew well.

"Did we miss it?" Magnolia yelled.

Daria rolled her eyes. "Mom, I'm right here. You don't have to yell."

Magnolia appeared in the doorway, flushed and smiling and holding hands with Martha. "We didn't miss it! You look ready to rock and roll, but that's been the case since you were born, baby girl."

Janis drank her champagne. "We avoided corporate takeover *again*, so what better way to celebrate us doing whatever we want by doing this. Rules are made up anyhow. All of them are. That's another piece of wisdom you can remind me I've said from time to time, Theo."

"Yes, ma'am," I promised. Beneath the table, Daria tapped her foot against mine.

"Shit, you're on in a minute," Elena said.

The crowd dissipated back into the other room, taking up various posts while Daria and I pulled on our headphones. I found her hand under the table and squeezed. Through the window, the community that had accepted us, loved us, cheered us on was watching simply because they could. And simply because we'd asked them.

I hadn't come from a biological family that showed up for me in ways like this. To have it here, to have this kind of unconditional love crowded in tight to watch my radio broadcast, was a type of magic that made it all worth it. They'd shown up, and I was permanently grateful.

"On in ten," Elena said.

We'd practiced this time on who would go first. So when the cue lights blinked on, I leaned down to the mic.

"Good evening and happy Thursday. It's been almost a week since we've been here live, so thanks for hanging in there during our unscheduled break. It was mostly due to my debilitating loss to Daria on the mini-golf course last week. A loss witnessed by so many of our members."

Daria was grinning, cute and cocky, with her chin in her hand.

"But…in all seriousness, before we get to tonight's calls, we need to disclose some personal news that we feel is important. You trust us every night with your fears and your secrets and the least we can do is be honest with all of you."

Her smile widened, and I was briefly enchanted. My office was still full of flowers, still full of Daria showing me the expanse of her love, how far she would go to meet me halfway in this relationship. I'd never known a romantic gesture to be so sincere. Never known one to fill me with such hope. But by now, I should be less surprised by the fact that Daria was remarkable.

"Daria and I have often been on opposing sides and viewpoints, even before we shared a show," I said evenly. "But over the course of working more closely together. Of listening to her. And learning. Of playing paintball and air hockey and losing terribly at mini-golf—"

She laughed softly but her eyes shone.

"I fell very much in love with my cohost."

I paused long enough for her to say, "Daria here. Just wanted to add that I fell very much in love with my cohost too."

There was movement in the other room. Everyone was

giving us some ridiculously excited version of a thumbs up or an air guitar.

"It wasn't planned," she continued. "And while Theo's all about the romance, my long-time fans know that dating, *loving*, again was not in the cards for me." Daria held my gaze. "Until it was."

"It turns out you've been calling in every night to get love advice from experts, but we don't know anything at all," I said.

She laughed. "We're messy, imperfect, contradictory humans that change their minds and grow, even when it's not according to our plans. We knew that lying about it didn't serve anyone, especially not us. We knew we had to disclose it. Theo and I have both learned so much from all of you—you're vulnerable and honest when you call, sharing more than we could ever ask for. I've learned that whatever I've felt these past five years, whether that's rage or confusion or curiosity—saying it out loud usually means someone else feels the same way. Keeping it a secret turns it into something shameful when I feel everything *but* ashamed of loving Theo."

We shared a smile for two beats of dead air, but neither one of us cared.

I dipped back to the mic. "There's no perfection or pretending with authenticity. We're going to mess up and change our minds. And learn new things and start the whole cycle all over again. It's the advice we would give to all of you. We need to live that advice ourselves."

"And this isn't going to be a show about us dating," she said, laughing. "Just need to make that clear. Nothing about the format or what we talk about will be different. Including that our relationship does *not* mean we will see eye-to-eye when we give advice."

I flashed a lopsided grin at Daria. "We would never disappoint our listeners by starting to unanimously agree because we're in love. That's our promise to all of you."

"Guys?" Elena chimed in. "I'm so sorry to interrupt this beautiful moment, but you've got a listener who called in, like immediately, and I think you're going to want to hear from them."

I raised an eyebrow at Daria. She shrugged and said, "Yeah, patch them through."

"Hey, it's Rachel!" came a cheery voice. "Oh, and Ted and Skyler are with me too."

"How are you three doing?" I asked, happily surprised. "Are you out there being brave with your new relationship?"

"Yeah, we really are," she said, "and that's why we called in. Because you and Daria *did something brave too!*"

In the background of the call came a lot of silly cheering. Daria's hands flew to her pink cheeks, her smile bright and breathtaking.

I held her gaze. "Yes, we did do something brave. And she was worth every risk."

DARIA

I could tell it was going to be a good show when it wasn't a show at all, but a retro roller rink party celebrating the birthday of my weird, grouchy boss.

If Theo and I ever made it, that is. We were no more than a minute walk from the roller rink we'd rented out for Janis's party. It was right next to the iconic Sunrise Beach Ferris wheel, which was spinning pink in the twilight, full of people. Per the request of *disco balls akimbo*, I wore my magenta glitter wig, a short black skirt, and knee-high, seventies-style socks I knew would look killer with the white roller skates.

The problem was that Theo had dragged me behind the abandoned lifeguard station, and his hand was currently sliding up that short black skirt.

"We're going to be late," I sighed, hitching my leg higher on his hip. I gripped his face and crashed my lips against his, my tongue stroking until he was pressing me back even harder against the creaky wood. The sultry night air caressed my skin while his palm smoothed up my thigh, fingers seeking and teasing.

"Time is a societal construct, Daria," he whispered, sounding amused and turned on at the same time. His mouth roamed the column of my throat. "I thought we weren't limiting ourselves to rigid definitions anymore."

I laughed. "Like the concept of *time*?"

His chest rumbled. I could feel his lips curving into a smile along my jawline. "Feel free to argue with me about it. I'm available for a discussion."

I pinned him with a sly look. "This roller-skating thing is a party. Not a competition."

"I know that."

"Then why are you dragging your feet?" I asked, crawling my fingers up his chest. "Not because you think I'm...*better* than you at skating?"

"That's...just a societal construct."

"Oh my god, you *are* worried."

Theo's large hands squeezed my hips as he rolled seductively between my legs. "Does it matter? I'm good at so many things."

I hummed under my breath. "It was one thing to have a scoundrel for a cohost, and now I've got one for a boyfriend."

His big body went still against mine. He used his finger to tip up my chin. "Daria Stone, what did you say to me?"

I fiddled with my earrings. "I called you my boyfriend. That's what you are, aren't you?"

His lips twitched in the dim light. "I'm desperately in love with you and two days ago, on the radio show we cohost together, I declared that love for everyone in town listening."

I swallowed. "So...you're my boyfriend then?"

He caught my lips for a searing kiss that turned into a low, sexy laugh. "All I know is that my girlfriend better have all of her sex toys out tonight when we get home."

"No empty promises," I whispered at his ear, my heart so light and buoyant it felt seconds away from floating free of my chest.

He ducked his head to catch my gaze. "Nothing would make me happier than to call you my girlfriend. Nothing would make me happier than to *be* your boyfriend." He lifted my hand to his lips for a kiss. "I want to reiterate that before we get back to your place and I keep you in bed with me for hours."

"I'd like that very, very much," I murmured. "The *being your girlfriend* part. And the *having sex for hours* part."

Theo kissed my forehead, threaded our fingers together and began walking us toward the rink with a devilish grin.

After Rachel had made me blush from head to toe, calling in to tell us we'd been brave, the rest of that show had gone better than either of us had imagined. A few grumpy emails had trickled in—people who either thought our dating was unprofessional *or* just a marketing ruse—but the overall reaction had been positive and supportive. We'd even received a deluge of fan mail from folks who appreciated how honestly we'd spoken about growth and change while being in the public eye. Their approval was a happy surprise, though not necessary.

It did remind me, yet again, that our listeners had never wanted Theo and me to be perfect representations of our opposing viewpoints, but flawed, earnest humans, there to listen when times were tough.

We strolled down the boardwalk—the roaring ocean to our left, surfers walking past carrying their boards, crowds of noisy tourists and people on skateboards. The warm evening held the scent of sunscreen and fried food, even more so when we got to Debbie's Roller Rink, where the staff of K-SUN and all of Janis's many friends were whirling around in skates, rainbow-colored and covered in glitter. Disco balls hung from the middle posts, casting the floor in a soft, multi-colored swirl.

Cliff was the DJ and he was true to his word—a synth-heavy Tears for Fears song floated through the hot summer air. To the right were the stations Elena and I had set up with Janis's favorite food and a giant birthday cake. Across the back of the rink was our banner: *92.1 K-SUN. Radio for the people.*

Janis skated past us in a bright yellow wig. "Grab skates, you two," she called over her shoulder. "Our destinies await on the roller rink!"

Theo shook his head with a laugh, gently repositioning my fake pink hair. I preened beneath his confident fingers, loving this new, open affection I'd never get enough of.

"Should we flip a coin to see who tells Janis she was right about us all along?" I asked.

"Never, she'll be insufferable," he muttered. "Besides, I need to start thinking of a gift for next year's birthday and declaring her *correct* about our true, romantic feelings is just the kind of present she loves."

Theo brushed one last strand of hair from my eyes and then I struck a pose. "So what do you think about my retro roller rink look?"

He dipped his mouth, breathing his next words against my cheek. "I think you are astonishing, Daria Stone. I might even get up the courage to ask you out on a date tonight."

"Oh yeah? What did you have in mind?"

He cocked his head. "Have you ever played paintball?"

"I see. You're looking for me to defend your honor. *Again.*"

He flashed a smug grin. "I changed my mind. Our date will be at the arcade where I will win, *again*, at everything."

I pressed up onto my tiptoes for a kiss. "Cannot believe you'd trash talk your girlfriend like that, Dr. Chadwick."

Our friends and coworkers spun by us in a blur of cheers and color. The lights of the Ferris Wheel mixed with the disco balls, sending sparkling light refracting over the roller rink like diamonds. Janis flew past again while, in the corner, I could see my mom and Martha scrambling together while laughing. Elena danced gracefully with her friends, looking even more badass in her long purple wig. And Des and Susannah couples-skated like professionals right down the middle.

We found a bench to pull on our roller skates. Theo lifted one of my feet and then the next into his lap, tightening the laces with a hand wrapped tight around my ankle.

"Is this the girlfriend treatment?" I asked.

"It's the Daria treatment," he said simply. When he finished, he dropped his head and kissed each of my knees before releasing my feet to the floor. I rolled them back and forth, feeling the wheels move. Then I hooked my finger in Theo's shirt and tugged him close.

There was one last thing I needed to say to my cohost.

"Do you remember Misty's question, the night we were at the arcade?" I asked.

"I remember all of my victories when I'm with you," he said mildly.

I nuzzled against his cheek and nipped his jaw, making him laugh. "Now who's cocky?"

He kept kissing up my neck, setting off a delicious shiver. "We said a lot of things to Misty that night. Which part in particular?"

I leaned back to catch his gaze. "You agreed that there were a lot of messages we get about love that can be fake. But that it takes courage to reach for what's genuine beneath that. I haven't stopped thinking about it. Especially because we were talking about soul mates."

Theo stilled.

"I can never support the concept of soul mates in that Hallmark-y, greeting card-type of way that *is* harmful in that it perpetuates the lie that you're only a whole person if you're married to another."

He tucked strands of my hair behind my ear and stared at me like I really was a marvel.

"I do believe in the power of choice," I continued. "I

choose to love myself, every day. I choose to love my mother. To love Janis and Elena and Des. To love this weird radio station and funky beach town and I love *you*, Theo Chadwick. I choose you and would choose you again and again. I don't know if that's what a soul mate is. I do know it feels like we're meant to be together."

He cupped my face with both hands, tipped my head back and kissed me. It was sweet, and quick, and I was still dazed and breathless after. "I would choose you too, Daria. Every hour of every day. I think I knew from the first moment we met."

I raised an eyebrow. "Even when we were arguing nonstop?"

His gaze lingered on mine. "My heart knew long before the rest of me that you were the one."

The music changed to something bright and upbeat, and Theo's lips curved into a crooked smile. He stood effortlessly, skating backward and bringing me along with him. With the setting sun, the colorful disco lights, the ocean breeze in his hair, he was too charming and handsome for words.

So I didn't say a thing, content to skate hand-in-hand around the rink surrounded by music, surrounded by our community, surrounded by the sounds of the boardwalk. He and I had already shared so many words at this point—and really, Theo was right.

Our hearts *had* known what they wanted all along.

We could never be experts on a feeling as wild and mysterious as love because it was as wild and mysterious as life itself. It didn't mean we shouldn't be greedy for every second and every lesson, eager to take up space with our loud, messy, jubilant passion.

I was never going to fully understand it, so I might as well crank the music up high and dance while I was here. Or, like tonight, might as well skate around a roller rink with my radio family, covered in glitter, beneath a bunch of spinning disco lights.

And holding hands with Theo, who loved every loud, messy, and jubilant part of me. As I loved every single part of him.

We were only human, after all.

EPILOGUE

THEO

Two years later

*D*aria looked especially beautiful wearing her headphones tonight.

"Did you plan on ending our first *nationally syndicated* broadcast with a marriage proposal question?" she asked.

I chuckled, shaking my head. "I can't help it if the people want my engagement advice. Call it a niche."

"Vibrators are, for *sure*, still my niche," she said. "Right, listeners? Should we do another poll to see which one of us has the best niche expertise? Or should we do it the old-fashioned way and take this to the arcade?"

"My most recent and humiliating loss at the pinball machine *will* be avenged."

She shrugged. "We'll see about that."

Beneath the table, Daria hooked her feet around my ankle with a cheeky smile. I caught her hand, gave her fingers a squeeze.

"But to get back to Daria's original question, I had no

plans whatsoever. That doesn't mean that Daria and I aren't both over the moon in the studio right now. This is *Love and Life Advice*'s first night on K-SUN as syndicated programming, and we've already been hearing from new fans all across the country."

"It's easy to toss around words like *dream come true*," Daria added, "but we really mean it. We hope you'll keep tuning in every Thursday, Friday and Saturday night to hear Theo and I talk to callers about love, sex and relationships and maybe fight a bit. But only a little."

I arched an eyebrow. "What's your definition of *little?*"

Two years ago, Daria teasing me about an on-air argument would have been our actual reality—the sound booth thick with an awkward tension, our conversations sharp and stilted. Now, she and I sat here three nights a week and had conversations with listeners that felt as easy as breathing and just as vital.

But that was why we'd waited as long as we did, learning how to be together as a couple *and* as cohosts here in Sunrise Beach, where our local following celebrated our relationship and Des now had multiple folders filled with the fan fiction we received.

When Janis brought us into her office a month ago to give the news that All Star Media was back with another syndication offer, this time saying *yes* felt right. It meant charting a new course for our careers and broadening the base of support for K-SUN, though at the center nothing had changed. We were still two human beings, giving the best advice we could, and learning from each other every single day.

It helped that a few months after Janis's roller rink birthday party, Daria's agent sold her manuscript, new ending and all, and her book was releasing in three months— already to a lot of early fanfare.

The response she'd gotten from her early readers had

been unanimous—Daria's imperfect story about choosing herself after betrayal made them feel seen in a world that often ignored them. She and I would be taking *Love and Life Advice* on the road in the fall so I could support her on her book release tour.

Not that she needed much help from me. Daria was as funny and down-to-earth with her readers as she was with her listeners and her influence only continued to grow.

My eyes darted up to the clock, aware of our time constraint. Daria pressed her lips together, barely concealing her excitement. We'd hatched this spontaneous plan together this morning, sitting on the beach with coffee, her back pressed to my front and my arms holding her close as we watched the waves crash against the shore. We'd bought a house a year ago, not too far from K-SUN and the board-walk, and discussed most of our major life decisions at that very spot.

And this one was more major than most.

I winked at my gorgeous cohost. "Sadly, we are just about out of time for tonight, but we'll be back tomorrow with more *Love and Life Advice.* Oh, and we forgot to mention that we'll be signing off from our show a little differently from now on."

Daria touched her mic. "That's right, we are. You are now listening to Daria Stone-Chadwick."

"And I'm Dr. Theodore Chadwick-Stone," I said with a grin. "Thank you, as always, for tuning in to 92.1 K-SUN, radio for the people."

We pulled off our headphones and waited, eyes locked. I heard Elena say, "What the fuck?"

And then Des, pushing open the mixing room door and saying, "Hey, what did you guys say?"

And finally Janis—who roared into the sound booth with, "Now what the *hell* is going on here?"

Daria threw her hands in the air and exclaimed, "Theo and I got secretly married over the weekend!"

The short pause was quickly overshadowed by the descent of what felt like the entire station pouring into the room, sounding as shocked as they were happy. Des couldn't stop hugging me and Elena was trying to rustle up some champagne.

Janis, meanwhile, was nodding at Daria and me like she finally realized we'd managed to keep one secret from her—a literal first.

"Nicely done, you two," she said. "Nicely done. I'm usually right about everything but I didn't see this coming."

In the commotion, no one saw Daria slip away, but it was technically my job to get everyone into the hallway, moving toward the breakroom. I accepted more congratulations and many hugs and handshakes. In the midst of the chaos, I looped an arm around Janis's shoulders as we shared a smile.

"Did you really get hitched last weekend?" she asked. "Because now I gotta scramble to find enough weed to bake you my own version of a wedding cake. It could take *weeks*."

"That's not necessary," I said. "Gift us a flamboyance of flamingos and we'll call it even."

Emotion rippled across her face—and this time she didn't attempt to hide it. "I can probably do that for the two people in this world I love the most."

My heart ached with happiness, and we hadn't even gotten to the best part yet.

"Are there pictures? Video? Did you elope?" Des asked, walking backward with us to the breakroom.

"What did Daria *wear*?" Elena yelled, still on her mission for champagne.

I slipped my hands into my pockets with an apologetic shrug. "See, that's the thing—"

"I'm coming, I'm coming, I swear," came Daria's sultry voice, slightly breathless from running. I watched her traipse down the hallway in her new, hastily arranged outfit—a short white dress, a gauzy veil and her boots, of course.

Even in the chaotic surge of our surprise announcement, the world hushed around me as my wife approached, her face full of joy and her blue eyes warm with her usual teasing affection.

Daria Stone *was* my love language. She was the woman who challenged me every day, who made me think, who changed me from an expert to an amateur and then just a man, hopelessly in love. She'd given me the bravery to change my mind and the courage to know myself better.

Having Daria's mother marry the two of us on the beach at dawn had been the easiest decision of my life. Nothing had prepared me for the moment we were officially declared husband and wife—not years of study, or giving advice, or contemplating caller questions.

I was an amateur, yet again, so overwhelmed with love for my bride that neither of us could hold back our tears.

It wasn't that we hadn't wanted our community with us. But given what happened to Daria on her last wedding day, she'd wanted our ceremony to be private and intimate, a moment for just the two of us.

Our first ceremony, that is.

I reached for her hand now and squeezed it. She grinned, reaching up to fix her veil.

"Yes, there are pictures," I said. "Yes, there's video too. No, we didn't elope. Mags married us on the beach at dawn and Martha was our witness. And as for the rest…"

Daria pushed open the door to the break room. Magnolia and Martha had transformed the space into a wedding reception—if a wedding reception was held in a slightly run-down radio station next to a boardwalk. There were white string lights, a buffet of food from High Frequency, and as soon as she saw us, Mags kicked the jukebox on with a cheer.

"Are we ready for the *surprise* wedding of Theo and

Daria?" she bellowed as the staff lost their minds. None more than Des, when he discovered Susannah and his parents there waiting inside, already seated.

"Theo," he said, pulling me in for another hug, "this is unbelievable. You did it. You found the one…and it was *Daria* this whole time."

"I'm pretty sure I would have known that sooner if I'd listened to you from the beginning," I admitted.

He grinned, slapping my shoulder. "Now who's the love expert?"

"Certainly not me," I said. "I'll sit with you and your parents after though and show you the video, I promise."

Next to me, Daria vibrated with happiness, already doing a little air guitar out of pure excitement. Mags gave a thumbs up and said, "Are you ready to do the damn thing or what?"

I cleared my throat and turned to Janis. "How would you feel about walking Daria and me down the aisle? It's just a reenactment, so nothing *too* serious."

"Or emotional," Daria added.

Her eyebrows shot to her hairline. "You want *me* to do it?"

"After all, you're the reason why we're together in the first place," I said. "Or have you already forgotten your ill-advised experiment?"

Janis laughed. "I never forget any of the incredible things that I've done, kid. But it just so happens that I'd do anything for the two of you. Anything in the world." She held out her elbows and turned to face Magnolia. "Let's go meet your destinies. Again."

I caught Daria's eye. She mouthed *I love you*. Then we were marching down the fake aisle with Janis as our coworkers cheered us on, this found family of ours that had only grown stronger in the past two years—Mags and Martha were blissfully happy, and Janis was keeping K-SUN afloat as our local support kept growing, our passionate members continuing to choose radio for the people instead of corporations.

Des and I still spent nights in this very room, planning out our shows with Elena. Though Daria was there now too, sitting next to me with her sly grin, making me laugh every chance she got.

We reached Magnolia at the end of the aisle. She was using a bunch of stacked milk crates, filled with records, as a makeshift podium. Janis released us but stayed nearby at the front, giving me a nod full of six years of memories.

And finally I was facing Daria—one eyebrow arched in feline amusement as I lifted her veil.

"Are you ready for our second wedding, Ms. Stone-Chadwick?"

She tilted her head. "I think we should do this every weekend, how about you?"

Mags raised her hands and the room quieted. "Thank you for coming to Theo and Daria's surprise wedding reenact-ment. Please note, *there will be karaoke* immediately following. And dancing."

"I'm singing back-up on *We Built This City*," Daria promised.

"That's because you're incredible, baby girl," Mags said. "But you all know by now that these two got hitched over the weekend, so they're already husband and wife."

The room erupted in cheers. Daria's eyes shone. Having a wedding every weekend was starting to seem like a brilliant idea.

"They did, however, wish to share their wedding vows with all of you, which they wrote." Mags tapped Daria's shoulder. "You go first, hun."

Daria exhaled a shaky breath. "Theo." Her voice broke the tiniest bit. "I vow to choose you, every single day. To learn from you. To grow with you. To love you with my whole heart, whether we're on a hiking trail together or sitting in sound booth C, talking to listeners for hours. You've shown me what true love is all about and it has changed my life forever."

She gazed at me expectantly, and though we'd said these exact vows only five days ago, this felt different too—declaring our commitment in front of the people we loved the most.

"Daria," I said, "you are as magnificent to me as the first moment we met. I didn't think it was possible to love you more each day, but here I am, loving you more than ever. Every morning together feels like a new beginning. Every moment, a promise, and every smile from you feels like the greatest gift. Being your husband is an honor."

There was a pause, and then Mags yelled, "You know what that means, folks. *Time to party!*" The jukebox was kicked off and dance music was turned on. "And you can kiss now."

The room did erupt into a party, but I didn't hear a thing. I cupped my wife's face and kissed her as ardently as I had on that beach. Kissed her until she laughed, wrapping her arms around my back and hugging me tight.

"Our love story was meant to be, Theo," she said, kissing me one more time. "Getting married twice proves it's true."

"I couldn't agree more," I murmured.

True romance was nothing like I'd imagined. It was singing along to K-SUN with Daria while we did the dishes at night. Or taking a bubble bath together while bickering over a listener question.

Or the simple joy of watching the sun set over Sunrise Beach from the top of the Ferris wheel.

And it was more than that—it was sharing a drink with Des and Elena at two in the morning after a show. Watching our coworkers fill our community pantry with food for our neighbors. It was Janis, staying late to help with a pledge drive and ordering us pizza, or the way Magnolia could play a certain song during her set and Daria's face would fill with love when she heard it.

It was all of this and more—always *more,* never less. And at the center of all of it was Daria Stone. My former rival. My wife. My destiny.

She'd been the magic, all along.

∾

BONUS EPILOGUE

DARIA

The night after their beach wedding at dawn

I balanced on a rock—barefoot and still in my loose white gown—and waited for my new husband to tell me when I could go inside the cozy cabin we'd rented in Big Sur following our sunrise wedding.

The ocean was a pretty, dazzling blue, crashing against a small slice of beach below the house. And the sun was just beginning its long ascent to the horizon. Through the windows, I could see Theo working hard at whatever adorable task he'd undertaken. His suit jacket was off, tie loose, sleeves rolled up to his elbows.

And on his left hand, he wore the thin gold band I'd placed on his finger less than eight hours ago.

My lips tugged into a smile when I caught him staring down at the ring with an affectionate look I knew well by now. It was the look I'd catch him wearing when he thought I wouldn't notice—like telling him a funny story while cooking dinner, or when he'd find me singing to our house plants, or after answering an emotional listener question.

Theo never told me that *unabashed, affectionate devotion* was a love language, but I'd learned early on in our relationship that it was his.

He swung around the side of the cabin, walking toward me, and my stomach dipped with anticipation. I could still hear his vows from earlier, feel the weight of them on my skin like a caress: *Every morning together feels like a new beginning. Every moment, a promise, and every smile from you feels like the greatest gift. Being your husband is an honor.*

We had something much more fun and public planned for our K-SUN family. But for now, the intimacy of a private dawn wedding followed by a few secluded days on the coast was the kind of romance a girl like me could appreciate. Theo understood how being left at the altar had shaped and changed me, yet two years of his adoring devotion had muted those memories so significantly that it was growing harder and harder for me to remember those old hurts and humiliations.

All I remembered now was the community that loved me through it. The radio station that took a chance on me and let me meet so many listeners who wanted to love themselves with a fierce passion. And Theo, of course, who looked so devastatingly handsome in his slightly disheveled wedding suit that I was blushing on my honeymoon night.

He was the kind of man who *always* showed up for the people he loved.

"Thank you for your patience, Ms. Stone," he said softly.

"That's Ms. Stone-Chadwick to you," I replied, wrapping my arms around his neck.

A sound of pure pleasure rumbled from his chest. "My mistake," he said, then dipped to scoop me into his arms. "Allow me to make it up to you? It's the least I can do as your husband."

A delicious thrill zipped up my spine. Nothing had changed between us since this morning. And yet *everything* had changed. It had less to do with the pretty silver rings newly adorning my left ring finger and more to do with the way choosing this kind of commitment felt as sweet as sinking into a hot bath on a freezing day. Comforting, safe, healing. *Euphoric.*

And warming me all over.

"Your new wife is quite demanding, or so I've heard," I said breathlessly, grinning as he carried me toward the house.

He nosed along my hairline. "If you're *more* demanding than you were as my girlfriend, I won't survive it."

"Poor husband," I crooned. "I'll ply you with electrolytes and energy bars."

He climbed the stairs and shouldered open the door. "Keep calling me *husband*, Daria, and I won't ever need them."

I opened my mouth to flirt back, but we were suddenly in the small, cozy bedroom. And it was now clear to me what Theo had been doing in here.

The space had been transformed.

"Theo," I breathed. "This is…"

He set me down gently, and there was a *swish* as the hem of my dress touched the floor. If I'd told him once, I'd told him a million times—I never wanted to see rose petals in the shape of a heart on our bed. Though I still brought him bouquets of wildflowers whenever I could, just to watch his face light up in delight.

But this wasn't that.

Floor-to-ceiling windows let in the view, making it feel like we were surrounded by gorgeous, rocky coastline on all sides. Dozens of flickering candles—stacked on tables and dressers—bathed the room in a pretty glow. The four-poster bed was draped in the most delicate fairy lights I'd ever seen. The same pattern adorned the ceiling, giving the appearance of dim stars. In small jars near the mirror were dried bunches of lavender, and when I dipped my head to examine them closely, Theo cleared his throat.

"I saved them from the day you filled my office with flowers," he said softly.

My head turned in total surprise. "You did?"

His throat worked. "You're the love of my life, Daria. I keep everything that you give me."

My heart leaped in my chest. It was funny, even after two years, the way this man continued to show me I was no expert at all—and a far better person for it.

I planned on being surprised and delighted by Theo for the rest of my life.

Slowly, I made my way to my husband, holding his gaze, surrounded by flickering light and ocean waves. My fingers trembled as I caressed his face, his lips as they curved into a grin. "I meant every word on the beach this morning," I whispered. "I meant every vow. Every promise." I took his hand and pressed it over my heart, and then he was on me. Pulling me toward him for a scorching kiss that stole my breath and curled my toes against the floor.

We parted just so he could spin me gently, pushing the hair from the back of my neck and pressing his lips there.

"*Daria,*" he breathed, over and over, his mouth tracing between my shoulder blades as his fingers worked down the zipper of my gauzy dress. Each inch of revealed skin had him groaning, had his hands smoothing down my body as the material floated softly to the floor, pooling at my feet. His breath seared me, hot at the base of my spine. His fingers curved around my thighs, tugging me to turn.

I did, already boneless with need. Already desperate with wanting the man on his knees in front of me, still partially clothed and gazing up at me with more love than I thought possible. And when he pushed me to lie facedown on the bed, bent at the waist and spread open for him, I did so eagerly.

With my face buried, I gave in to the temptation to *feel*: the soft sheets against my naked skin, the warm, fragrant air, the sound of Theo shifting behind me. His strong hands roamed up the backs of my thighs, spreading me another inch. His teeth nipped at the curve of my ass, and I jumped, pushing back for more.

His low laughter was rough as sandpaper, breath feathering across my skin. With firm hands, he tilted my hips up, leaving me open and exposed to him. His fingers gripped my ass cheeks, spreading them, squeezing possessively. He growled that same rumble of pleasure before pushing his face between my legs and groaning.

"I waited for you my entire life," he whispered, swiping his tongue along my slick skin. "My wife. My *everything*." He licked lightly at my clit, and my fingers curled into the bedsheets. "You should prepare to be worshipped every single goddamn day, Daria."

Theo pushed his tongue deep inside of me, and I cried out.

"But I...I already feel worshipped by you," I panted.

He fucked me with his tongue, in and out, while his index finger circled my clit. My body began to tremble, and every time Theo slowed his motions, I kept tilting the lower half of my body up, up, *harder* against his face.

He pulled back and flipped me over—letting me watch him strip out of his remaining wedding clothes till he wore nothing but a devilish grin. Then he curled his hands around my legs and dropped his mouth back to my clit, giving me long, firm strokes while I yanked on his hair.

"You already feel worshipped yet you always want *more*, Daria," he whispered, eyes on mine. "That's why I love you. You can always ask for more, and I'll always be ready to give it."

With my own smirk, I sat halfway up, propping my legs on his shoulders so I could grip his hair harder, rocking sensually against his tongue. Riding his face. Watching his eyes close in sheer pleasure as I ground against his mouth.

My head fell back. "So good." I sighed. "You're so *fucking good.*"

His tongue moved rhythmically with my body, each circle of my clit tightening my core, sending ripples of unbelievable ecstasy through every limb. I watched him reach down and grip his thick, hard cock, stroking up and down. He knew what I loved, knew that getting to watch him touch himself while pleasuring me was one of my favorite fantasies.

"Oh god, Theo," I moaned. "Fuck your hand faster."

He grunted, lashing at my clit while stroking his cock. I rocked and rocked my hips. His fist jerked up and down, biceps flexing with the effort. My orgasm felt like a bolt of actual lightning—I screamed, falling back, while Theo expertly licked me through the intense peak and the slow, rippling after-shocks.

But my husband was right. I *did* always want more. So before he could rise from the floor, I was sitting up and shoving his broad, naked body to the soft carpet. Straddling his hips, I fell forward for a searing kiss. Theo's hands tangled in my hair, his lips hungry and firm.

We parted, our breath mingling. "I love you so much," I murmured, pushing the hair from his forehead. His smile was the same one from this morning, the one that had burst across his face when I'd said, "I do."

I couldn't wait one more second. I sat up, taking his cock all the way inside me, so deep we both groaned with absolute relief. His hands curled around my hips, lifting me up and down, jaw tight, breath harsh.

"Oh, *fuck,* Theo," I hissed. "Yes, so good, *so fucking good.*"

He pushed up to sit, and I curved my legs around his waist. He was so deep I couldn't think, could only revel, bewildered, at the physical joining of our bodies. I wrapped my arms around his neck and rode him hard and fast, desperate for us to climax together.

He held my face with one hand, thumb pressing into my lower lip. Our eyes stayed locked, lips dancing close.

"So beautiful, you are so beautiful," he kept panting. A bead of sweat slid down his temple. My head fell back again, and his mouth dipped, tongue sliding up my throat like he'd never get enough of the taste of me. "I can feel how close you are."

"Together," I chanted. "Together, *please.*"

Not a second later, we came in a rush of cries and a sloppy, shuddering kiss that dissolved into breathless laughter. We collapsed back onto the carpet, staring up at the twinkle lights—until we turned to look at each other. The shared astonishment had my heart doing those same backflips that had become a daily routine ever since that first, argumentative game of paintball.

It had been love all along, of course.

Theo smoothed the hair from my face and kissed the tip of my nose. "We did something very brave today."

I grinned. "That we did. Our listeners will be very proud." I curled onto my side, felt the smooth metal of his wedding band on my skin. "How does that make you feel?"

"Ready to take on the world. And you?"

I pressed a sweet kiss to Theo's lips. "Ready to do the same."

A NOTE FROM THE AUTHOR

Dear Reader,

Thank you for tuning in to K-SUN FM—radio for the people. I hope you enjoyed your hosts-slash-lovebirds, Theo and Daria!

If it isn't obvious (and I think it is), RIVAL RADIO is my "loosen up and have *fun*" book. I've spoken quite a bit about the creative burnout I experienced in 2021 (an experience shared by many other writers), which included an inability to tap into the freewheeling, madcap joy that's involved in storytelling. So when I sat down to begin drafting a story idea I'd been marinating on for about six months—something about enemies who give love advice for a living, falling in love with each *other*—I let go of some of my usual techniques and instead let myself feel my way through with curiosity instead of judgment. The fact that RIVAL RADIO contains a lot of my favorite things is no coincidence—radio stations, ragtag crews, grumpy-but-loveable bosses, nostalgia, beach towns. And we all know that writing spicy, enemies-to-lovers banter is the cherry on top of the board-walk sundae.

So it's hard to narrow down a list of favorite scenes but

I'll give it a try: every scene between Janis and Theo (when she tells him he is *extraordinary* at the very end, I lose it every time); the paintball scene, which was the most joyful and wacky thing I've ever written and was totally based on my intense love for *10 Things I Hate About You*; Daria's relationship with Mags and Mags falling in love with her friend Martha; when Theo explains the love languages to Daria while sitting in a patch of sunshine (after she tries to sneak away after leaving him food); *every single time they argued—* and I cannot stress that enough; when Theo is watching Daria walk away after they have sex in his office and he sees the sunrise; Daria filling his office with flowers and all of their coworkers already guessing they were stupid in love; sex toys sex toys sex toys SEX TOYS; when they're playing air hockey at the arcade and they accidentally agree with one another; the juke box named Stevie Nicks; when they tell their listeners they fell in love and Rachel calls in to tell them they'd done something brave…

…okay that's like the whole book!

Writing Theo and Daria falling head-over-heels in love brought me so much joy. I hope they brought you a little bit too. When it comes to this being-a-human thing, none of us are experts. So I hope you get to sing a little, dance a lot, and roller-skate beneath disco balls while eating a funnel cake, because life's too short not to.

Love,
Kathryn

ACKNOWLEDGMENTS

RIVAL RADIO wouldn't exist without the support of my amazing community. I'm lighting up the airwaves with my abundant thanks to:

Faith, my best friend and developmental editor, the Mary to my Stede. We're finally free. Long may we roam!

Jessica Snyder, my story and line editor, who has a knack for plot, stakes and detail that continues to amaze me (and always leaves hilarious comments sprinkled throughout the manuscript). This book had *way* fewer sleep-deprived voice mails involved than the last one, but if it had, I know she'd have listened to them—and responded with kind yet brilliant suggestions every time.

Jodi, Julia and Bronwyn, my beta readers, who continue to impress me with their ability to spot the gaps, the pacing issues, the character nuances and all the missing pieces that make a book whole. Working on RIVAL RADIO with the three of you was *so much fun* this time around and I'm so grateful to call you my friends.

Mel and Lizette, my sensitivity readers, who were very kind to offer feedback and notes on Des and Elena, respectively. Thank you for providing perspective and grounding to these characters I love and for sharing your experiences. Any mistakes made in this text are my own.

The *giant* and *gorgeous* support system that gets me through every book: the Hippie Chicks (who are the *literal best*), Joyce and Tammy (also the literal best), Lucy, Claire, Pippa, LJ, Avery and Stephanie, who continue to be some of the best people in our romance community, and Tim, Rick and Dan who are directly responsible for the beautiful book you hold in your hand. When I say I couldn't do this without you all, I absolutely mean it.

For my parents and brother, the original supporters of independent radio (WXPN!). In so many of my favorite memories growing up, WXPN is playing in the background.

And finally for Rob, my husband, my soulmate, my favorite weirdo. Spoiler alert: I'm stupid-in-love with you and am probably making you a mix-tape and/or filling your office with bouquets of flowers as we speak. Thanks for always being down to barrel through this life together. Now let's go chase some sunrises...

HANG OUT WITH KATHRYN!

Sign up for my newsletter and receive exclusive content, bonus scenes and more!
I've got a reader group on Facebook called **Kathryn Nolan's Hippie Chicks**. We're all about motivation, girl power, sexy short stories and empowerment! Come join us.

Let's be friends on
Website: authorkathrynnolan.com
Instagram at: kathrynnolanromance
Facebook at: KatNolanRomance
Follow me on BookBub
Follow me on Amazon

ABOUT KATHRYN

I'm an adventurous hippie chick that loves to write steamy romance. My specialty is slow-burn sexual tension with plenty of witty dialogue and tons of heart.

I started my writing career in elementary school, writing about *Star Wars* and *Harry Potter* and inventing love stories in my journals. And I blame my obsession with slow-burn on my similar obsession for The *X-Files*.

I'm a born-and-raised Philly girl, but left for Northern California right after college, where I met my adorably-bearded husband. After living there for eight years, we decided to embark on an epic, six-month road trip, traveling across the country with our little van, Van Morrison. Eighteen states and 17,000 miles later, we're back in my hometown of Philadelphia for a bit... but I know the next adventure is just around the corner.

When I'm not spending the (early) mornings writing steamy love scenes with a strong cup of coffee, you can find me outdoors -- hiking, camping, traveling, yoga-ing.

BOOKS BY KATHRYN

BOHEMIAN

LANDSLIDE

RIPTIDE

STRICTLY PROFESSIONAL

NOT THE MARRYING KIND

SEXY SHORTS

BEHIND THE VEIL

UNDER THE ROSE

IN THE CLEAR

WILD OPEN HEARTS

ON THE ROPES

RIVAL RADIO

Printed in Great Britain
by Amazon

81311758R00215